3 4143 11006
KT-500-466

THE NIGHT
IN
QUESTION

Also by Laurie Graham

The Man for the Job
The Ten O'Clock Horses
Perfect Meringues
The Dress Circle
Dog Days, Glenn Miller Nights
The Future Homemakers of America
The Unfortunates
Mr Starlight
Gone With the Windsors
The Importance of Being Kennedy
Life According to Lubka
At Sea
A Humble Companion
The Liar's Daughter
The Grand Duchess of Nowhere

THE NIGHT IN QUESTION

LAURIE GRAHAM

Quercus

First published in Great Britain in 2015 by

Quercus Publishing Ltd
Carmelite House
50 Victoria Embankment
London EC4Y 0DZ

An Hachette UK company

A CIP catalogue record for this book is available from the British Library

HB ISBN 978 1 78206 974 4
TPB ISBN 978 1 78206 975 1
EBOOK ISBN 978 1 78429 641 4

10 9 8 7 6 5 4 3 2 1

Typeset by CC Book Production

Printed and bound in Great Britain by Clays Ltd, St Ives plc

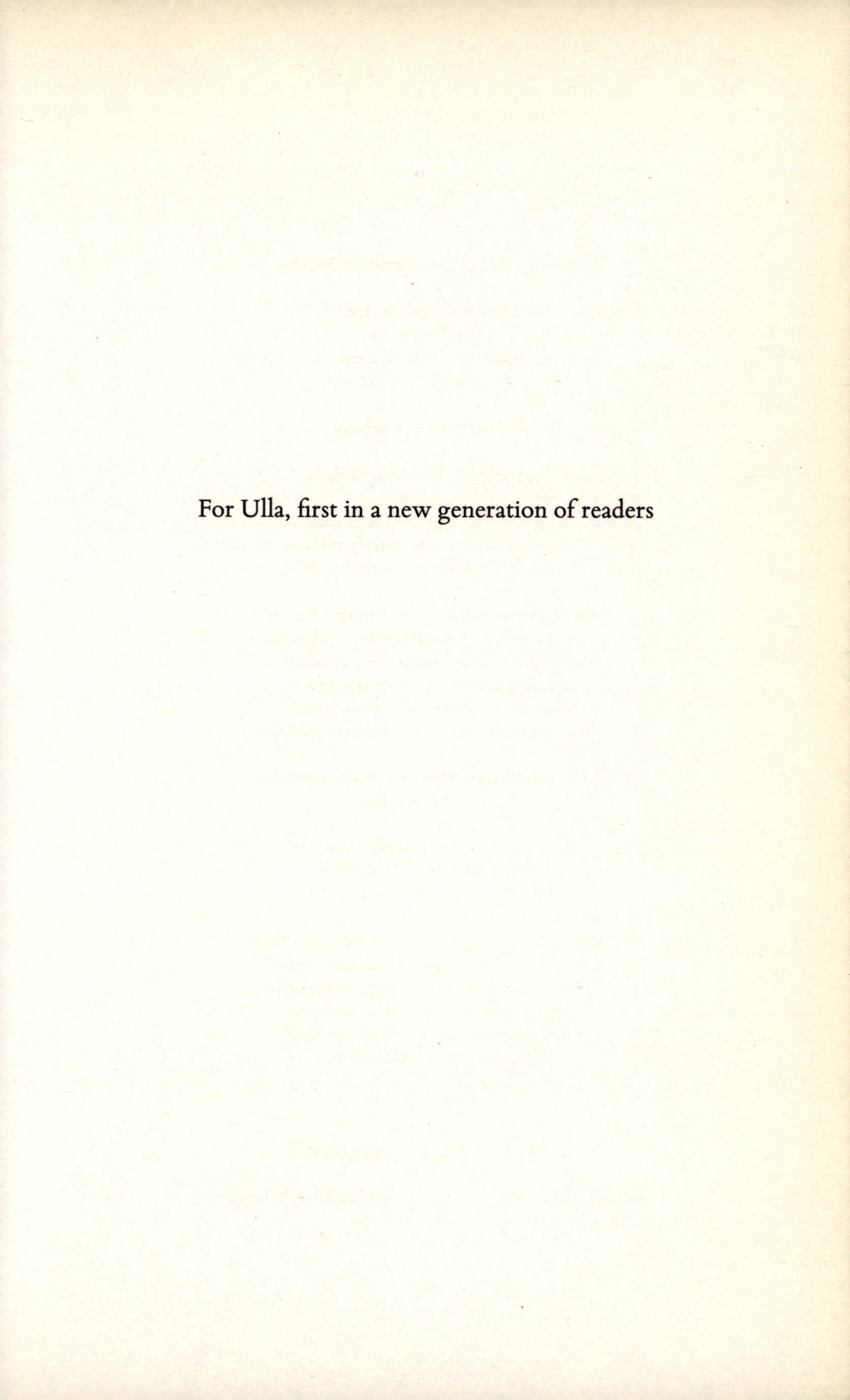

For Ulla, first in a new generation of readers

SPITALFIELDS
WHITECHAPEL
COMMERCIAL STREET
HANBURY STREET
BRICK LANE
BUCK'S ROW
BISHOPSGATE
SPITALFIELDS MARKET
COONEY'S DOSS HOUSE
GOULSTON STREET
WHITECHAPEL ROAD
COMMERCIAL ROAD
LEMAN STREET
BERNER STREET
BATTY ST
HOUNDSDITCH
MITRE SQUARE
1 Martha Tabram
2 Mary Anne Nichols
3 Annie Chapman
4 Lizzie Stride
5 Kate Eddowes
6 Mary Kelly

I don't powder my face till I've had the ten-minute call. I like to have one last thing to do, something to distract me from the shakes. You can't prevent them, but you can decline to pay them much attention. So I have my little routine. I rub eau de cologne on the back of my neck, then I tie an Indian shawl under my chin to keep the powder off the front of my gown and, once I've started powdering, woe to anyone who tries to strike up a conversation with me.

The young ones are the worst, the girls particularly. They do their turn and then they come off full of bubble and chatter, with never a thought for them that's still waiting to go on. Tittering and squealing. It's like trying to compose yourself in a monkey house. Boys seem to be more circumspect, and the old-timers are like me. We may be depended on for patter and jollity on stage, but just before we go on we require silence. I've often thought theatres should have two dressing places. One for Before and one for After.

So I tie on my shawl and while I'm powdering I make a gargoyle of myself in the looking glass. I don't mind what I see. The passing years are on my side. Not like some. I've seen faded beauties drummed off the stage in tears. If good looks were your ticket, audiences will show you no pity once they've faded. Men don't want to be served mutton when they can get chicken. But if you're a comic it's a different matter. The worse I make myself look, the more they laugh, and it has another advantage: if they happen to see me on the street without my rouge and lamp black they never know me.

The next call comes.

'Miss Allbones to the stage.'

Sometimes you only have one stairway to climb, sometimes you have to walk a country mile. Every venue is different. I've played halls where the only way to reach the stage was to go outside, through puddles and God knows what else and risk catching your death. And I've been lost a few times too, when I first started out in proper theatres, took a wrong turning and nearly missed my cue. But gradually your feet remember even if your brain doesn't. You can go back to a theatre after many years away and trust your feet to convey you safely to the wings.

The wings. Not pleasant places, I will say. They smell of rubber and turpentine and fear. What little space there is is cluttered with ropes and hoses and bad-tempered gas men and lime-boys. And you don't want to get on the wrong side of them. A cross word and they might give you too much light and show you to disadvantage. Or they might extinguish you entirely and leave you in the dark.

But the wings are where you must wait and observe something that can never give you any pleasure: the closing minutes of the act that's gone before you. Say the artiste is being very well received? Then the audience don't want him to finish. He's set the bar high. How can you follow that? On the other hand, if he's dying on his feet he's putting the audience in a bad mood and you'll have the job of winning them back. He can't win. He may be your dearest friend in the world, but not when you're in the wings waiting to go on after him.

Then off he comes, pushing past you, dripping sweat and either beaming like a loon or cursing the day he ever took up the profession.

That's the moment. There can be no turning back, no crying off sick because you've got two ears on your head. The chairman taps his gavel.

'Ladies, gentlemen and . . . lawyers, tonight for your delectation, a magisterial mélange of music and merriment, *pause for good-natured groans*, a banquet of bathos, burlesque and badinage, *wait for it*, *wait for it*, I give you, *gentle drum roll*, *if Bones hasn't fallen asleep*, the inimitable, the incomparable lionesse comique, Miss Dot Allbones!'

1

So this is how it all started. It was a Friday the first time she claimed me. I know that because Valentine was waiting for me in a hansom. He had rooms in Dalston at that time but on Fridays he'd usually come home with me for a glass of bubbly and a bite to eat. Any other night of the week I could ask my manager, Monty, if I felt in need of company, but on Fridays Monty has to eat dinner with his mother. It's a Hebrew custom.

I kid him about it. I say, 'Would it really kill you to miss Friday dinner once in a while?'

'No, Dot,' he says, 'but it would likely kill my dear mother.'

The thing was, some nights I was quite happy to go home alone, but some nights I wasn't. I can't explain it. I'm not a silly woman. I don't suffer from the vapours. I can step out onto a stage in front of a thousand faces but coming home to an empty house, in the dark, sometimes it gave me the jitters. When I was a kiddie my brother Albert used to think it a great lark to hide in the ginnel along the back of our house and jump out at me, so perhaps I should blame him.

Now Victoria Park, where I was living, is a superior kind of area, not dangerous like Whitechapel or Wapping. But there was a passageway at the side of the house, with a door leading to the back yard and another set of rooms, and it was as dark as a coal hole round there. I'd have preferred to keep that door bolted but Mr Earp, the gentleman who lived at the back, used to say it wouldn't be convenient to his callers. I don't think he ever had any callers, but what could I do? He paid his rent and he was entitled to do as he pleased with his door. So, daft as it may sound, I was happier when I had a gentleman to see me home, even if it was only a scaredy cat like Monty Hyams, or a slip of a lad like Valentine. It put my mind at rest.

Sometimes there was no gentleman available. If I was playing second house I might ask, 'Who takes drink with Miss Allbones tonight?' but the old hands would already have had a nip or three from their flask, before, during and after as you might say. They wanted to go home, and the younger ones didn't want to keep company with an old-timer like me. They had their sweethearts to attend to. But Valentine didn't have a sweetheart. He was a bit backward in that respect, or so I thought, so I was always glad to see his name on the playbill. Valentine St John, Genuine Male Soprano, because then I knew I'd have company for Friday night.

We were both playing the Griffin Hall in Shoreditch. I'd been engaged for the last two weeks of June and the reason I was delayed coming out that night was that Jimmy Griffin had commenced arguing about my fee. He said the houses had been very poor, the box was down and we must all be prepared to take a cut.

I said, 'Your houses are poor because you don't hire enough decent supporting turns.'

Jimmy Griffin can be as tight as a duck's arse. Nobody wants to see clog-dancers in this day and age, nor spoon-players. They'd as soon watch rain run down a window pane. People expect value, but I can't carry a show on my own. I'm good but it doesn't matter how good you are if your audience has got the hump by the time you go on.

'Well,' Griffin said, 'I'm afraid I shall have to talk to Monty.'

'Yes,' I told him. 'You do that.'

Valentine had a cab waiting for me at the end of the passage and I was hurrying to get to it when suddenly she appeared in front of me. She gave me quite a fright, stepping out from the shadows like that.

'Is it Dot?' she says. 'Is it Dot as used to be Little Dot? From Wolverhampton?'

I've never glossed over my humble origins. Make a feature of them, is what I say. You must use whatever you've got. But still, she caught me by surprise, speaking of Wolverhampton.

'Yow wouldn't remember me,' she said. 'I used to live across from your house. It's Kate, off Bilston Street.'

I never should have recognised her. What had it been, fifteen years? No, more like twenty. And time hadn't been kind to her. When I think what a corker she used to be. When I was a nipper I'd have given anything to have her curls and her pretty face.

She took off her bonnet.

'Now do yow know me?' she says. And I did. Well, it was more the set of her that was familiar, and her Black Country way of speaking. I've quite lost it myself.

'Never expected to see me again, did you?' she says. 'I'll bet yow didn't even know I was in London.'

Well I hadn't thought of her in years. I asked her how she was, though it was clear from the look of her that she wasn't doing well.

'I see you're going on all right, Dot,' she says. 'I hear you're getting a hundred pounds a week.'

That's the way people talk. A hundred pounds a week, two hundred, even three hundred. They just think of a number and double it. And they never reckon on your outgoings, or the weeks when you have no engagements. There's nothing steady about being an artiste.

I said, 'A hundred a week? You should go on the halls yourself, Kate. You're quite a comic.'

'Oh, Dot,' she says, 'I do wish yow'd lend me sixpence for my bed tonight.'

She said she'd been sleeping at the casual ward in Mile End but she was hoping to get a bed at Cooney's that night. Then I felt badly for her. Nobody lodges at the Casual if they can help it, nor at Cooney's.

I said, 'Is it sixpence for a bed in that rat hole?'

'No,' she says, 'it's fourpence for a single, but if I have another twopence I can get a drop of rum to help me sleep.'

So I gave her a shilling for her honesty and she called down all the blessings of heaven on me.

'Yow'm a good 'un,' she says. 'I've often observed it's the ones with the plainest faces that's got the kindest hearts. God bless you, Dot. Tararabit.'

And off she trudged, down towards Spitalfields Market.

Valentine said, 'Jiminy Christmas, Miss Dot, did you know that woman?'

I said, 'I did. That was Kate. I'll think of her last name presently. She used to pass for a beauty. I used to study her, across the street. Played with her a few times too, before she got too old for playing.

And now look what she's come to. Begging for the price of a bed in Cooney's. What a shock. What a come-down.'

He said, 'She wasn't here by chance, then. She'll have seen your name on the playbill and laid in wait for you. You know, I wonder you never thought of changing your name. Spongers are the worst when they know you. They know how to play on your heart strings.'

Valentine changed his name, of course. There surely cannot be a man alive who came into the world as Valentine St John, not in Wigan at any rate, but Valentine's quite cut-glass these days and I've never managed to get it out of him what name he started out with.

'That person,' he says, 'is dead and buried.'

There was a time, years ago, when I did think of changing my name. I tried Dolly Du Charme for a while, when I was playing the Birmingham theatres, but I found it didn't suit me so I went back to Dot Allbones. People like that, somehow. It sums me up. Our dad used to say, 'I've seen more meat on a horsewhip.'

Valentine said, 'How much did you give her?'

'Only a shilling, poor creature.'

'Too much,' he says. 'You'll be seeing her again. You know what they say. Pay a beggar, keep a beggar. Now, shall we be off? Your cold cuts'll be curling at the edge. And I cannot *abide* warm Bolly.'

Valentine loves his glass of Bollinger. Well so do I and I shall have it as long as I can afford it. There's nothing better after all those hours in a stifling theatre. And he was right about the cold cuts. I had this girl, Olive, who came in daily. I didn't need more than that. She'd come in of an afternoon, flick her duster around, donkey stone the front step once a week. She was a good girl. Clean and quiet, and honest. She never pocketed any of my trinkets. The only problem with Olive was that there was always one last thing she'd omit to do. Like, she'd forget to put the hall runner back after she'd mopped the linoleum, or she'd forget to lay a damp tea cloth over the supper tray to keep everything fresh and dainty till I came home.

I hardly ate a thing that evening. Artistes are generally hungry after a show. It's a well-known phenomenon. It was explained to me once, how it's caused by nerves. You're wound up, tight as a fiddle string before you go on, which saps you without your realising it. Then you come off and feel like you could eat a ferret with the measles. But that evening I didn't have much of an appetite. Perhaps it was seeing Kate. I think it was.

Valentine said, 'You're not your usual self, Miss Dot.'

I said, 'You know Griffin's talking about cutting wages?'

'Well,' he said, 'let him try. I shall walk out and he'll never engage me no more. I'm booked for Collins's and then the Liverpool Adelphi. I'm on the up and up, so Jimmy Griffin had better not threaten me.'

I didn't like to point out that Collins's Music Hall hardly amounts to being on the up and up.

He said, 'And as for you, he wouldn't dare. You're a star. Griffin wouldn't have a show without you, and he knows it. It's an idle threat. I wouldn't give it another thought.'

One good thing about Valentine is he knows when to apply a bit of soft soap.

I said, 'Anyway, Monty deals with all that side of things. He'll tell him what's what.'

'Quite right,' he said. 'Make Monty Hyams earn his percentage. Miss Dot, I've been thinking.'

'Beginner's luck,' I said.

We had a laugh.

'But seriously,' he said, 'I'm thinking of giving up my digs.'

'I thought you liked it there?'

'I did. But there's a type moved in upstairs and he's not very clean. When he's passed through the front hall there's a horrible whiff. It hangs about for ages. You know me, Miss Dot. I'm very particular about cleanliness. And he has no consideration. I think it's generally known in the house that I'm in the theatre. I work late hours and I must have my sleep, but he's clodhopping about above my head at five in the morning.'

'And then does he go to work?'

'I suppose he does, but he takes his time about it, back and forth, back and forth, and always with his boots on. Well, once I'm awake I can't get back off. I'm a wreck. So I was wondering. About your spare room?'

I'd always kept that room made up in case my brother Albert should think of visiting me, though he never did. It was a handy place to hang my gowns too, my theatricals, not my day wear.

I said, 'It's hardly suitable for a lodger. It's a small room.'

'And I'm a small person,' he said. 'We get along, don't we, you and me? Sometimes I wouldn't even be here. Two weeks and I'll be off to Liverpool. I'd be a phantom lodger.'

Anybody else, I'd have said no at once. I've lived alone too long to be accommodating other people. Sometimes I stay all day in my wrapper, until it's time to go to the theatre.

I said, 'I couldn't allow a lot of hot food brought in. I don't want the smell.'

'Strike me down if I was ever to do more than coddle an egg,' he said.

'And if you required your bits and pieces taken to the wash-house you'd have to come to an agreement with Olive.'

'We'd be company for each other, on a Sunday, say, or when we're between engagements.'

'But only by prior appointment. No coming into the parlour unannounced. I like to take a bath in here on Sunday afternoons.'

'My eyes will be averted.'

'And sometimes I have callers.'

It's only Tom Bullen, but if you're going to take in a paying guest it's as well to have everything on a clear footing from the start.

'You'll find me the very soul of discretion,' he said. 'And when you've thought about the rent, be so good as to write the figure down on a little billydoo. Friends shouldn't talk about money. Now, Miss Dot, it's not like you to leave a custard tart.'

'You have it. I've no appetite tonight.'

'Is it Griffin who's upset you? Or seeing that person?'

Kate from Bilston Street. I did keep thinking about her.

I said, 'Anybody can go to the bad, I suppose. Look at Chip Carver.'

'Who's he?'

'Novelty siffleur. Well, he was. Before your time. He was highly successful, though you wouldn't think it to see him now.'

'What happened?'

'Lost all his teeth.'

'That was bad luck. And he had nothing else to fall back on?'

'No, more's the pity. He does a bit of message-carrying nowadays. I see him sometimes, on the street. He keeps very cheerful, considering, but that's my point. A bit of bad luck, a wrong turn here or there. How many misfortunes, how many wrong turns does it take before you end up like Kate, sleeping at Cooney's?'

'A great many,' he said. 'And it's hardly a prospect that should worry you.'

'But you get to forty, Valentine, and you do start to wonder who'll look after you when you're too old to work. When you're alone in the world, like me.'

'You'll never be alone in the world,' he said. 'You'll always have me.'

I said, 'I remember when men used to turn to look at Kate. She was very bonny. And she didn't care what anybody thought of her. I remember when she was the talk of our street.'

'Oh do tell,' he said. So I did.

2

I'm a Wolverhampton girl, Black Country born, bred and buttered. My granddad was an ostler at Moxley colliery and my dad worked at the Bilston Steel. I was the youngest of four, but by the time I came along there was only my brother Albert left at home and he was in long trousers. My sister May had gone away to Birmingham to be in service and the oldest boy, Titus, had died from the cholera. I was a bit of an afterthought, you might say. Our mam probably believed she was safe from getting any more babies.

'I thought I had a growth,' she used to say. 'I thought my days was numbered until you started wriggling about.'

There was some dispute from our dad that he'd fathered another child. He swore Mam must have been carrying-on with some other man. Where he thought she found the time for any carrying-on I do not know, but once my father got an idea in his head it took more than plain horse sense to remove it.

Albert reckons the arguing went on all the time Mam was carrying me.

'That bab's never mine. Yow'm a trollop, Jessie Allbones, no two ways.'

'And yow'm barmy, Allbones. You go the Onion Fair and come

home so kaylied you fall up the stairs and then yow don't even remember poking the fire.'

Apparently the matter was settled the minute I was born because I was the very image of Dad – long and thin and bald as a badger – and he never called Mam a trollop again. That was 10th June 1847 and today is the 7th March 1889, so now you can calculate how far over the hill I've travelled.

I reckon I must have been about five when Kate came to live on Bilston Street. Everyone was talking about it. She was a poor orphan, took in by her aunt and uncle who lived across the street from us. Kate's parents had left Wolverhampton and shifted to London, hoping to make a better life, but I suppose all they found was the same life in a bigger city. Then they both died.

'Well,' Mam said. 'That's London for you.'

Kate's parents had left a number of children who had to be farmed out to any relations kind enough to take them, or be put in an orphanage. Kate dropped lucky. Her aunt and uncle gave her a home and treated her as if she was their own. It all went well for a start. People on Bilston Street took to her at once. She had a cheerful, open kind of face, not shy in the least or sorry for herself as you'd think a poor orphan might be.

'A most likeable girl,' everyone said.

She was soon out on the street playing with us. Her cousins were just little babs so she needed playmates, and then before you knew it, she was in charge. She was the one who decided when it was time for a new game. We'd all be playing knucklebones, then out she'd come with a length of clothes line and that was that. Next day everybody'd be skipping.

I was fascinated by her. I think it was her hair, thick and dark red with a natural wave. My hair has always been a disappointment. That's why I make a feature of my hats. Kate would have been ten, going on eleven, but she seemed older. She was always kind to me. When you're the tail end of a family you can feel a bit of an oddity, but she took to me. I put my heel through my skirt hem one time, playing hopscotch, and I was afraid I'd get a larruping from Mam. But Kate said, 'Don't blart. Blarting don't get you anywhere,' and she fetched a needle and thread and mended it for me and made a good job of it too. I still got a larruping, when the mend was discovered, but Mam did concede it was very neatly done.

But then, after a year or two, Kate stopped playing in the street. It seemed like overnight she'd turned into a woman. That was when Albert and his friends started noticing her. They'd dribble their football up and down in front of her house, hoping she'd come out so they could have a peep at her bay window.

She was always a bit forward, I suppose. Perhaps that was the cause of her going astray. Some people stopped finding her likeable, particularly the women.

Mam used to say, 'Yow keep your trousers buttoned, Albert Allbones. That one's got trouble wrote all over her.'

When Kate finished her schooling, she went to work in the japanning room, at the same factory where our mam worked. Nearly all the women round our way did. I suppose I'd have ended up there too, if God hadn't given me the knack of making people laugh. I shouldn't have liked it, day after day the same, all those women together chuntering about their babbies and their grandbabbies and their insides, but you do what you have to do. There was always plenty of work to be had in Wolverhampton. A girl could earn three or four shillings a week in the factories.

A bonny figure can take a girl far, if she keeps a sensible head on her shoulders, but I think the thing with Kate was that she was restless. She didn't want to spend her whole life on Bilston Street. Well neither did I. She had her looks and she was no fool, but she thought a man was her ticket out of there, which goes to show she wasn't so clever. Men are all very well, as long as you don't depend on them entirely.

Every lad from Willenhall to Coseley was sniffing round her and I'm sure our Albert was one of them, but she wasn't interested in boys. She took up with an older man.

'Thirty, if he's a day,' Mam said, 'and Irish!' She said it like she'd swallowed a dose of worm syrup. 'After everything the Edderses have done for that girl.'

We didn't like the Irish. There were none on Bilston Street but it was one of our rules, just in case we encountered any. Mostly the Wolverhampton Irish lived around Caribee Island where the rents were cheaper, so we were always warned not to set foot in that quarter of town. Mam said the Irish spent all their money in wobble shops and kept donkeys and stalled them inside their houses. Worst of all, they were Catholics.

I'm sure Kate got the same warnings I did, but it didn't deter her. She took up with an Irishman called Conway and went to lodge with him on Herbert Street and everyone put on their sympathetic face when they saw her aunt and uncle. You'd really have thought there'd been a death in the family.

We didn't see Kate again for a long, long time after that. Albert heard a few things, which Mam said he wasn't to speak of but what she actually meant was he wasn't to repeat them until she had time to put on a clean pinny and sit down to listen to all the particulars. Kate was apparently doing very nicely. Conway wasn't one of those ditch-digging micks. He had a bit of an army pension for one thing, *and* he was a writer. A writer! And not the literary kind that lives on bread and water and dies in an attic. Tom Conway made a good living at the gallows ballads. He composed them and then Kate hawked them, at the executions.

'Hawks them with her other wares on display,' our Albert used to snigger. 'Well I'd buy a sheet, just to have a free gander at them dumplings.'

It would have been a travelling life of course. I don't know how far afield they'd have gone. Shrewsbury, Worcester, wherever there was to be a hanging. It'd be a bit like the business I'm in. No two weeks are the same. You must go wherever you can get an engagement. But then, as was bound to happen, Conway got her in the family way. We heard she'd had a girl. A baby must have clipped her wings for a while. I believe her aunt did go to help her, during her lying-in, but it wasn't much talked about. Kate faded from our lives.

I had my own engagements by then. By the time I was fifteen, I was quite well established. The way it started was as follows: a contest was got up one year, just before Christmas, an entertainment to be held in the back room of the Boot and Star. That was 1853, so I'd have been six. It was a penny to take part and the prize was a cockerel, plucked and drawn and ready for the oven, and as I was forever performing to myself in Mam's bit of bedroom mirror, Dad said we might as well invest a penny and try to make something of it.

I sang 'Cherry Ripe', and when that didn't seem to be delighting everyone to my satisfaction, I did a quick switch to 'Over the Hills and Far Away', complete with actions and facial expressions until I was lifted down off the table and informed that my time was up. I won the cockerel though, so we had a good Christmas dinner and my Dad got stars in his eyes.

He said, 'I reckon our Dot might do well on the boards if we train her up a bit. I reckon she'll keep us in our old age.'

I continued going to the Ragged School, I'll give my father credit for that. He wanted me to know my letters. But any time a turn was required, I was proposed for it. I became quite a regular at the Prince of Wales and whatever I earned was put into a jar on the mantelpiece, to pay for the new costumes I seemed to need every other week because I was growing fast. Shooting up like a lupin fed on horseshit, as Dad used to say. By the time I was ten I towered over Mam, by twelve I could look Dad in the eye. I was late becoming a woman though, and even then I didn't have a lot to show for it, no bosoms, no hips, so the boys weren't much interested in me.

'One thing about our Dot,' Mam used to say. 'She'll never bring us no heartache.'

Unlike Kate, who'd pitched up again with two children and another one on the way. She'd had a falling out with Mr Conway and was hoping her relations would take her in. But her uncle had passed away by then and her aunt was struggling to get by. I suppose she was in no mood to pick up the mess Kate was making of her life. She sent her on her way, and I do believe that was the last time I'd seen her, trudging off down Bilston Street with her swollen belly and a pair of skriking kids running after her. Until the night she claimed me outside Griffin's.

3

Monty and Griffin had words about money. According to Monty he came out on top of the argument, but that was a cock-eyed version if ever I heard one because the net of it was that Griffin cancelled my December engagement.

'Never fear,' Monty says. 'I'll find you another spot. Plenty of time. Have you thought of pantomime?'

He knows I'm not suited to ensemble work. I'm a solo artiste. I write my own patter. I can't share a stage. And anyway it was daft, empty talk because July's too late for pantomime bookings, unless somebody's had the misfortune to fall under a tram, and nobody likes to work in dead men's shoes.

I said, 'A season at the Paragon is what I'd like.'

'You and everybody else,' he says. 'The Paragon's a tough nut to crack.'

'Twenty-five years I've been at this game, and twenty of them at the top. The Paragon ought to be begging me.'

'But those twenty-five years,' he says, 'may be the problem. An artiste gets to a certain age. Places like the Paragon, they're looking for fresh blood. No offence, Dot, but you're no ingénue.'

Well, I never was the ingénue, even when I could have been. That's not my line.

I said, 'When was the last time you talked to the Paragon about me?'

'Allow me to know my business,' he says. Which was no answer at all. 'Many artistes of your age would be glad to rest up a bit.'

Artistes with rich husbands. Artistes with nothing better to do than lie on a couch eating violet creams.

I said, 'I can't afford to rest up. I need to see my engagement book filled, and not with penny gaffs. I have rent to pay.'

'And bills for French champagne,' he says. 'Perhaps you should make some economies. You live higher than most.'

Not that he ever refuses a glass when it's offered.

I'll tell you about Monty Hyams. He was my booking agent and manager. Monty handled other turns, of course, novelty acts mainly, but nothing of my calibre. I was the jewel in his crown and he'd have done well to remember it. Monty and I had been together since '75. He took over from my brother Albert after Mam took badly and he had to go back to Wolverhampton to look after her.

When I first started out, I mean properly started out, playing places like Holder's Concert Hall in Birmingham and the Moor Street Adelphi, I was managed by Uncle Si. He wasn't a real uncle. He was a friend of the family, as they say. A friend of the family who watched me grow up and start to make a name for myself and thought: 'I'll have a slice of that, thank you very much.' It was quite some time before we twigged that he was pocketing more of my earnings than had been agreed, but as soon as it was discovered Albert and some big lads from the steel works invited him down a dark alley for a knuckle sandwich and that was the last we saw of Uncle Si.

After that, Albert said he'd manage me. You can trust family. Albert had his percentage, of course, but he was never a money-grubber. As long as he had enough in his pocket for a beer he was satisfied. Perhaps I'd have gone to the very top, up the West End, if Albert had been a bit more industrious, but we did well enough. The thing about a brother is loyalty. When I was married to Hamish McHendie, Purveyor of Hibernian Hilarity, which I was for two years, three months and eight days of misery, Albert always stood up for me. But then Dad passed over and Mam went downhill. He said, 'No sense you giving up all this, Dotty. I'll go home and look after her. I can probably get set on at the steel again. I'll find something.'

So then Monty Hyams bid to take me on and he had a good reputation. Straight as a billiard cue, people said, and I will say I never doubted his honesty. He never tried any funny stuff. He was a queer bird though. You never saw him with a sweetheart. I suppose he had his needs like any man but how he catered to them I do not know.

He owns two houses on Berner Street. He used to live in one of them and his mother lived in the other. She must be about a hundred and twenty and if the seventh angel came to earth and sounded the last trump, Monty wouldn't dare miss Friday dinner with her.

I had begun to wonder, though, if he was doing right by me, if he was getting me the bookings and the fees I deserved. He seemed to spend an awful lot of time looking for new artistes. He'd say, 'I have to, Dot. I have to keep myself apprised of changing fashions, otherwise I'm liable to find myself with a book full of dead wood.'

I said, 'I hope that's not a knock at me.'

'Not at all,' he says. 'But I'll give you an example. As you'll recall, there used to be plenty of work for plate-spinners. You'd find one in every line-up. Not any more. You can't give them away. But lady weight-lifters and lady wrestlers, I could use another dozen of them.'

Amazonia was his latest acquisition. *Authentic and exotic warrior maiden*. The only true word in that billing was 'and'.

So Monty and Griffin had words and I got the chop.

I said, 'That wasn't supposed to be the outcome. So who's he bringing in instead of me?'

'For December? I couldn't say.'

'Not Bella Delmere, I pray.'

'Who?'

'The one with the rabbit teeth.'

'She's not Bella Delmere. Hasn't been for a year or two now. She goes as Marie Lloyd these days, but I don't think she's working at the moment. I heard she was in the family way.'

I said, 'Good. That'll hobble her. By the time she gets her figure back, they'll have forgotten her.'

'I wouldn't bank on that, Dot,' he says. 'She has a very strong following.'

Bella Delmere, whatever she calls herself, is nothing but a winking skirt-dancer if you ask me. I don't know why people make so much of her.

I said, 'Then I suppose you've offered Griffin your Amazonian maiden in place of me.'

'Nothing's been decided. Griffin's having a revamp,' he said. 'He'll choose the turns he wants in his own good time.'

I always know when Monty's wriggling. He twiddles his moustache.

'And anyway,' he says, 'December's a long way off.'

I'd written to Albert to tell him I'd bumped into Kate, to see if he remembered her.

I should say I remember her, he wrote. She ran off with an Irishman. I'm sorry to hear she's fallen on hard times but I can't say as I'm surprised, Dotty. She wasn't exactly a lady. You'll understand what I mean.

Nothing much to tell you. I'm going along all right, not too bad for an old-timer, just laid new linoleum in the front bedroom. Ezra Dick gave me a helping hand, you probably don't remember him, he used to work at the Springvale furnace, got a wall-eye, very nice man. Our May is pretty middling from what I hear. I haven't been to see her. I got a card from her last back end, said she was sinking but, Dotty, she's been sinking for years and it's a fair old traipse to Small Heath. I suppose I shall have to go when they bury her. Any road, remember me to Kate if you should see her again. Now you've given her money, I daresay you will.

Valentine moved into my spare room the Sunday before he went off to his Liverpool engagement. He brought his own sheets and his own tea kettle.

He said, 'All I'll require from you is a key, and a scuttle of coal in case the nights turn chilly.'

I heard him go out around three. I was in my hip bath, just getting my final rinse, so I was decent by the time he came back.

He called through the door, 'I've brought a poppy-seed cake from Friedman's if anybody's feeling peckish.'

Olive whispered, 'Mr St John seems very nice. He's paid me in advance for doing his shirts, and he won't even be here next week.'

So then we all had tea and cake in my parlour. Valentine insisted Olive should join us before she went home. She grew quite flushed, laughing at his little quips. She thought he was paying her attention, I suppose. Well I put her straight about that before she left.

I said, 'Mr St John is an artiste, a top-liner sometimes.'

'Oh I know,' she said. 'Everybody's heard of Mr St John.'

I said, 'Just don't act giddy around him. He's only trying to put you at your ease.'

'I am at my ease,' she said. 'And, Miss Allbones, I think it'll be a great comfort for you to have a younger person about.'

That was how our Sunday teas came about. Valentine was clearing away the teacups – he wouldn't hear of Olive doing it, 'you get off home,' he told her – and he said to me, 'Well that was very pleasant. We must do it again, when I get back from Liverpool. You know Friedman's make a very good apple cake.'

I said, 'Here you go. You haven't even unpacked your hair brushes and you're taking over.'

But I didn't mind, not really. And then that Monday he was gone early, slipped away to go to the railway station and I never heard a thing. I reckon he must have carried his boots and tiptoed out in his stockinged feet.

4

I was booked for two weeks at the Marylebone. It had been a while since I played there. It's not a bad hall, more commodious than Griffin's at any rate. With Valentine away in Liverpool, it was in the back of my mind who might keep me company when it came to Friday night. I mean, I have my standards. I'd sooner go home alone and risk an attack of the jitters than share a cab with some I could mention. Men with bad breath. Boys with no conversation. Pontificators who keep a lady waiting. Gas men are always the last to leave. Bandsmen wait for no-one. Last strain of 'The Queen' and they're out of the door. And the trouble at the Marylebone was they were all new faces. Thursday night, second house, Tom Bullen was in. I recognised his laugh, and he came round afterwards, to compliment me on the show. I've known Tom for many years. He's a newspaper man. Not the kind who writes the stories. He's one of those who finds the stories.

'Cracking turn, Dot,' he says. 'As usual. You had me laughing till my sides ached. Can I press you to brandy and soda?'

I said, 'Not tonight. Monty's waiting to see me home. How about tomorrow?'

'It'll be my pleasure,' he says. So that was Friday settled.

Come Friday he sat right through the show again too.

He said, 'I won't lie to you, Dot, it wasn't just you I came to see. I wanted to have another look at them Irish acrobats.' The Flying Flahertys. They do this act, they pretend to miss their footing or lose their bearings. It's quite comical.

I said, 'I didn't know you liked that kind of thing.'

'No,' he says, very confidential. 'But I heard a little whisper the police have got their eye on them.'

I said, 'The Flahertys? Are you sure? I know their act's a bit ropey but they're surely not that bad. If anybody in the show needs locking up it's Madame Celeste.'

He laughed.

Madame Celeste La Rue, Lady Baritone – well I call her Cissie because I knew her when she was plain Cissie Roundtree – to be candid, she's more of a freak show than a true artiste. She should be in a circus. And she's a nightmare to work with when space is tight. She expects hanging room for her gowns, and a place for her doggie's basket, and that's before you've allowed room for her own substantial self. Every time I see her she appears to have grown another chin. And her voice! Valentine calls her The Dying Bullfrog. He's quite convinced she's a man. Any time he knows Cissie and I are appearing at the same hall he urges me to take a peek but I never do. Some things are best left shrouded in mystery.

So Tom saw me home that Friday night and all he talked about was the Flying Flahertys. He'd heard they were secret Fenians.

'Fenians!' I said. 'Surely that's ancient history?'

'Short memory you have,' he says. 'Have you forgotten Gower Street? Have you forgotten Dynamite Saturday?'

I hadn't forgotten it. 1885. Every week there'd been a new panic on, Irish arrested, plots uncovered, dynamite found. There was a bomb went off at the Gower Street station. You'll never catch me riding on one of those underground trains. It's not natural. Give me a tram any day. I like to see a bit of sky when I'm travelling. Then three bombs went off in one afternoon, two at Westminster, one at the Tower, and all people talked about was Fenians. But three years had passed and it seemed to me the Fenians had gone quiet.

'Gone quiet, maybe,' says Tom, 'but not gone away. Don't you worry though. Scotland Yard never sleeps. They have their eyes and ears.'

I said, 'Well I won't believe it of the Flahertys. They're lovely boys.'

'Of course they are,' he says. 'That's their front. That's how they lull us. Next thing you know they'll be blowing us up. You keep your eyes open. You see anything of a suspicious nature, you let me know.'

I said, 'What, like Jerry Flaherty rolling a barrel of gunpowder down the street?'

'You may scoff. When Paddy and his friends start up again don't say I didn't warn you. I shall receive your apology with good grace.'

Tom Bullen's always looking to be first with a story. That's his trade. He hears something and runs with it to the papers. It doesn't matter if it turns out to be nonsense. Papers must have something to fill their pages and it's all soon forgotten. Anyway, it all ends up wrapped round fried fish.

Tom had always been keen on me. On and off, over the years,

we'd had our moments. One glass of the bubbly and he came over very amorous that evening.

'You're a fine woman, Dot,' he says. 'Budge up so I can sit beside you.'

I told him he could have one kiss and be on his way. I don't mind it sometimes but I wasn't in the mood. Then he commenced bargaining with me.

'As long as it's not just a peck on the cheek,' he says. 'A proper kiss and a cuddle, that's all I ask. I'm a gentleman, you know that, but I'm only human.'

I'm afraid we had a bit of a tussle. That can be a drawback of not wearing stays. Men sometimes get over-heated if they sense they're within reach of the finishing line. But I had the last word. I need my sleep after a show, and between you and me I don't think Tom had got much starch in his dickey. I'd say he'd had a few, earlier in the evening.

It must have been after one o'clock when I got him out the door.

'How are you fixed for next Friday?' he said.

'I don't know, Tom. I might have other plans.'

'That's the ticket, Dot. Keep me in suspense. What a woman!'

I said, 'By the by, did I tell you I have a lodger now?'

That sobered him up.

'Where?' he says. 'What, upstairs? Is she in? Has she been listening to all our private business?'

'It's not a she, it's a he, and no, he's not in. But he could have been, just so you know.'

'But who is he?'

'Valentine St John.'

'The one who sings like a girl? I didn't know you were looking for a lodger.'

'I wasn't. But Valentine wasn't happy in his old place. He suggested moving here and I thought I'd give it a try.'

'I'm the one you should give a try. I'd move in with you tomorrow.'

'So you've often told me, but that would be an entirely different arrangement.'

'Well,' he said, 'I suppose if you must have somebody living under your roof, just as well he's only a boy. He won't be trying anything with you. Has he got a sweetheart?'

'No.'

'Is he a powder puff?'

'I have no idea.'

'You should ask him. When you take in a lodger you need to know these things.'

'He's clean, he's quiet, he pays his rent.'

'That may be so. But say you had an engagement out of town, you don't want to come back and find your home turned into a molly-house.'

After the Marylebone I was engaged for the Forester's in Mile End. There promised to be a fair line-up. Dickie Dabney and his Mathematical Crows, Stefan the Mentalist, Lionel Neve the blind pianist, Babette the Living Doll. Also Monty's new artiste, Amazonia. I was looking forward to watching her. She was supposed to bend iron bars and carry full-grown men off the stage. Of course, as it turned out, they weren't iron bars at all. They were lead pipes. And the men she carried, volunteers from the stalls, weren't volunteers. They were plants. Weedy little stooges who weighed next to nothing.

Monday afternoon I got to the theatre and what did I find? Amazonia had top billing.

Lottie Cherry runs the Forester's. She used to be half of the Cheery Cherry Twins. I played Hoxton Varieties with them years ago but Lottie's in management now. She was in the office.

I said, 'There seems to be a misprint on the playbill.'

'No,' she said. 'It's what was agreed.'

Not with me it wasn't.

'Backsides on seats,' she says. 'That's the only business I'm in. If the public wants lady weight-lifters, lady weight-lifters is what I'll give them, top of the bill. Monty told me you'd been advised of the change.'

Monty had never said a word to me, the varmint. I put my hat back on.

Lottie said, 'Don't run off, getting yourself into a state. It's not going to make any difference. Go downstairs. Have a glass of seltzer. Put your feet up for half an hour.'

But I couldn't settle till I'd had it out with him, and I guessed where I might find him. Monday afternoons he likes to get his hair trimmed, at Farbstein's on Chicksand Street. And there he was, in the first chair, towel round his neck. Everything fell quiet, of course, when I opened the door. It's not a place ladies go to. Old Farbstein said something into Monty's ear and he turned.

'Dot?' he says. 'Whatever are you doing here? You look a bit flustered. Everything all right?'

'Amazonia. Top of the bill.'

'Ah,' he said. 'Well the thing is, I'm afraid Lottie insisted on it.'

See, that's what you're up against. Management blames the agents and agents swear the management wouldn't have it any other way.

'And you never even warned me. Those playbills were printed and everybody and his Aunt Sadie knew, except me.'

'I thought I did tell you. It must have slipped my mind.'

Slipped his mind! Then he changed his story.

He said, 'I knew this is how you'd be. I knew you'd have a fit. But you've got second billing, Dot. There's artistes who'd kill for that. Why can't you be satisfied?'

'Get me second billing at Drury Lane and I will be satisfied. But not at Forester's. I've been the top-liner there for years.'

'Perhaps so,' he says, 'but times change. There's a lot of interest in Amazonia just now.'

'She'll be a five-minute wonder.'

'Then she's entitled to her five minutes. I have to live too, Dot. I have to eat. You're not the only artiste on my books, may I remind you.'

I could understand it if she was easy on the eye. Men love a flash of a girl's knees. They'll come back hoping to see a bit more the next time. But these fleshings Amazonia wears, there's nothing left to the imagination. She looks like a five-foot sausage. Uncooked.

I said, 'She's not even exotic. Amazonia! She's blummin' Blanche Smith. She's from Dewsbury.'

'I'll thank you not to spread that about.'

I said, 'I don't need to. They all remember from two years ago, when El Gerardo used to saw her in half. It's a pity he ever put her back together.'

Farbstein stood there with his clippers in his hands and his mouth open.

Monty said, 'Get to the theatre, Dot, there's a trooper. I'll be round later. We can talk about this after the show.'

But what was there to talk about? The damage was done. Once you start to slip down the playbill it's very hard to clamber back. Next thing you know you're down at the foot of the page and the only thing below you is the line that says *Disorderly persons will be expelled*.

When Monty dropped me home that night, the gas mantle was lit in the front hall. You could see the flicker of it through the glass.

He said, 'I suppose that daily girl of yours left it burning. What a waste of money. You should train her better.'

But I knew it wasn't Olive. She'd have been gone long before it got dark.

I said, 'It'll be Valentine. I'm expecting him back from Liverpool.'

'Valentine?' he says. 'You mean St John? How long has this been going on?'

'He's lodging with me, and just as well. If you carry on giving my top spots to Blanche Smith, I shall be glad of a bit of rent from Valentine.'

'Well,' he said, 'that sounds very cosy. How's he doing these days? Who represents him?'

I said, 'He represents himself and he's doing very nicely. He's just had a week at the Liverpool Adelphi.'

He pulled a face. Golders Green's about as far north as Monty ventures.

'Liverpool?' he said. 'Why would he go there?'

'Because he's from that part of the world. I suppose he still has a following up there. It must have been worth his while. He wouldn't travel all that way and go to the expense of digs if it wasn't a paying proposition. Valentine's no fool. And he keeps himself in work. Not always top drawer, but he's not often idle. He cultivates all the theatre managers. He writes letters and he goes from hall to hall making sure they don't forget him.'

'Why does he put himself to all that trouble? I could do that for him.'

'Never mind about him. You pay proper attention to *my* engagements.'

'Your problem, Dot, is you need some new material.'

'And your problem, Monty, is you hang around the office waiting to see the takings counted instead of watching me. I *have* new material. "Naughty but Nice". "In the Hands of my Solicitor". "Mary Plucker Sparrowtail". I ring the changes.'

'"Three Acres and a Cow". How many years have you been singing that?'

'My public expects it.'

'Then give it to them for an encore, should you ever be asked for one.'

We parted very cross that evening.

I said, 'I won't require you to come in tonight.'

'Nor any other night, I suppose,' he said. 'Now you've got a lodger. Well that suits me. I need to get home to Mother. She's not at all well.'

Valentine heard my key in the lock and came out from the scullery. He was bright-eyed, polished as an apple.

'There you are!' he said. 'I thought you were going to sit out in that cab all night.'

'I was having words with Monty.'

'Get your coatee off and come and tell me all about it. The Bolly's nice and cold. Olive forgot to put a tea cloth over your bread and butter but I think I've managed to resurrect it.'

It was comforting to have someone to come home to. I told him about Amazonia.

'You've been robbed, Miss Dot,' he said. 'The woman's an abomination! But she'll soon be forgotten. This time next year who'll even remember her? Novelty turns never endure. Now, cheer up and see what I've brought you back from Liverpool.'

Rose fondants. It was only when he got up from his seat to fetch them that I noticed the fob chain on his waistcoat.

I said, 'Is that a pocket watch you're wearing?'

He brought it out to show me properly, a half hunter in a gilt case.

I said, 'Who did you knock down for that?'

'It's a present,' he said. 'From an admirer. No, not an admirer. A follower.'

Well! Valentine's a dear boy and he does have talent, but a pocket watch is a considerable gift.

I said, 'A follower? What's her name, Lady Rosebery?'

'Him,' he says. 'He's an American gentleman, very well connected, very cultured. Dr Townsend. He's a connoisseur of the male voice.'

'So it went well in Liverpool.'

'Full houses. They'd have extended my engagement but, of course, I had prior commitments. I'm at Gatti's and the Canterbury from next Monday.'

'You're not working this week?'

'No. Frank says it's very important to rest a voice like mine.'

'Who's Frank?'

'Dr Townsend.'

'He knows about voices, does he?'

'Oh yes. He says I must be very cautious not to get nodules on my cords. He says they're easily acquired and hard to get rid of.'

'And what was this American doctor doing at the Liverpool Adelphi?'

'He'd just landed, sailed from Boston. He saw me billed as a genuine male soprano and came to my second show. He was so impressed he delayed his journey to London. He came in every night, and bought me dinners.'

'And a pocket watch.'

'Yes. But, Miss Dot, he's in London now. We travelled down together. First class! Frank insisted. You must meet him. You'll find him a most entertaining raconteur. So I was wondering, how would it be if I invited him to our Sunday tea?'

It has been my experience that a person who gets billed as 'a most entertaining raconteur' is generally a disappointment and I'd already decided to dislike this particular one, going around handing out pocket watches to impressionable boys, so I thought I might as well take a look at him and confirm my opinion.

I said, 'If you vouch for him, Valentine, I look forward to meeting him.'

'Oh good,' he said. 'I'll go down to Friedman's early and get a plum cake. We'll have a proper little soirée.'

A week in Liverpool and he comes back speaking French.

5

On the Friday I did a rash thing. I invited Tom Bullen to Sunday tea. Well I didn't see why Valentine should have a friend there and me not. To be honest I was starting to regret that I'd agreed to the arrangement. All I'd heard from Valentine that week was 'Frank this' and 'Frank that'.

Tom said, 'Tea? I'd sooner come home with you now and have something stronger.'

I said, 'Not tonight. I need my beauty sleep.'

He said, 'If you get any handsomer, Dot, I shall need to shade my eyes.' He can be a silly old ta-ta.

'What's the occasion on Sunday? It's not your birthday.'

'Valentine's got a friend coming to call.'

'A sweetheart?'

'No. It's an American gentleman. A doctor.'

'That's handy. I've a toenail that's turned black. I might ask him to take a look at it.'

'You keep your boots on. I don't want toenails on display in my parlour, black or otherwise. Anyway, I don't know what kind of doctor he is. In fact, I can't quite make out his story. If he's American and he's a doctor, why isn't he in America doctoring?'

'Leave it to me, Dot,' he said. 'I'll fathom him. That's my profession. You pour and I'll get the story of his life.'

Sunday afternoon, we were all assembled but it got to nearly four o'clock and there was no sign of Dr Townsend. Valentine tried to keep a cheerful face but I could see he was disappointed. I was about to send Olive home with a slice of cake, when he arrived, and a great commotion he made about it too. No apology or explanation, hardly a Good Day even, just a wet handshake and in he strode, struck a pose against my mantelpiece and commenced to hold forth.

He was a tall man. Tom reckoned six foot, I'd say more. Ginger, with watery eyes and a walrus moustache that could have done with trimming. Perhaps it was his height made him give the impression he was looking down his nose at me, but I don't think so. I've observed many men in my time. I soon detect when a man has no appreciation of women. He hardly addressed me, and as for Olive, I don't think he noticed she was there. Frank Townsend was playing to Valentine and Tom, and he was quite the showman. I know it when I see it. His pauses and his little gestures. It was all very studied. And he had a fund of stories. He appeared to have been everywhere and know everyone.

'As I once remarked to Mr Lincoln . . .'

'As Sam Grant used to say to me – I'm speaking of General Ulysses S. Grant of course . . .'

He might have been an admirer of Valentine's voice but he wasn't averse to the sound of his own.

Tom asked him what brought him to London.

'Business affairs,' he says.

'Oh,' says Tom, 'Then I must have misunderstood. I thought you were a doctor.'

Valentine said, 'He is. Frank's a herbalist.'

'Indeed I am,' says Townsend. 'Oriental herbalist and purveyor of patent medicines. My profession requires ingredients from the great markets of Asia and Africa. Nowhere better to purchase them than the ports of London and Liverpool. I brave the Atlantic crossing twice a year, for my sins. But travel brings its rewards, sir. Only the day after I docked at Liverpool, I happened upon young Valentine at the Adelphi Theatre of Varieties. What a talent! What a find!'

Tom asked him where he was staying.

'I make the Charing Cross Hotel my principal residence,' he said, 'but when I'm doing commerce with the warehouses I find it more convenient to lodge in Whitechapel. Such colour, such character! It quite reminds me of our great metropolis of New York.'

He took two cups of tea and said he must be off. He had an appointment to view a room on Batty Street.

'I have a bachelor temperament,' he said. Not that anybody had asked him. 'My needs are simple. A bed, a desk, an armchair. But regarding landladies, I'm more particular. I require them to be mute and invisible. I pay my rent and, in exchange, I expect silence. Not always easy to find. The ladies can run on so.'

Damned cheek. He'd have given Henry Irving a run for his money, that one.

Tom said, 'Sounds like you'd be better suited to a monastery than rented rooms. What's that place in Mile End, Dot?' He winked at me. 'St Audrey's, is it? St Ann's?'

'A monastery would be eminently suitable but for one thing, sir.

The curfew. The monastics keep strict hours and what red-blooded man can visit London and forgo the delights of the supper rooms and theatres? But I have every hope that the chatelaine of Batty Street will prove to be a woman of few words. Her name has a German sound to it and they are a taciturn people.'

He made it clear he expected Valentine to leave with him.

'You must come and advise me, dear boy,' he said. 'Two heads are better than one.'

I think if Frank Townsend told Valentine to jump in the Limehouse Cut he'd be inclined to do it, but he did hesitate. That tea party had been his idea, after all. I'd even taken my bath half an hour earlier, so as to oblige him.

He whispered, 'Leave the tea things, Miss Dot. I'll clear them away when I get back.'

I said, 'Never mind a few cups and saucers. But as you're going in that direction, be so kind as to see Olive home. Not right to her door. Just drop her on Whitechapel Road. The kind of street she lives on all the neighbours'll be talking if she steps down from a hansom.'

'Well,' Tom said, when they'd gone, 'I don't know about you, Dot, but I could do with a proper drink.'

'What did you make of him?'

'A blusterer. I never met such a name-dropper.'

'He seems to have money. An oriental herbalist who buys pocket watches for artistes he's known for five minutes.'

Tom said, 'I'll fathom him. I reckon there's a story there. Did you observe the ruddiness of his complexion?'

'Too much whisky?'

'Or that florid cast so common among the Irish.'

'Townsend's not Irish.'

'He may have kicked the bog dirt off his boots, but I smell a Fenian.'

'You've got Fenians on the brain. Where does he get all his money? First-class railway carriages from Liverpool, rooms at the Charing Cross Hotel . . .'

'That's what I'm saying. Don't you know where the Fenians get their money, Dot? From America. From American-Irish who're quite happy to pay for dynamite as long as it's not blowing up their houses. I think I might call at Leman Street tomorrow, mention our Dr Townsend to Bill Thicke. It can't hurt.'

Bill Thicke's a sergeant at H Division. Tom Bullen cultivates them all, so he can be quick off the mark if there's a crime story.

I said, 'I think you're wrong, Tom. If he was bringing money to Fenians, surely he'd slip in quietly, do the deed and be gone. And the look of him, the size of the man, that great drooping moustache. You'd notice him at once if he passed you on the street. He must be remembered everywhere he goes. No, there must be more money to be made at Oriental herbalising than we realise. Anyway, whatever he is I didn't like him.'

'Me neither. I never trust a man who uses twenty-guinea words in conversation. In Parliament, or on the printed page, that's where they belong, not at a tea party. I hope you'll say something to young Valentine.'

'Such as?'

'Warn him to end the association.'

'Because I didn't like his friend? What am I to say to him? Tom Bullen thinks Frank Townsend's up to no good, based on him having money and a red face? I can't do that.'

'There is another aspect, Dot, but it's no topic for a lady. I'll have a word with Valentine myself.'

'What aspect?'

'Unnatural practices. I'll say no more.'

'Tom, I've been twenty-five years in the theatre so there's not much I don't know about. But Valentine's not like that. He's not much more than a boy.'

'That may be true. All the more reason to warn him. Nobody gives you a watch like that lest they want something in return, and if Townsend's not a sodomite I'll eat my hat.'

I don't know what time Valentine came in. Tom gave up waiting and went home. I gave up waiting and went to bed. One thing about Valentine, at night he's very light on his feet. It's the mornings when he makes his presence known, first with his gargling and then with his vocal exercises, but not early. It's usually getting on for noon before he starts.

I said, 'What became of you last evening?'

'I'm sorry, Miss Dot,' he says. 'Time got away from me. I went with Frank to view those diggings on Batty Street, then we fetched some of his things from Charing Cross, and then we went for a late supper.'

'He took the room then? The landlady wasn't too much of a chatterbox?'

'No, he's very happy. Very well suited. And didn't we have a lovely tea party? Frank found you all most congenial.'

'He certainly has some stories.'

'And you didn't hear half of them. He's had such an interesting life. Montreal, New York, San Francisco, London. He's been everywhere. It makes me realise how little I've seen of the world. Wigan, Rochdale, Oldham, Blackpool. Did I mention Rochdale?'

I said, 'Valentine, there's something I must say.'

'I know, I know,' he said. 'I shouldn't have gone off and left you to clear the tea things. I felt badly for doing it, and it won't happen again.'

'Very well,' I said. 'Then we'll say no more about it.'

Nor about unnatural practices, and the dangers of taking up with men you hardly know. It didn't seem the right moment. I don't imagine it ever does.

6

Monday was a bank holiday. When people have a day off it can go either way. They might come to the theatre, they might not. In August, generally, they stay away. If the weather's warm, people don't want to be sitting indoors. They'd sooner bring a chair out onto their front step and fetch a jug or two from an alehouse. But that particular Monday the weather turned cool and then it came on to rain. We were full for the second house.

I had words with Amazonia. It was bound to happen so I thought I'd give her cause and get it over with. We had a nice crowd in, very jolly, so I gave them an encore of 'Beautiful For Ever' and I took my time over it too. She, of course, had been called up, ready to go on. I could see her out of the corner of my eye, standing in the wings, sweating in her sausage suit.

'Hurry up, you old has-been,' she says, as I came off. 'They've had enough of you.'

Lol Withers, the gas man, was standing there.

I said, 'What's this blocking my way, Lol? The Human Polony?'

He chuckled.

I said, 'You mind the butcher's dog doesn't run off with you, Blanche.'

'Monty'll hear of this,' she says.

She went running to him as soon she came off.

He said, 'Dot, I want a word with you. I'll thank you not to upset Amazonia. You quite threw her off her stroke speaking to her that way, and just as she was about to go on.'

I said, 'She started it.'

'Time you grew up,' he says. 'It's up to you older artistes to set the tone.'

I said, 'You wouldn't expect a person who parades around like an oatmeal pudding to be so sensitive.'

Lottie Cherry was in the cubbyhole by the artistes' entrance.

'Nice show, Dot,' she says. 'There was a person asking for you just now, said she was an old friend but she looked a bit rough to me. I told her to wait outside.'

It was drizzling rain, nothing much but it can soak you in a minute. They were huddled close to the wall, Kate and a man.

'Oh, Dot,' she says. 'It's me again. I was hoping to see you.'

Yes, I thought. And hoping for another night's doss money, no doubt.

But I was wrong.

'Me and John have both been in work,' she said. 'So I wanted to pay you back that shilling you loaned me.'

I didn't take it of course. I never lend. As long as I've got it you can have it and keep it. If the day comes when I haven't got it, I hope people will remember me kindly.

'Ah yow'm a good sort,' she said. 'I told him you wouldn't want it but he likes us to pay our dues when we can.'

John Kelly was Kate's new husband. Whether they were truly married I cannot say, but I don't know that she was ever clergy-married to Tom Conway either. She wasn't the kind of woman to worry about a wedding ring. Kelly was a few years younger than Kate I'd say, or perhaps he was just holding up better. Another Irishman. He hardly opened his mouth. Sometimes people lose their tongue when they find themselves face to face with a famous artiste.

Monty was squeezing my arm, urging me to get along but I was in no mood to humour him. He should have thought of the consequences before Blanche Smith got her name printed above mine.

I said, 'I'm glad to see you, Kate. Me and Monty were just going to a chophouse for a bite. Why don't you and Mr Kelly come with us?'

Monty's face was a picture.

I said, 'Close your mouth before you catch a fly. You owe me.'

And off we all went to Stott's for a slap-up. Veal chops, syrup tart and French claret wine. Monty had his mardy face on but not for long. Kate charmed him out of that, asking him the story of his life, asking him all about his dear mother. She soon cottoned on to what's closest to Monty's heart.

Indoors, in the lamp light she did look a bit rough, but nothing that a dab of Pond's cold cream wouldn't help. There was still something about her. She was quite bonny really, for what, nearer fifty than forty, and hardly any grey in her hair.

John Kelly was quiet. He'd answer you, very polite, but he didn't volunteer anything. He wouldn't take any drink either. He said he had to be at Spitalfields by four, for the call-on. Any later than that he might lose a day's work. He did portering or sometimes he just minded carts, whatever he could get. Kate was working too, sweeping and scrubbing floors for somebody on Wentworth Street.

She said, 'It's a very busy time of year, do you see, for Mrs Gully. I'd say she'll need me for a good few weeks yet.'

She spoke of Mrs Gully as though I should know her. That's how they are in Whitechapel. Everybody expects to know your name and your business. Not like Victoria Park. Mr Earp had rooms at the back of my residence and I hardly knew him from a bar of soap. I wouldn't have wanted to.

I asked Kate what kind of trade this Mrs Gully was in.

'Oh babbies,' she says. 'Poor little babbies that can't be kept by their mothers. She's mowed out just now. Too many really. Her daughter's had to come in to give her a hand. There's been a lot of hop babies this year.'

The unintended hop babies. The Whitechapel women go hop-picking towards the back end of the summer, down to Kent. They can earn good money. Sometimes their husbands go with them, but sometimes they don't and that's when the women are liable to go astray. Perhaps it's the country air makes them reckless. Then they come home with more than hop money under their apron.

I have heard of people like Mrs Gully. Some of them have lying-in houses, where the babies are born and left behind, some just take babies in, for a fee. A lot of them die. A few drops of paregoric in their milk. I suppose it's easily done. Some of them might get sold on, the lucky ones, placed with people who want a child but can't seem to get one the usual way. I suppose some good comes of it.

Kate said, 'Very kindly hearted, Mrs Gully. She never turns a bab away, not even a sickly one.'

I wanted to ask her what had become of her own babies but I feared there'd be some sad story there.

Monty was going to order another bottle. I'd never seen him so mellow. But John Kelly said, 'Kate's had enough.'

She didn't like that. She turned on him, so sharp.

'Kate's not had enough,' she said. 'Why don't you mind your business? Why don't you bugger off to work and stop spoiling the party?'

And he did. He got up, he thanked Monty for his dinner though he'd eaten very little, and off he went.

'Pay no heed to him,' she says. 'He's not my keeper. Let's have another little drink. The trouble with Kelly is he worries too much. He worries about money, worries about tomorrow. What's the point? What will be, will be, eh, Monty?'

And Monty agreed with her. I had to smile. Monty Hyams worries the sun won't rise. But he was in his cups. Kate had loosened her neckerchief and he was enjoying the view to the south.

I said, 'Still, not a bad thing to have a man looking out for you, Kate. Claret can leave you with a thick head.'

'True, true,' she says.

That's the thing about drunks. One minute they'll argue black is white and then they'll turn around and agree with everything you say.

She said, 'John's very fond of me. His wife passed away and he likes to have somebody to care for. When he's had a day's work he always brings me a little something. A twist of tea or a bit of ribbon. He puts up with the sharp side of my tongue. I will say that. He never complains. He's blessed with a mild nature, do you see? He's very amiable. Like your Monty here.'

He nearly choked on his syrup tart, to hear himself described as *my* Monty.

I said, 'Monty's not my husband.'

'Isn't he?' she said. 'Well good luck to the pair of you any road. As long as he's not anybody else's husband, eh? But you should pluck him off the bough, Dot, before somebody else does.'

Poor Monty. I don't know which was worse, to be mistaken for my husband or for a fruit ripe for harvesting. I asked her if she remembered Albert.

'Course I do,' she said. 'Lovely lad. He broke his foot one time, jumping off a wall.'

That wasn't my Albert. That was Amos Willetts, but I let it go.

The rain had stopped when we came out of Stott's. She wouldn't hear of us dropping her.

'I shall walk,' she said. 'It's a nice fresh night now.'

I said, 'Will you go to your usual place?'

'Not tonight,' she said. 'I'm too late for Cooney's. But don't you worry. I know how to lift the latch at Mrs Gully's. I can sleep on her settle. Get an early start.'

I said, 'Come to the show one of the nights. I'll leave two tickets for you on the door.'

'I'd like that,' she said. 'Yow'm a good 'un, Dot. Yow'm a diamond,' and off she staggered.

Monty said, 'Will she be all right? Where does she live?'

'She's going to this Mrs Gully's tonight, where she chars, but usually she lodges at Cooney's, or the Casual Ward.'

'The Casual!' he says. 'God Almighty, Dot, what were you thinking of, making me sit next to her? What if she's lousy?'

'She looked clean enough to me. A bit threadbare, but that's no crime.'

'Well now I can't go home to bed,' he says. 'I'm probably infested. I'll have to sit up and wait for the bath house to open and you'd better do the same.'

I don't go to public bath houses. The very idea.

I said, 'I don't think Kate's lousy. I was only thinking how decent she keeps herself considering her circumstances. But you're right, Monty. You were sitting very close to her. You were very cosy.'

'We were not,' he said. 'I was being polite, that's all. I didn't even want to go to Stott's. I had no intention, but you had to go and open your big mouth, inviting strangers to dinner. And now you tell me that person sleeps at the Casual.'

'Sometimes.'

'And the Irish weasel that was with her?'

'I don't know where he sleeps. He had good shoulders on him for a weasel.'

'Black sorrow if my mother should ever hear of this,' he said, and he never spoke to me the rest of the way home.

7

I had clothes in my wardrobe I hadn't worn in years so I thought I'd look out a few things for Kate. She was shorter than me, and stouter, but a good-quality garment can always be let out. I wasn't palming off anything shoddy. I parcelled up two cotton shirts and a black wool coat with a rabbit fur trim and took them to the theatre. I thought she'd be sure to come to the show the next night, but she didn't.

Lottie said, 'The tickets you left at the door? They weren't took up. What do you want me to do with them?'

I said to leave them. Kate and John Kelly were sure to come, some other night.

'Monty seeing you home?' she says.

He was, but he wasn't coming to the theatre to collect me. He'd gone to the Pavilion to look at some fire-eater he was interested in so I'd agreed to walk down to Whitechapel Road to meet him.

'You mind yourself,' Lottie says. 'There was a woman murdered last night.'

'On Whitechapel Road?'

'No, on Wentworth Street,' she said, which gave me pause. I knew somebody had spoken of Wentworth Street recently but for a second or two I couldn't think who. Then I remembered.

I said, 'Have they named her?'

'I don't think they have. But there's been plenty gone to the dead-house today to take a look at her. Somebody'll know her. It'll be in the paper tomorrow morning.'

'An acquaintance of mine was walking to Wentworth Street last night. We'd been to Stott's for dinner.'

'Very nice. Then I hope your acquaintance got home safe. A hundred knife wounds, that's what I heard. Well it doesn't take a hundred jabs to kill a person. That's plain vicious. That was done by somebody who was in a fury. Her husband more than likely.'

Lottie has a low opinion of husbands. She's had three and she seems to have prospered but she never speaks fondly of any of them.

Monty said he knew nothing about the murder except that there had been one. He said he'd been too busy fumigating himself all day to listen to gossip.

I said, 'And I'll bet you never found a thing. Not the tiniest flea. How was the fire-eater?'

'I've seen better. And don't change the topic. I don't want you involving me in any more dinners with people who sleep in kip-houses. The thought of it has made my mother quite ill.'

I said, 'Why did you even tell her?'

'Because Mother and I have no secrets,' he says. 'Tuesday's not my usual day for the wash-house. She was bound to ask.'

Do you know something? I've never met Monty's mother, not once in all the years he's managed me. I've spied her at a window, just gazing out, and I gave her a cheery wave the first time I noticed her but she didn't wave back so I didn't bother again.

I said to him once, 'I don't think you've got a mother. I think that's a manikin in a white wig sitting in the window. I reckon you've got a dancing girl locked up in that house.'

'Damnation, Dot!' he says. 'You've discovered my secret.'

I said, 'The murder happened near Wentworth Street.'

'And? What is it to you?'

'Kate was walking that way after we left Stott's. Don't you recall? She was going to Wentworth Street.'

'Her and many others,' he says. 'Shouting and arguing and carrying-on till all hours. You'd think people in Whitechapel didn't have beds to go to.'

'Some of them don't. It couldn't be Kate lying in the morgue, could it? John Kelly would have claimed her by now, wouldn't he? He'd have missed her.'

'How should I know? Why do you even think about these people? They're nothing to do with us. Treating them to dinner, giving them theatre tickets, just because you lived on the same street as her, how many years ago? You'll soon beggar yourself, Dot, if you start feeding every stray dog.'

Is that how it goes? Keep a tight hold on what you have and the Devil take the rest of them? I don't think so. How many slips between any of us and sleeping at the Casual?

I said, 'You can't take it with you, Monty. Haven't you ever felt the pleasure of passing a bit of it along? And she's not a stray dog, no more than you might be some day. Her name's Kate.'

He looked at me quite puzzled. I might as well have been speaking Chinese.

There was a murder reported in the paper on Wednesday. It was on page three and I never would have seen it only I took a sheet of

Dickie Dabney's *Echo* to shine up the mirror in the dressing room and the words 'Mysterious Tragedy' caught my eye.

A female, identity unknown, estimated to be about forty years of age, had been brutally done to death. She'd been found in the buildings on George Yard, on a first-floor landing. I couldn't place George Yard. Dickie said it ran between Whitechapel High Street and Wentworth Street. I still couldn't place it. I showed Monty the story when he came in.

He said, 'You know the White Hart? That's on the corner of George Yard. It'll have been some old prossie. If they don't know who she is then she evidently didn't live in the buildings and if she didn't live there what was she doing on that landing in the middle of the night? It's clear enough. She was just an old whore going about her dirty business.'

By Thursday morning the poor murdered soul had a name, or rather she had two names. Valentine fetched in the newspapers, after he'd done his vocalisations. One said she was Emma Turner, the other had her as Martha Tabram who sometimes went as Emma Turner and was known at Satchell's Lodging House on George Street.

I said, 'Well at least it wasn't Kate. She was out late on Monday night. Monty stood us supper, and she would insist on walking home.'

'Supper, eh? So you're quite pals again, after all those years?'

'We were never exactly pals. Everybody played together. All in together girls, never mind the weather girls. But it is nice, talking to somebody who remembers Bilston Street, remembers the people, my mam and dad. It takes me back, hearing her speak.'

'When was the last time you saw Bilston Street?'

'Seven, eight years. I went back when Albert had a bad turn with his chest. Wasn't expected to live, but he proved them all wrong. He's still there, in the old house. I doubt anything has changed. Do you ever go back?'

'To Wigan? Wild horses, Miss Dot. It would take wild horses.'

'No family you'd like to see?'

'No family. Now, let's read about this horrid murder.'

One report said Mrs Tabram had received more than twenty knife wounds, the other, more precisely, said thirty-nine. Not a hundred anyway. A cab driver who lived in the buildings had seen her body when he came home from his work at about half past three, but the lamps were extinguished by that hour and he'd presumed she was passed out, drunk, and thought no more of it.

It was starting to get light when she was properly discovered. A man had come out of his dwelling, going to the docks for the call-on, and seen her lying in a pool of blood. He'd run to find a constable and the constable had sent for a doctor who had pronounced life extinct. Twenty-guinea words, as Tom Bullen would say. She was dead.

Valentine said, 'Well she came to a bad end, didn't she, and you can be sure money was the cause of it. Either her trick decided she was charging too much or she tried picking his pocket. What lives those women lead, going with any man who'll strike a bargain with them.'

Friday night, Blanche – I cannot bring myself to call her Amazonia – was in a fine old mood. One of Dickie Dabney's crows had relieved itself on the leg of her fleshings. I love those birds. Dickie says they can read his mind but I think that particular one must have read mine.

'Fooking creatures,' she says. 'Look at that! It's ruined me leggings. I can't go on wearing that. And what's the fooking point of crows anyhow? You can't even eat them.'

Dickie went straight to Lottie Cherry and complained about the language Blanche had used in front of his birds. He can be very particular about that. Personally I wouldn't have bothered. They weren't likely to repeat what they'd heard. They're *mathematical* crows, not parrots. Anyway, all the years they've worked the boards there can't be much they haven't already heard.

Lottie came down to try and restore peace. It takes a lot to get her out of her cubbyhole but Blanche was her star turn, so-called, and she didn't want her rattled. But Lottie's fond of Dickie too. We all are. He's a true showman and a gentleman.

She said, 'Amazonia, dear, just rinse it under the tap. It's only bird lime. And I don't ever remember us having a mishap with Dickie's birds before.'

'That were no mishap,' she says. 'Somebody put that bird up to it. They've all got it in for me. It was intended.'

I said, 'How could it be intended, you foolish creature? They're just birds. When they have to go they have to go.'

Then Dickie joined the fray. He said, 'Pardon me, Dot, but I must contradict you there. My crows aren't *just* birds. Not at all.'

So that's the last time I speak up on his behalf.

Lottie says to Blanche, 'How would it be if I found you your own little place to keep your fleshings?'

'You mean my own private dressing room?'

I looked at Lottie. All the years I've played the Forester's I've never been offered my own room, not even as a top-liner.

'It's only a small place,' she said. 'Very small. But you might be happier there. Save any more mishaps.'

I guessed then where Lottie was thinking of. Blanche was beaming.

'And it'll be just for me? Nobody else allowed in there?'

Lottie said, 'Just for you. That's all there'll be room for. You'll have a longer walk to the stage, but I think you'll be better suited.'

She said she'd try to have it prepared for the following night.

Would it have a screen and a chamber pot, Blanche wanted to know. Also, she'd require a good mirror and an oil lamp that didn't smoke.

I said, 'And her name on the door, Lottie. Don't forget that. Once you've moved all the pails and mops and rat poison out of there. In fact, you might have to widen that doorway, to accommodate the size of her head.'

Blanche said, 'I'll fooking kill you, Dot Allbones. You and them birds.'

And Lottie said, 'Dot, do be gracious. Be an example to a young artiste.'

Me be gracious! And Blanche is no young artiste. She won't see twenty-five again.

Lottie said, 'By the way, your friend's in.'

I thought she meant Tom.

I said, 'Already? Are you sure? He's supposed to come to second house.'

'No, not Tom Bullen,' she said. 'The person you left tickets for.

That woman. But she's on her own. She wanted to know if that meant she could see the show twice. And she wanted to know could she come round, between houses. What do you say?'

I said, 'Of course she can.'

'She's all right, is she? You'll vouch for her? She's a bit shabby-looking and you know I don't care for strangers wandering around the back of my theatre.'

'Unless it was to be Prince Eddy.'

'Prince Eddy would be a different matter entirely. I could do with a bit of royal patronage. Very well, I'll let her come round then, after the first house.'

Kate was wearing a different bonnet.

'It's new,' she said. 'Well, new to me. Kelly treated me. He got it for me from the pawnbroker's. I haven't been feeling too good this week. I have worked but it's been a struggle. I've a ginny kidney, do you see, and that causes me to get out of puff sometimes, when I'm bent over scrubbing. I don't know why it should be, but there it is. I'll never make old bones. Oh but Dot, that was a bostin show. I come over quite peculiar, knowing you for a real person and then seeing you up there on the stage. I told everybody sitting near me. I said, "I knew her when she was a little tyke on Bilston Street." They must have thought I was mad. They probably thought I'd had a few. I don't mean to be funny but it's not very nice back here, is it? I thought you'd be stretched out on a couch eating bonbons. Can you smell a horrible smell?'

Blanche said, 'That's Dickie Dabney's stinking fooking crows. But I'm getting my own accommodations tomorrow. I'm top of the bill, me.'

I said, 'It's not the crows that smell at all. It's sewers and sweat and cat piss. That's theatres for you. That's what we put up with for a few minutes in the limelight.'

Kate said, 'Ah, but what a few minutes! I can see why you do it, Dot. When they all join in with your choruses. When they stand up and shout for more. That must lift you. I remember when you used to sing in the Prince of Wales on a Saturday night, when you were still a nipper. "I'd be a Butterfly". You used to do it with all the actions and all them fancy high notes.'

Well that took me back. 'Butterfly' was one of my first pieces. I couldn't sing it now. My voice has dropped, along with a lot of other things.

I said, 'I'm glad to see you. I've been wondering about you, since that murder on Wentworth Street. Did you know that poor woman?'

'No,' she said, 'never heard of her. They say she lived at Satchell's.'

'You'd wonder how it could happen. All those people going in and out of the buildings and nobody saw anything. Nobody heard her cry "Murder!"'

Kate said, 'They probably did. Round our way you can't hardly sleep for cries of "Murder!" Nobody pays any heed though. Anyhow, they've got him. They've caught him.'

That was news.

'Oh yes,' she said. 'He's a soldier, apparently. She'd been seen drinking with some guardsmen and I suppose she went off with one of them. Quarrelling over money, that's what it always is. Then he'll have run her through with his bayonet. But they have him locked up now in the guardroom at the Tower. So that's that. He'll get his neck stretched.'

Kate got her information off the street where a story changes with every retelling, so what she told me turned out not to be quite the case. Martha Tabram had been seen drinking with soldiers and she might even have gone with one of them, for a fourpenny touch. It was a trade she'd been known to engage in. But that soldier was never found, though they questioned a great many of them and lined them up in front of people who'd seen the company she was keeping on the night she died.

Kate took the clothes I'd parcelled up. She hesitated, but I could see she wanted them.

'It's John,' she said. 'He don't like us to be charity cases.'

I said, 'A gift from a friend isn't charity. And how's he to know? Just wear them. Men never notice.'

'He does. I'll tell him Mrs Gully found them. I'll say they were left behind by one of her customers.'

Tom was late. I was about to give up on him and ask the Chucker-Outer if he'd kindly ride with me to my front door when in he bounced with a bunch of violets and a gleam in his eye.

'Sorry, my lovely,' he says. 'I was detained on a matter of business. But here I am. What's it to be tonight? A bottle of the bubbles and a nice bit of tongue?'

Tom said he doubted what Kate had told me about the killer being caught.

'If they've arrested a soldier, it's news to me and that can't be right. I'm the man who obtains the news. If you want to know the latest, apply to me.'

'And what is the latest?'

'Murdered by persons unknown. I doubt we'll hear any more

about it unless he comes forward and confesses. They do that sometimes, even years later. They suddenly decide to get it off their chest. Worried about the fires of Hell, I suppose. But then sometimes they're never caught.'

What a terrible thing. If you have the misfortune to be murdered, you'd like to think they'd catch the villain and make him pay the price.

Tom said, 'She didn't suffer, at any rate, poor old trollop. She never knew what hit her.'

I said, 'How do you know?'

'Because I've seen the mortuary photos,' he says. 'Joey Martin showed me them. He was called out to take them on Tuesday morning. She looks as peaceful as a sleeping baby.'

'After thirty-nine stabbings?'

'That's what I'm saying. You'd never think it to look at her face. You'd think she was dreaming of her next tot of gin. Did you speak to young Valentine about his American friend?'

'No. It's not my affair. If he's being shown a good time, who am I to begrudge him? Townsend'll be gone back to America soon enough so let Valentine enjoy it while it lasts. He has a sensible head on his shoulders.'

'Is he at home tonight?'

'I don't know. I'm not his keeper. He probably won't be. He's not working this week so he might be out, enjoying himself.'

'With Frank Townsend, Oriental Herbalist and Friend of Presidents and Generals. He took that room on Batty Street, then.'

'How do you know?'

He tapped his nose. 'I'm not at liberty to say.'

'You've been snooping.'

'It's called "making discreet enquiries", Dot. That's what I do.'

Tom didn't outstay his welcome that evening. He made a bid or two for my garters, which I don't mind, it's nice to be wanted, but then he came over very sleepy. Whether it was the Quieting Syrup I put in his champagne while he was answering a call of nature, I cannot say. He's a big man and I only used a very few drops.

8

It was a week before I saw Kate again. I'd been for a blouse fitting on Leman Street and it was a pleasant evening so I thought I'd take a slow walk to the Forester's. I never mind getting in early for a show. I like an empty theatre, listening to the quiet of it and then feeling it start to wake up. When I was a girl, just starting out, doing turns at the Prince of Wales, Mam used to fuss around me, tying my hair ribbons over and over and talking about anything that came into her head.

Dad used to say, 'Shurrup your chuntering, Jessie. Can't you see the girl's collecting herself?'

And Mam would say, 'Shurrup yourself, Allbones. I'm only keeping her mind off her nerves.'

But I didn't have any nerves, at least not till just before I went on. I was always raring to get up on that table and set them laughing. Dad was right. I was collecting myself. I was running through everything, picturing the moves and faces I was going to make. I still do it.

I was nearly at Baker's Row when I spotted Kate, weaving her way towards me. She was drunk. There was nowhere for me to duck out of sight of her, only that stinking alley that runs along the side of the Pavilion Theatre, and I wasn't going down there. I'd have passed by on the other side if I could, for I hate to see a woman so far gone in drink. But there was no avoiding her. She might have been stewed but she'd seen me clear enough. She was wearing the little coat I'd given her. It was tight across her shoulders but it looked well enough. Her new bonnet was all askew.

'Dot,' she says. 'There you are! I knowed I'd see you. I felt it in my water. Come with me to the Black Bull. I'm going to buy you a glass of porter.'

I told her I never drink before a show.

'But I've got money,' she says. 'And I want to buy you a drink. My friend, Dot. My dearest friend.'

I said, 'If you've got money go and buy yourself a hot dinner. Something for you and John Kelly.'

'John Kelly!' she says. 'Pah! John Kelly can get his own dinner.'

Well I commenced to walk away. It grieved me to see her like that. But then she ran after me, crying and calling herself the greatest fool that ever breathed.

I said, 'You are a fool, Kate, and I've no patience with it. Now if I take a drink with you, will you promise to keep your money for food and lodging?'

She promised and I walked her past every alehouse until we got to Bethnal Green Gardens and I bought her a cherryade.

'You tricked me there,' she said. 'I thought you meant to buy me a proper drink.'

But she was good humoured about it.

I said, 'You've had more than enough. However did you come to this, Kate?'

'I don't know,' she says. 'Conway. It was that bugger ruined me.'

'Did he give you the taste for drink?'

'Drove me to it more like. And took my babbies from me too.'

So then I heard her story. She'd had a girl and two boys.

'All growed, of course. My Annie's got three babs of her own, so I'm a grandma now. She's in Bermondsey, got a nice husband. She's done all right for herself. I don't see them though, not as much as I'd like. I can't blame her. I've been a worry to Annie. I haven't always kept to the straight and narrow.'

Her two boys were altogether lost to her. They'd gone to live with their father.

'I call them boys, but they're men by now,' she said. 'Bloody Conway. He said it was their choice, to go with him, but he'd been dripping poison in their ears. He's no saint. Why would they go with him? And I don't know where he is. In London somewhere. Annie knows but she's not allowed to tell me. As if I'm going to cause any trouble. What harm would it do for me to see my boys? And to think I was ever daft enough to mark myself with that bugger's name.'

She pulled her coat off to show me her arm. There were letters, tattooed in blue ink. I couldn't make them out.

'It's a T and a C. It's gone a bit fuzzy over the years but it'll never go away. Every time I roll my sleeves up, there's his initials. Were you never married, Dot?'

I told her about Hamish McHendie. A five-minute wonder. I was never the type men dote on. No golden ringlets, not much in the way of curves, but I had plenty of chances. It happens in the theatre. Once you're through the artistes' entrance, you leave the rest of the world behind, and things can get very cosy backstage.

You have your moments. The trouble is, when you step back outside you wonder what possessed you. There was a conjuror, Mr Mystery. We were playing the Walsall Imperial and he cut a very tasty figure on the stage. It's not every man that suits a top hat. We used to go in the carpenter's shop between shows. Not very romantic, nor very comfortable, but we couldn't get enough of each other. He seemed a bit of all right, Mr Mystery, but not in the cold light of day. After the show closed, it turned out he was just a vain little runt. McHendie was different. At least I thought he was. He took his time courting me, pretended he hadn't even noticed me. Very clever. He reeled me in. Then we got married. Everybody said we made the perfect couple. Two comics. Which just goes to show 'everybody' doesn't always know what they're talking about.

I said, 'I tried it once but it was soon over and it didn't end well.'

'No kiddies then?'

'No, no kiddies.'

'Well it wouldn't have been convenient, would it, for a person in your profession?'

It wouldn't. I've often wondered. But there's no sense poring over What Ifs.

I said, 'But you've got John Kelly now. He seems like a decent man.'

'He is,' she said. 'Boring though. One thing about Conway, there was never a dull moment. John's as quiet as a chapel mouse. All he longs for is a little house and a bit of garden, so he can grow potatoes and cabbages. I don't know as that'd suit me but I can't see it ever happening so I don't worry about it. I reckon we'll be stuck here till they put us in our shrouds.'

She asked me to sing her a song.

'Not one of your comical ones,' she said. 'Sing me a sad one. I love a good cry when I've had a drink.'

I sang 'Home, Sweet Home', very quietly. I don't give free performances in Bethnal Green Gardens.

'Beautiful,' she said. 'It's not the excellence of your voice, Dot. You won't mind my saying I've heard better. But it's the feeling you put into it. You make them laugh and then, quick as anything, you make them cry. I observed that the other night. You've got a knack, no doubt about it. See, now you've got me going.'

There were sparrows taking a dust bath. I could hear a hurdy-gurdy playing somewhere close by. She wiped her tears on her sleeve.

She said, 'Did you ever go back to Bilston Street?'

'Not in years,' I said. 'My brother Albert's still there. But what'd be the point?'

'None at all. I didn't go back. Well, I did once. When I was desperate.'

'I remember. I saw you. You were expecting.'

'I was. I was carrying Georgie, but my aunt told me not to trouble her again. She said I was a disappointment to her. She said I'd been given every advantage, which I had. I had no answer to that. It was my own giddy fault for going with Conway. My sister Eliza, you never knew her, but when our dear father passed away Eliza was sent to the workhouse in Bermondsey. She had it rough. But look at her now. She's in clover.'

'Where is she?'

'On Thrawl Street. You might know her. Mrs Frost?'

'I don't know anyone in Whitechapel, apart from Monty.'

'Her first husband was a butcher, name of Gold. I never knew him. That was when I was with Conway, when we were travelling. Mr Gold passed away and now she's married to Charlie Frost. He works down the docks. Well I suppose they're married. He's strict chapel so I don't think they'd be living over the brush. I reckon Mr Gold must have left Eliza quite comfortable. She has a whole house, big enough for lodgers.'

'Couldn't you live with her instead of at Cooney's?'

'Bless you, no. She won't have me an inch inside her front door. Charlie Frost's a Wesleyan and she makes out she's the same but I reckon she enjoys a nip as much as the next person, when he's not looking. But as I said, she had things harder than I did. Perhaps she holds that against me. I mean, she'll say Good Day to me, if she happens to see me, but that's as far as it goes. As for my boys, if they were to pass me on the street I'm not sure I'd know them. I'm always on the lookout. I see a young feller and I study his face, but London's a terrible big city. There's a lot of faces to study. It's a hopeless case really.'

'I should get to the theatre. Are you sober now?'

'Pretty much. I have my wits about me. The few I have left!'

'Will you go to Cooney's and get a bed for the night?'

'Yes,' she said. 'Or the White House.'

'Is the White House better?'

'No different, really. But you can have a double there, if you've a husband or a gentleman friend. If you're in the mood for company.'

'I see.'

'Or I might just buy a rasher or two of bacon for Kelly.'

I said, 'Don't let me find you staggering about the street again, Kate. I hate to see it.'

'You won't see it,' she said. 'You won't see me at all for a bit. We're going hop-picking, me and Kelly, down to Kent, and when I come back you won't know me. I'll be as brown as one of them darkie minstrels. And I'll have plenty of jingle in my pocket.'

I said, 'Good. As long as you don't drink it away.'

'I won't swear to that,' she said. She set her bonnet straight and gave me a smile. 'Hop-picking's thirsty work, you know?'

We parted at the Forester's and she continued on towards Whitechapel Road, slow but straight.

'Tararabit, Dot,' she said.

I followed the gas men in.

I said, 'Lottie, I'm thinking of making a few changes to my programme this week.'

'Why?' she says. 'I don't want you causing inconvenience.'

'No inconvenience, I just thought I'd lighten the mood. I'll cut "Granny Snow" and "Just Like the Ivy". And after "Naughty but Nice" I'll finish with the Sniff Song.'

Lottie says, 'I don't see why you must change anything. You can get laughs with "Just Like the Ivy". Gertie Kemp does.'

Gertie Kemp gets laughs for entirely the wrong reasons.

I said, 'I know what I'm doing, Lottie. Trust me.'

'I do trust you,' she says, 'but you must have a word with Tad. See if he's agreeable. And don't go over-running your time and upsetting Amazonia again. It's bad enough I've had to provide her with private accommodations.'

It was the first time I'd ever heard a broom cupboard called 'private accommodations'.

I went down to the pit to see Tad. He's the leader of the Forester's musical ensemble. Ernesto Tadolini. Tad has the most perfectly spherical body I've ever seen. How he balances on his piano stool, I do not know. It must be a finely judged thing.

I wrote out my new running order for him. He studied it so hard, twitching his great eyebrows up and down, puffing a silent tune with his lips, you'd have thought it was a Queen's Bench summons. That gave me an idea. I asked him for plenty of euphonium for the Sniff chorus, for extra comic effect. He sucked his teeth.

'First 'ouse, it can be, Miss Ollerbonez,' he says. 'Second 'ouse it cannot be. Second 'ouse euphonio must go quick quick to 'oxton Britannia. We hask Signor Ho'Leary hinstead. Bassoon it can be nice.'

I said, 'Bassoon it can be nice, but not if it misses its entrance, which O'Leary is guaranteed to do.'

Tad swore by all the saints that he'd make sure the bassoon paid attention but, of course, it went haywire. I could see O'Leary was snoozing. Bones prodded him with a drumstick and he woke with a start and shouted 'feck off' which raised a great laugh, so then I made a feature of him. Every time the chorus was coming up I called down to the pit, 'Are you awake, Mr O'Leary?' or 'Trouble you for a few more notes, sir?' They loved it, and once he was awake O'Leary didn't mind it at all. When you play the bassoon I suppose it's not often you get an ovation.

On that Monday Amazonia – Blanche, that is – came into the theatre all of a pother.

'Well here I am,' she said. 'I suppose you heard what happened to me on Saturday night?'

Nobody answered her but she carried on anyway.

'I was followed, that's what. By a man.'

I said, 'And what did this blind man look like?'

Everybody laughed. Lionel Neve, who of course *is* blind, threw his hands up and said, 'It wasn't me, Dot, I swear!'

And Babette the Living Doll, said, 'Blanche, don't you have a broom cupboard to fuck off to?'

But there was no offending nor stopping Blanche till she'd finished her story.

'What happened was, I went out from here, Saturday night, couldn't find a hansom, they was all rattling past, taken, so I started walking. Got to Mile End Road, still no cabs. It was raining, if you remember. Then I got this horrible feeling there was somebody behind me. I couldn't hear no footsteps. It was just a feeling, but I'm very sensitive to feelings. I stopped a couple of times and turned round. Nobody there. Well, I know there was somebody, in the shadows. He must have ducked in a doorway when he seen me turn. So I shouts "Murder!" and ran, and do you think I could find a policeman? Not till I got to Stepney Green. By which time I seemed to have thrown him off. Then a bobby did very kindly walk me the rest of the way home, but I haven't slept since, not a wink. I've told Monty he'll have to see me home this week, till my nerves are steadier.'

I said, 'Then you'd better join the queue. Monty generally sees me home.'

'Why do you need seeing home? You've not been followed and nearly murdered.'

'He sees me home because it's agreed between us and has been for many years. I'm his principal artiste.'

'That's what you think.'

'And I doubt you'll be seeing Monty tonight anyway. He's got a new turn trying out at the Queen's in Poplar.'

'Then Lottie'll just have to have a hansom waiting for me, after second house. My nerves are still jangled from Saturday.'

Lottie said, 'I'm damned if I know what's wrong with the pair of you, afraid to go home without a man. You should put a sad-iron in an old stocking. Anybody troubles you, just give them a whack.'

Dickie Dabney said, 'Is that what happened to your three husbands, Lottie? Did they get too close down a dark alley?'

She chuckled.

'No,' she said. 'I reckon I just wore them out.'

I hardly saw Valentine that week. He was playing first house at Gatti's in Lambeth, then second house across the street at the Canterbury. I've done worse in my time, rushed from Camden Town to Borough, sweating like a blacksmith, to play second house. You do it when you're young, when you're starting out, but I won't do it any more.

Sunday morning I heard him up and gargling. Next thing he tapped on my door to say he'd be out all day, going up West to enjoy the sunshine and take a turn in Hyde Park. He was wearing a new suit, grey with a chalk stripe, very dapper.

I said, 'Look at you, all dressed up like a Christmas goose.'

'Do you like it?' he says. 'Made to measure, at Olinsky's.'

I said, 'The coat's cut a bit snug.'

It's the new fashion, apparently.

'Bespoke suits? What brought this on? Have you got yourself a sweetheart?'

He blushed.

'I don't have time for sweethearts,' he said. 'But Frank said I owed it to my public, to be nicely turned out at all times.'

Which didn't make much sense because Valentine always performs in a tailcoat. What he wears on the street is of no importance. People don't recognise you once you step off the stage. You don't want them to.

'Frank Townsend. So he's still around?'

'Oh yes. He'll be here for some time yet. He has a lot of business to attend to.'

'Funniest doctor I ever met, crossing the Atlantic, staying away from his consulting rooms for months. I go to Dr Baptie if I need a physician, which I hardly ever do, and I doubt he travels beyond Clapton from one year's end to the next. You can depend on finding him at his rooms.'

'But Frank's not your everyday doctor.'

'You're right there. Doctors don't usually give advice on what a person should be wearing. Apart from recommending red flannel vests.'

'Anyway,' he says, 'you have to understand, things are done very differently in America. It sounds like the most wonderful place. I might get some engagements there next year. Frank says they'd love me in New York. He knows the right people too. He could put in a word.'

I said, 'And I suppose Frank paid for your new suit?'

He said, 'I know you don't approve.'

I didn't deny it.

He said, 'Let's not quarrel, Miss Dot.'

And we didn't quarrel, but the matter hung between us and I didn't like that. There were times when I began to regret his moving in. If he'd only stayed in his Dalston diggings I wouldn't have had to know about Frank Townsend. And Tom Bullen wasn't helping matters, poking around, asking questions.

'I must tell you, Dot,' he says, 'I've come by some information. This Frank Townsend is known to the police. I had a word with Bill Thicke. They know him as Townsend and they know him as Tumelty.'

'Known to the police for what?'

'For coming and going.'

'Is that a crime now?'

'For going under two names. Why would a man use different names? Because he's up to no good. And Tumelty, that's Irish. Just as I said.'

'So he might be a Fenian.'

'Or I'm a Chinaman.'

'But you don't think he's known to the police for the other thing. The unnatural practices.'

'I'm not saying that. A man could be both. It's not a vice the Irish are known for but this Tumelty's *American*-Irish. He could be a great many things.'

'Should I tell Valentine what you found out?'

'You should not. From what you tell me they're as thick as thieves. He'd be sure to warn him, frighten him off before the police have a firm reason to nab him. No, you must say nothing. The scoundrel must be allowed to start what he came to do and then be apprehended. But don't have him in your house, Dot.

No more tea parties. You wouldn't want to breathe the same air.'

'He bought Valentine a bespoke suit.'

'There you are! The man definitely has tendencies. So the sooner this comes to a head the better. We have to hope the police make their move before young Valentine's entirely corrupted.'

So then I was on pins. I was relieved to think the police were keeping an eye on Frank Townsend, Tumelty, but I wished I could say something to Valentine. He noticed, of course. He kept asking me was I feeling all right. I told him I wasn't sleeping well.

He said, 'I think it's because you eat so late. Since I've started eating luncheon, I find all I want of an evening is a bit of bread and milk. Then I sleep better.'

'Luncheon!' I said, 'That's a big word for a cup of tea and a soft-boiled egg.'

'Oh no,' he said, 'I eat more than that now. Frank recommends a substantial meal in the middle of the day. We generally go to the Midland Grand or the Great Eastern.'

I said, 'Do you indeed. And where does Dr Townsend get all this money for luncheons? Does he print his own banknotes?'

He laughed.

I said, 'I'm serious, Valentine. Does he have family money?'

'I think so.'

'You don't seem to know much about him considering how much time you spend with him. What do you talk about?'

'The places he's been to, the people he's met. He's a very interesting man.'

'Well he's certainly got you bewitched. I have another question. Is he Irish?'

'Up to a point.'

'What does that mean?'

'His forebears were Irish. Is that why you don't like him? I know you have prejudices.'

Not true at all. I can take an instant dislike to a person of any nationality and why not? Why waste time trying to warm to a hopeless case? But Irishness doesn't bother me particularly, nor Scottishness, in spite of McHendie. I take people as I find them.

'And is his name really Townsend?'

That struck home. Valentine's an easy book to read.

I said, 'Because I heard he sometimes goes under a different name.'

'Who says?'

'I can't remember. Somebody mentioned him. A big, tall American with bags of money. As you say, he knows a lot of people.'

'So what if he does use another name?' he said. 'Blanche Smith calls herself Amazonia these days. Cissie Roundtree calls herself Celeste La Rue.'

'That's different. That's an accepted thing among artistes, as you well know. But what kind of turn is Frank Townsend? A magician, I suppose. He seems to conjure money out of thin air.'

'Miss Dot,' he says, 'Frank has connections in very high places and you and your friends would do well not to pry. If it's convenient to him to go under more than one name, that's no affair of mine or yours.'

'And there are more things in heaven and earth, Horatio. How long does Dr Frank plan on staying?'

'I don't know.'

I said, 'All this time away from his consulting rooms. I hope his patients don't desert him.'

'I've nothing more to say about it. Now I'm going to change the topic. I'm trying out a couple of new songs and I'd appreciate your opinion.'

So he ran through them, not in full voice but enough to give me an impression. 'If Somebody There Chanced to Be' and 'The Sun Whose Rays'. My opinion was that they were very nice but one per show would suffice. A little of Gilbert and Sullivan goes a long way.

9

Valentine secured an engagement at the Paragon at very short notice. He'd been in Ludwig's on the Monday morning getting his hair trimmed when he happened to hear that Stanley Walters had fallen and broken his knee, so he went round to the theatre directly and they engaged him for their second house. He came home cock-a-hoop, and with good reason. The Paragon was a prestigious engagement.

I said, 'So instead of the Tadcaster Tenor they'll be getting the Wigan Warbler.'

'And as you're resting this week you'll be able to come and see me.'

I said, 'I don't know about that. I suppose Dr Frank will be in every night?'

'Not at all,' he said. 'He's far too busy. Well, Saturday I'm sure he'll try to be there, for my last performance.'

'Then I'll come on Thursday, if that suits.'

'It does,' he said. 'I need to spread my little band of claqueurs across the week.'

I was happy for Valentine but I dearly wished I could get an engagement at the Paragon. Monty always reckoned it wasn't my kind of theatre.

He said, 'You appeal to a different type of audience, Dot. Ordinary people. The man in the street. The Paragon's not to everybody's taste.'

He was happy enough to come with me though.

The Paragon stands where Lusby's used to be before it burned down. It's a beauty of a theatre, as fine as anything up West. With the balcony and the steep rake they can seat five thousand, and they do. It has crystal gasoliers they can raise up to the ceiling before the show begins, and a nice cool garden promenade either side of the stalls. Me and Monty were glad of that promenade. Thursday was one of those close, thundery nights, when you need a storm to clear the air. My gown was sticking to my back by the time we got there.

It wasn't a bad show. The Marvellous Eugenes on the flying trapeze, a negro banjo troupe, d'Alvini the Illusionist, a juvenile burlesque, far too young. She should have been at home in her nightgown. Valentine got a very warm reception. Of course it was generally known he was standing in at short notice, but he was on top form anyway.

Monty said, 'He's put on a bit of weight.'

He had. All those luncheons with Frank Townsend.

He said, 'It suits him though. He's altogether better-looking than I remembered. Didn't he used to have pimples?'

'He's outgrown them. He's blossomed.'

'He has. I wouldn't mind having him on my books. I might have a word with him.'

I said, 'Save your breath. Valentine didn't need you to secure himself an engagement at the Paragon. He got it by enterprise, by being quick on his feet.'

'Pure luck,' he said. 'If Stan Walters hadn't fallen.'

We had a couple of seltzers in the bar while we waited for Valentine to come round. There had been a rumble or two of thunder during the show and when we came out it had been raining. The pavement was shiny and the night felt fresher, but there was a strange smell in the air and over towards the river the sky was glowing orange. Something was on fire. An old fellow stopped to tell us.

He said, 'There's a warehouse a-fire at Shadwell dry dock. That's tar you can smell.'

He'd been down to have a look at it.

'There's boats alight too,' he said. 'You can feel the heat of it on the Ratcliffe Highway. I never got no closer. And there's another blaze going, Surrey side. Lightning bolt caused them, I daresay.'

Valentine said, 'Oh I love a blaze. Let's go down there and watch.'

But I didn't care to. Fires trouble me. I remember our mam talking of one that happened on Dudley Street. 'Whole family burned to a cinder. It smelled just like roasted meat.' Any time she caught me larking about with a lit candle, I had to hear that story.

Anyway, I wasn't feeling tip-top. Sluggish. It's always the same when I'm not working. It's the audience that gives me my pep. We took a cab and left Valentine to walk down towards the docks.

I said, 'I won't ask you in tonight, Monty.'

'Suits me,' he said. 'I need to get home and look in on Mother. She's not well.'

I don't know what time Valentine got in. I didn't hear a peep out of him till he commenced his gargling at eleven.

★

Olive came in during the Friday afternoon, just to bring in my clean sheets and mop the floors.

'Have you heard?' she says. 'There's been a terrible murder and the body was chopped all to pieces.'

She had her information from women at the wash-house so as soon as she'd finished mopping, I sent her out to buy the evening paper, to get the story straight.

'Couldn't get the *Standard*,' she said. 'But the *Echo* has it, and the *Advertiser*, so I bought them both. It's horrible. Her head was nearly separated from her body.'

We sat and read the accounts together. A woman's body had been found at four o'clock that morning in Bucks Row. An unfrequented thoroughfare, the paper said. I'd never heard of Bucks Row but it seemed to me a thoroughfare is a thoroughfare. Somebody has to be frequenting it.

According to the *Echo*, the body had been discovered by a constable, not in actual pieces but grievously hacked about. Her throat was cut from ear to ear, and her belly had been slashed but, mysteriously, no blood stains had been found.

Olive said, 'Then she must have been killed in another place and carried to Bucks Row.'

I said, 'There'd be drips, surely?'

'Not if her blood had ceased to flow. It curdles, Miss A., once the life has gone out of you.'

Olive had a brother who worked at a horse slaughterer's yard. That's how she came to know such gruesome facts.

The woman's identity was unknown but her petticoat had the laundry mark of Lambeth workhouse, so she was presumed to be one of those unfortunates who went with strangers for immoral purposes.

I said, 'So until she has a name there'll be another crowd of ghouls going to the dead-house to have a look at her.'

Olive said some had gone already, first thing, women she knew from the wash-house.

'But nobody recognised her?'

'Oh no,' she said. 'The wash-house I go to, they're respectable people. They wouldn't know a person of her kind.'

'Then why did they go to view her?'

'Something to do, I suppose.'

There are some pitiful people in this world, with nothing better to do than gawp at a nameless soul on a mortuary slab. People had gone to Bucks Row too, to examine the pavement for gore, though it was stated quite clearly that there was none, and to interview a night watchman from the goods' wharf who had heard nothing and seen nothing but he was the best they could do to slake their thirst for information.

I said, 'I hope you've more sense than to go looking at murdered bodies.'

'I wouldn't dare,' she said. 'I have to go home directly my work's finished. Our dad'll give me a hiding with his strop if I stay out.'

By Saturday morning the murdered woman had been named. Enquiries had been made at Lambeth workhouse and the superintendent had gone to the Whitechapel mortuary to see if she recognised her, which she did. She was Mary Anne Nichols, well known in Lambeth though she hadn't been seen there in recent months, and as soon as word of her name got out there were plenty in Whitechapel who claimed acquaintance with her. It's a funny thing, how you could have hardly a friend in the world, but get yourself murdered and they'll be round you like flies on yesterday's fish. Mary Anne Nichols had been lodging on Flower and Dean Street. I wondered if she'd been at Cooney's. I wondered if Kate might have known her. She was in her thirties and she was known to take drink. In other words she was like a hundred others who perched in that rookery.

It came on to heavy rain that evening. Valentine went off early to the Paragon and I closed the curtains. There was a murderer about and I didn't care for the idea of him peering in my window and seeing me all alone. I read the newspapers front to back. A woman had died of carbolic poisoning in Liverpool. The Prince of Wales was in York for the running of the Ebor Handicap, and was expected to stay on in the north for a week of grouse shooting. An indifferent hop-harvest was predicted in Kent. A man had been questioned for leaning against a lamp post on Worship Street in such a manner as to excite suspicion, and had exchanged blows with the investigating constable. No charges had been preferred. F Division of the Metropolitan Police had formed a brass band, with the intention of giving free concerts in park bandstands, for the entertainment and moral uplift of the poor. Their instruments had been paid for by personal subscription and not out of the public purse. Mr Simmons the balloonist had perished. He had planned to cross the English Channel and then continue on as far as Vienna, but the wind had turned unfavourable and the venture had come to a bad end in a barley field in Essex. As the papers said, it won't be long before someone steps up to fill Mr Simmons's shoes. There's good money to be made at aeronauticals, if you live long enough to enjoy it. There's nothing so guaranteed to draw a good crowd as the likelihood of seeing somebody perish.

10

My next engagement was at the Pavilion. It's not a bad theatre. The audience can be a bit rough and ready, but I've played worse and the backstage arrangements are quite commodious. I knew I wouldn't get top billing – I never do if the Norbury Nightingale is playing – but that week I didn't even get second line. That went to Coco, the Burned Cork Humorist. He's one of Monty's turns.

I said, 'I see the way the wind's blowing.'

'Not at all,' says Monty. 'It's just according to the clientele. Coco was very popular when they had him here in April. A very great success. You can't argue with the public. They know what they like.'

'They like me.'

'They do. But you've been around for many years now and Coco's still a novelty. You're still well thought of.'

I said, '"Well thought of" won't buy the baby a new bonnet.'

'You're getting your usual fee. Just be grateful you're working. Think back, Dot. How many acts have you seen come and go? How many did you start out with that have faded away? You're third from the top at the Pavilion. Be thankful. And while I think of it, I won't be in on Wednesday and Thursday this week, so you'll have to make other arrangements about going home.'

'Why?'

'Because Thursday's Rosh Hashanah. I'll be having dinner. The night before and the night of.'

'So you'll be free on Friday instead?'

'No. Friday is still Friday. Just because it's New Year don't mean Shabbat's cancelled. What about Valentine? Can't you ride home with him?'

'Don't worry about me.'

'I'm not worried about you. As a matter of fact, I think it's pure silliness a woman of your age expects a chaperone every night. It's not as though you have to *walk* to Hackney. And I have a life too, you know? It's not always convenient to me to see you home.'

I said, 'Have you got a sweetheart?'

He scowled.

'What's that to do with anything?' he says. 'You just mind your own affairs. You have to master your fears, Dot. Look at what happened to Amazonia. Followed by a shadowy figure all the way to Stepney Green but she's got over it.'

I said, 'Well if your authentic warrior maiden's everything she's cracked up to be, I'd have thought she'd have turned on any man daft enough to follow her and chucked him over her shoulder. Or smiled at him. Her face would stop a seven-day clock. But don't trouble yourself about me. I'll be all right. Even if a woman did get her throat cut, not five minutes' walk from here.'

'She got her throat cut wandering down an unlit street in the middle of the night. And we know what type she was. Women like that are asking for trouble.'

I said, 'No, Monty, she was asking for fourpence, for a tot of gin or a bed for the night.'

'Well, well,' he says. 'You've come over very charitable all of a sudden. You'll be opening a mission hall next. I suppose this is your dosser friend's doing? I suppose she's been bending your ear. "Oh, I've got a ginny kidney". "Oh, my wicked husband robbed me". Well those people get no sympathy from me. I'd like to see the lot of them cleared off the street. They give the neighbourhood a bad name.'

'I think anybody can fall on hard times, Monty.'

'Not if they're sober and thrifty.'

'How about the men who go with them? It takes two to do business.'

'Men have their needs.'

'So do women, for money to pay for their food and lodging.'

'But to get back to the point, Thursday's a High Holiday so I won't be in before Saturday night. Just take a cab. Nobody's going to harm you.'

The line-up at the Pavilion was as follows: Marguerite, the Norbury Nightingale, Coco the Comical Darkie, The Inimitable Dot Allbones, The Pearly Pierrots, Ida the Infant Prodigy (who's not an infant at all, she's just stunted. She must be thirty-five if she's a day). Also Randolph Bailey the Cycling Trumpeter, Fritz and his Yodelling Dachshunds, and a new vent act, Clarence and Percy. Percy's the doll. He's about the size of a five year old, made of wood, with a china head and a horrible chuckle. Well of course it's Clarence who does the chuckle. But I don't like vent manikins. They give me the hoo-hahs.

Valentine was still at the Paragon, retained by popular request.

I said, 'Monty's not around much this week. Shall you and me share a cab home? It wouldn't be out of your way to swing by.'

'Ah,' he said, 'this week's a bit difficult. I have some prior commitments.'

I've known Valentine to race across town after his second show just to oblige me, but not since Frank Townsend came on the scene.

He said, 'Why don't you ask Mr Bullen? He always seems very willing.'

Which annoyed me greatly. When I ask a favour of a person all I want is a Yes or a No. I don't want them making obvious suggestions, trying to shift it onto somebody else. I'm not daft. I can fathom things for myself. I was so cross I thought, 'Sod them all. I'll take Lottie Cherry's advice and carry a smoothing iron in a sock. And my sharpest hat pin.'

On Wednesday afternoon I was in Packer's, on Berner Street, buying apples when I saw Kate go by, walking at a good clip. I called after her.

I said, 'I thought you were off to the hop-picking.'

'We are,' she said. 'We'll probably make a start tomorrow, when John finishes work. We should be there by Sunday.'

'I'm glad to see you with your bonnet on straight today.'

'Why?' she said. 'What can you mean?'

But when I reminded her about finding her tiddly on Whitechapel Road, about sitting with her in Bethnal Green Park till she sobered up, she laughed.

She said, 'I reckon you've been a-dreaming, Dot. I ain't took a drink in weeks.'

That's the way my father went in the end. The ale shrivelled his brain so he never could remember drinking the stuff.

She said, 'I'll be glad to get away, Dot. It's quite shook me up, about Polly Nichols getting murdered.'

'I thought her name was Mary Anne?'

'I couldn't say. I think that was her name on paper, but I only ever heard her called Polly.'

'Were you friends with her?'

'No, not friends, but I used to see her in the Frying Pan. She'd go in there for a warmer, before she went to business.'

'You mean with men?'

'Yes, she did do that. I don't know as she had any other trade. But she was always clean and tidy. Not like some of them. She kept herself nice. They're burying her tomorrow, poor soul, but not on the parish. She's getting a proper send-off. Her husband's stepped up to pay for it, and her father. What a thing, though. There's plenty of houses and people on that street and yet nobody heard a sound. They say it's because her windpipe was cut.'

It made me shudder to hear her say it.

'He must have taken her entirely by surprise.'

'Oh yes. He'd probably got his old todger out and then when she went to attend to him he cut her. But they say she looked peaceful in the dead-house, so she didn't suffer. I hope she didn't. I shall be glad to get away to Kent, Dot. Try to forget about it.'

'I read it's been a poor year for hops.'

'Has it? Well never mind. We shall have some larks anyhow. It's hard work but we have hot dinners and lovely sing-alongs of an evening. Last year we even had a magic lantern show, in the parish hall. It'll be a proper holiday.'

*

Wednesday evening we had a very sparse second house. You can't see your audience, the footlights prevent it, but you can hear them. The openers soon let you know. Randolph Bailey was the first back down with a long face.

'Like a graveyard,' he said.

The Infant Prodigy thought it was because of the Nichols woman's murder.

She said, 'Nobody wants to be out late, not till they've caught him, it stands to reason.'

Randolph said, 'That's rubbish, Ida. She was a doxy. Her type are always getting killed. They put themselves in harm's way. Normal people don't have anything to fear. Anyhow, it's safe as a mother's arms around here. Gas lamps every few steps. No, if the takings are down it's not because of any murders. It's the Norbury Bloomin' Nightingale that's the problem. She's not suited to a venue like this. There's no warmth about her. And she don't always hit her note neither. Have you noticed that, Dot?'

I had. Anything above top E, she'd sidle up to it. That's the trouble with styling yourself a soprano. The years catch up with you.

Ida said, 'I know nobody's going to get murdered in the Whitechapel Road. But on their way home, *that's* what I'm saying. Down dark alleys, places where he might be lurking. Anyhow, it's the thought of him that's put the wind up people.'

I said, 'Ida, would you please not talk about dark alleys and murders. I have to go home to an empty house.'

'Consider yourself lucky,' she said. 'It's standing room only where I live. But you'll be all right, Dot. He won't be going out murdering tonight. It's their New Year. The Jews. Rosh Nosh. I don't know why they can't have it in January, same as the rest of us, but there it is.'

I said, 'It's called Rosh Hashanah. What's it to do with the murders?'

'Well, he's one of them, obviously. The murderer.'

'How do you work that out?'

'Because Hebrews can make theirselves invisible. It's a well-known fact. That's how he gets away with it. He says some of his mumbo jumbo, turns invisible, and then cuts them down. So I reckon we'll be all right this week, on account of it being Rosh Nosh.'

The world according to the Infant Prodigy. She's as dizzy as a spinning top but you can have a laugh with her. I did think of asking her if she fancied coming back with me for a bite but then off she went with the Pearly Pierrots. They were meeting two gentlemen followers at the Criterion Supper Rooms. So that was that. I was nearly the last to leave.

A theatre after a show can be a melancholy place. Before a show it's different. Everything has a rosy glow. But afterwards you notice the scuffs and the dust and the cracks. It empties out and all that's left is ghosts. I've never seen one, but I do believe in them. I was playing last house at the Green Dragon, many years ago, and as I was putting my coat on I heard somebody singing 'The Rose of Tralee', very, very faint. I asked the chairman who it was and he said, 'Oh, that'll have been Pat Connolly. Take it as a compliment. He must have enjoyed your turn. He's been dead ten years and he doesn't come back for everybody.' And Chip Carver once swore to me that whenever he played at the Alma in Islington he was attended by the shade of an old comic called Baddeley. Chip wasn't a fanciful man.

He said, 'He's never showed himself to me but I know him by the smell of his hair oil and the creak of his shoes. He stands right beside me and it doesn't trouble me. In fact I'd miss him now if he wasn't there.'

Old songsters and dead comics. I suppose they can't stay away. That's the theatre for you. They must keep coming back to do one more turn.

So there I was, with the last of the gas men leaving and Ma Marks waiting to lock up.

'Terrible box this week,' she said. 'If it carries on like this I don't know what we'll do. You on your own tonight? Don't Monty usually squire you home?'

'Rosh Hashanah,' I said. 'Dinner with his mother. Anyway, night after night, it gets that you have nothing to say. It's like being married. So I put a stop to it. I decided I'd as soon talk to myself.'

'Me too,' she said. 'Since Marks passed away I like to go home, take my corsets off and have a damned good scratch. Good night then, Dot. Mind how you go. There's some terrible villains about.'

I stepped out into Whitechapel Road and hailed myself a cab. There are times in a lady's life when it's to her advantage to have mastered the two-fingered whistle. I just wished I'd remembered to wear a longer hat pin.

11

I sang all the way home, to keep the jitters away. 'Thou Hidden Source of Calm Repose', 'Depth of Mercy', anything I could remember from chapel, and I kept the trap open, so I could hear the driver's wheezing.

He called down, 'Madam, are you intoxicated?'

I said, 'I am not.'

'Then if you must sing can't it be something a bit cheerier?'

So I gave him 'The Sniff Song', which caused him to laugh.

'Not bad,' he says. 'Not bad at all. With a bit of polish you could go on the halls.'

I'd told Olive to leave a gas mantle burning in the front hall. I thought she might forget but, as the cab stopped, I could see the flicker of it through the glass.

'Oh good,' I says to the driver, 'my husband's still up and waiting for me.' I said it nice and loud, just in case the slasher who'd done for Mrs Nichols happened to be hiding in the shadows.

'Up and waiting?' he said. 'I wouldn't allow any wife of mine to be out so late. Don't you read the papers? There's dangerous people about.'

'Not around here.'

I said it more to encourage myself than for his information. I suppose there are murders in Hackney but they'd be private affairs, done behind closed doors and with poison, probably. Not with a sharp knife. People who live in nice houses don't want gore on their rugs.

'I couldn't speak to that,' he says. 'I'm a Stepney man myself, but if you ask me you can find wickedness anywhere. Bid you goodnight.'

Off he clattered. It was very dark. There was hardly a fingernail of moon, and when I lost sight of his coach lamps the road was quite empty. I wished then I'd asked him to wait, just till I was safely inside. He'd seemed a kindly sort.

I had my hat pin in one hand and my key in the other.

'Now, Allbones,' I said to myself, 'answer me this. Why would a cut-throat travel all the way to Victoria Park to lie in wait for you when he has all those courts and ginnels in Whitechapel to choose from and plenty of gin-soaks willing to go off with any man?'

It was a very satisfactory argument. Then I heard the door to the back yard swing on its hinges and my guts turned to water.

There was a knack to my latch-key. Valentine was always saying I should get it seen to. Sometimes it opened first turn, sometimes you had to jiggle it a little. Monty had the hang of it. He generally managed without any trouble. But Monty was at home, sleeping off a brisket dinner.

The yard door swung open, not loud, but unmistakeable, and from the corner of my eye I saw something move. I can't say I let out a scream. It was more of a strangled croak, and I dropped my hat pin and my key. But *he* screamed. Actually, he did more than scream. He appeared to levitate clean off the ground and let out an almighty cry, and then when he'd fallen back to earth he braced himself against the wall and clutched at his chest.

'Oh God help me and save me,' he says. 'Miss Allbones, it's you. You gave me such a fright. A sudden insult to the heart. The very thing I've been warned against.'

It was my neighbour, Mr Earp, in his nightshirt and slippers, threatening to die of shock. But he didn't. He survived to tell me the reason he was creeping about in the dark. He was looking for his tabby cat.

'She will stay out late,' he said, 'though I've begged her not to. Now my heart is beating much too fast, and irregular. Be so good as to bring me out a chair. I must sit down. My head's spinning. My sight's growing dim.'

I said, 'I can't help you. You gave me such a jolt I dropped my key. You're the one should be helping me. If I don't find that key I shall have to come in and take shelter in your rooms.'

That cleared his head. He commenced peering about for my key.

'Don't you keep a spare?' he said. 'Hidden in some secret place?'

'I do not. I don't believe in it. There's no such thing as a secret place a burglar hasn't already thought of. So without my key I'm locked out until my lodger comes home.'

'Ah, yes,' he said, 'the person who sings scales. Up and down, up and down. He never seems to progress to anything tuneful. So he's your lodger. I thought perhaps he was your pupil.'

'I don't have pupils. I'm a solo artiste and so's Mr St John. That's him warming up you'll have heard, but he does it at half-voice. If you want a full performance you'll have to go to the Paragon and pay your shilling.'

'Not I,' he said. 'I stay indoors at night. Nothing good ever comes of being out after dark.'

I found my key but I'd grazed a knuckle casting about for it by the doorstep and so I let fly a certain word. Nothing too warm, but it scandalised Mr Earp.

'Miss Allbones!' he says. 'I thought you were a lady! Now I can feel the palpitations coming upon me again.'

I said, 'Then you'd better go in. You don't want to die in the street, and all for the sake of a kitty cat. And in nothing but your nightshirt.'

'Oh don't say such a thing. If I just steady myself a moment against the sill, the crisis may pass. No, no, I feel it coming on again. I think my legs may fail me. Miss Allbones, if I should expire be so good as to bring out a cloth to cover me decently, an old shawl would do or a bed coverlet, until a litter can be found to bear me away. And please have me taken to St John's. I'm known to the mortuary custodian there.'

I said, 'Mr Earp, you must go inside at once. I want no dying on my doorstep tonight. I'm too tired to wait up for the dead-cart.'

I helped him to his door, right through that dark passageway, and I was so struggling not to laugh at him, juddering along on his matchstick legs, that I never gave a thought to who might be lurking there. There's nothing like a daft old valetudinarian to take your mind off your fears. I closed the curtains though, the minute I was inside. It was the thought of being watched. That was what he must do. He'd watch them first.

Olive had left poached salmon sandwiches, enough for two people, but I scoffed the lot, and a whole jam tart, and a pint of lukewarm Bolly. There was a nice letter from Albert too.

You mind yourself, Dotty. I know you'd never venture down a dark alley on account of your nerves but you must still be careful. By the sound of things London's getting to be a terrible dangerous place. Brummagem's not much better. There was a man strangled his wife in Nechells because she didn't have his dinner ready. There was a woman drownded her bab, says she has no recollection of doing it. Whatever's the world coming to? Did I tell you about the new linoleum?

I slept late. I heard Olive let herself in.

'Miss Allbones,' she calls up to me. 'I have last night's *Star* in case you didn't see it. All about the murderer. An arrest seems inniment.'

I said, 'Good. Put the kettle on. And it's "imminent", Olive.'

'Yes,' she said, 'exactly what it says here.'

We sat and read together. Since Mrs Nichols's murder, several women had come forward, to say they'd been attacked in recent weeks too but had managed to escape from their attacker. *Women of a low type*, the *Star* said. They'd gone with a man to do their business and then found he suddenly grew violent and threatening. There was a description. He was short and bull-necked and he sported a black moustache. Sometimes he wore a leather apron, such as a cobbler might wear, and he'd been seen to brandish a trimming knife. It said police investigating the deaths of Martha Tabram and Mary Anne Nichols were now looking closely at men engaged in the boot and slipper trade.

Olive said, 'But he sounds like half the men in Whitechapel. What are they going to do, round up all the boot-menders?'

I said, 'Those women must know who he is. They have their regulars I'm sure, and everybody knows everybody in Whitechapel. I'll bet the police already have a name. They just can't say, until he's arrested.'

'Why not?'

'Because if his name was published while he was still at liberty he'd have a mob at his door, ready to string him up.'

'Serve him right. He'll hang anyway. My dad says why should hangmen get paid so handsomely when there's men in the street who'd be willing to do it for nothing.'

I said, 'But, Olive, what if a mob went to the wrong house? What if they hanged the wrong man?'

'I don't know.'

'No, well think about it. Even a murderer must have a trial. And if the *Star* can publish this much you can be sure the police know even more. I'll find out from Tom Bullen when I see him. He gets the stories practically before they've happened.'

'Is Mr Bullen the gentleman who came to tea? That Sunday when Mr St John's American friend was here?'

'Yes, that was Tom. And what did you make of Dr Townsend?'

'I don't like to say.'

'You can do. You can speak your mind.'

'Mr St John's very nice.'

'He is. But that doesn't mean we have to like all his friends.'

'Well, I thought Dr Townsend wasn't very polite. When you're in company you should make light and pleasant conversation with everyone present and not talk about yourself all the time.'

'Quite right.'

'Also, you should have topics you can talk about, in case you find yourself with someone who seems shy, so you can put them at their ease. Topics of general interest. I read that in the *Girl's Own Paper*. And since you've asked me to speak my mind, I didn't like riding in the hansom with him and Mr Valentine neither. I'd as soon have walked home.'

'Was Dr Townsend unkind to you in the hansom?'

'Oh no. He didn't speak to me at all. But he was watching me all the time, on the sly, and I didn't care for it.'

'I should think not. I'm sorry.'

'Mr Bullen was nice to me though. He even held the door while I carried the tea tray to the scullery. I suppose he's one of your admirers?'

'I don't have admirers, Olive. Now you'd better get on with your work. The front step needs scrubbing, and while you're out there keep your eyes peeled for a hat pin I dropped last night.'

'Oh, Miss Allbones,' she said, 'I didn't mean to be impertinent when I spoke of Mr Bullen. Only I did find a gentleman's trouser button under the couch. And anyway, I'm sure you must have a lot of admirers.'

She came clanging and sloshing through the front hall with her mop and pail.

'I'm afraid I didn't find no hat pin,' she said. 'I'll bet a magpie had it. They'll take anything that glints. Mr Valentine's late starting his doh-ray-mes today. Is he resting this week?'

Valentine wasn't resting. The reason we didn't heard him warming up his voice was that he'd overslept his usual time. He'd come in very late and woken me, banging about, not his usual quiet self at all.

I said, 'I believe he went up West last night. Tap his door and ask him if he's ready for his shaving water.'

'Up West,' she said. You'd have thought she was speaking of Samarkand.

'I should like to go there some day,' she said, 'just to see it. I've been as far as Bishopsgate but I'd like to go a bit further. I'd want to come home though. I wouldn't care to go so far away I had to sleep in one of those hotels.'

'Why not?'

'Because other people would have slept in the bed before you. People you didn't know.'

'I think they change the sheets, Olive, unless it's a very disreputable hotel.'

'Do they? Well I'd still want to come back to my own bed.'

Funny really, because I knew for a fact Olive didn't have her own bed. She shared it with her sisters.

Monty came by before the first show. He was on his way to synagogue. Actually, he'd gone out of his way because he worships at Duke's Place. He reckons you get a better class of person there than you do on Goulston Street.

I said, 'I suppose I should wish you Happy New Year.'

'Thank you,' he says. 'I thought I'd better drop in, make sure you got home without being murdered.'

'So you were worried about me.'

'No. Just doing my good deed for the day.'

I said, 'As you can see, I'm well. Though that bank clerk who lives behind me nearly killed me with fright, creeping about in his nightshirt.'

'Did he? What was his game?'

'He was looking for his cat. He screamed like a girl when he saw me standing at my door. I was struggling with that key. You know how it sticks sometimes. He said he had a dicky heart and was quite liable to die after the shock I'd given him. He'd given me a fright too but it was really quite diverting, him standing there with his thin bandy legs. So I believe I've conquered my fear, Monty, just like you said I should. I shall go home alone in future and you can eat as many dinners with your mother as you please.'

'That's commendable, Dot,' he said. 'I'm very glad to hear it.'

I said, 'And you might think of shaving off that moustache. Now I study you, you're quite the image of this boot-mender the police are seeking.'

'What boot-mender?' he says. 'What are you talking about?'

'The man who's been attacking women. Believed to be the murderer of the Nichols woman and possibly the Tabram woman too. It was in the papers yesterday. He's short and thick-set, with a foreign complexion.'

'I'm not short,' he says. 'And I'm certainly not thick-set.'

I'm afraid he is, but I let it pass.

'He also has a black moustache and is known to wear a boot-maker's apron. Do you own an apron, Monty?'

'What a comic you are,' he said. 'Well then, it's a good thing I'm not required to be your chaperone any more. I shall have all the more time to put my apron on and go out at night terrorising doxies.'

We had a laugh. The next time I saw him though, on the Saturday, he had shaved off his moustache. I wouldn't say it improved him, but it did give him a much-changed appearance. But then, by Saturday, a lot of things had changed.

12

It wasn't in the morning papers. I knew nothing of it till I got to the Pavilion on Saturday night and walked in with one of the Pearly Pierrots.

'What times we live in,' he said. 'What horrors.'

Another body had been found, a woman, most horribly mutilated, in a yard behind a cat's meat shop on Hanbury Street. Backstage was a-buzz with it. *Three* bodies had been found, according to Mrs Marks. No, it was as many as *five* according to the Infant Prodigy, and they were all so slashed that their own mothers wouldn't recognise them.

Mrs Marks thought it had to be the work of a butcher.

'Who else would know how to go about cutting them up? How else could he go home covered in blood without his wife remarking on it?'

Ida was still of the opinion that he had the power to make himself invisible. A Jewish butcher. But the general verdict around the dressing room was that when the police finished quizzing the boot-menders, all Smithfield men and all Aldgate shochets should be taken in for questioning.

Monty came by.

I said, 'I told you you wouldn't be required.'

'Fair enough,' he says. 'I just thought I'd offer. Considering what occurred last night.'

'I'll be all right. A cab, door to door, like you said I should.'

'Only, for your information, I won't be available much till this man's caught. I'll be going out on patrol.'

He'd just come from the Crown in Mile End. A builder called Lusk had called a meeting there, of local traders and householders, and a Vigilance Committee had been set up. Men were going to commence patrolling the streets, in pairs, until such time as the murderer was caught.

I said, 'How is that a job for shopkeepers? More police is what's needed.'

'All very well to say, but who's to pay their wages? No, George Lusk's right. It's a citizen's duty to assist the police and protect his own streets. A constable on his beat, how often does he come around? Twice in an hour? A felon only has to wait to see him pass, then he can commit a crime at his leisure. But not any more. From now on we'll have committee members out there every night.'

'And you'll be going out with them?'

'Certainly. I'll take my turn.'

'Your mother won't like that.'

'Nevertheless.'

'And were there really five killed last night?'

'Five?' he said. 'Where did you hear that?'

'Mrs Marks.'

'Ma Marks should take more water with her drink. No, there was only one killed last night, but one's too many.'

'I thought you wanted all the prossies cleared from your neighbourhood?'

'I do. But murders are bad for trade, Dot. Unless you happen to own a newspaper. I wish I'd had the foresight to invest in one. Theatre boxes are down. I doubt you'll get many in tonight's show. People are very uneasy.'

Perhaps the reason there was talk of more than one body was because there was more than one name being bandied about. As soon as the body was found and the alarm had been raised, people flocked to the mortuary to see if it was someone they knew. One said the corpse was her friend, Annie Chapman, another named her as Mrs Sivey, several just knew her as Dark Annie. All one and the same person as it turned out. She was a widow, formerly employed at White's, finishing doilies and antimacassars, but now sunk to dossing at Crossingham's Lodging House, another sad creature living hand to mouth, hour to hour. Generally sober, according to Crossingham's custodian, but if she had money on a Friday she'd spend it on rum.

She'd been seen on Saturday morning at two, going out at that dead hour to try and earn her doss money. Seen at two, found at six, still warm but lifeless.

Monty said, 'When will these women ever learn?'

'When men stop offering them the price of a drink for two minutes' work. What's a woman to do when she's too old to go charring?'

Ida said, 'I don't know why somebody don't open a proper whorehouse. It'd do a roaring trade. You might think of it, Monty. I'll bet you've got a bob or two to invest.'

The rims of Monty's ears turn red when he's embarrassed.

Ida said, 'Don't give me that old-fashioned look. A nice clean knocking-shop. You'd make a fortune. Better than having them at it like dogs in your back yard and then ending up dead. You wouldn't have to go out on no midnight patrols then. You could stay at home and count your money. And drabs like Annie Chapman wouldn't need to go out getting murdered at two in the morning.'

'All I want,' he says, 'is the filth cleared off my street. I remember when this was a respectable place.'

I said, 'Well we can't make perfection of human nature, Monty. Some must have their drink, and some must have the other thing. These patrols? What will you do if you stumble upon him?'

'Summon the police. We'll have whistles.'

'How about a cosh?'

'No coshes. Our job is just to detain any suspect.'

'But how? He's not going to stand there obligingly waiting for a constable to come. You should arm yourself. You'd better borrow one of Blanche's lead pipes.'

'You may scoff,' he says. 'You'll be grateful when we've nabbed him.'

Ida said, 'The thing is, Monty, when word gets out about these patrols, he'll probably clear off somewhere else.'

'Good,' he said. 'I hope you're right. But I don't think he will. If he's local he'll want to stay where he knows his way around.'

'Is he local?'

'How else does he disappear so fast?'

'Magic,' says Ida. 'Jewish magic. I reckon he's one of your tribe.'

'Oh yes,' he says. 'And how did you come to that conclusion?'

'Come on, Monty,' she says. 'You know what I mean. All them

funny things you get up to with your long scarves and them boxes you strap on. Magic powers.'

'Better watch out then, Ida,' he said. 'There's a lot of us about.'

Monty was right about the audience. We had very few in that night, but if you ask me it wasn't because people were afraid to be on the streets. It was because they had something more entertaining to go to. For a penny you could view the very place where Annie Chapman had been done in. Clarence the vent had passed along Hanbury Street on his way to the theatre. He said it was thronged with people waiting their turn to enter the passageway and go into the yard where the body had been discovered.

'Fastest-selling ticket in town,' he said.

Ida said, 'And I'll bet the murderer's one of them. I'll bet he's standing there, listening to what everybody's saying. He'll be relishing the excitement he's caused.'

Clarence said costers had set up their carts.

'Hot pies, whelks, baked murphies. You name it, you can get it. It's like a regular fair. And there was a drayman trying to get his horses to the forge for shoeing, but he couldn't get through the crowd. The police were trying to move people on but they'd no sooner cleared a thoroughfare than the street filled up again.'

'Who's pocketing the pennies people are paying to view?'

'Whoever owns the yard, I suppose. And the houses opposite are offering viewings from their upstairs windows. I don't know how much they're charging. I can't see there'd be much to be gained by gawking from up there but I suppose people must make hay while the sun shines. It's not every week you get a murder on your doorstep.'

Someone had even been sharp enough to write a ballad and have it printed for hawking. Clarence had bought a copy.

Dark Annie went out strolling, hoping for a crumb to eat.
Her belly thought her throat was cut.
Then she turned down Hanbury Street.
'Twas there she met the wicked cove who flashed a deadly knife.
Then Annie's throat was truly cut. Extinguished was her life.
Oh was ever there such crimes, in these or other times?
These horrid dirty doings still increase.
Though our taxes we must pay, getting heavier every day,
Still we ask ourselves the question
WHERE'S THE POLICE??

It made me think of Kate. Ballad-hawking was her old trade, when she was married to Tom Conway. I asked Clarence who he'd bought it from.

'Some minstrel,' he said. 'I don't know if he composed it himself but he was wandering about, singing it at the top of his voice.'

'Not an Irishman, by any chance? Getting up in years?'

'I couldn't say. He was no Gilbert Duprez, that's for sure. Just some chancer with the arse of his trousers worn through.'

Valentine didn't come home that night. I'd quite have liked to sit and jaw with him a bit, like old times. I'd have liked him to make sure the windows were shut and the doors bolted. I gave it till midnight and then I turned in. I was too tired to stay awake worrying about murderers.

⋆

Sunday morning, the streets had been aired before I heard his key in the lock and then the door closing, very quiet.

I called out to him. I said, 'You don't need to creep in. I'm up and decent and sitting in my parlour wondering if I still have a lodger.'

He put his head round the door.

'Miss Dot,' he says. He'd brought in poppy-seed rugelach from Friedman's. 'Cracking day out there. Everything all right with you?'

'Well you're alive, that's something. I thought I might have to go searching the infirmaries for you. Or the dead-house.'

'You've no need to worry about me,' he said. 'I've plenty of acquaintances. If ever I was to meet with an accident, somebody would inform you.'

'I'm glad to hear it. It just strikes me as very odd, to pay for a bed and then not sleep in it.'

Well then he squared up to me.

He said, 'I pay my rent. It's surely my business where I spend the night. I'm a grown man.'

What could I say? I'd never come close to quarrelling with Valentine, at least not until we lived under the same roof.

I said, 'I was worried about you.'

'Were you?' he said. 'That's nice.'

He gave me a hug.

I said, 'If I'm not mistaken, that's Trumper's Extract of Limes you're wearing.'

'It is,' he said. 'How come you know that?'

'I have a good memory for smells.'

'As worn by an admirer, I suppose.'

There was somebody, many years ago. He was a Hon. The nearest

I ever got to being a rich man's sweetheart. Bertram, only everybody called him Booby. He preferred to come east for his entertainment. I reckon he thought himself quite the adventurer, wandering as far as Whitechapel. It was nice while it lasted but then he found a new fancy, a younger bit of stuff. I always remember his cologne though. It's a pleasant, fresh fragrance.

Valentine said he'd been in the West End, with Frank Townsend. Dinner at Rules, then out till late at a private club on Vere Street.

'So you haven't slept?'

'I did, a bit,' he said. 'I took the couch in Frank's room.'

'On Batty Street? You might as well have come home.'

'No, no. At the Charing Cross Hotel. He still keeps his room there. He only stays at Batty Street when he has business nearby, at the docks, at the warehouses. Now what about this latest murder, Miss Dot? I suppose you've heard all about it.'

'Too much. It was all anybody talked about last night.'

'What baffles me is why nobody hears anything. Not when the Tabram woman was killed, nor Mary Anne Nichols, and now this one. From what I've heard, there's a dozen people lodging in that house on Hanbury Street and yet no-one heard Annie Chapman cry out. It makes no sense.'

'Because her windpipe was cut. Kate told me. He took her quite by surprise, I suppose. But he does seem to have the luck of the devil.'

'Well that will run out. One of these nights they'll catch him at it. I heard they're bringing in extra police.'

'And they've got up a Vigilance Committee.'

'What's one of those?'

'Local men. They're going to go out in pairs at night, on the lookout for suspicious characters. Monty's volunteered.'

'Monty Hyams!' he said. 'On patrol? Will his mother allow it?'

'I don't think she's been consulted, but Monty's determined to play his part. He was quite ardent for it last night. You know, people are saying this killer must be a madman, but I beg to differ. I'd say he must be perfectly in his wits. How else does he do these deeds and then slip away, cool as you like?'

'But of course he might not be the kind of lunatic who runs about gibbering and foaming at the mouth. Bear in mind, Miss Dot, there's other kinds of insanity. A man might have a hidden type of madness that only slips out from time to time.'

'Like at full moon?'

'Yes. Only it wasn't, was it? Last Friday night it was as black as Newgate's knocker. There was no moon at all. But what I'm saying is, mad people don't always look mad. Most of the time he might seem as normal as you or me. You might pass him in the street and never give him a second look. Frank explained it to me. He's seen cases of it. Two souls inside one body, that's how he described it. Like the play that's on at the Lyceum. *Dr Jekyll and Mr Hyde*.'

'Which has had very poor notices.'

'It has.'

'Well I'd prefer this Whitechapel murderer to be a regular lunatic, so we can all recognise him when we see him.'

He started to laugh.

He said, 'I just had this vision of Monty going out on patrol. *With cat-like tread, upon our prey we steal*.'

'More like, *a policeman's lot is not a 'appy one*.'

'Will he be armed with a billy club?'

'No, just a lantern and a Hudson whistle. Mrs Lane from the Britannia has put some money up, apparently, and Benny Redman's purchasing them. He's getting them at cost.'

We laughed so much I thought my ribs would crack.

He said, 'I think I might get my head down for an hour or two.'

'No luncheon with Dr Frank today?'

'No,' he said. 'Not today.'

I said, 'Valentine, have you learned any more about him?'

'Such as?'

'Where does he get his money?'

'He's a doctor.'

'So you say. But he never does any doctoring. And even doctors who go to their office every day don't make a pile.'

'I bet royal doctors do.'

'I bet they don't. You don't think the Royals settle their bills on time, do you? And anyway, where are Frank Townsend's patients? The other side of the ocean blue.'

'I don't know. Perhaps he made good investments.'

'Is he a Fenian?'

'What does that mean?'

'You know what it means. The Irish cause. Does he congregate with Irishmen? With dynamiters?'

'Jiminy Christmas, no,' he says. 'What ever gave you such an idea? Frank doesn't mix with those types. He's a very refined man, and very well connected. You'd be surprised at some of the people he knows.'

'Try me.'

'I can't name names. But you'd be surprised.'

I said, 'Well I have connections too, and a little bird told me Frank Townsend is known to the police. What do you say to that?'

'I think your little bird has the wrong end of the stick. That'll be Tom Bullen, I suppose. "Known to the police" is one thing. "*Acquainted* with policemen" is quite another, and I'm not talking about constables. Frank is acquainted with the upper echelons.'

'So you're telling me that he chums around with senior police officers? He's down at the docks buying Oriental herbs. He's eating luncheons and going to theatres. He has money to burn and yet his patients back in New York haven't seen him in months.'

'I won't be drawn into a quarrel, Miss Dot. I'm not saying another word.'

I said, 'Just be careful, Valentine. Between you, me and this teapot, nothing about Frank Townsend adds up.'

'It saddens me to say it,' he says, 'but I think you're jealous. I think you're put out because I'm not at your beck and call any more. Frank observed it at once when he met you.'

I said, 'I'm surprised he claimed to observe anything at all, he was so busy holding forth. But you're right, we shouldn't quarrel about him. I'm very fond of you and I'm sure I'm only saying what your mother would say. Have a care. That's all.'

'Yes, well,' he said. And he went to bed. Nine o'clock on a beautiful Sunday morning and he couldn't keep his eyes open.

13

I went out for a walk in Victoria Park, just up as far as the bandstand. I paid for a chair and sat down next to an old boy sunning himself. The band was playing 'Mother's Advice'.

I said, 'That's my song they're playing.'

'Oh yes?' he says. 'I prefer a nice Viennese waltz myself.' And he moved to another seat.

He didn't realise he was talking to Dot Allbones. I suppose he thought I was some lonely old maid setting her cap at him. I sat for an hour and listened to the music, then made my way back. I met Mr Earp on the corner of the street, out for a constitutional, long winter coat and a muffler.

I said, 'Aren't you stifled in all those clothes?'

'Oh no,' he says. 'I feel draughts most acutely. I'm never too warm.'

I said, 'Well I'm glad to see you're still with us. You seemed in a bad way the other night.'

'I was,' he said. 'I may tell you my nerves are still quite raw. And of course I caught a head cold, which I very much fear will settle on my lungs.'

'But you found your cat?'

'I did.'

'Then you had more success than I did because I still haven't found my hat pin.'

'Miss Allbones,' he says. 'You had a caller, just as I was coming out. A person hammering at your door.'

'I left Mr St John resting. Perhaps he didn't hear.'

'No, no,' he says. 'Your Mr St John had already gone out. He had company himself and then they went out. I heard the door bang.'

I said, 'Are you sure?'

'Oh yes. He had a gentleman caller.'

'Was it an American voice?'

'That I couldn't say. Only that it was a very *loud* voice. And then they left, which is when the door was banged. The whole house trembled, Miss Allbones. A picture I have on my wall quite shifted on its hook.'

Silly old fool. He'd probably had his shaving mug to the wall, all the better to hear things and complain about them. Sitting in his rooms from Friday night to Monday morning with nobody for company but a cat, you'd have thought he'd have welcomed a few signs of life.

I said, 'But you must agree, Mr St John is usually a very considerate neighbour.'

But Mr Earp wasn't in a mood to concede anything.

'And then,' he says, 'hardly had that pandemonium died away than another person came hammering at your door.'

'How long ago?'

'Just now. Mr St John's commotion had given me a crippling headache, here, like a steel band screwed tight across my brow, so I thought I'd come out, to take a little air. And there was a person knocking most persistently on your door. I told him you were almost certainly away from home and he said you almost certainly weren't, this being your day of rest.'

I thought it had to be Monty. He pays no heed to Sundays.

'Was he thick-set, about forty? Sallow. In a beaver hat?'

'No,' he says. 'It was an older person, with grey whiskers and a rather florid complexion. He was wearing a green ulster and a yellow ascot. Not that I made a close examination of him, you understand?'

Tom Bullen.

I met him walking back towards Mare Street and it was hard to say which looked the worse for the heat, the bunch of dahlias he was carrying or Tom himself.

'Dot,' he said, 'you're a welcome sight. I've been hammering on your door.'

'So I heard. My neighbour buttonholed me to tell me your particulars and complain about the noise.'

'Yes, he spoke to me. Funny old dodderer. But it's not like you to be out this time of day on a Sunday. Olive turned up just as I was giving up on you. She had her key and she said I was welcome to go in with her and wait, while she was heating up your bath water, but I didn't like to presume.'

I said, 'Are the flowers for me or are you visiting a cemetery later?'

I dislike dahlias, but I did take pity on Tom. He looked all in.

I said, 'I have lemonade at home, if you're fit to walk back with me.'

'The sight of you,' he said, 'has revived me. And if you've a drop of brandy in the house to fortify the lemonade, it would be most welcome. Tell you what, why don't we send Olive home. I can scrub your back for you.'

I didn't send her home. It takes more than a sorry-looking bouquet for a man to gain admittance to my toilette. I made him wait in the scullery until I was done.

We talked about the killings. We talked of other things too, but we always came back to the killings. Tom had been to Annie Chapman's inquest. It had opened that morning at the Working Lads' Institute.

'I've covered some terrible stories in my time,' he said, 'but I've never seen the like of this. You wouldn't think one human could do it to another.'

'I read that her rings were missing. So was it done for robbery? You wouldn't expect a woman like that to have anything worth taking.'

'She didn't. They were brass rings, but those who knew her say she was never without them. And her rings weren't all he took.'

'What?'

'Parts.'

'What do you mean?'

'I'd rather not say.'

I said, 'Damnation, Tom, you can't start a story and not finish it.'

'Female parts.'

'You mean her bosoms?'

'No. Lower down.'

'Her womb? Taken away?'

'Gone. Not a trace.'

'Did you go to view her?'

'I went with the jury. I felt I should. I have to be in possession of the facts. I spoke to Mrs Simmons as well, to confirm what I'd been told.'

'Who's Mrs Simmons?'

'A nurse at the dead-house. She's worked there for years. If you want to know the whys and wherefores of a corpse, she's your woman. She'd washed Annie Chapman and tidied her up and the parts were definitely taken.'

'So he is a madman.'

'Has to be.'

'And how long must that have taken him? It's not like snipping off a lock of hair. You do read of murderers doing that, for a kind of keepsake. But a womb? Whatever can he have wanted with that?'

'Let's say no more about it, Dot. It makes me queasy to think of it. Pour me another brandy, there's a darling.'

'There'll be more killings, I suppose.'

'Guaranteed. He won't stop till he's caught. His blood's up. The Nichols woman was cut worse than Martha Tabram and Annie Chapman was worse still.'

'What about this boot-mender everybody's talking about?'

'Leather Apron? I don't put much store by it. That story started with a couple of prossies and, take it from me, they're not to be relied on. Half of them are stewed, half of them are puddled. One of them says a man in a cobbler's apron threatened her and before you know it they're all saying the same thing. Every cobbler in Whitechapel will be fearing for his good name. And for his neck.'

'They say he has a dark moustache. Monty's shaved his off.'

'I don't blame him. An idea gets around and the next thing you know, there's a mob running amok. That's how innocent men get strung up. A moustache you can grow again but you can't bring a hanged man back to life.'

'What was said at the inquest?'

'Not much. There was a statement from the man who found her. A John Davies. The coroner had him tied in knots.'

'Why, what wrong had he done?'

'None at all, except to discover the corpse, poor sap. He's a porter at Leadenhall Market. He'd gone into the yard to use the privy before he set off for work, saw Annie Chapman sprawled on the ground with her skirts akimbo, and went out into the street to call for help. He got two men from the case-makers a few doors down, and they ran to fetch a constable. Only Davies omitted to find out the men's names. Well why would he? They were just men who happened to be standing nearby, having a smoke before they started their work. What were they to do with anything? But Wynne Baxter, he's the coroner, he says, "You should have discovered their names, my good man," and Davies said, "I had my work to go to." "Never mind your work," says Baxter. All very well for him sitting on his well-paid backside. "Your work is of no consequence compared to the importance of this inquest." You could see Davies was fit to thump him, only he daren't. Punch a coroner and you'll have time to regret it, sitting in the lock-up with a black mark against your name. Then they had the identification. There was a woman who was a friend of Annie Chapman's, and the night watchman from Crossingham's Lodging House, where she'd been dossing.'

'Did they give her a good character?'

'A good character? Living at Crossingham's?'

'Well was she liked?'

'She wasn't disliked. Well, she had been in a fight, a few days before.'

'With a man?'

'No, with another woman, over a piece of soap. Got her eye blacked. You see what these women are like, Dot? Very quick with their fists and their boots.'

'Not quick enough, apparently, otherwise Annie Chapman wouldn't be dead.'

'True. He must be a very smooth talker, and not rough looking. He must have them quite beguiled. Then in he goes with his knife. The night watchman from Crossingham's said the Chapman woman had been a willing worker at one time, hawking penny dreadfuls and bits of crochet, but not recently. He said, to the best of his knowledge, she'd had a husband who used to send her a bit of money but then he'd died and she'd quite let herself go. Seldom sober. He reckoned she'd had a good skinful on the night in question. One thing that did surprise me: he said when she went out to earn her bed money on Saturday morning she went off through Paternoster Passage. Now that runs from Dorset Street towards Brushfield Street, which was quite the contrary direction to where she was found.'

'I don't think I've ever been on Dorset Street.'

'I should think not. It's no place for a lady.'

'So is that it then, for the inquest?'

'No, no. There's a lot more to be heard. But it's adjourned till Wednesday. I'd say Baxter wanted to get home for his Sunday dinner.'

'Valentine says they're bringing in more police.'

'Yes. Abberline's back on his old patch. Inspector First-Class Abberline, if you please. He turned up at Leman Street last night, so there's a few noses out of joint there.'

That was a piece of news. I've known Fred Abberline since the 70s. He was based at Leman Street for years, but not in uniform, in plain clothes, as they say. He seemed to be very highly thought of. His wife liked the halls. He'd bring her to a show sometimes and they'd come round afterwards, for a few words. They lived in Shoreditch in those days but then he was promoted to Scotland Yard and they left, moved out to Clapham, I believe. Gone up in the world.

'So Fred Abberline's in charge now?'

'That's the latest. It seems a lot of trouble to go to over a few old prossies. Not exactly going to be missed, are they?'

'I read the Nichols woman had children. Probably Annie Chapman did too. Everybody has somebody who'll miss them.'

'Still, not exactly an adornment to society, were they? Not to warrant sending an Inspector First-Class from Scotland Yard. It could be because of the cutting. People get very alarmed about stabbings. I mean, it's one thing to give a scrubber a warning tap, if she tries to cheat you. You know what they're like.'

'No, what are they like?'

'They'll try dipping a man's pockets while his mind is on his pleasure. So I'm told. I can't speak from personal experience. But this slashing is something vicious. There appears to be a violent person on the loose and you can never find a constable when you need one. On the other hand, Abberline could have been sent here for a different reason entirely.'

'Such as?'

'Fenians.'

'Not Fenians again. Can't we just concentrate on catching murderers?'

'You may scoff, but a murderer only kills one at a time. A Fenian can blow up an entire street. Is Valentine still chumming around with that American?'

'He is. They had supper at Rules last evening. Two dozen Colchester oysters, then on to a private club on Vere Street.'

'Private club? That'll be a molly-house or my name's Mary. But he does come home at night?'

'Not last night. He spent it on Townsend's couch.'

'Couch, my eye! Oh, Dot, you must speak to him.'

'You told me not to. You said the police were watching Townsend, Tumelty, whatever his name is, and I mustn't say anything that might cause him to bolt.'

'I meant you shouldn't speak of the *Fenian* business, not the other. There's no reason you shouldn't warn young Valentine about perverse practices. In a motherly way. Mind you, if he's stayed the night in Tumelty's rooms, it's probably too late. He's probably been corrupted. Does he look like he's been corrupted?'

'I don't know. How can you tell? He has started wearing a billycock hat.'

'I don't know why you find it amusing. It's a felony, Dot, what those types do. If that young man's not careful, he could end up in gaol.'

'If he's not blown up first.'

'Precisely. Tumelty might have explosives stored in his rooms. Sometimes they go off when they're not supposed to. And consider this, what better time to be plotting and dynamiting than while the police are distracted? They're dashing about looking for Jack and while their backs are turned, the Fenians'll be getting to work. You know he might even ask Valentine to bring the stuff here for safekeeping. Have you thought of that? You could be blown sky-high. Does Olive clean his room?'

'When he asks her to.'

'Then tell her to be very careful. Tell her to come to you if she finds anything of a suspicious nature.'

'Olive doesn't need telling. She's as sharp as a tin tack. And Valentine's no fool. Townsend's got rooms up West and rooms on Batty Street. I'm sure Valentine would think it very strange if he asked him to keep anything here.'

'If he's had his head turned with dinners and presents, he might not be thinking straight at all.'

'You're letting your imagination run away with you. Now stop fretting. Why did you call him Jack?'

'Who?'

'The killer. You said the police are running around looking for Jack.'

'Did I? It was just a name. As good as any other. It'll do for now, till we know his real one.'

He loosened his collar.

'Dot,' he says. 'You and Monty, do you have an understanding?'

'He's my manager.'

'I know that. But is there more than that between you? Of a sentimental nature?'

I laughed.

I said, 'You surely know that Monty is tied to his mother's apron strings. And anyway, he's not to my taste.'

'Ah,' he said, 'and is there anybody who is to your taste? Could there be? You shouldn't be alone in the world.'

'I'm not the marrying kind, Tom.'

'How do you know till you've tried it?'

'I did try it, a long time ago.'

'I didn't know that.'

'Not many people do. I was married to Hamish McHendie.'

'Never heard of him.'

'He was a comic. Quite successful, not in London. In Birmingham and further north. But he was no joke to live with.'

'Did he beat you?'

'Only once and I turned round and hit him right back.'

A man doesn't have to use his fists to injure you. If he's clever he can lay you low just by what he says. That was McHendie. He could have an audience in fits but it was a different story at home. He had an unkind mouth on him. I believe it was because I overtook him. There came a time when I got higher billing than he did, and more money. We were pretty comfortable. But the better I did, the nastier he grew. And you know what they say. Once bitten. Once beaten.

I said, 'McHendie was thought to be quite a catch. All the girls were after him but he deigned to show a bit of an interest in me. He said I made him laugh. But the honeymoon was soon over. He didn't find me so comical when I got top line at the Prince of Wales and he had to settle for the Leicester Alhambra. So I left him.'

'What became of him?'

'Dead. A twisted bowel. That's going back a few years. I didn't know for a long time. I probably still wouldn't know only I happened to bump into his brother on a tram. He said "I suppose you heard about Mac?" Funny really, I was a widow and I didn't even know it.'

'And you've never been tempted to try again?'

'No. When I was shot of McHendie, I decided to stay single, to be on the safe side. I've done all right. I've had my admirers.'

'And here sits one of them. I'm not codding you, Dot. You know I have feelings for you.'

Now, as I recalled, there had occasionally been talk of a Mrs Bullen, though he never seemed in a hurry to go home to her.

I said, 'But, Tom, surely you have a wife? Or did she pass away?'

'She might as well have,' he said, 'for all the wife she is to me. To speak plainly, Dot, we live more as brother and sister these days.'

How many times have I heard that from a man!

'And is it Mrs Bullen who starches your collars and polishes your boots?'

'That's her job.'

'Well collars and boots are just two things I do for no man, and there are plenty more besides, so don't talk of throwing over a good woman for a roll in the hay with me.'

'I'd do it though, Dot, if you were to say the word.'

'I have said the word, Tom. The word is No.'

14

Monday night was one of the worst houses I could ever remember. We'd had murders before, and fogs and fevers, but it had never kept people from coming to a show. Quite the opposite. The worse things were outside, the more people liked to be entertained and have their mind taken off their troubles. But that Monday people were finding cheaper entertainments. For a start there was Hanbury Street, where you could still go for a penny gawk at the back yard where Annie Chapman had been butchered, and then a rumour spread that the man they call Leather Apron had been found and arrested, so people swarmed down to Leman Street to assemble outside the police station and pass the evening there.

Randolph the Cycling Trumpeter had come that way and said there was a considerable crowd hoping to see this Leather Apron.

'Some of them were shouting out a name, so they appear to know who he is.'

'What name?'

'Pisser.'

'Never! Nobody has such a name.'

'Well it was something like that. And the best thing for him will be to get charged with a crime and kept in the cells because if the police let him go he'll never come through that throng in one piece. Don't matter what the police decide, I'd say that crowd has him charged, convicted and measured for the drop.'

'So he's done for whichever way it goes.'

Ma Marks said, 'Many more houses like tonight we shall all be done for.'

I guessed where that remark was leading.

'Because if they don't catch this perisher soon,' she said, 'and get him off the streets I shall be forced to make economies.'

The Infant Prodigy said, 'You'd better not try keeping me out of what I'm owed. I have bills to pay.'

'We all have bills to pay, Ida, and yours are nothing compared to mine. Theatres eat money and I can't pay out what I don't have.'

I said, 'One bad night, and you're talking about economies? What kind of penny gaff is this? And what about the nights when there's so many wishing to see me you have them standing in the aisles? What reward do I get for that?'

Ma Marks said, 'If that occasion should ever arise, Dot, I'll be the first to offer you a bonus.'

The Norbury Nightingale said, 'Yes, and pigs will fly.'

It wasn't entirely clear whether she was casting doubts on my popularity or on the likelihood of Ma Marks keeping her promise, but I didn't lower myself to question her. The Norbury Nightingale indeed! More like the Strangled Goose. She claims this damp summer has affected her pipes but, the fact is, she always was a second-rate squawker and now she's certainly had her day.

Ma Marks said, 'Well, if things are no better tomorrow night I shall think of closing till next Monday. It's a short week anyway.'

It was a short week because Saturday was the Day of Atonement,

Yom Kippur as they call it, a very particular day for the Hebrews. Ma Marks is of that persuasion, though not in a big way. She's not like Monty with his Friday dinners. But it's always been the custom for the Pavilion to be dark the day before Yom Kippur and on the day itself, out of respect.

Ida said, 'I'm damned if I can see why we should close at all. If there's days when the Jews aren't supposed to go to see a show, so be it. Nobody's forcing them. I gave up humbugs one year, for Lent, but I didn't go round causing misery and hardship to sweet shops. And anyway, this thing they do every year, what's any of it to do with kippers? I thought they were supposed to go all day without eating.'

As Randolph said, so much for the Infant Prodigy.

Monty came by just before second house.

I said, 'The box is down and Ma Marks is talking about making economies. She's threatening to close for the rest of week.'

'She's not the only one,' he says. 'I was just at Griffin's and they only had a handful in for first house.'

I said, 'Even with Blanche headlining? Dear me, has the authentic warrior maiden lost her touch?'

'Business is bad everywhere, Dot. Don't be mean. Amazonia's still very popular. It's these murders. They've upset the whole apple cart. You all right? About going home?'

Monty's a funny one. He complained when I expected him to ride with me every night and then when I managed without him he seemed a bit put out. But I had no intention of going back to our old arrangement. I told him I'd be having supper with Tom Bullen, though I knew that was highly unlikely. Tom would be hanging around at Leman Street, catching any crumbs of information about Leather Apron.

Monty said, 'Bullen, eh? How's his wife?'

I didn't rise to it.

'Well if you're sure,' he said. 'I was passing this way anyway so I just thought I'd offer.'

I said, 'You're very good. Very considerate. And, Monty, now the police have captured this Leather Apron, it'll be safe for you to grow your whiskers again.'

'Dot,' he says, 'shaving off my moustache had nothing whatsoever to do with any of it. I just happened to be in the mood for a change. And, as a matter of fact, I've received several compliments.'

I couldn't think who from, apart from his mother. In my opinion, Monty's face benefits from a moustache.

Clarence the vent said he was going out to Leyton to his new diggings, if I'd care to share a hansom.

I said, 'Very well. As long as that doll of yours stays in his box.'

'Miss Allbones!' he says. 'His name is Percy and he's tucked up for the night. He's sleeping, so he shouldn't have heard you, but please don't ever refer to him as "that doll".'

The cabbie said Leather Apron was still being held by the police.

He said, 'I'll take you Brick Lane way. You won't care to see what's going on at the corner of Thomas Street.'

'Why, what is going on?'

'People who ought to know better, queuing to see pictures. Of the deceased. The Chapman woman. With her throat cut. A penny for a peep. I don't know what the world's coming to.'

Clarence said, 'I can't say I give any credence to this Leather Apron story. A boot-maker, a local man known to so many people? How could he be going out at all hours, and coming home with blood on his person? The way people live in Whitechapel, you'd only have to contemplate breaking wind behind a closed door and your neighbours would know about it. No, this slasher, whosoever he may be, he's not a local man.'

'Then what is he?'

'Quality,' he said. 'You see if I'm not right. He'll be somebody from up West, who rides about in his own equipage. How else does he fly the scene so fast?'

And a voice from inside that damned doll's box said, 'He must have wings.'

Clarence resumed his theorising when we reached Victoria Park. He asked our driver for his opinion.

'Somebody riding in a private turnout?' he said. 'In Whitechapel? No, that would have been noticed. And he don't make his getaway in a hansom, that's for sure. A driver always knows if he's carrying a wrong 'un. We may look like we're sitting up here minding on our own business but there's not much gets past us. No, I think this fellow goes on foot. With a good, long stride and wearing his dancing pumps, for a quiet tread. And I'll tell you what else I think. When they ketch him, I predict they'll find he's an educated man. He'll be a physician, or a sawbones.'

Clarence said, 'Why should that be?'

'Because of what he does.'

I said, 'He means because of the parts that were taken from Annie Chapman's body.'

The cabbie said, 'I do. Which cannot be the work of no ordinary man. He wouldn't know how to go about such a thing.'

Clarence said, 'He might have an idea. We all know where the heart is.'

'But it wasn't her heart he took away.'

'What was it then?'

I said, 'A female part. He cut it out, as clean as a whistle.'

'Miss Allbones, no more! I don't recall reading that. You seem to know a terrible lot about it.'

'I have a friend. A gentleman of the press.'

The cabbie said, 'As the lady says. He went straight to that part and cut it out. In a dark yard. With working people up and about and liable to catch him at it at any minute. No, he has to be a medical man. Mad of course but still, a person with particular knowledge.'

Clarence said, 'It's a damned good theory. I like it. Though I still think he must have some kind of private conveyance, to come and go so easily.'

I said, 'The pair of you ought to put your ideas to the police before they send this Leather Apron to the gallows. He's just a Whitechapel cobbler but everybody appears to think they've caught their man.'

'Police!' the driver said. 'They couldn't catch cold if they ran around barefoot in a blizzard. To Leyton next did you say, sir?'

And as Clarence climbed back into the cab, I heard that doll's voice say, 'Night, Miss Dot. Straight in now, and bolt that door.'

15

Tuesday night was as bad as Monday. Even the Norbury Nightingale's claque weren't in.

I said, 'What's happened to your gallery boys? Did you forget to pay them?'

'I pay no gallery boys,' she said. 'I don't need to.'

Clarence whispered to me, 'That's true. Those boys she gets in are doing penal servitude. I hear they're given a choice. A year of hard labour or two years listening to Marguerite every night.'

Ma Marks announced that she'd decided to close after second house.

'Until next Monday. At the earliest,' she said.

It didn't affect me. It was my last week anyway. I was due back at the Marylebone for the following week, top billing, but Ida was supposed to have two more weeks at the Pavilion.

She said, 'What do you mean, "at the earliest"? I need to know how I stand. And if you ask me, come next Monday night people'll be clamouring for entertainment. Once the Chapman woman's been buried, they'll soon lose interest in murders.'

Ma Marks said, 'Unless there's another one. The police have let Leather Apron go, so we're no further forward there.'

That was the word on the street and Tom confirmed it. John Pizer had been released. He'd gone home.

I said, 'And the crowd didn't tear him to pieces?'

'Not at all. They were dancing and cheering. His friends and relations started it, and then everybody else joined in. When I came away, they seemed set to dance him all the way to Mulberry Street. Very good-natured.'

'But weren't they baying for him to be hanged yesterday? I shall never understand human nature.'

'Don't even try, Dot. Have you ever observed the behaviour of a flock of sheep?'

I said, 'No. I'm from Wolverhampton.'

Tom thought John Pizer had only been arrested to stop people criticising the police.

He said, 'Bill Thicke's known Pizer for years. He knew where to find him. And people do call him Leather Apron. But he's not of the criminal type, and he's not swift of foot neither, to be murdering women and then disappearing into the night. He's just a boot-finisher. He may go with doxies. He might even be an unpleasant character. But a murderer? I don't think so. Bill's not letting on but I reckon Abberline told him to bring Pizer in, to throw a bone to the public, to try and calm things down. And it's worked.'

Ma Marks said, 'Till the next time.'

Ida said, 'Yes. He's still out there.'

But Tom said just because the Leather Apron story had come to naught didn't mean the police weren't following other lines of inquiry.

'Such as?'

'Annie Chapman's murder. There were sightings. Suspicious-looking men.'

That raised a laugh. Suspicious-looking men are ten a penny around Whitechapel.

A passer-by, on her way to work at Spitalfields Market early on Saturday morning, said she'd seen a man and woman in conversation on Hanbury Street and when she heard of the murder she'd gone to the dead-house on Montagu Street to view Annie Chapman's body and had recognised her at once as the very same woman.

Now I count myself a good observer of people. It's my business to catch their little mannerisms. That's why my skits are so successful. But if I was up so early in the morning, plodding my weary way to work, and happened to pass an old jade arguing with her husband or bargaining with a johnny, I'd no more remember the particulars of her face than I would a lamp post. But this person claimed to be such a hawk-eye she had clear recall of the man too and had given a description of him to the police.

'He was foreign-looking,' Tom said. 'Dark-complexioned, with a beard and a moustache, and wearing a low-crowned hat.'

'She must have taken a long look at him.'

'Not only that, but she says she can put a time to it. She was up at five, washed, dressed, had left her lodgings and was passing the Weaver's Arms when she heard the brewery clock strike the half.'

I said, 'The police should engage that woman to be a detective constable. She'd soon have every felon locked up.'

The other report was of a man seen drinking, early that same morning, in the Prince Albert on Brushfield Street. Tom said we'd certainly read about it in the morning papers. The publican's wife, a Mrs Fiddymont, had served a man who had a smear of blood on his hand. Furthermore, he'd been wearing his hat pulled down, as though he meant to conceal himself, and she hadn't cared for his glowering demeanour and his rough appearance.

Ma Marks said, 'If you keep an alehouse on Brushfield Street, it must be a rare thing to serve anybody that doesn't look rough.'

Ida said, 'And if you commit a murder, you don't go into an alehouse with blood smears on your hands. You find a tap and wash yourself. And who's to say a murderer must look like a murderer? The ones you need to worry about are them as look meek and mild. Like vicars. Have they brought any of them in for questioning?'

I said, 'Last week you wanted all the Jewish butchers questioned.'

'Them too,' she said. 'Quiz them all.'

Mrs Fiddymont's story ran as follows. When the blood-smeared drinker left her establishment, she'd sent one of her neighbours to follow him, though for what particular reason the papers didn't say. It was surely too early for her to have heard that another murder had been committed, and drinking a glass of ale is no offence, even at seven in the morning and with a glowering demeanour. The man was probably just a worker from some knacker's yard.

The neighbour had gone behind the man as far as Bishopsgate before he tired of the chase and left off pursuing him. He described him as ginger-haired, closer to fifty than forty, with a moustache and ill-fitting trousers. Whether they were too baggy or too long or too short, the report did not say. In any event he sounded nothing like the dark and foreign character seen talking to Annie Chapman on Hanbury Street.

★

Annie Chapman's inquest was resumed on Wednesday. On Thursday I sent Olive to buy the newspapers while Valentine was still warming up his tonsils. Then we all had tea and toast while we read the reports.

'Two whole pages in the *Daily News*,' she said. 'I wonder if he's reading them himself? If he can read.'

Valentine said, 'I'll bet he does. I'll bet he buys every edition, and snips out every mention of his deeds and sticks them in an album.'

Olive said, 'Then he must certainly be a bachelor.'

'How so?'

'Because if he had a wife she'd want to know what he was thinking of, wasting money on so many papers and clipping out murder stories and leaving a mess on her kitchen table.'

Those who had given evidence to the inquest on the Wednesday were the packing-case men who had gone to fetch the police, and some of the people who resided at the house where the body had been found. The packing-case men must have cursed their bad luck. They'd just happened to be standing on Hanbury Street, waiting to go in to their work, when the alarm was raised. But they were still obliged to attend the inquest, and lose half a day's pay.

One of them, a Mr Holland, had run to Spitalfields Market, but the constable on duty there said he couldn't leave his post, not even if a body had been discovered, and had directed the man to walk up Commercial Street where he would certainly find an officer available to go to the scene of the crime. But Mr Holland had gone back to Hanbury Street without finding a single constable. He said he thought it was a disgraceful thing, to find no men on the beat, and for a constable to refuse to attend a dead body, and he'd made an official complaint, but Mr Wynne Baxter, the coroner, gave him short shrift. He'd said it wasn't for a box-maker to question the procedures of the Metropolitan Police and, anyway, other officers had been found, without too much of a delay, and they had gone to Hanbury Street to secure the scene of the murder. So that told Mr Holland.

Then a Mrs Richardson had been called. She rented the house on Hanbury Street and lived there with her grandson in two of its rooms. She ran a case-making business from the cellars and let the other rooms to tenants, about fourteen of them as far as I could calculate, though it wasn't a very large house. It must have been like an ants' nest inside those walls.

Mrs Richardson herself had heard nothing until the clamour went up when Annie Chapman's body was found. She said she hadn't slept well that night and would have heard if anyone had gone through the passage from the street to the yard. It was a sound that was familiar to her. The coroner had quizzed her on that point. He'd said, 'You mean people regularly go into your yard who have no business there?'

'Yes. Quite often.'

'For immoral purposes?'

'Oh no,' she'd replied. 'I should never allow that. I'd say they get caught short, on their way to work, and need to avail of my privy.'

Her son had given evidence too and somewhat contradicted her. John Richardson said he didn't live at Hanbury Street but he was in the habit of calling in at his mother's house on his way to work, to make sure her workshops were secure. He'd begun the practice after her cellars had been burgled some time previously and good tools taken. He said he often found women in the yard entertaining men and he always turned them out onto the street. On one occasion, he said, he'd found a couple inside the house, going at it on the first-floor landing. He made his mother look a fool or a liar. Either way, I'll bet he got what for when they left the inquest.

According to the papers, John Richardson had gone to Hanbury Street just before five, on his way to work at the market, and had found everything in order. He'd sat for a moment on the yard steps, to try and trim a piece of leather that was flapping from his boot, and would certainly have seen Annie Chapman's body if it had been there. The coroner wanted to see the knife he'd used to cut his boot. Richardson said he hadn't brought the knife with him to the inquest. He said it was just an old fruit knife, it had proved too blunt to cut his boot leather anyway so he couldn't see that it would be of interest to the inquiry, and the coroner said, 'It is not for you to decide what is relevant to this inquest. Fetch the knife.'

Valentine said, 'Who is this idiot, wasting time on fruit knives?'

Mr Wynne Baxter. County Coroner for Middlesex and very highly thought of, according to Tom.

I said, 'I don't think he can be an idiot, to have risen to that position.'

But Valentine said, 'Don't you believe it. It's not what you know. It's who you know.'

Of course the people most likely to have heard if Annie Chapman cried out when she was attacked were the tenants who lived in the back of the house. There was a Mr Walker, a tennis boot-finisher, who had a ground-floor room with his imbecile son, and above him were the Misses Copsie, two sisters, who worked at Cohen's, packing cigars. But none of them was called to be questioned. I thought that rather odd.

The last to give evidence on Wednesday was John Pizer, thirty-eight years of age, a bachelor, and a shoe and slipper-maker. He agreed that he was sometimes known as Leather Apron but he said so were other men who wore such an apron for their work.

Olive said, 'That's true. My uncle's a cabinet-maker and he wears one. Well, he did, but lately he hasn't dared to.'

John Pizer said that he had been at his brother's house on Mulberry Street since the day before Annie Chapman's murder and hadn't set foot outside its door until Sergeant Thicke had gone there on Monday to arrest him. The coroner asked him if it was usual for him to remain indoors for so many days on end and Pizer said he'd done it on his brother's advice, because there had been so much talk of Leather Apron ever since the Nichols murder and he feared he was the object of a false suspicion.

The hearing was adjourned till the following day.

Valentine said, 'Shall we have a fresh brew and some more toast? I'm famished.'

'What, no fancy luncheon with Dr Townsend?'

'Not today,' he said. 'Frank's been very fatigued these past few days. He's resting up.'

I said, 'Well if you want more tea you'd better make it yourself. We've been sitting here reading about murders for quite long enough. Olive needs to get on with her work.'

It was her day for swabbing the passages and giving the back kitchen a good bottoming. Valentine was appearing at the Royal

Cambridge on Commercial Street. He said he'd go in early and eat at Brumpton's, rather than get under Olive's feet.

He said, 'Will you wait up for me tonight, Miss Dot? I shouldn't be late. We haven't had one of our tray suppers for a long time.'

Not my fault, I'm sure.

He said, 'Enjoy your afternoon off. It's all right for some!'

But, of course, the thing about being an artiste is it's very hard to enjoy an afternoon off. Sundays, yes, fair enough, but not on a Thursday when by rights you should be working. It makes me nervous. You do hear of people giving up the theatre, shifting to the country, to Walthamstow to grow onions, but in most cases it's the theatre that gives up on them. I pray it won't happen to me. I hope I shall keep going till I'm ready to drop. They can carry me on in my box, I'll give them one last performance of 'Forty Fousand Frushes' and then they can screw the lid down.

I decided I'd walk down to Mare Street and get Mrs Sullivan to attend to my corns. I was in the front hall, arranging my hat, when Olive came looking for me.

'Miss Allbones,' she said, 'I'm afraid we've got a bit of a pong. I think it's in the sink. I've put soda and hot water down the plug hole but I can't seem to get rid of it.'

I don't know what she thought I could do about it but I went through to the scullery anyway. All I could smell was soap and toast. We stepped out into the back yard. I never go out there. The flags were wet where Olive had emptied her bucket and there was something, a slight whiff, sweetish, not pleasant but not too bad.

I said, 'It must be the drains, with the warm weather. It'll probably disappear as soon as we have a cold snap.'

I happened to look up. Valentine's window was wide open.

I said, 'No wonder Mr Earp complains about his warbling. He should keep that window shut and show a bit of consideration. Run up and close it, there's a good girl.'

'Oh I don't like to,' she says. 'Mr St John told me he must have fresh air. And I only go into his room when requested.'

I said, 'You *are* being requested, Olive.'

But she still didn't budge. I went up myself and pulled down the window sash. First time I'd set foot in that room since he moved in. I will say he kept it nice and tidy.

Olive gave me a bashful look as I came down the stairs, as well she should have. I thought perhaps I was getting too soft with her, allowing her to sit down and look at the papers with me. It was Valentine who started it with his Sunday teas but I was the one paying her wages. He just bunged her a few shillings for washing his shirts and getting his collars done.

'Oh, Miss Allbones,' she says, 'just look at that.'

A great fat blowfly hovered between us and then landed on my hand. I hate flies. I don't know what God can have been thinking of.

I said, 'Now before you do another thing, roll up one of those newspapers and send this filthy creature to meet his Maker.'

'I will,' she said. 'And I'll be sure to put a tea cloth over your supper tray. And when I come in on Sunday I'll bring another can of Jeyes, in case you still have that pong.'

Trying to get back in my good books.

16

Annie Chapman was buried that Friday. It was a quiet affair according to the papers, no mourners, no coaches. An elm coffin was brought for her from Hawes's on Hunt Street and she was transported very early from the dead-house, before many people were about, and whatever family she had, such as hadn't washed their hands of her, waited for her at the cemetery in Forest Gate. The inquest dragged on. John Richardson's fruit knife was taken into custody. The state of the Whitechapel mortuary was strongly criticised.

Tom said, 'It's not really a proper mortuary. It's just a shed out the back of the workhouse and, between you and me and the newel post, Bobbie, the attendant who's in charge of it, he's not all there. He's a bit touched. Perhaps it's from being surrounded by corpses.'

The only thing of real interest in the inquest report was the police-surgeon's evidence. Dr Bagster Phillips. He'd seemed reluctant to go into all the grisly particulars of the state of Annie Chapman's body, even when the coroner pressed him to say more.

I said, 'What, did he think it was too gory for the general public?'

Tom said, 'They did clear the room of ladies before he continued. Phillips is a nice old chap, very decent, very proper. And he's a very experienced police-surgeon. He has his way of doing things. He has his reasons. For one thing he always likes to keep back a few details, a few things that only the murderer could know. It can help sometimes, for a prosecution. And, of course, if you tell the public everything you run the risk of imitators. But what makes sense for the police, Dot, don't make sense for the newspapers. So although I can understand Bagster Phillips's point of view, I was glad when Wynne Baxter pushed him to say more. The public don't want to read about fruit knives. They want to read about gizzards.'

I'm afraid Tom was right. I even found myself skimming over the dry details and going directly to the gory stuff. Dr Bagster Phillips surmised from the swelling and protrusion of her tongue that Annie Chapman had been stifled before she was cut. He had also noted an abrasion on the ring finger of her left hand and an indentation likely to have been caused by the habitual wearing of a ring and those who knew her said she wore three, just brass and of no value, though no ring was found on her. The doctor said the cutting weapon was likely to have been a very sharp knife with a thin, narrow blade. Her bowels had been thrown about her body where she lay. That her womb had been taken, I already knew from Tom.

The inquest had been adjourned again, for a full week.

I said, 'Why don't they finish it? What else is there to investigate?'

'There's a neighbour who might have heard something. There's passers-by who might have seen something. Nothing much. No, this one's gone right off the boil. It'll be "wilful murder by person or persons unknown" and everybody'll go back to business as usual.'

I said, 'I hope you're right. I can't afford any more cancelled shows.'

He used the moment to slide his arm around my waist.

'Ah, Dot,' he says, 'if you'd only let me take care of you. You'd find me a good provider.'

There are times when I could almost give in to Tom. There are times when it's very comforting to feel a man's arms around you, even if he does have a wife in Mile End.

We'd both fallen asleep. It was Valentine coming in that woke me. All it takes is one wet day and that front door swells and sticks in its frame. Tom was still spark out. I roused him.

I said, 'You'd better go home.'

'What's the time?'

'Must be about five. The sky's starting to get light.'

'Just another half hour,' he says, and snuggles back under the counterpane.

I said, 'Valentine's home.'

'So?'

'I don't want him knowing you're in my bed.'

'He's your lodger, Dot. This is your house. You can do as you please. How about working up an appetite for breakfast?'

Which led to a bit of a tussle. I mean, a bit of slap and tickle can be very nice first thing, when you're feeling rested, but I didn't want Valentine to hear us.

I said, 'Put your trousers on. Your wife'll have a search party out looking for you.'

'Ah, Dot!' he says, 'Don't mention her. Now you've gone and made me lose my morning vigour.'

So that put paid to that. I had such a thick head. He went down to the scullery to fetch me a glass of water. One thing about Tom, he can take a knock-back. He doesn't sulk. He knows I say Yes more often than I say No.

'Right,' he said, 'first stop, a coffee stall. Second stop, Leman Street. Find out what mischief has been occurring while I've been enjoying the pleasures of your boudoir.'

He was lacing up his boots.

He said, 'By the way, sweetheart, I think your cesspit needs emptying.'

But there was no cesspit. It was a superior, modern property, with proper drains.

'In that case,' he said, 'I reckon you must have a dead rat. It's probably behind a skirting board.'

I can tell you there are no rats in my house, dead or alive. We don't even have mice. I put down Everton mints to keep them away. A mouse can't abide the smell of peppermint.

Valentine had noticed the smell too.

'Yes,' he said. 'Now you mention it. It's probably gas coming off the Hackney marshes, with this warm spell. We shall just have to splash on extra cologne. Roll on winter!'

If he had heard Tom's voice that morning or the creaking of the bed springs, he never mentioned it. Perhaps I was daft. I was entitled to a bit of comfort, after all. If Mrs Bullen didn't care for Tom's attentions any more, there was no reason I shouldn't enjoy them. But that was between me and Tom. And Valentine was such a boy. I didn't wish to scandalise him.

*

It was as Tom had predicted. By the start of the next week, people were losing interest in the Whitechapel murderer. They were ready for some cheerful entertainment and that's what I gave them. I played to full houses at the Marylebone, even on the Monday when you might have expected things to be a bit slow, and Valentine said the Pavilion appeared to be open again too.

It was a decent line-up at the Marylebone. Dickie Dabney and his Crows, Madame Celeste La Rue, Blind Lionel who plays the piano, Betsy Ash who does stilt-walking and juggling, and the Mad Margolinskis engaged at the last minute to replace the Flying Flahertys. According to Lol Withers, the gas man, one of the Flahertys had had his collar felt by plain-clothes policemen and the whole troupe had scarpered.

I said, 'So they *were* Fenians?'

'That's the story. Found to be in possession of an alarm clock and a pair of pliers.'

'I did hear a rumour about Jerry Flaherty, but I put no store by it. He seemed such a nice boy. Was it just him the police questioned?'

Lol said, 'I couldn't say, Miss Allbones. All I know is the lot of them's gone and we'd have been in a right old fix if the Margolinskis hadn't been unexpectedly available. And, between you and me, I'd sooner watch them anyway. I never found the Flahertys so very comical.'

The Margolinskis are sand-dancers. Dan and David, and they have a sister, Deborah, who appears with them sometimes. They're a nice act, very good-humoured people. I rub along very well with Betsy Ash too. She doesn't stand on her dignity like some I could mention. The thing about Betsy is she doesn't really need to keep working. She has a couple of admirers, wealthy gentlemen who keep her comfortable, so she's not the kind to try elbowing other artistes out of her way. Tuesday night she had Reggie Scrope-Lyttleton in. He's only a Hon., but he's got plenty of jingle to spare. If he doesn't pay her rent I'll bet he keeps her in stockings and bath salts. Wednesday night it was the Duke of Bedford. Hastings, as she calls him.

I said, 'How do you make sure they don't both turn up the same night?'

'Well,' she said, 'I *am* a juggler! But, actually, we have an agreement. They both know they're not my one and only. It suits them. You know what lads are like. Never happier than when they're playing with somebody else's toys.'

Of course Hastings Bedford is hardly a lad. He must be pushing seventy.

She said, 'Doesn't matter. Give me an old boy any day. They're more generous and they're not in such a hurry.'

There's truth in that. Tom can be very considerate of a girl's needs.

I said, 'Someone told me that Prince Eddy's one of your followers.'

She laughed.

'Not likely,' she said. 'I have been presented to him, but he wasn't interested in me. You can tell at once, can't you? I think a thruppenny upright round a dark corner might be more Prince Eddy's style. Or perhaps he's of the other inclination. I don't know. Anyway, I'm evidently not his type and he's certainly not mine.'

'Even though he'll be King some day? That'd be a feather in anybody's cap.'

'But, Dot,' she said. 'Have you never studied him?'

'I've never even seen him.'

'You haven't missed anything. He's not all there. Up top. There's nothing going on. Well I mean, a bit of how's-your-father is all very nice but what about before, and after. You want a bit of conversation too.'

We were a happy band that week. We all got along, except for Cissie Roundtree. She doesn't like me because I forget to call her Madame La Rue. What does it matter? Backstage, scrub the slap off our faces, we're none of us what the audience sees.

Thursday night it was so close and muggy I went outside before second house, onto the passageway by the artistes' entrance, just to try and get a breath of air. They say there used to be gardens where the Marylebone stands, with lovely trees and arbours. Nothing now but hansoms and horse droppings.

I was about to go back down when I heard the most desperate screams coming from below. I fairly ran down those steps and when I reached the bottom there stood Cissie, wide-eyed, hair on end. She looked like an owl in a thorn bush and, to make matters worse, she was wearing nothing but her combinations. She had her little dog in her arms. It's one of those terriers with the long hair. You can't see their feet. They always seem like they're moving on castors.

'Dot, help me!' she cries. 'Baby's dying.'

Next thing I know, I'm holding the dog. Cissie's shaking and weeping.

I said, 'What's happened to him?'

'He's choking, Dot,' she says. 'Quick, save him. Do something! Before it's too late.'

Well what was I to do? All I could think was to give his middle a good squeeze, which I did and it caused the ungrateful little hound to cough out the cause of his blockage all over my new canvas boots. That was when Dickie Dabney appeared.

'Give me that dog,' he says. 'I'm going to strangle him.'

Cissie grabbed Baby from my arms and held him to her.

I said, 'Dickie, calm down. What's he done? Chewed your top hat?'

'That little fiend,' he says, 'has eaten my Nero. He's eaten my best boy.'

It appeared that the mess on my boots was the earthly remains of Dickie's star crow, Nero. Amazing. If you'd asked me who'd be the victor in a scrap between a crow and Cissie's lapdog, I'd have put my money on the crow.

Dickie said he'd go to law. Cissie said she might do likewise, seeing that value of her doggie was vastly greater than that of a scabby old bird and it was Dickie's carelessness, leaving a bird to wander free, that had nearly cost Baby his life.

'Scabby old bird!' he said. 'My crows have performed at Marlborough House, I'll have you know. My crows earn a living. Nine years and Nero never once missed a show.'

Cissie said a bird could never have the value of a dog, particularly a highly bred dog like Baby, who was her constant companion, family even, like a child to her. I don't know. All I'd ever seen that dog do was lie in his basket licking his commodities.

Dickie was beside himself. I was really afraid he might take a seizure. I took his arm.

I said, 'Let me send out for a nip for you. What do you like? Brandy? Rum?'

'No, no,' he says. 'No drink, Dot. I don't hold with it.'

But he did agree to a dose of my Quieting Syrup, after he'd perused the label. Black Drop is guaranteed not to contain the demon alcohol.

He said, 'I'm inconsolable, Dot. I don't think I can go on for second house.'

I said, 'You have to, Dickie. Remember what you told me, years ago?'

He looked at me.

I said, 'After I found out McHendie had spent my rainy day money and I was in pieces? Remember what you said to me?'

'No.'

'Think not of yourself, Dot. Think of your public. When you're an artiste you must save your tears till you get home.'

'Did I say that?'

'You did.'

'Where?'

'We were in Brum. At the Queen's, on Snow Hill.'

'Fancy. And you've remembered it, all this time.'

Of course I hadn't remembered it exactly. I had to polish it up a bit. It might even have been somebody else who said it to me. Still, whatever it takes to get a man back to the footlights.

He said, 'And I was right, wasn't I? I never spoke a truer word.'

So he did go on, and he paid a very moving tribute to Nero. I was watching from the wings and I saw several people bring out their handkerchiefs as he spoke. It was a sensible thing to do because it made everyone very forgiving when his act turned out a shambles. Well it was bound to. The other crows had witnessed Nero's demise. They were too shocked to concentrate on their calculations. And anyway, take away one card and the whole house is liable to collapse. Dickie will have to train up a replacement. It could take months.

I said, 'Cissie should compensate him for his loss.'

Betsy said, 'Cissie wouldn't give you the skin off her cocoa. I just hope we can get her out of here tonight before her doggie-wog starts shitting feathers.'

17

Friday night, Tom turned up, intending to squire me home. Hoping for a reward, I'm sure. He commenced nibbling on my neck as soon as we were in the cab.

I said, 'I'm tired, Tom.'

It was the truth. I mean, I was fond of him, but I couldn't be romping every night of the week. Sometimes it's just nice to have a warm body beside you, but if Tom got frisky there was no stopping him. Then, as soon as he'd had his pleasure, he'd go out like a light. He'd spread himself across the bed like a rabbit squashed on the high road and I'd be left huddled on the edge. When I'm working I need my sleep.

'What you need is a nice drop of Bolly,' he says.

We were coming up Bishopsgate, just by White Lion Street, when I spotted Kate. Well it was my old coat I recognised first because Kate wasn't striding out in her usual style. She was walking like an old woman. I told the driver to stop.

Tom said, 'Now what?'

'Old acquaintance,' I said. 'I'll just say hello. But if she's the worse for drink I shall tell the cabbie to drive on.'

Kate wasn't drunk.

'Just puffed,' she said. 'And I've got a gammy foot. I've got a great hole in my boot. Too much walking!'

I said, 'Did you go to Kent?'

'Been and come back. We were too late getting there. They'd set on all the pickers they needed. I told Kelly we should have gone sooner but he'd got a bit of portering at Smithfield and he didn't want to give it up. Ah well. At least we got out of here for a few days. Kent's very pretty. Meadows and hedgerows. We've been living off blackberries and Queen o' the May. Kelly knows all that country stuff, what you can eat, what'll kill you.'

'Do you have your bed money for tonight?'

'I do. I charred for Mrs Fiddymont today.'

'At the Prince Albert?'

'Yes. Do you know her, then?'

'No, but I remember her name. She was in the papers, after this last murder. She was the one who served a man drink and noticed he had blood on his hands.'

'That's right, she did. The morning Annie Chapman was found. We heard all about that of course, even in Kent. So there's another terrible thing. What a world. I hear there's a reward going so perhaps I'll win that. I know a few likely individuals. I could give the peelers a few names.'

'Could you?'

'No, not really. But I can dream. A hundred pounds, Dot. Think of it.'

Tom was getting restless.

I said, 'Are you living at Cooney's?'

'I am,' she said. 'Cooney Mansions! Next stop, the grave! Night, night then, Dot. I can see your friend's eager to get off. Tararabit!'

Tom said, 'I thought she'd never stop rabbiting. I thought you'd never get rid of her.'

'I didn't want to get rid of her. A friendly word costs nothing. And what's it to you?'

'You said you were tired. Who is she, anyway?'

'Kate,' I said. 'And a warning to us all.'

'How so?'

'She used to be the best-looking girl on Bilston Street. Raised nice, finished her schooling, married a man with a trade and a bit of money. And now look at her. Scrubbing floors to make her bed money for the night. Hobbling back to Cooney's with a hole in her boot. What size feet would you say she has?'

'Dot,' he says, 'all I saw of her was her face and if that's Bilston Street's idea of beauty, it's a sad thing. She looked to me like an old drab.'

'That's my point, Tom. A person's fortunes can change.'

'Not if they're prudent.'

'That's what Monty always says.'

'Does he? Then, for once, I agree with him. How is Monty? I don't see him about much these days.'

'He's a very busy man. Evenings he goes out on patrol with this Vigilance Committee. And bear in mind it's that time of year for Jews. All those holidays. First they have New Year, then they have Yom Kippur, and now it's the next thing.'

'Sukkot.'

'That's it. When they put the shed in the yard behind the Lodzer synagogue. And a lot of waving.'

'Waving?'

'Branches and greenery.'

'Ah yes. I can tell you about that, if you're interested. It's to recall the time when greenery was a precious thing, when they lived in the desert.'

'And now they're on Goulston Street. Not a lot of greenery there neither.'

'Yes. Still, they do love their holidays. But you're right, Dot. You'd think they'd spread their high holidays out a bit, across the year.'

I said, 'Is Cooney's on Dorset Street?'

'No, Cooney's is on Flower and Dean Street. Why?'

'I have a pair of boots that might do for Kate.'

'Then you must give them to me to take there. You can't go wandering into a place like that.'

I told him I'd think about it. Tom means well but I've never cared to have a man telling me what I can do.

As we walked through the front door he said, 'Oh, Dot, you haven't got rid of that smell.'

I couldn't smell anything.

'That's because you're habituated to it. You need a rat-catcher. I know a man. Leave it to me.'

I said, 'When I decide I need a rat-catcher I'll let you know.'

'Well,' he says, 'it's quite unpleasant. You wouldn't want to be giving any of your tea parties with a smell like that in the house.'

*

The big story in the papers that week, for want of any more murders, was about Sir Charles Warren, top of the tree of all the London police. Would he resign or wouldn't he?

Tom said, 'He damned well should. Nobody likes him.'

I said, 'Perhaps he doesn't need to be liked, as long as he gets the job done.'

'But he doesn't get the job done. He rubs people up the wrong way. He was never right for that position. See, Warren's an army man. That's a particular mentality. Always fussing about uniforms. Boots polished, belt buckle centred. But you can't treat your beat bobby like that. He's not on a parade ground. He's walking the streets, dealing with house-breakers and cut-throats. And look at these chief constables Warren's brought in. All army cronies. No police experience. And surplus to requirement. When you've got four good wheels on your wagon why would you tack on a fifth one? They should send him back to Africa. Let him deal with Hindoostanis, that's more in his line.'

'I think the Hindoostanis are in India.'

'Don't quibble, Dot. Africa, India, the sooner Warren's gone the happier everybody'll be. The man's a martinet.'

He didn't stay long that evening. He said the smell from my scullery was making him feel bilious. So then I started to imagine a smell. It wasn't the sink. Olive kept that sparkling clean. I was about to slide back the bolt and have a sniff of the back yard and then I thought of Annie Chapman. What if that villain had wandered out as far as Hackney? What if there was a body lying out there? I waited up for Valentine and as soon as he stepped into the front hall I called out, 'Stop! Can you smell anything?'

'Don't think so,' he says. 'Maybe. A bit. Is it gas?'

I asked him to go up to his room and look down into the yard, in case a body lay there.

'Miss Dot,' he says, 'how could a murderer get into our back yard except by passing through this house?'

But he humoured me and went to look.

'Nothing there,' he said. 'It's probably a bit of gristle caught in the drain. Now let's have a cup of cocoa and a natter about cheerier things. We've all got murders on the brain.'

Saturday morning I looked out a few more bits for Kate. A chintz skirt, two cotton chemises, never worn, and a pair of laced boots, not new but quite good enough to get her by while she had her old ones mended. I took the horse tram down to Bishopsgate and went to the Prince Albert first, thinking I might catch her there. There were beer casks being delivered. One of the draymen looked at me.

He says, 'You all right, lady? You look like you've took a wrong turning?'

Well in I went. I rather like the smell of yesterday's ale. It reminds me of when I was a girl, starting out, doing a turn in the back room at the Boot and Star with Mam and Dad looking on. The Prince Albert taproom was deserted. I suppose most of their trade is market hands, when they've finished work for the day.

A man was wiping glasses. He cocked his head.

'Snug's through there,' he said.

I said, 'I'm not drinking. I'm looking for Kate.'

'Who?'

'Kate Conway? She chars for you sometimes.'

'You mean Kate Kelly. Missus,' he calls, out through the back, 'did Kate Kelly come in today?'

'No,' came a woman's voice. 'Never turned up.'

I asked the quickest way to Flower and Dean Street.

He smirked. 'Flower and Dean Street? You sure? Doing good works are you? Working for some charitable institution?'

'Do I turn after the church or before?'

'Go to the end of this street and turn right. Past Christ Church, past the Queen's Head, then keep left. Don't make the mistake of going down Shepherd Street.'

'Why?'

'Jew boys. Shepherd Street, Tilley Street, Palmer Street, anywhere round there. That's their patch. Anybody not of their nation, they'll give you trouble, don't matter how respectable you are.'

'I'll keep it in mind.'

'Be sure you do. And watch your pocket, lady. I wouldn't let my wife venture down Flower and Dean, not for a big gold watch.'

Flower and Dean Street runs from Commercial Street to Brick Lane. It's not a long street nor particularly narrow. There were gaps of cleared land along it too, and it was a fine, sunny day but no light seemed to penetrate. There were a great number of people out, sitting on doorsteps, leaning against walls. I suppose they have to be, until it's time to claim a bed for the night. Where else are they to go if they have no work? I didn't care for the feel of it. Not so much of danger. More like hopelessness. A dead end, even though I could see Brick Lane up ahead of me, busy with people and carts.

I walked down the middle of the street and every head turned to watch me. They wouldn't have recognised me, of course, even if they'd had the privilege of seeing me perform, but I was too well turned out for that neighbourhood. They couldn't help but gaze at me.

The problem was finding Cooney's. Those houses all look the same. I asked a woman with a child on her hip.

'Other side of the street,' she said. 'Just before the corner. Spare a penny for the baby?'

I didn't have a penny. I gave her a sixpence.

'God bless you, duchess,' she said. 'He's had nothing, only a rusk this morning.'

I said, 'Is he your grandbaby?'

She laughed. 'Grandbaby!' she says. 'Not yet, I hope. Do I look that old? I'll be thirty come Christmas.'

I'd thought her my age at the very least.

I said, 'No, you don't look old. It's me. I have bad eyes.'

The door to Cooney's was open. I stepped inside and the sour smell made me catch my breath. I wished I'd thought to sprinkle a little lavender water on my handkerchief. There was a small room to the right. A man came out, in his shirt sleeves.

'Help you?' he says.

'I was hoping to find Kate Kelly.'

He looked at me.

I said, 'Or she might go as Conway?'

'I know who you mean,' he says. 'You mean John Kelly's missus. I reckon she's down in the kitchen. She in trouble?'

'No. I'm a friend.'

'If you say so. Through that door and down the stairs.'

★

The cellar steps were steep and wet. They looked to have been scrubbed recently. The further down I went, the more the odour improved. I'd sooner smell mildew than unwashed clothes any day. The kitchen was cool and dark. There was no fire burning. There was a man asleep on a settle, snoring, and a figure sitting in the hearth, dozing, mouth open, leaning against the chimney breast. Kate.

She opened her eyes at once.

'Who's there?' she said.

I said, 'It's Dot Allbones.'

'Dot? In Cooney's basement?'

'I brought you a few things. There's a pair of boots.'

She got to her feet, wiped her mouth with the back of her hand. She looked terrible. Grey and dropsical. I gave her the parcel. Then she started to cry.

I said, 'Don't be daft. It's not much. The boots have been worn, but not much. The skirt too.'

She said. 'But I'm ashamed for you to see me here.'

She opened the package and put the skirt on at once, over what she was already wearing.

'Look at that,' she said. 'What a handsome piece of cloth. Daisies and what would you call those?'

'I'd say they're lilies. How many layers are you wearing now?'

She smiled.

'This one makes four.'

'Won't you be too hot?'

'I'm never hot. Feel my hand.'

It was cold as clay.

'Any road, there's no armoires at Cooney's, Dot. If you've got it you wear it. There's some light-fingered buggers about. And this is a quality garment. I dussen't let this one out of my sight.'

'Try the boots.'

They were too big for her but she insisted they were perfect.

'I'll rob a pair of socks off Kelly. That'll fill them out.'

She started bringing things out of her pocket. A comb, a thimble, a piece of soap no bigger than my thumb, a mustard tin.

I said, 'You carry mustard?'

'No,' she said. 'It's an old tin, but it's a good place to keep my valuables.'

She opened it to show me. A pawn ticket and a twist of paper.

She said, 'I've got a brew of tea in here I'd make for you but I shall have to go out for hot water. There's none here this time of day.'

'I don't need tea. Do you have your bed money for tonight?'

'Yes. I swabbed the steps here for Mrs Wilkinson so that'll pay for tonight and Kelly'll see me all right for tomorrow. He's working at Leadenhall Market.'

'I went to the Prince Albert first. I thought I might find you there.'

'Did you? I'll bet my name was mud. But I couldn't have worked there today, Dot. Not down on my knees scrubbing. I'm so out of puff.'

'Will you just sit here all day?'

'Nothing else to do.'

'Come out for a stroll. Give your new skirt an airing. We can get a bite to eat.'

'I haven't got much of an appetite.'

'You should have something. How about a slice of cake from Friedman's?'

'I might do. I'll walk with you though, Dot. It'd be nice to have your company.'

'What about that broker's ticket in your tin? Do you want to redeem it?'

'No, no. I was gave it by Em Birrell, when we were in Kent. It's for a shirt that was her late husband's and she thought it might do for John Kelly, but I'd say it'd swamp him. Em's husband was the size of a bear.'

She rolled the two chemises back in their wrapping paper and tucked them in her waistband. I guessed what she intended to do with them. As we left, the man in the shirt sleeves appeared again.

He said, 'You've perked up.'

Kate said, 'I have. That's what a visit from a friend can do for a person. And do you notice my nice new skirt?'

'I do,' he said. 'You'll have the gents after you, wearing that.'

'And do you see who my friend is? This is Dot Allbones.'

'Is it?' he says.

'Star of the halls,' she said though I tried to hush her. 'She's at the Marylebone theatre this week. Pavilion, Forester's, she plays them all.'

'Well fancy that. Let me fetch Mrs Wilkinson.'

I dislike to be pointed out. If people recognise your name they're liable to expect a free skit there and then, like you might turn on a tap, and if your name doesn't register with them you have to put a good face on it.

The wife appeared, wiping her hands on her apron.

Wilkinson said, 'We have company, Mary. Friend of Kate's here. An artiste, off the halls. Her name's Dot Allbones.'

Kate said, 'Dot's a top-liner these days. But I've known her since she was knee-high to a flea.'

Mrs Wilkinson peered at me.

'We love a show, me and Fred, but of course evenings is our busy time. It's hard to get away. And tickets are such a price.'

I was glad she'd gone straight to the point. Sometimes people take for ever. They go all round the houses, hinting about complimentary tickets.

I said, 'Well if ever you're passing, just ask for me at the stage door and I'll see what I can do for you. We should be off, Kate. I've a few errands to run.'

We were half out the door.

Mrs Wilkinson said, 'I tell you who I'd love to see. That warrior maiden. Ammonia. Do you know her at all?'

I said. 'Oh, you mean Blanche. Yes, I know her well. Blanche Smith. She's a Dewsbury girl. Used to be a conjuror's monkey before she went solo.'

'No,' says Mrs Wilkinson. 'That can't be her. I mean the one that can lift a grown man. Ammonia.'

Kate and I turned onto Brick Lane.

She said, 'Is that warrior maiden really from Dewsbury?'

'She is.'

'What a swizz. I thought she was from the jungle. Nothing's what it seems, is it?'

18

We went to Smith's dining rooms. I had a pie and gravy. All Kate would take was a glass of milk.

I said, 'Are you tired? Do you want to go back? I have to go along Whitechapel Road now. It'll be quite a step.'

I needed to go to Miss Rosen's, to collect some ostrich feathers I was having dyed for one of my stage hats.

'Where's Miss Rosen's?'

'In that court between St Mary's tube station and the old Jewish Theatre.'

'Then I shall come with you,' she said. 'I do love nosing around a haberdasher's.'

She did too. She was all over the shop, picking up ribbons and cotton reels and bits of lace and turning them over.

I said, 'Do you remember when you mended my skirt?'

'No. When?'

'When you lived on Bilston Street. I tore it, jumping about, and you mended it for me.'

'Did I? That's a long time ago. But I used to make all my babbies' nightgowns, all their little shirts. I was quite handy. I wasn't a bad mother, Dot. I just drank some rotten rum one time and it knocked me sideways. I was never the same after that.'

Miss Rosen was hovering, listening in, watching to see that Kate didn't take anything. My ostrich feathers weren't right either. I'd asked for crimson but they'd come out more of a russet shade.

'I suppose you'll want them sent back?' she said. She looked like she was chewing on a bar of soap.

Well russet feathers were no use to me. It's not a colour I wear. But I didn't leave her establishment without spending a few coppers. I bought a bit of ribbon with jet beads, just the end of a roll but it was enough for Kate to trim her bonnet.

I said, 'Have you got needle and thread at home?'

'At home!' she said. 'I leave nothing at Cooney's. No, I have them here, in my mustard tin. I've got everything but a caged linnet in these pockets.'

She took my arm.

'Yow'm a pal, Dot,' she said. 'It feels like a birthday, promenading about with you. And in a new skirt.'

'When is your birthday?'

'Buggered if I can remember. April, some time. I don't suppose you feel like getting a little drink?'

'You know I don't. Think of something else you'd like to do.'

'Let's go to Barry's, to the penny show.'

She'd heard there were tableaux set up there, depicting the murders. Annie Chapman, Polly Nichols, Martha Tabram. I wasn't keen, but Kate predicted it'd be good for a laugh and though it didn't seem right to say it when those poor women were mouldering in their graves, she was right. Barry's show was a laugh. It was nothing but old wax manikins splashed with red paint. Tom Barry would put his own mother on display if he thought people would pay to look at her. We should have asked for our money back.

Kate said, 'What do you think then, about this slasher? Is he a Whitechapel man? I reckon he must be.'

'Some people think he's from up West. That he comes this way for a cheap bit of business and then makes his getaway in a carriage.'

'No. I reckon it's somebody who know every ginnel and cut-through. That's how he gets away so easy. And who could that be? A bobby, that's who.'

'That's a new one. Butchers, boot-menders, surgeons. I've heard all those ideas. But not a policeman.'

'Listen, I've given it a lot of thought. Hundred-pound reward. That's worth racking your brains for. It has to be a bobby, on his beat. Say you're Polly Nichols, out late looking for business. If you meet a copper you might not be exactly pleased to see him but you wouldn't think you were in any danger, would you? How's it go? *If you want to know the time, ask a policeman?* Now, say she knows him, say she knows he's a copper who's on the take, she might offer him a quick touch, on the house so to speak. To keep him sweet. Only when her guard's down he lamps her one or stifles her, and then in goes his knife. Then he continues on his way. By the time somebody finds her, he's at the other end of his beat.'

'But he'd have blood on his hands.'

'There's plenty of taps. He could go into any back yard to rinse his hands.'

'What about blood on his tunic?'

'I'm still pondering that.'

The Penny Show is just by the Red Lion. I could see her eye keep wandering in that direction.

I said, 'I have to be on my way to the theatre now, Kate.'

'Course you do. Oh but I've had a bostin afternoon. It's really taken me out of myself. John won't be too happy. He'll think I've been gallivanting. But I couldn't have worked today. I'm not a slacker, Dot, but I just couldn't have.'

'Have you been to the infirmary?'

'Oh yes, many a time. They're sick of the sight of me. Nothing they can do. All I'm fit for is Winthrop Street.'

'What's at Winthrop Street?'

'Harrison's. The glue factory. So I might as well enjoy life while I can, eh?'

She still had the package tucked down the waist of her new skirt.

I said, 'If you don't need those chemises, if you'd sooner hock them, I won't mind.'

'No, I shall try them,' she said. 'And if they're too tight I'll take them over to Bermondsey, to my Annie. She's slender, like you.'

'Please yourself, Kate. They're yours now. But if you do pawn them, don't spend it on drink.'

'I won't,' she said. 'It does me no good, I know that. Well it does, for five minutes, and then I pay for it. Then my bad kidney gives me gip.'

By the time I took my leave of her, we'd progressed as far as the Black Bull. I hailed a cab and, damn me, who should step out of it but Frank Townsend. He didn't notice me, of course.

'Dr Townsend,' I said. 'Good afternoon.'

Then he looked, but he still made out he didn't remember me. Perhaps he didn't. Some people are very unobservant. Me, I never forget a face or a voice or a way of walking.

I said, 'It's young Valentine's landlady. You came to Sunday tea a few weeks back. But I think perhaps I have your name wrong. Is it Townsend, or is it Tumelty?'

He tipped his hat, just about, but he never said a word, and he fairly pushed past Kate.

'Oi,' she called after him. 'You mind who you're jostling.'

He strode off down New Road, heading to Batty Street I suppose, to his lodgings.

She said, 'Who was that?'

'The friend of a friend.'

'Then whatever have you done to offend him?'

'Not a thing, except see straight through him.'

'Well he's got the hump with you. If looks could kill. And he shoved me aside like I was a street arab.'

I climbed up into the cab.

She said, 'You've cheered me up no end, Dot. Come and see me again. Tararabit now.'

Monty was waiting for me when I got to the Marylebone.

'There's been a development,' he says, 'vis-à-vis Griffin's. Now, I know you said you'd never work for Jimmy again.'

'He started it. He was the one tried to cut my money.'

'He was going through a shaky patch.'

'He was the one cancelled my next engagement.'

'Dot,' he says. 'I don't need a history lesson. Would you be willing to play Griffin's next week or would you not?'

'Why, who's he insulted this time?'

'Nobody. It's Amazonia. She's not well.'

'She got a bun in the oven?'

'No. She's ricked herself.'

'How much?'

'I don't know. It's her back.'

'I don't mean how much has she ricked herself. I mean, how much is Griffin paying?'

'I'd have to talk to him.'

'You should have done that before you came here. Well, I'll want whatever Blanche was getting plus extra for stepping in in his hour of need.'

'I'll see what I can do.'

'Fair enough. You see what you can do and then I'll see what I can do. Saturday night, Monty, I'd have thought you'd be out on patrol, out catching murderers.'

'I do my bit. I generally do Mondays.'

'And how long do you think you'll keep this up?'

'Till we catch him.'

'Of course, he might move away. I would if I was him. I'd go somewhere they weren't expecting me.'

'No, he's not gone. He's still around.'

'How do you know?'

'I can't say.'

'But you know something?'

'My lips are sealed.'

'Too late for that. How do you know he's still around? Is it you? Monty Hyams, the Whitechapel Fiend.'

'Yes.'

'Stop jesting. How do you know he's not moved away?'

He chewed his lip for a minute.

'A letter's been received. But it's not generally known so don't go gossiping about it.'

'A letter from the murderer?'

'Apparently.'

'To the police?'

'To the papers.'

'What did it say?'

He shook his head.

'Did it say "I'm still here"? "You can't catch me!"'

'Something like that.'

'Have you seen it?'

'I'm saying no more.'

'Then I shall ask Tom Bullen. He'll know.'

'You're still thick with him? I wonder his wife doesn't have something to say about that.'

I said, 'Mind your own business, Monty. Which is to get me a fair fee from Jimmy Griffin. I won't work for buttons. And give Ammonia my condolences.'

Tom was waiting for me at the end of second house.

He said, 'And where did you get to this afternoon? I went twice to your house looking for you.'

I said, 'Was I expecting you?'

'You never mentioned you'd be going out.'

'Because I didn't decide till I got up this morning. And I'm a grown woman, Tom, free to come and go as I please.'

'No need to get uppity. I was worried about you, that's all. You usually rest up of an afternoon.'

'Was it just a social call?'

'It's always a social call, Dot. But I wanted to warn you not to be going home on your own at night. I'll escort you. Even if I'm not here when you come off, you wait for me. I guarantee I'll come. Don't take any risks. I reckon we're due another killing from old feller-me-lad.'

'Is that what the letter said?'

'Oh!' he said. 'How come you know about the letter?'

'Monty had heard about it. Have you seen it?'

'I have. As a matter of fact, it was sent to my office. For my attention.'

'Did it have your name on it?'

'Not exactly. It was addressed To the Boss. Which is me.'

Tom can play the turkey-cock at times.

'And what did it say?'

'That he's down on whores and he won't stop ripping them till the police buckle him. And that when he killed Annie Chapman he bottled some of her blood, to use for writing, only it congealed so he'd had to use red ink instead.'

'Was it well written?'

'It was done in a fair hand, but it wasn't the work of an educated person. A stranger to the apostrophe, shall we say?'

'And where's the letter now?'

'At Leman Street. Abberline has it.'

'How could he have bottled Annie Chapman's blood? Surely blood just oozes, or drips?'

'Or spurts. He cut her throat, don't forget.'

'Even so. Bottling blood *and* cutting out her parts. How did he have the time?'

'I don't know. I'm just telling you what his letter said. So where did you get to this afternoon?'

'Cooney's. I went to take Kate those boots.'

'Dot!' he says. 'Didn't I offer? Didn't I beg you not to go down there?'

'Well I lived to tell the tale. Things are hardly ever as bad as you make them out to be. You're a newspaper man, Tom. You like to make every molehill into a mountain. Cooney's wasn't so bad, apart from the smell. I walked the length of Flower and Dean Street and nobody harmed me.'

'Then you were lucky. And you went inside Cooney's?'

'Yes. I spoke to the deputy and his wife. The Wilkinsons. They seemed nice enough. Is there a Mr Cooney?'

'Oh yes. Johnny Cooney. You know the Sugar Loaf on Hanbury Street? Of course you wouldn't. But that's his pub. He's got doss houses on Brick Lane as well, and on Thrawl Street. You know they blame the Jews for bringing the neighbourhood down but I don't know of any yids that own lodging houses. Cooney, and McCarthy and Lewis, they're all Irish and they're all in together, marrying each other's sisters and cousins, keeping it in the family. McCarthy's the one. He's lord of the manor round Dorset Street. He's got the whole place tied up. Coal yards, pubs, chandlers. But you'd never see him set foot in any of his houses. He'll send a bag man to collect the takings. Cooney too. Whoever would have thought it, eh? Micks with money!'

19

Sunday morning about eleven, Valentine rapped on my parlour door.

He called out, 'You in, Miss Dot? How about a tea party this afternoon? I thought I'd go down to Friedman's, get a cake.'

I went out to him.

I said, 'All right, but just you and me. I don't want your doctor friend here.'

'I know that,' he says. 'Anyway Frank's not even in town.'

'Well he was in town yesterday because I saw him on Whitechapel Road.'

'When?'

'Five-ish.'

'But he's in Liverpool.'

'Not any more. He nearly knocked my friend off her feet. And when I spoke to him he looked at me like he didn't know me from Adam's cat.'

'Well then it can't have been him because Frank certainly remembers you. What friend were you with?'

'Kate.'

'The one who waited for you that night outside Griffin's? You're chumming around with her now?'

'Hardly chumming. I'd just taken her a pair of boots I never wear.'

'But you know what I mean. She's not exactly your kind of company. Given her way of life.'

'She does a bit of scrubbing, that's all.'

'And lives at a doss house and mixes with all kinds.'

'You mean unlike us theatrical types? All straight out of the top drawer.'

'Well if it was Frank you saw, and I very much doubt that it was, I'm not surprised he didn't stop to converse with you. Jiminy Christmas, a professional man doesn't want to be seen anywhere near a woman like that. In broad daylight!'

He was just rattled, to think his friend had come back from Liverpool without telling him. There had been a time, not so long ago, when Valentine spent every spare minute with Townsend. Tumelty. Whoever he is. But I was glad to see things seemed to have cooled between them, just a bit.

I said, 'Anyway, let's have tea and a natter, just you and me. After I've had my bath.'

'And Olive?' he says. 'I like Olive.'

Olive used to come at about twelve on a Sunday, heat the water, set up the clothes horse with towels for my greater privacy and fill the tub for me in my parlour. It saved her carrying jugs of water up the stairs and in the winter I'd have a bit of a fire in the hearth. Then, when I was done, I'd go up to my bedroom to get dried and dressed while she cleared everything away and emptied the bath water into the back yard.

I heard her drag the tub along the passage. I heard her slide the bolt on the scullery door. Then I heard her scream. Not just a little shriek, like she'd do when she'd seen a spider, but a proper scream that went on and on. I wasn't even half dressed. All I had on was my knickers and my health corset. I ran down in my dressing gown and nearly did the splits skidding on water that had slopped over the rim of the bath. By the time I got to the yard she'd left off screaming and commenced whimpering instead. The yard was black with flies and so was she, head and shoulders.

I said, 'Wave your arms.'

But waving her arms didn't help and neither did waving mine. The flies would lift off her and land on her again at once. Then they began to land on me. I called up to Valentine but he was still out. I did the only thing I could think of. I went to the meat safe and brought out everything I could find. Half a veal pie, some sliced ham, a bit of brawn. That did the trick. The flies began to desert Olive. They prefer dead flesh to live meat any day.

The front door banged. Valentine was back.

'Put the kettle on the hob, Olive,' he says. 'I've bought an apple cake.'

I shouted to him to come out to the yard.

'Great heavens,' he says. 'What's happening? Is it a plague?'

Olive was still sobbing. I sent her in to wash herself and wipe her eyes. Valentine and I watched the flies jostling on the plate of meat.

'Fascinating,' he said. 'Pity about the pie though.'

'Desperate measures. I had to do something. Olive was covered. She came out to empty my bath tub and they swarmed all over her.'

'Poor girl! We'd better get rid of them now, while they're congregated on your meat.'

'And how do we do that?'

'Throw a coal sack over them, tie it up and put it out for the vestry van.'

'I don't have a coal sack.'

'Miss Dot,' he says, 'every back yard has a bit of sacking. It's just a question of finding it. But now look. There's more flies still arriving and you can see where they're coming from. See Mr what's-his-name's window?'

Mr Earp's window was open a crack. The inside of the pane was thick with flies but some of them were coming out through the opening and making straight for the plate of meat. It was as though they could hear a drum beat summoning them, or a bugle.

Valentine said, 'I don't like the look of that at all. He must have an infestation. Somebody had better knock at his door and tell him.'

'You go. You're the man.'

'No you go,' he says. 'He doesn't like me. He complained to me one time about me warming up my voice.'

I got dressed while Valentine poked about in the yard for something to smother the flies. Then I went round to Mr Earp's and hammered on his door. There was no reply. I called through the letterbox. Nothing. Valentine and Olive came peeping round the side gate, very free with their advice but I noticed they kept their distance.

'See if there's a key hidden.'

'I wouldn't let myself into his house even if there was one. I hardly know the man.'

'When you opened the letter flap was there a bad smell?'

'I was calling his name not sniffing for smells.'

'What about fetching the landlord? He'd have a key.'

'All the way from Muswell Hill, on a Sunday? I don't think so.'

Then Olive said, 'We should ask Mr Warlord what to do.'

She said the Warlords were the people in the house across the street. They had three sons and a spaniel and Mr Warlord was a magistrate.

'So he'll be able to advise us,' she said.

I said, 'How come you know so much about them?'

'Because my cousin Ethel does their laundry.'

I didn't see what Mr Warlord could bring to the situation, but Olive seemed to think a magistrate would have the answer to everything so Valentine crossed the street and came back with Mr Warlord, very rosy-cheeked and in his carpet slippers. I don't believe I'd ever seen the man before in all the time I'd lived there. That's what happens when you work theatre hours. By the time you get up, your neighbours are at their work and by the time you come home they're a-bed.

Mr Warlord said, 'I believe your neighbour is an elderly gentleman? I have seen him about, but only to say Good Day. I know nothing about him. Does he go away?'

'I don't think so. But it'd be hard to tell. He never makes any noise.'

He peered through the letterbox. 'Oh my!' he says, 'I don't care for the smell of that. Not at all. I think some mishap must have occurred. I'll send my oldest boy up to Hackney to find a constable.'

He padded back across the street and a few minutes later we saw his lad go off towards Mare Street. I told Olive she should go home, considering the fright she'd had, but of course she wanted to stay and see what mishap had befallen Mr Earp.

Valentine said, 'Then let's have a brew while we're waiting, there's a good girl.'

She said, 'Mr St John, I reckon one of them flies went down my gullet. Do you think I'll die?'

'Not if you take a slice of apple cake,' he says. 'It's a sovereign cure.'

We went indoors.

Olive said, 'I suppose Mr Earp might have gone away. He might have left a rasher uncovered. Meat soon goes off in this weather.'

And Valentine said, 'You're right, Olive, it has been very muggy. And, Miss Dot, that would account for the smell that was troubling you. Mystery solved!'

So we sat and acted cheerful and pretended the problem was a bit of mouldy bacon even though we knew in our hearts that a man like Mr Earp would never have been so careless. Two hours passed before a constable appeared and by that time there was standing room only in my parlour. Monty was the first to arrive.

'Good news, Dot,' he said. 'Everything's settled with Griffin. You open tomorrow.'

'Blanche's fee and something extra for short notice?'

'Yes. Are you all right? You look quite distracted.'

With everything that had happened, I hadn't pinned my hair. Hadn't even combed it.

'I am distracted. We're waiting here for the police to come. We think we might have a body lying next door.'

'A body?' he says. 'Then I'd better come in until the police get here. I am on the Vigilance Committee, you know.'

I said, 'Not that kind of body, Monty. I don't think there's been a murder. It's just the old gentleman who lives round the back. He's not answering his door and there's flies and a smell.'

But Monty was already across the threshold and then Mr Warlord, who must have been keeping watch, mistook Monty for a detective and came hurrying back across the street too. Tom was the next to arrive, with a bunch of Michaelmas daisies.

'Oh,' he said, when he saw the tea things laid out, 'I didn't realise you had company.'

I said, 'Unexpected company. You're the writer. What do you call a herd of crows?'

'Are you playing parlour games?'

'No, but we're all assembled here like carrion crows, waiting to find out if my neighbour is lying dead in his bed.'

Olive went to make more tea.

Tom said, 'Well now, if you're speaking of birds, Dot, it'd be a flock, not a herd. But for crows there is another word they use. It's something comical and it's on the tip of my tongue. An "unkindness"! That's the word.'

Mr Warlord said, 'I must correct you, sir. An "unkindness" refers to ravens. A "murder" is the word for a community of crows. I happen to know because my wife has been reading Mr Poe's story, *The Murders in the Rue Morgue,* and that very word came up.'

So we sat like a murder of crows, with Tom and Monty glowering at each other. Valentine presided over the teapot, Mr Warlord was all congeniality and very appreciative of the apple cake, and Olive stood by the window watching for the police.

Tom said, 'We could wait a long time for a constable on a Sunday. Why don't we just break the door down?'

Monty said, 'And get billed for its repair? Not likely. I'll have no part in it.'

'Well that's what the coppers'll do when they get here.'

'Then let them. Let them pay for it. How's Mrs Bullen these days?'

It was getting on for four o'clock when the police came. Two boys from the Clapton Square station. One of them went into my yard to try and see through Mr Earp's window. He came back with a fly on the rim of his ear. The other went directly to Mr Earp's door.

I said, 'Waste of time. We've already done that.'

Monty said, 'You have to appreciate, Dot, procedures must be followed. What if the old gentleman's sleeping? You can't just barge into a person's residence.'

But the constables hadn't come equipped to barge in anywhere. They said one of them would now have to go to the fire station to fetch an axe.

'No need for that,' said Mr Warlord. 'I have an axe in my garden.'

And because Mr Warlord was a Justice of the Peace it was agreed that his axe would be an acceptable tool for staving in Mr Earp's door. Olive had her coat on.

I said, 'You get off. Your family'll be looking for you.'

'Not yet,' she said. 'I can't go home with half a story. They'll want to know if Mr Earp's been murdered.'

Mr Earp hadn't been murdered. I didn't go in to look at him. It didn't seem right. He was a very private person. And Valentine didn't go either. He didn't have the stomach for it. But Tom went in, and Monty, and Mr Warlord. They said he appeared to have died peacefully in his armchair and then been set upon by flies.

PC 27J said, 'The deceased seems to have been there quite some time. I shall have to go back to Mare Street and ask for a police surgeon to attend.'

And the words had no sooner left his mouth than another figure appeared at the front gate and Valentine said, 'Oh but here's Frank. He's a doctor. Perhaps he can save you the trouble.'

Frank Townsend.

I said, 'What's he doing here? I told you not to invite him.'

'I didn't invite him. He's here quite by chance. I hope you're not going to make a scene.'

I didn't. But Tom commenced trying to make mischief at once.

'Not Townsend at all,' he murmured to PC 114J. 'That's Tumelty. You'll know all about him.'

'No,' says the bobby. 'Know what?'

He was only a youngster.

'Francis Tumelty,' says Tom. 'American-Irish and a person of interest. H Division will confirm that if you care to enquire.'

Frank Townsend had stopped short when he caught sight of the constables.

'Frank,' says Valentine, 'you're the very man we need. Dot's neighbour has passed away and the officers require a doctor to certify he's dead.'

But Townsend held up his great pink hands.

'Not my province, dear boy,' he says.

Mr Warlord said, 'Not that kind of doctor, eh?' and Tom said, 'Doctor, my arse.'

Monty said, 'I think what the gentleman means is it's a job for the police surgeon. He's quite right. You can't have just anybody interfering with a body. The old man may seem to have died of natural causes but he might not have. He might have been poisoned, or stifled. Police procedures have to be followed. I'd have expected you to know that, Bullen.'

And Mr Warlord said, 'Yes, Mr Hyams is quite right. Constable, we should secure Mr Earp's door as best we can. I'll stand guard over it until a surgeon can come. And in the meanwhile I suppose we must try to discover whether the poor man had any family.'

I said, 'I don't think he did. He had a cat he was very fond of. I wonder where she is? She sits on my windowsill sometimes but I haven't seen her lately.'

Olive said, 'You shouldn't worry about a cat, Miss A. If you don't feed them for a day or two they soon go off and find somebody else who will.'

'But as a matter of fact he did once beg me that if ever he should expire on the street, I was to send word to St John's. He said he knew the custodian of the mortuary there.'

'Well then, that's what we must do, as soon as the police surgeon has attended.'

Monty said, 'Why did he charge you with such a job when he hardly knew you? Did he expect to die?'

'I think he did. Every minute. He was quite a nervous person. He enjoyed very poor health.'

The murder of crows began to disperse. Olive hurried off home with her story. Frank Townsend wisely came no closer than the front gate so Valentine pulled on his coat and hat and left with him. Mr Warlord brought a ladder-back chair out from his house and kept company with PC 114J to guard Mr Earp's broken door while PC 27J reported to Mare Street. And I was left with a tray full of dirty teacups and Tom and Monty bristling at each other.

Tom said, 'Shouldn't you be making a move, Monty? Won't Mrs Hyams be missing you?'

Monty said, 'My mother is never alone. She has Mrs Gutkin reading to her. But I daresay you're eager to get off. Sunday afternoon, a time for family. Your wife will be getting anxious. I'll stay with Dot, make sure she's all right. She's had a shock.'

I said, 'Dot *is* all right. It's poor old Earp who's not.'

Tom patted my hand. And then he said, 'To speak plainly, Monty, if you're waiting for me to leave first you'll wait a long time. Dot and I like to have sexual relations when we get the house to ourselves.'

Poor Monty. I thought we might have another death on our hands. I thought he'd die of embarrassment. He was scarlet, fumbling about for his bowler hat, bumping into the coat-stand in his rush to get out of the door. He didn't even say goodbye.

Tom looked like the cat that got the cream.

I said, 'That wasn't nice. Whatever his faults, Monty's a gentleman. Saying a thing like that to him! I don't know how I shall look him in the face next time I see him. And he'd have left in a minute or two anyway, if you'd only been patient.'

'Come and sit on my lap.'

'I will not. You keep yourself buttoned up. There's a corpse next door, and a constable within earshot, and Mr Warlord.'

'That'll make it all the more exciting.'

'Not for me, it wouldn't. What a day. And now I have to think what skits to do tomorrow night.'

'I thought you were off this week?'

'I was but Jimmy Griffin was in a hole. The authentic and exotic warrior maiden pulled a muscle so he begged me to help him out.'

'You swore never to work for him again.'

'That was before this murderer emptied the theatres and reduced my earnings. I need the money.'

'You should let me look after you. How about a little drink?'

'As long as you're not hoping it'll get me into bed, because it won't.'

'On my mother's life.'

'Your mother's long dead. I remember when you buried her.'

I joined him in a glass of sherry wine.

'Fancy Tumelty turning up like that. Did you see his face when he spotted the coppers?'

'He had no business coming here anyway. He cut me in the street yesterday. Not that I wanted to converse with him but when you've been a guest in a person's house you don't cut them. And what's he doing here all these weeks? He calls himself a doctor. What patients does he have? I wouldn't let him near me even if I was at death's door.'

'He's no doctor.'

'What was it Mr Warlord said? "Not that kind of doctor." What other kinds are there?'

'There's Divinity. The Bible.'

'Well Townsend's not one of them.'

'No. Doctor of Hog Swill more like. But he still seems to have young Valentine on a string. "Come with me, dear boy," he says, and Valentine goes running.'

'Not for much longer. Valentine says he'll be going back to America soon. What I don't understand is if the police have their eye on him, as you say, why haven't they collared him?'

'Ah. Let's just say it's complicated.'

'Either he's a Fenian or he's not.'

'Oh I don't think there's any doubt that he is. But it might suit the police to keep him around. He could be careless and lead them to some of these dynamiters. Or there's another possibility. He might *choose* to lead them there. Sometimes a betting man backs more than one horse.'

'Why would he do that?'

'To get paid by two paymasters. Think about it. He could be taking money from the Americans, for being their messenger boy, and then double-crossing them. Taking money from the Metropolitan Police as well. That'd explain why he's always so flush.'

'Do the police give money away like that?'

'They do if it buys them good information.'

'So he might actually be on our side?'

'No, if I'm right, the only side he's on is his own.'

'Well I can never like him, doesn't matter whose side he's on. Did you know the Flahertys have scarpered?'

'Yes, and you laughed when I told you they were Fenians. The Flying Flahertys have fled. That's not easy to say after two sherries.'

Someone knocked at the front door. It was the constable.

He said, 'We've just about finished next door. I thought I'd better let you know.'

I asked him to step inside. It struck me, as we went in, that Tom looked very much at home, a man taking his ease in his own parlour, and PC 114J must have thought so too.

'Mr Allbones,' he starts.

I said, 'There is no Mr Allbones. Tom's just a friend. Just visiting.'

'Ah,' he says. 'I beg your pardon. Well, Miss Allbones, the deceased has been removed from the premises and taken to St John's in accordance with your instructions. We'll secure the door to his accommodations to the best of our ability. About the landlord?'

'Mr Frimley.'

'Are you likely to see him?'

'No, I never see him. My manager, Monty Hyams, who was here

earlier, he pays my rent and deals with all that kind of business. And if I know Monty, he'll be on his way to Muswell Hill in the morning, to break the news.'

'Because the property will need to be cleaned and aired. It's very unpleasant in there.'

Tom said, 'You should get a reduction in your rent, Dot, until it's been done. You can't be expected to live next to an insanitary smell and still pay in full.'

I said, 'That's what Monty'll be thinking. That's why I guarantee you he'll be on Frimley's doorstep first thing.'

'And you know of no family the deceased might have had?'

'None.'

It's a funny thing how you carry your name through life, Dot Allbones, Tom Bullen, Mr Earp, but the minute they put coins on your eyelids you're just The Deceased.

He said, 'Mr Hyams is your manager, you say. Can I enquire what kind of shop you keep, Miss Allbones?'

Tom jumped to.

'Young man,' he says, 'this is no shopkeeper. You are in the presence of a luminary of the boards, a bright star in the firmament of the music hall. This is the great Dot Allbones!'

'Is it?' he says. 'I'm very sorry. I don't know much about the halls. But I'll bet my mother will know your name. I'll write it down now, so I don't forget it.'

Which he did. First time my name has ever been written in a bobby's notebook. As far as I know. He was on his way out.

He said, 'About the deceased. You think he worked for a bank?'

'I believe so.'

'He couldn't have been a haberdasher? Or a hatter?'

'I'm quite sure he wasn't. I always wear notable hats, but Mr Earp never remarked on them, not once. Why do you ask?'

'He had a table in his parlour, set out with ribbons and combs and all kinds of notions. It was all very orderly, like a showcase in a shop, I'd say. Ladies' gloves too.'

Tom said, 'Sounds like there was more to Mr Earp than you thought, Dot. A bit of a collector of ladies' gewgaws. Anything saucy, Constable? Any unmentionables? It's always the quiet ones, isn't it? Always the ones you least expect.'

I was about to close the door. I was just thinking I should tell Olive the front step was overdue a scouring, and then my mind went back to that night I came home alone and Mr Earp was creeping about in his nightshirt, looking for his kitty cat.

I said, 'Constable, on that table, did you happen to notice any hat pins?'

'I don't know. I think there was an earring.'

'Because I dropped a hat pin out here one evening and I never did find it.'

'I'll have a look for you. What was it like?'

'Filigree and green glass. It's not of any value but I was fond of it.'

Tom was draining the last of the sherry.

I said, 'There's no more.'

'But if I know you there'll be something drinkable in your pantry. So now what do you make of your quiet bachelor gentleman? Ladies' gloves. Hair combs. I'll bet he had a few stockings as well. The old goat!'

'I'm surprised you didn't notice that table while you were round there. It's not like you to miss a tasty detail.'

'You're right. But the stench was too powerful for me to linger, Dot. I took one look at him and I had to get out of there. But let's not talk about it. I know you. You'll dwell on it.'

'Not very nice though, is it? To be dead in your armchair and nobody misses you. How long had he been there? More than a week.'

'I don't know. Come to bed.'

'It's broad daylight.'

'All the better to see you, my dear.'

'If he'd kept a dog it wouldn't have happened.'

'What's a dog to do with it?'

'If he'd kept a dog we'd have known something was up because it would have barked and barked.'

'Or got hungry and ate him. Come and cuddle up to me at least. You're not the only one who's had a shock.'

We'd just got comfortable when the door knocker went again.

'God Almighty!' Tom says. 'Can't a man be allowed five minutes for a bit of pleasure!'

It was PC 114J again.

'Is this it?' he says, and there in his hand was my lost hat pin.

I gave him one of my new portrait postcards for his trouble, and signed it of course. He said his mother would be very pleased.

Do you know what I did with that hat pin? I wrapped it in newspaper and put it out for the vestry cart. I found I didn't want it in my house, reminding me of Mr Earp and his odd ways.

'Right,' said Tom. 'Anyone else taps at that door, you're not in. I'll gag and bind you if I have to. Now come over here and sit on this.'

One thing about Tom. He knows how to take a girl's mind off unpleasant thoughts.

20

Valentine didn't come home that night and when I saw him on Monday morning I found him quite frosty with me.

He said, 'You put me in a difficult situation, Miss Dot. You and your friend.'

'What's Tom done?'

'Yesterday. I heard what he said to that constable. A person of interest. I'm not deaf, and neither's Frank.'

'Tom wouldn't have said it if it wasn't true.'

'There you go again. You've taken against Frank though I'm sure I don't know what he ever did to offend you.'

'He's rude, for one thing.'

'I don't find him so.'

'And none of his stories add up. Do you really believe he's a doctor?'

'I know he is. I've seen his bag of instruments. Miss Dot, I can't live where my friends are insulted.'

I said, 'Are you giving me notice?'

'I'm thinking of it. I don't want to but I suppose it may come to it.'

'We used to be good pals, Valentine.'

'We did. And I'm sure I'm not the one causing difficulties. And if you must know, it's not just about your attitude to Frank.'

'What then?'

'I suppose *your* friend stayed the night again.'

'Tom did stay. What does that matter to you?'

'It's embarrassing.'

'What, that I have a sweetheart?'

'You know what I mean.'

I did know what he meant. Tom can grow very enthusiastic and he doesn't care who hears him. So I looked at things this way. Townsend-Tumelty will soon be gone, and Tom Bullen has a wife waiting at home, whatever he may say about her, but Valentine has always been a true friend and so have I, so we shouldn't quarrel over passing fancies. That's how I put it to Valentine and we agreed a truce. He'd keep his friend from my door and I'd keep Tom Bullen on a shorter rope.

He said, 'I couldn't stop thinking about Mr Earp last night.'

'Neither could I. That's the reason I let Tom stay. It was nice to have company.'

'But he's not likely to move in?'

'Never. The advantage of Tom is he does have to go home once in a while.'

'If he didn't have a wife would you live with him?'

I didn't have an answer for that. I was very fond of Tom but sometimes, when he went home, it was like getting a caraway seed out from between your teeth. You don't always realise how much it's been annoying you until it's not there any more.

*

Jimmy Griffin greeted me like I was his best friend in the world.

'Pleasure to have you back, Dot,' he says.

I said, 'You've changed your tune. Last time I was here you told me I wasn't worth my fee.'

'Monty drives a very hard bargain,' he says. 'But I know I can rely on you. Not like some I could mention.'

'How's her ricked back?'

'Is that what he told you?'

'Not that I believed him. I suppose she's in the family way.'

'Oh yes. It's in the bag.'

I knew most of the other turns that were engaged for the week. Clarence and Percy, the vent act, the Infant Prodigy, a plate-spinner who's been around since the Creation, and the Mad Margolinskis.

There was a tenor I'd never worked with before, a Mr Sylvester, a Canadian gentleman. He did songs from operetta. 'Night and Day', 'Let Us Drink', 'A Wand'ring Minstrel I', that type of thing. He hadn't been long in London so he was new to Griffin's penny-pinching, but he soon learned. He'd requested a moon effect, which made sense. If you're doing 'Fair Moon, To Thee I Sing', it helps to have a moon to sing to.

But Jimmy said, 'I'm afraid that won't be possible. I can't run to the expense of another lime-boy.'

Poor Mr Sylvester. He was quite put out but you could see he didn't want to make a fuss, being new to the venue.

I said, 'Jimmy, if you got rid of that old plate-spinner you could afford to give Mr Sylvester a moon.'

'People like plate-spinners.'

'No, *you* like plate-spinners because they're cheap. But they've had their day.'

Ida said, 'What about a disc of baker's paper with a lantern behind it? I've seen that done.'

I said, 'So have we all, Ida. In a penny travelling show on the back of a cart. I think Mr Sylvester was hoping for something better than that in a London theatre.'

'Causing trouble already, Dot?' says Jimmy.

Well I wasn't worried what he thought. He was lucky to get me.

I said, 'I'm a dream to work with compared to Ammonia, and you know it.'

He laughed.

'Ammonia,' he says. 'I like that! I shall call her that next time I see her.'

Mr Sylvester never got his moon though.

The murders were back in the papers that Monday. The inquest on Mary Anne Nichols had resumed. I thought it was all finished but they had to have one last day, so the coroner could sum everything up and the jury could reach a verdict. Clarence read out to us from the *Daily Telegraph*.

> Mrs Nichols, known to her acquaintances as Polly, was forty-seven years of age and known to live an irregular life.

Ida said, 'That's a fancy way of saying she was a prosser.'

I said, 'More to the point, she never knew where she'd be sleeping from one night to the next.'

And a voice from that bloody doll's box said, 'Unlike me.'

> Mrs Nichols was last seen at two in the morning, inebriated and making her way down the Whitechapel Road.

Spent her bed money on drink, no doubt.

> Her body was discovered just before four o'clock and the police are satisfied that she was murdered where her body was found, on Bucks Row. The first constable on the scene thought he'd felt a faint pulse though she was certainly beyond help, and if she'd been dragged there, or carried from some other place, there would surely have been a trail of blood. As to how her assassin had escaped detection, Mr Wynne Baxter, the coroner, said it wasn't so very surprising. There were often blood-stained slaughtermen in that quarter of Whitechapel, coming from their work.

Ida said, 'I never see blood-stained men on the street.'

Clarence said, 'That's because you don't get up till dinner-time.'

Annie Chapman's murder was mentioned too, though that inquest was still proceeding. The police surgeon said he believed the same weapon could have been used in both cases. It would likely have had a long, narrow blade such as you'd find on a boning knife. Everything seemed to point to a man accustomed to working with carcases. But what could have been his reason for committing more than one murder? A jealous quarrel can end violently. Nothing new in that. But a man doesn't engage in jealous quarrels every week. Robbers can kill you if you put up a fight instead of giving them what they want. But what can you take from a woman who has nothing?

Ida said, 'And Annie Chapman's bits he took, of her insides. What's his game? What can he have done with them?'

And a dark voice from Percy's box murmured, 'Fried them with a bit of chopped onion.'

Ida screamed and I jumped.

I said, 'I wish you wouldn't do that, Clarence. It's not funny.'

'Sorry, ladies,' he says. 'I thought he was still asleep.'

I don't know how Clarence does that. He's very good.

He said, 'Well some murderers like to have keepsakes. I suppose this one just likes giblets.'

'And her brass ring,' says Ida. 'Not worth a light. Makes your blood run cold, don't it?'

It did. I kept thinking of Mr Earp and my hat pin.

The verdict on Mary Anne Nichols was that she had been wilfully murdered by a person or persons unknown. There was a piece about Mr Montagu's reward too. Sam Montagu is the Member of Parliament for Whitechapel. He doesn't live in Whitechapel, of course. He's a wealthy man, come up from nothing through banking. He keeps a big house in the West End. But he's well thought of, and he'd offered to put up a hundred pounds of his own money for information leading to the apprehension of this murderer, which was more than the authorities had done.

The Home Secretary said the Government was disinclined to offer rewards. He said rewards attracted low types, not to mention fantasists and time-wasters. I thought it was a weak excuse. The police are quite accustomed to dealing with such people. It's their daily bread. And what did it matter who got the reward if it led to the arrest of the murderer? If he was a lunatic, as seemed likely, it might take another lunatic to identify him. Or a mad doctor, who knew of a patient's episodes and had his suspicions.

The general opinion seemed to be that Mr Home Secretary Matthews was a stuffed shirt who would do well to take a walk around Whitechapel some dark night and acquaint himself with the man in the street.

Tom thought differently.

'Sam Montagu's reward will be enough,' he said, 'if there's anyone who can name the villain. A hundred pounds, Dot. That's not to be sniffed at. No need for the Government to put up more money. Matthews isn't the problem. The police are the problem. They're going about this quite the wrong way. They don't give out information the way they used to.'

'I thought Fred Abberline was in charge? You always got along with him.'

'Don't speak to me of Abberline,' he said. 'He's changed. Gone all "Scotland Yard" on us. Since he's back at Leman Street there's no cooperation. He should be keeping people like me fully apprised, not shutting us out. Getting anything out of him, it's like getting a tick off a dog.'

'Perhaps he has his reasons.'

'And what could they be?'

'Perhaps they think they're closing in on the murderer and they don't want him to know they're on to him.'

'Rubbish. They're not closing in on anybody. They need help and we're the ones that can give it. For instance, if they have a description of a suspect the papers can publish his likeness and it'll be seen by thousands over their morning tea. Or say they have an unnamed victim.'

'They don't.'

'But say they did, Dot. Same thing. Publish a likeness and before you know it you'll have a name. They say people don't want to read about gizzards and blood and slashings. Well that's not my experience. In my experience, the more gore there is the more papers we sell. And those who don't wish to read the grisly details aren't obliged to. They can turn the page and read the fashion notes.'

I said, 'Tom, this is going to sound daft but you don't think it could have been my neighbour, do you?'

'That old gentleman? The murderer? Never! What gave you such an idea?'

'Those things he had in his house. Gloves and combs. My hat pin. Whoever killed Annie Chapman took her rings.'

'Well, for one thing, that constable said nothing about any rings.'

'He said nothing about my hat pin till I asked him. He might not have noticed any rings.'

'True. Some of those constables couldn't find a hole in a ladder. But your Mr Earp couldn't have murdered those women. He wouldn't have had the strength. I've seen the corpses, Dot. They were all sturdy women. And rough. You'd need to be sure of yourself to pick on any of them. The kind of places they were living they'd know how to give as good as they got. By the way, what's your landlord doing about Earp's room? Has he had everything cleared out?'

'Not that I know. He told Monty all it needs is a good airing.'

'It needs more than that. That chair the old man died in, he should burn that.'

'He wanted to know if Olive was available to wash the floors and windows. I told him no, she is not. Let Frimley find his own char.'

'Olive might be glad of the extra money.'

All very well for him to say. Have her laying out my supper tray after she's been cleaning up after a dead man? Not likely.

'Well,' he said, 'if Monty's not taking care of things for you, you let me know. I'll be happy to have a word. Or we could move? Have you thought of that?'

I said, 'What do you mean, "we"?'

'You know. Get a little place together.'

'What about your wife?'

'Then you wouldn't need to have a lodger.'

'I like having a lodger.'

'Still, it's something to consider.'

I was very unsettled that week. I was happy to be working, even if it was for Jimmy Griffin, but nothing seemed quite as it should be. There'd been the upset of Mr Earp. There was Valentine keeping company with Frank Townsend. And there was Tom. I could feel him getting his feet further and further under my table, always wanting to know where I was going and what I was doing. 'I care about you, Dot,' he'd say. 'You'd find me a good provider.' I've always provided for myself. But in my profession sometimes you don't know where your next engagement is coming from. I never minded that, years ago. But lately I'd started to think, what if there isn't a 'next engagement'? I'd seen so many fall by the wayside.

Ida's about my age. She's single, she's no chicken.

I said, 'Do you have something put by for your old age? For when you can't work?'

'Can't really say that I do,' she said. 'My Mum always paid into a burial club, so her funeral would be paid for. She'd sooner have gone hungry than miss paying her burying money. So I have kept that up. Habit really. I pay it once a week at the Horn of Plenty. But I don't have much else. I shall have to find myself a rich admirer. Not much chance of that though, working at Griffin's.'

'I played the Marylebone with Betsy Ash. You know she's got two followers, I mean *dedicated* followers, and they're both rolling in money. One's a duke, the other's a Hon. I reckon they try to outdo one another, who can spend the most money on her.'

'And she's nothing much to look at, is she? Don't her ears stick out?'

'I haven't noticed that. I do know she sports quite a balcony and that's something generally appreciated by the boys.'

'Funny though, in a stilt walker. You'd think a bosom would throw her off balance.'

'She's very jolly, very easy to get along with. I suppose they find her agreeable company.'

'And then, once the lamp's turned down, the set of her ears don't signify. So we need to find ourselves a couple of dukes, Dot. Any ideas?'

'I don't think many of them venture this far east. We might have more success at that if we were appearing at Drury Lane.'

'I tell you what though, Dot, for me it don't even have to be a duke. I'd settle for a banker. Anybody with a bit of jingle. He can be as ugly as sin with a pecker the size of a haycorn. Just as long as he wants to spend his money on me.'

Ida's a featherbrain, but she does cheer me up.

21

Annie Chapman's inquest was resumed on the Wednesday. Valentine brought in the *Daily News*.

I said, 'It's time they laid all that to rest. We've heard it all before.'

'True,' he says. 'Although I don't remember reading this before. *Her possessions were arranged around her on the ground*.'

'Her rings were taken.'

'Yes, but there were other things. Listen. *A tooth comb. A piece of muslin cloth. And an old envelope with pills in it*.'

'All she had in the world.'

'Well, all she had in her pocket.'

'That's what I mean. She lived at Crossingham's. When they live in places like that they keep everything in their pockets. They can't leave things behind. It's not the Charing Cross Hotel.'

'You seem to know a lot about it.'

'I've seen how Kate lives at Cooney's. Not the actual place she sleeps, but I've seen how she carries on. Everything's in her pockets. Bits of soap and string, her pipes and her baccy, and her tea and her sugar. What a life.'

'You have to wonder why they keep going. If it was me I reckon I'd throw myself off London Bridge.'

'Not Kate. She's the cheeriest soul you could wish to meet. Sometimes I think I'd like to do something for her, but what? She's a demon for the drink and if she won't stay out of alehouses, what's the point of giving her money?'

'None at all. She's lucky you even think of her.'

'No, she's not lucky, Valentine. For one thing her health is quite ruined.'

'Sounds like Annie Chapman wasn't long for this world either. It says her lungs were found to be diseased, and her brain. Everybody knows your private business once you're dead, don't they? There's no secrets. And these bits and bobs that he laid out on the ground. What was he thinking? Cutting out her you-know-what, and then arranging her things. He could have been discovered at any minute. Why would he spend time doing that?'

'Because he's mad.'

'I suppose he must be. Funny though, when he's killing them, when he's slashing them, he must be very savage, but afterwards it seems he acts as calm as you like. Setting those things out like dainties on a plate.'

'And then walks away as cool as you like and disappears. You know some people think it's not a man doing it?'

'A woman?'

'No, something, you know, not of this world?'

'You mean a diabolical spirit entity?'

'Something like that. Load of nonsense if you ask me.'

'Still, it'd get the police off the hook, wouldn't it? A power beyond their control. It's probably them that started the idea.'

He went up to his room to do his vocalising. He was appearing in Stratford East, at the Theatre Royal, so he left the house before

I did. It was only after he'd gone that I picked the paper up and finished reading where he'd left off. There was something else new. About Annie Chapman's womb.

Mr Wynne Baxter, the coroner, had received a letter from someone employed in a hospital museum. I never knew of such a place. It's where future doctors go, apparently, to learn about body parts. The person who'd written the letter was a custodian, the curator, who said he had information that might be of interest to the coroner in the case of Annie Chapman. So Wynne Baxter had paid him a visit. Here's what the paper said:

> Some months ago, a gentleman, an American involved in the sphere of medicine, called on the curator and asked to purchase certain preserved organs, particularly specimens of the same part as that removed from the body of Annie Chapman. The American gentleman said he was engaged in the preparation of a book for students of human anatomy and was willing to pay as much as £20 per specimen. The preserved parts were to be shipped directly to America. The curator told him that he could not possibly fulfil such a request and the gentleman had gone on his way. Furthermore, the curator has since heard by way of his professional grapevine that another hospital museum was approached with the same request.

It was altogether a very strange story. No names were given.

I said to Tom, 'An American doctor? We could provide them with a name.'

'We could. And I did. I reminded Bill Thicke about Tumelty.'

'What did he say?'

'Nothing. He just tapped his nose.'

'And you left it at that?'

'Of course I did. I know how to read Bill. So I followed a different line of enquiry. I went round to the London Hospital. I know Openshaw, who runs the museum there. I thought it might have been him that wrote to Wynne Baxter but he swore it wasn't. He said he knew nothing of the matter. You should see some of the things they've got in there, Dot. Shelves and shelves of glass jars. Lungs and hearts and things with two heads. I tried not to look.'

Tom had spoken to two other curators, at St Bartholomew's Hospital and St Thomas's. They both said the story was nothing to do with them. The Middlesex Hospital had declined to answer any questions.

'So you think the Middlesex was where it happened?'

'Seems likely.'

'Then why don't they own to it? If they didn't sell him anything, they've done nothing wrong. It's not their fault if some oddity goes around trying to purchase pickled wombs.'

'People don't always realise how it looks, refusing to say anything to the press. But it's one of the strangest stories I ever heard and I've heard plenty. If it was Tumelty, what would he want with body parts?'

'Perhaps he boils them down to make one of his oriental remedies.'

'And another thing, why come all the way to London on an errand like that? Why not buy them in New York or Boston? No, it doesn't add up. It can't have been Tumelty. I don't care for his type, never did from the first time I clapped eyes on him, but dynamite's his trade. I'm sure of it. And he's not the only Yankee in London.'

'You can see why that letter was sent to the coroner though. A man goes about trying to buy wombs and then that's the very part that was taken from Annie Chapman's body.'

'True. The only thing I can think, to make any sense of it, is that somebody at the Middlesex, a museum clerk maybe, or a porter, heard twenty pounds was being offered and went off quietly to earn himself a bit of money.'

'What, murdered a woman and risked his own neck for the sake of earning twenty pounds? I'll never believe that.'

'People have killed for less. But you're right, Dot. I don't really give it any credence. I don't understand why Wynne Baxter even mentioned it. It just muddies the waters. Where is this American? Didn't he leave his calling card? Anyway, the inquest's closed. Five days it dragged on, and we all knew from the very start what the verdict would be. You have to feel sorry for the jury. I hope they got their fee paid promptly.'

On Friday afternoon I was on my way to Miss Rosen's, to see about my crimson feathers, when Kate hailed me from across the street. She was with two other women, younger, rough-looking. Kate lifted her skirts to show me she was wearing the boots I'd given her.

'Dot!' she cries, 'these new boots are bostin!'

Bostin! That's a word you don't much hear outside of Wolverhampton. We had to shout, the street was so busy.

I said, 'You look better today.'

'I am. I've been charring at the Nag's Head.'

She was laughing and acting the giddy goat. I reckon she'd been doing more in the Nag's Head than scrubbing floors. Spending her money as fast as she earned it.

I said, 'I'm at Griffin's for another week. Shall I leave a ticket for you?'

'Smashing,' she said. 'I'll come Monday or Tuesday. I'm going to Bermondsey tomorrow, to see my Annie.'

I was about to ask her if I should leave a ticket for John Kelly too, but then two growlers came along, piled with baggage, and blocked my view. By the time they'd moved on, Kate had disappeared. Into the Blue Anchor, more than likely. The women she was with had the look of topers.

There was an incident in Dalston that night. I heard about it from Tom when he turned up at the theatre the next day. First, two women had cried murder. They said a man had pulled a knife on them and when they cried for help he'd run away.

Ida said, 'Two women at the same time? If that was our Whitechapel slasher, he's getting cheeky.'

It didn't sound anything like him. How could he murder a woman with her friend standing by? But since the Annie Chapman killing people had murder on the brain.

Tom said, 'They were just a pair of prossers. I reckon they'd tried to pick his pocket and he'd raised his hand to fight them off. He was soon caught and he had no knife on him.'

'He could have thrown it away.'

'He could have. Nothing was found. I think he was just some poor sap on his way home. All he had in his pocket was a corkscrew. Whoever heard of murder by corkscrew? But the word spread. You know how it is. The first time of telling, two women had cried murder. Next thing you hear, two women have actually been murdered. People came out onto the street.'

'You'd think they'd stay indoors if they were frightened.'

'Not frightened, Dot. Excited. Not a lot happens in Dalston.'

'And what were you doing there at that hour of the morning?'

'Working, sweetheart. Following up a story which I'm not at liberty to divulge. And then the writing was discovered, around three o'clock.'

According to Tom there had been an arrow chalked on the pavement, towards the Shoreditch end of Kingsland Road. Then two pieces of writing.

'The first part said "Look!" and the next part, a bit further on, said "I am Leather Apron. Five more and I will give myself up." And there was a drawing too. A man with a knife, and a woman. It was no work of art. More like something a child might draw. But there was no mistaking what it was.'

Clarence said, 'It was probably young lads did it, having a lark, trying to put the wind up people.'

And an unkind thought crossed my mind. 'Young lads having a lark, or just a press man trying to freshen up an old story on a slow night.'

Tom said, 'You might be right, Clarence, but one thing I do know, there's a madman still out there. It's been three weeks. How long before he gets the itch to kill again? So I'll see you home, Dot. Better safe than sorry.'

I said, 'No need. I'm having supper with Valentine.'

'Oh,' he says. 'I see.'

Ida winked at me. She said, 'You can see me home if you like, Tom.'

It isn't often you see Tom Bullen lost for words.

'Well,' he says, eventually, 'I do have to go to the office just now. I might be a while.'

She said, 'I'm just codding you. I make my own arrangements, never fear. And any Leather Apron crosses my path, he'll get my knee in his crown jewels.'

22

We had such a downpour in the night it woke me, rain drumming on the roof. Then I lay there going over a new piece I was considering.

I'm going to sing a little song, if you will list to me.
It's not too short and not too long, as you will quickly see.
I don't say my song will please you, though your verdict I don't fear.
It's the kind of song you read about but very seldom hear.

I had a beau called Marmaduke, who lived on Regent Street.
He'd the handsomest of figures and the neatest dancer's feet.
Such pearly teeth and manly lips, and raven locks had he.
The kind of beau you read about but very seldom see.

It was one of Mr Lloyd's songs and it had too many verses but I was thinking I could do something with it. I don't know what time it was when I eventually drifted off. I know the sun was streaming in when Valentine tapped on my door.

He called, 'I'm going down to Friedman's. Apple cake or plum?'

★

It got to one o'clock and he still hadn't come back. Not that I'm that bothered about cake. But Olive hadn't turned up either and I do look forward to my Sunday bath. It was getting on for two o'clock when they came bundling in together in a state of high excitement.

'Shocking news, Miss A.,' says Olive. 'There's been more murders. Two of them at least.'

'There's police everywhere,' says Valentine. 'And people out on the streets. I've never seen anything like it. I had to use my elbows to get into Friedman's. Waste of a journey that turned out.'

He'd bought a plum cake, then he'd bumped into Olive and been so busy talking about the murders he'd left the package on the tram seat. But he did have a copy of *Lloyd's Weekly*. They'd printed a special edition. There was nothing in *Reynold's* or the *News of the World* so they'd been caught napping. Tom wouldn't be happy.

Olive didn't seem in any hurry to put her apron on. She appeared to think a couple of murders were the occasion for her to partake of another tea party.

I said, 'First things first. Light the gas under my bath water and find us something to eat. Then we can read about murders.'

She made toast. There was a jar of bloater paste and a bit of potted beef.

The first body had been found in a yard off Berner Street, the very street where Monty lived, just before one o'clock. The second was found barely an hour later, in Mitre Square. I couldn't place it. Valentine said it wasn't really in Whitechapel.

'It's nearby though,' he said. 'Just off Aldgate, behind St Katherine Cree. I suppose strictly speaking it's in the City. But these killings could be the work of the same man. Berner Street to Aldgate, I'd say a person could walk it in ten minutes.'

The woman killed on Berner Street had had her throat cut but she hadn't been interfered with as poor Annie Chapman had. It was a different story at Mitre Square.

Completely disembowelled, the paper said. *A sickening spectacle, with the victim's face cut about and organs scattered around her lifeless body*.

I said, 'So they don't know if it was all the work of one man? The killing on Berner Street might have nothing to do with the other one.'

'But look at this. It says the police have reason to believe that the Berner Street assassin may have been disturbed before he could fulfil his savage intentions. Have reason to believe. What do you think that means?'

'That somebody saw him running away?'

Olive said, 'Yes. Scared him off. So then he went and found somebody else and a quieter place to do what he'd set out to do. The fiend! Now I won't sleep tonight.'

I said, 'Then stop your ears and go and see how my bath water's progressing.'

Valentine said, 'Your friend Tom will know if the police have a witness.'

'He might not. He's been complaining about them lately. Since Abberline's been in charge at Leman Street, Tom doesn't get information like he used to. Funnily enough, he was only saying last night we must be due another murder. He thinks it's like an urge the killer gets. It builds up, he does a murder, then he calms down again for a while. So I suppose he's not likely to be out on the prowl tonight. Still, you won't catch me venturing down any dark alleys, not any night. And you mind yourself too, Olive, now the evenings are drawing in.'

Valentine said, 'And here's another thing. I'll bet the murder at Mitre Square isn't even on Leman Street's patch. If it's in the City, they have their own police. That could be a good thing, if it was the same man killed both those women last night. Twice as many heads to help catch the demon.'

'Or twice as much running in circles. Two heads aren't always better than one. One thing I do know, this'll be bad for business. Everybody'll be paying a penny to see the gore at Berner Street and we'll be playing to empty theatres.'

I was right. Nobody was interested in going to a music hall when there were the sites of two murders they could visit.

Ida said, 'How much do you bet me Griffin won't turn the lights off after the first house and send us home? We'll all be out of pocket if they don't hurry up and catch this murdering bugger.'

She'd brought in the *Daily News*. It was twice its usual thickness.

'Here,' she says. 'There's plenty in this to give you nightmares.'

Neither of the murdered women had been named. The one found at Berner Street was reckoned to be about thirty-five years old, of slender build and pleasant features, but betraying signs of an irregular life. She had been dressed in black, with a carnation posy pinned to her coat. Her bonnet had been padded out with newspaper to achieve a closer fit.

'And listen to this,' says Ida. 'This'll curdle your blood. *Her body was still warm when the police arrived at the scene and so swiftly had death come upon her, she had a packet of liquorice cachous still clutched in her hand.*'

A lot of people had gone to the mortuary on Cable Street to view the corpse and several names had been put forward to the police.

One was Dolly Warden from Brick Lane, but Dolly Warden had turned up, alive and well. Another was Lizzie Stride from Flower and Dean Street who nobody had seen since she left her lodging house on Saturday evening with sixpence in her pocket. The corpse had also been claimed by a Mrs Malcolm, who said the murdered woman was certainly her sister, Elizabeth Watts, an incorrigible drunkard and wastrel in spite of the many occasions she had personally gone out of her way to treat her with Christian charity.

Ida said, 'What a way to speak of the dead. God save me from the charity of a sister like that.'

The paper explained where the murder had occurred. I was quite well acquainted with Berner Street, on account of Monty residing there. Monty's house is across the street from the George IV. If you walk up the street towards Commercial Road and cross Fairclough Street, there's a beer house, then a greengrocer's, then a gateway into Dutfield's Yard. It's directly across from the new Board School.

The murder had been carried out in that very yard, just inside the gates. The property next door to the yard was said to be a Jewish club where they held socials and gave lectures to improve the mind. It was the club steward who'd found the body. He lived in one of the houses in the yard and had come home late from Crystal Palace Market. He sold trinkets there. He was driving his cart back through the gates when something had caused his horse to shy. He'd struck a match and seen the body but thought it was just a woman passed out drunk, then he'd looked closer and noticed the blood. There had been a sing-song going on in the club room so he'd run upstairs at once to summon help. Then somebody had gone to find a constable.

The woman killed on Mitre Square was estimated to be in her

forties, of buxom build, five feet in height and with reddish-brown hair. Several persons had already attended the Golden Lane mortuary but firm identification was hampered by the terrible injuries done to the woman's face. That was something new. He hadn't marked Annie Chapman's face.

The body had been found by a constable, an officer with the City of London Police. He passed through the square regularly on his beat, approximately every fifteen minutes, so he could say with certainty when the murderer must have struck, and lest there be any suggestion that he'd been snoozing in the back room of an alehouse instead of walking his beat, he had a witness who could vouch for his time-keeping. At around half past one he'd spoken to the night watchman at Kearley and Tonge's warehouse and passed in his tea can for hot water so that a brew would be ready for him the next time he passed.

Fifteen minutes later, he'd done his rounds, came back into the square and stumbled upon the terrible sight. The square itself had been deserted, although there were a few people about on Aldgate. They have a Jew market there on Sundays and the first costers were starting to arrive. No-one had seen or heard anything of the murder. A City constable who happened to live on Mitre Square had slept quite undisturbed until the commotion of whistles and voices and heavy boots had woken him.

There were pages and pages. I didn't have Ida's patience to read every word of it. There was even a doctor's opinion, from a Dr Forbes Winslow, an eminent expert on lunacy. I wonder where they found him? He recommended that the police bring in experienced asylum warders to assist them in the identification of the killer.

Ida said, 'This doctor says the murderer is likely to present a cool and rational exterior to the world, except to those well-versed in the cunning traits of maniacs. What does that mean?'

Clarence said, 'It means he doesn't have horns and a tail. He's probably quite personable. That's why these women go with him. This one who was killed on Berner Street, with a nosegay pinned to her coat? Who gave her that? No Leather Apron, that's for certain. He'll be a more refined type of gent. And even though he's mad, he won't appear to be, not to you and me. That's what this doctor's saying.'

'But if he's personable why would he need to go into a stinking yard to get his jollies?'

'Because, Ida, it's not his jollies he's after. It's the killing. *That's* what he likes. That's what makes him a maniac.'

'Thank you, Professor Clarence.'

And a voice from the box said, 'When's Percy going to get his jollies?'

Monty came in. He was a sight, rings under his eyes. He needed a shave.

He said, 'I'm going away for a bit, Dot, till this murder business has died down. Mother's found it all very upsetting. I'm taking her to Herne Bay tomorrow morning.'

'It didn't exactly happen on your doorstep, Monty. It was the other end of the street.'

'Quite close enough. Have you seen Berner Street today? You can't move for gawkers and ghouls. We won't get any sleep till they lose interest and go home.'

'What about your patrols?'

'My mother's health is more important.'

'Do you know the fellow who found the body?'

'No. Why, should I know him?'

'It says in the papers he's the steward of a Jewish club. I thought you might know him.'

'Not our kind of people. They're Socialists, Dot. Russians, Polacks.'

Ida said, 'Still, Jews though. Where are your people from then, Monty?'

'Hoxton,' he says.

23

Griffin didn't close us down.

'We'll see if we get more in tomorrow night,' he said. 'Perhaps we should work something into the show. Keep things topical. You got any humorous songs about murders, Dot?'

What a reptile he is.

The papers were nothing but murders. I reckon the world could have stopped turning and it wouldn't have been reported. Ida brought in the late edition of the *Star*. The inquest had opened on the woman killed in Dutfield's Yard and she'd been named as Lizzie Stride, even though there was still some doubt as to who she really was. The woman killed on Mitre Square was still unnamed. A few sightings were reported too.

On Berner Street a woman had been on her doorstep taking the air late on Saturday night and seen a man go by carrying a black bag. In the Three Nuns on Aldgate, a man with a black bag had been noticed. He'd been enquiring as to the best place in that neighbourhood to do private business with a woman. And another man had been seen, tête-à-tête with a woman on Duke Street, which runs just behind Mitre Square. He was described as young and fair, with a neckerchief and a bargeman's cap. But no black bag.

Ida said, 'Makes your head spin, don't it. They can't all have been him. I don't see how they're ever going to catch him at this rate.'

That's how we all felt. Five women dead and the police didn't even know what kind of man they were looking for. Was he tall or short, or young or old? I'm sure that was why the City Police were so quick to organise a reward. Now he'd moved onto their patch they wanted him stopped, and quick.

The Lord Mayor had proposed the reward on behalf of the City Corporation. Five hundred pounds for information leading to the arrest of the Mitre Square murderer. Five hundred pounds! As Clarence said, 'If that doesn't get somebody to point the finger, nothing will.'

Another three hundred pounds had been put up by City businessmen and offered to the Home Secretary for use as a government reward. But Mr Matthews, who apparently doesn't understand the value of three hundred pounds to Whitechapel people, said he was still of the opinion that no useful results would issue from the offer of a reward. The cheque had been returned to them.

And then there was the postcard. It had been delivered to the Central News Agency, where Tom worked, on the Monday morning. There was a picture of it in the paper. A messy-looking scribble, all smears and smudges.

I was not codding dear old Boss when I gave you the tip, you'll hear about Saucy Jacky's work tomorrow double event this time number one squealed a bit couldn't finish straight off. Had not the time to get ears for police thanks for keeping last letter back till I got to work again. Jack the Ripper.

It was written in red ink and believed to be by the same hand as the letter already received and published. Well of course I knew about the letter because Monty had spoken of it and Tom had actually held it in his hand, but I hadn't seen it published.

Ida said, 'Yes you did. It was in yesterday's paper. *Dear Boss.* Remember?'

I must have grown weary of reading before I got to it.

It was Olive's day for cleaning out the kitchen range. I thought she was sure to have used that very newspaper for the ashes, but my luck was in. It lay in one piece on the scullery floor, where she'd polished the boots and then forgotten to clear it away. I found the letter. It was quite an epistle.

> *Dear Boss, I keep on hearing the police have caught me but they wont fix me just yet. I have laughed when they look so clever and talk about being on the right track. That joke about Leather Apron gave me real fits. I am down on whores and I shant quit ripping them till I do get buckled. Grand work the last job was. I gave the lady no time to squeal. How can they catch me now. I love my work and want to start again. You will soon hear of me with my funny little games. I saved some of the proper red stuff in a ginger beer bottle over the last job to write with but it went thick like glue and I cant use it. Red ink is fit enough I hope ha. ha. The next job I do I shall clip the ladys ears off and send to the police officers just for jolly wouldn't you. Keep this letter back till I do a bit more work, then give it out straight. My knife's so nice and sharp I want to get to work right away if I get a chance. Good Luck.*
>
> *Yours truly*
>
> *Jack the Ripper*
>
> *Dont mind me giving the trade name*

PS Wasnt good enough to post this before I got all the red ink off my hands curse it No luck yet. They say I'm a doctor now. ha ha

It didn't look to me anything like the hand on the postcard. It seemed like the work of an uneducated man, or someone passing himself off as unschooled. I was never a great scholar but I learned where to put an apostrophe. We'd have been whacked with a ruler at Salop Street if we'd turned out such a letter.

I read on. Somehow you always find something of interest in an old newspaper that's been under your boots or lining a drawer. There was a full description of the woman who'd been killed on Mitre Square and still lay unclaimed at Golden Lane mortuary.

> Age about 40, height five feet, dark auburn hair, hazel eyes. Clothing – black jacket with imitation fur collar and three large metal buttons, brown bodice, thin white vest, green alpaca petticoat, grey linsey underskirt, brown ribbed stockings, mended at feet, a pair of laced boots, dark green chintz skirt patterned with Michaelmas daisies, coarse white apron (part cut away), black straw bonnet trimmed with jet beads, large white handkerchief round neck. Two pawn tickets, one, for a man's shirt with the name Birrell, White's Row, the other, for a pair of boots, with the name Kelly, Dorset Street. The police had visited both addresses and found them to be false. The deceased had the initials T. C. tattooed in blue ink on her left forearm.

Well then my blood ran cold. I tried to read it again but the words came up at me all jumbled. I heard the front door close. Valentine always comes in very quietly if there's no light burning in the parlour. He must have started to go up the stairs. He leant over the banisters.

'Miss Dot?' he calls. 'Are you in the scullery?'

I came out to him. I couldn't speak.

'What?' he said. 'Whatever has happened? You look grey. Have you had bad news?'

I gave him the paper.

I said, 'It's Kate.'

'What is?' he says.

'The one they found in Mitre Square. Kate from Bilston Street, from Cooney's. She was wearing the skirt I gave her.'

I don't know what I'd have done if Valentine hadn't been there. We may have had our ups and downs but he was a perfect comfort to me that night. First thing he did, before he'd even taken his coat off, was light the gas fire in the parlour and close the curtains. It wasn't a cold night but I felt chilled to the bone.

'Now,' he said. 'Let's look at this. It might not be your friend. That skirt you say you gave her, was it made for you, bespoke?'

'No, I got it at Marshall and Snelgrove.'

'There you are then. There'll be any number of them, identical.'

I said, 'It's not just the skirt. It's the broker's ticket. I know Kate had it. It was for a dead man's shirt. She told me a woman called Em Birrell gave it to her when they were in Kent for the hop-picking. I remember distinctly. And there's the name printed in yesterday's paper. Birrell. And Kate had those letters inked on her arm too. T. C. So it's certainly her. I shall have to go to the dead-house and give them her name. Will you come with me?'

'Of course I will. But tomorrow. We can't go now. They'll be locked up for the night.'

I don't think dead-houses ever close, but I was in no great hurry to go. At that moment I wasn't sure my legs would have carried me. Valentine made me hot milk and brandy.

He said, 'If we go it'll just be her face they show you. Just a quick look and you'll be able to say at once if it's her. And they'll have tidied her up. She'll look like she's sleeping.'

He meant well. He was forgetting what it had said in *Lloyd's Weekly*. *A sickening spectacle, with her face cut about.*

I said, 'You go to bed.'

'And leave you up and tormenting yourself? I will not. We'll sit here and try to talk about cheerier things. Remember Babette? The Living Doll? She's got new teeth.'

'She needed them.'

'She did. But the thing is, Miss Dot, they're not a perfect fit. Far from it. They click when she's speaking and they move about. They really draw your eye. So Clemmie, you know Clemmie who's one of the Pearly Pierrots? She offered her some of her Corego Dental Powder. It's a fixative. And Babette says, "Fixative! I don't need no bloody fixative. These are the teeth God gave me!" and as she said it her top plate dropped clean out of her mouth. Clemmie says, "In that case, Babs, you should apply to God for your money back." I had to leave the room. I laughed so much I thought I'd die. Sorry. I didn't think.'

I said, 'What time should we go to the mortuary?'

'Not before nine o'clock. And listen, by then somebody else might have identified her. There's no sense putting yourself through a thing like that if you don't have to. What name did she go under?'

'Edders or Kelly. Not Conway at any rate. At Cooney's they know her as Kelly. That's her man's name. John Kelly. I don't know if they're married.'

'Well if she has a husband surely he'll have missed her by now?'

'He should have. But they're not always together. They don't lead a regular life. They're not exactly Darby and Joan.'

'"Darby and Joan"!' he says. 'I haven't heard that in a long time.'

He coaxed me to sing it with him, trying to calm me. Trying to take my mind off going to the dead-house.

Old Darby, with Joan by his side,
You've often regarded with wonder.
He's dropsical, she is sore-eyed,
Yet they're never happy asunder.

I said, 'From what Kate told me, it depends on what work they've had. If they're short of bed money, one of them might go to the Casual Ward for the night. Or back in the summer, when she was working at that lying-in house, she'd spend her money on drink and then go back to Mrs Gully's and sleep on the kitchen settle. He might not have missed her yet.'

'Well I suppose you must prepare yourself for the worst but don't run too far ahead. This is yesterday's paper. He'd certainly have missed her by now. But if she was Kate Edders and her husband's name is John Kelly, why does she have TC written on her arm?'

'Because once upon a time she was married to Tom Conway. Love's young dream.'

'That's another lovely song.'

'It is, but I'm in no mood to sing it. Conway lifted her out of

Bilston Street, took her travelling. I think they had good times together, until they didn't any more. I don't know why things went bad. I never knew him. But she showed me those letters on her arm one time. We were sitting in Bethnal Green Park and she rolled up her sleeve to show me. So it is her. I know it is. Don't try to tell me any different.'

'Then I'm very sorry,' he said. 'We'll go to Golden Lane in the morning.'

He looked all in.

He said, 'We should go up. Even if you won't sleep.'

I did though, funnily enough. I lay on top of the counterpane with my clothes on and went straight off and when I woke up all I could think was that I'd had some kind of bad dream that had left me feeling sad.

Then Valentine came tapping at my door and as soon as I saw his face I remembered about Kate.

'Miss Dot,' he says, 'I've been out for the morning papers. You won't need to go to the mortuary after all. She's been named.'

24

I sat in bed and read it.

> The Mitre Square victim has been identified as Catherine Eddowes, aged forty-six, recently resident at a common lodging house on Flower and Dean Street.

Eddowes. I'd never seen it written before.

I could hear Valentine banging about in the scullery.

He shouts up, 'I suppose I'd be wasting my time to offer you anything but tea?'

I said, 'You suppose right.'

It seemed to me I should go to Golden Lane anyway. I was worried what they might do about burying Kate. It wasn't likely John Kelly had any funeral money put by. There was the sister she'd spoken of, and the daughter in Bermondsey, but family don't always step up.

Valentine said, 'So what are you saying? Are you willing to pay for a funeral?'

'I'll chip in, if nobody else has offered.'

'Well, if you'll take my advice you won't rush in. Give others time to think on and do their duty. You could write a letter to the mortuary. Say you're willing to contribute but only as a last resort. I'll deliver it by hand if you like. No need for you to go to a place like that.'

'I should see her though. Make sure they've tidied her up, made her decent.'

'I'm just afraid you'll get embroiled. If you go there and tell them you knew her, who knows where it might lead? You could be summoned for the inquest.'

'I don't care if I am. I shall go to the inquest anyway.'

'Oh, Miss Dot,' he says, 'I do wish you wouldn't. It's bound to affect you, seeing a friend lying dead and cold. I dread the thought of it and I didn't even know her. Us artistes have to be careful of our nerves.'

I said, 'It's not the dead you have to fear, Valentine. It's the living. But don't you worry about coming with me. I'm quite composed.'

'Well,' he said, 'let me think about it.'

I slipped out quietly while he was upstairs doing his thinking. The last thing I needed was Valentine fainting on me. It was strange to be out and about so early in the day. Ten o'clock in the morning I'm barely moving as a rule.

The City mortuary was a fair old step. I took the horse tram as far as Old Street. It had been a long time since I was in that neighbourhood. I played the Ironmonger's Arms one time, when I was new to London. Anything for a couple of quid. It's still there and from the look of it the years haven't improved it. I had to ask for directions to the mortuary. 'By the brewery,' they said. 'Just follow the smell of hops.' Kate would have smiled at that. She loved the smell of an alehouse.

I thought dead-houses were always hidden away in churchyards. You can't just build them anywhere you please. People don't want such a thing next to their place of residence. But the one at Golden Lane is quite a fancy establishment. There was a clerk in the front office, in a morning coat and a long face. I don't suppose you'd find employment in such a place if you had a jolly smile.

I told him I'd come about Catherine Eddowes. That I wanted to ask about the funeral arrangements.

'Monday afternoon, at one o'clock,' he says. 'Are you family?'

'A friend. How's it to be paid for? She had no money and not much in the way of family.'

'More family than many have,' he said. 'And our good Mr Hawkes has offered to furnish the hearse at his own expense.'

Mr Hawkes apparently owned a funeral parlour on Banner Street but he was also a vestryman at St Luke's, and a generous Christian.

He said, 'And did you wish to view the deceased?'

Well, then I hesitated.

'There's no doubt it is her?'

'None at all. She's been identified by several who knew her. Were you a close acquaintance?'

I said, 'I knew her from a girl. We grew up on the same street. And then our paths crossed again this year, just a few months back. You know, I think I will see her. I think I should. Does she look very bad?'

'Her face was cut. You'll have read that in the newspaper. We've made her presentable. We do our best. We always do our best.'

★

They have a viewing chamber at Golden Lane. You wait outside until they're ready for you. I suppose they have to fetch the body from the cold store, and then they bring you in, very solemn, and speak in whispers.

I said, 'You'll have had a lot of people here to look at her, before it was known who she was.'

'Not very many,' he said. 'Most of them went to Cable Street to look at the other body. The Berner Street murder. It was more convenient to them than coming here. But we had a few come from up West. They couldn't possibly have known her, of course, but I daresay they had nothing better to do on a Sunday evening.'

We went in. And do you know, the first thing I thought was 'That's not Kate!' I must have let out a little cry because he kindly offered me a chair.

Her hair was loose, and filthy, from her being on the ground, I suppose. And its colour had faded. How she used to toss her curls going along Bilston Street. She knew all the lads were looking at her. Our Mam used to say, ''Er thinks 'er's the kipper's whiskers. I'd rein her in if 'er was mine.'

The face seemed thin and flat, the cheeks quite sunk, but it was Kate. And what an abomination he'd made of her with his knife. Her nose was cut through, and her cheek, right down to the corner of her mouth. He'd even cut her eyelids. Her throat was covered but I knew from the papers what lay beneath the cloth.

I said, 'They reckon he did all this, and took her parts, in just a few minutes?'

'So it seems. In as long as it took the constable to walk his beat.'

'And is this what he did to Annie Chapman and the others?'

'I couldn't speak to that. She's the only one we've received here. He's a savage beast, that's all I'll say.'

She looked so scrawny lying there. I'd always thought of her as buxom, but as the gentleman pointed out, in life she had gone about wearing a great number of garments. What was it she'd said? 'There's no armoires at Cooney's, Dot. If you've got it you wear it.'

He saw me to the front door.

He said, 'I hope you won't mind my enquiring, madam, but were you by any chance ever in the theatrical line?'

I admitted it.

'I thought I knew the voice! I've seen you at the Marylebone. But I first saw you many years ago at the Pied Horse.'

I said, 'That *was* many years ago.'

Nearly twenty if I recall. Those were the kind of engagements our Albert used to get me. The Ironmonger's, the Pied Horse, the Green Dragon.

He said, 'You were only young but you used to play an old lady. You sang a song about your lost beauty.'

I'm not quite what I used to be
When I used to be young and gay.

'That's the one. You made it very comical.'

'I still sing it. Only these days I don't have to draw greasepaint lines on my face.'

He smiled. Long, horsey teeth.

I was back out on the street when it occurred to me I could have offered him tickets. He'd been very considerate. And then I remembered there were tickets at Griffin's that I'd left for Kate. He could have had those. But I didn't go back. I hadn't the heart for it. When I turned onto Old Street, there was Valentine hurrying towards me.

'Jiminy Christmas,' he says, 'thank goodness I've found you. You shouldn't have crept out without telling me. I'd never have let you come on your own.'

'You needn't have troubled.'

'Now I feel terrible.'

'I'm all right. And anyway, it wouldn't have been right for you to look at her. You didn't know her. She's had enough strangers gazing at her.'

'So you did see her?'

'I did.'

'Was it awful?'

'Yes. No. I don't know. Ask me tomorrow.'

'Well I'm still sorry I let you go alone. It's just that I've never seen a corpse. I wasn't sure how I'd hold up.'

I said, 'Never seen a corpse! Where have you been all these years?'

On Bilston Street going to see the dead was a very popular pastime. You'd get offered a cup of tea at the very least, or something stronger, so people would go to viewings even if they'd hardly known the deceased. When our Mam passed over, we kept her on the sideboard for two days and nights and we got through three bottles of Morning Dew. She was very well liked. Mind you, it was winter.

I said, 'But what about your mother and father? Are they still living?'

'Never knew them. St Joseph's Home for the Fatherless and Destitute, that's where I was dragged up.'

It was the first time he'd ever mentioned that. I'd always thought he just didn't like his family. It hadn't occurred to me that he didn't have one.

He said, 'I have seen bodies. I've seen people run over in the street. But not close up. Not anybody I knew. Anyway, Miss Dot, I'm very sorry for your loss.'

I said, 'It isn't really a loss. It's just a shock.'

Valentine says, 'So what now? Are you going home?'

'I don't think so. Now I'm out I think I'll take a walk to Mitre Square.'

'Miss Dot!' he says, 'is that advisable? Why upset yourself?'

But I'd done the hardest part. If I could look at the cuts on Kate's poor face, I could certainly look at the place where she'd died. In fact I wanted to. I was bound to keep picturing it in my mind anyway, so better to see the actual spot.

I said, 'Look at me? Am I upset?'

'You're a rock,' he says. 'Well if you're determined, I shall come with you.'

He put his arm in mine.

'And afterwards I'm going to take you to the Great Eastern for a decent luncheon. Apart from milk and brandy, I don't believe a thing has passed your lips since yesterday.'

Valentine knew exactly the way to go to reach Mitre Square. I wouldn't have had the first idea.

'Along Ropemaker Street,' he says, 'past the railway station and across Bishopsgate.'

'How come you know all these places?'

'When I first came to London I spent every minute I could

walking about, I was so thrilled to be here. I mean, Wigan wasn't a bad town. They'd got the gas lights, and there was plenty of work. But it was nothing like this. I used to walk about London and pinch myself, to be certain I wasn't dreaming.'

We turned onto Duke Street.

I said, 'This is where Monty goes to church.'

'Synagogue,' he says. 'It's called the Great Synagogue. Very fashionable, I believe. All the top Jews go there. There it is, across the street.'

You'd never have known it was a synagogue. There was no tower, no steeple. It was just a building with a little sign set in the wall.

Valentine stopped.

He said, 'Miss Dot, we're nearly there. Now, are you sure you want to see it? We can go home if you'd sooner. I shan't mind.'

You could pass Mitre Square and never know it was there. We turned down a narrow passage alongside the Great Synagogue and the square opened before us, quite small. The buildings seemed too big for it somehow, great overbearing counting-houses in that little space. It was a beautiful sunny morning but the square was all in shade. I believe it would have made me shiver even without knowing what terrible thing had occurred there. There was a constable talking to two women.

'He'll know where it happened,' says Valentine. 'We'll ask him.'

Not only did the constable know the spot, he was standing beside it.

'Yes,' he said. 'Here is where the victim lay. Her head was toward the fence, her feet toward the square.'

He had it off pat. How many people had he told it to? It was certainly a handy little corner to commit a crime.

I said, 'It must be very dark here at night. Are there no lamps?'

'Oh yes,' says the constable, 'there's three. One on the corner where you came into the square, one on the corner of Mitre Street, which I grant you does nothing to light this spot, and one across the way, do you see? In front of Kearley and Tonge's? But that one does give a rather inferior light. But there's really no call for more illumination. There's only one house on the square that's occupied, the rest stand empty. This is a place of commerce, so after the hours of business very few people pass this way.'

One of the women said, 'Except the type who met her end here.'

That riled me.

I said, 'And what type would that be?'

Valentine put his hand on my arm.

He said, 'My friend knew the person who was murdered.'

So then they became quite interested in me. Who was I, in my good serge coat and my velvet tam o'shanter, to know *that* type of person?

She said, 'Only one thing a woman'd be on the streets for at that hour.'

And the other said, 'Yes. When decent folk are in their beds. They entice men into dark corners. This place is known for it.'

She pulled her shawl around her, very satisfied with herself and Valentine murmured, 'Let it alone, Miss Dot. Don't be upsetting yourself.'

There were no blood stains on the ground. You'd never have known what had happened there. A man was carrying timbers out from Heydemann's yard and loading them onto a cart. Business as usual. I'd have liked to stand quietly in that place for a moment, to think of Kate and hope she hadn't suffered, but there was no chance of that. Those two old witches chattered on to the constable. He seemed to know them well. Perhaps they made a habit of going to the scenes of murders.

Well, no matter. I intend to go back some day, when everybody else has forgotten about Mitre Square.

We made our way along Houndsditch to the Liverpool Street railway station. I was in a fury.

I said, 'Kate wasn't the type they were suggesting. She was a drinker but she didn't go with men. She scrubbed floors for her money.'

Valentine said nothing.

I said, 'And what I can't understand is what she was doing anywhere near that place. Whitechapel was her neighbourhood, and Shoreditch. She must have taken a wrong turning.'

He said, 'I know you were fond of her.'

'I wasn't *fond* of her. Well yes, all right. We went back a long way, me and Kate, and when I was a nipper she was always kind to me. People weren't always nice to me. The other kids on our street. Jealous, I suppose, because I was getting engagements, because I had a future. And when I saw her again, that night she was waiting for me outside Griffin's, it broke my heart to see how low she'd fallen and how cheery she was about it. The only time I ever saw her sorry for herself was when she told me how her children were lost to her, her boys. And even then she soon dried her eyes. You couldn't help but like her, Valentine. You couldn't help but think there but for good fortune goes any one of us.'

'Yes,' he said, 'I see that. And nobody likes to speak ill of the departed, but what if she was short of her bed money? What if she'd had no work that day? They say men will pay fourpence. That's not bad money for a few minutes' work. So if a man approached her? No offence, Miss Dot, but why wouldn't she go with him?'

And then, as we walked along, it came to me how it must have happened.

I said, 'The last time I saw Kate she said she was going to Bermondsey to see her daughter. That's what it is. She went to Bermondsey, came back over London Bridge and took a wrong turn.'

But he still wouldn't have it.

He said, 'You don't take a wrong turn into Mitre Square. You've seen it. You have to know it's there to find it. And if she was coming from London Bridge all she had to do was take Fenchurch Street. That would have brought her straight to Aldgate and Whitechapel High Street.'

'But if she'd taken a drink or two, she might have gone astray. She might have asked for directions. She might have had the bad luck to ask that villain. And then he led her into that dark place, as if to show her the way.'

'Yes,' he said. 'I suppose it's possible.'

By which he meant he didn't think it was possible at all. He changed the subject.

'By the way, have you seen Monty this week?'

'He's gone away. Taken his mother to Herne Bay until things calm down.'

'Then I wonder if he's read this morning's paper. You know Mr Simkin, who keeps the chemist's shop on Berner Street? He was attacked. Struck about the head with a hammer.'

'Is he dead?'

'No, and the villain was caught. He didn't even try to get away. Too addled with drink, most likely. But still! I mean, nothing bad ever used to happen on Berner Street. It used to be quite respectable.'

The Great Eastern has a beautiful dining room, with a thick carpet and good, heavy table linens, and it's filled with light from the glass dome high above you. Valentine was greeted like quite the regular. The head waiter asked him if Dr Townsend would be joining us.

'No,' says Valentine, 'but we'll take his usual table. I notice it's not occupied.'

I said, 'I hope he's not likely to turn up.'

Valentine said he knew for a fact that Frank Townsend was in the West End.

I said, 'What a charmed life that man leads. Nothing but luncheons and theatricals. A doctor without a single patient to trouble him.'

'Don't start,' he says. 'I'm determined not to quarrel with you after the morning you've had.'

The only thing about eating in dining rooms is the waiters will hover and bob about. They remind me of those birds that dibble and dabble about in the wet sands at Margate. And I don't care for having my napkin opened for me and dropped in my lap. Do they think a person is helpless? Valentine ordered a dozen Colchester Natives and a pint of Perrier-Jouet.

'Very good, sir,' says the waiter. 'And for Mother?'

I said, 'Mother will have ham and eggs and a pot of black tea.'

We did have a laugh about that.

25

Tom came by after first house.

He said, 'I'm sorry I haven't been around for a few days.'

'Haven't you?' I said. 'I can't say as I'd noticed.'

'Highly comical,' he says. 'You ever thought of going on the stage, Dot?'

He'd heard that I'd been to Golden Lane. The gentleman clerk who'd assisted me there was an acquaintance of his.

'Sidney,' he said. 'Known him for years.'

One of these days I shall hear of somebody Tom Bullen hasn't known for years.

'In my business a mortuary man is a useful person to know and Sidney's a cut above the usual. I was there this afternoon about a body that washed up at Custom House Stairs. He says, "Tom, we had a famous visitor here this morning. A lady, a star of the halls. She came about the Mitre Square woman." Well I never dreamed he meant you. When he said your name I thought he had to be mistaken. "Oh no," says Sidney, "the deceased was known to Miss Allbones." And then of course I started to make sense of it. She was the old trollop you spoke to by White Lion Street that time. The one you gave the boots to.'

'Kate.'

'Now do you see what I meant, about not going to places like Flower and Dean Street? You risk life and limb.'

'She wasn't killed on Flower and Dean Street.'

'You know what I mean. They live in a different world, those women, and it was no place for a lady like you. And you shouldn't have gone to see her body either, not on your own at any rate.'

'I wanted to make sure there was somebody to pay for a proper funeral.'

'Yes, Sidney said. But she had family apparently, and anything they can't pay for, Hawkes'll supply gratis.'

'It's a pity her family didn't do something for her when she was living. Paying for a coffin, that's cheap grace.'

'Dot, there are some people you can't help. And the trade she was plying, can you blame her folks if they didn't want to see her? Would you want somebody like that in your house?'

'I don't know why everybody insists she was in the habit of going with men. She cleaned floors, washed windows, helped out at that lying-in house. Some days she didn't even have the strength to do that. And John Kelly, that was a husband to her, he seemed quite decent, quite proper. I can't believe he'd have let her work on the streets.'

'Then what was she doing on Mitre Square? Answer me that. The police let her go at one o'clock. If she had her bed money for Cooney's, she had no reason to turn towards Aldgate.'

I said, 'What do you mean, the police let her go?'

'Didn't you hear?' he says. 'She'd been in the lock-up on Bishopsgate, drunk and disorderly. They kept her there a few hours till she'd sobered up. One o'clock they let her go. But Mitre Square's in the contrary direction to Flower and Dean Street. I'm sorry, Dot, but there's only one reason a woman goes into a place like that in the dead of night.'

'She might have been looking for drink.'

'There's no alehouses on that square. It's just a quiet corner where prossies take men.'

There was no point arguing with him. He didn't know Kate.

I said, 'Do you remember she joked with me about getting that reward? Said she had a few names she could give to the police.'

'A lot of people are *saying* that. Nobody's doing it though. All that money on the table and I reckon the police are no further forward than they were after he killed the first one.'

'Kate could have met somebody she knew. Fallen into conversation, walked along with him. I can't believe she'd have gone with a stranger. She was no fool. She'd lived rough for too long.'

Tom said, 'Well if anything's known of her habits it'll come out at the inquest. It starts tomorrow.'

'I know. I'm going to attend.'

'Then you'll need to be there early. The Stride woman's inquest is adjourned now till Friday afternoon so there's sure to be a lot of interest at Golden Lane. It'll be standing room only. Your best chance is to go with me. I can get you in. I'll meet you at the tram terminus on Old Street. Nine o'clock, no later.'

Ida came in.

She said, 'I don't know, Dot Allbones. Luncheon at the Great Eastern. Gentlemen followers calling on you between shows. They're like wasps round a jam pot with you.'

'Oh yes?' says Tom. 'And who's been taking you to hotels?'

I said, 'Never you mind who. And don't say *hotels* like that. It was a dining room. A person does have to eat.'

Ida said, 'Tom, you're in the know. That Lizzie Stride, do they think it was the same man killed her that killed Dot's friend?'

'It appears so. That's what his letter said. Double event.'

Ida said, 'But according to the papers that letter came to your office on Monday morning. Well, everybody and their Aunt Nellie knowed there was two dead by then. I could have written that letter. Turn your face to the wall, Tom. I have to change my bodice. I'm in a muck sweat.'

I don't think Ida's got anything that would interest Tom. She has a pigeon chest. She's altogether of a very odd build. Her body's a normal size. It's her legs that make her appear so short. I never saw anybody so bandy, but she's very cheerful about it. 'Look at them shins,' she says. 'They wouldn't stop a pig in an alley.' And of course that's why she's able to pass herself off as the Infant Prodigy.

Tom said, 'I take your point, Ida, but I think it's the same man. I mean, what are the chances, two in the space of an hour and both with their throats cut? He'd have had to get his skates on, admittedly. The Stride woman was still warm when they found her, but she hadn't been interfered with. Not like Kate Eddowes.'

'You mean he hadn't taken any of her parts.'

'Correct. He cut Lizzie Stride's throat and then he scarpered. So it seems to me he was disturbed before he'd finished. You know, he could even still have been there in that yard, about to finish his evil business, when Diemschutz turned up and spoiled his fun.'

'Who's Diemschutz?'

'The steward of the club. He drove his cart in, looked to see what had caused his pony to swerve, and saw the body. Then he went indoors, to fetch help. So the killer could still have been there, in the shadows.'

'And ran off when Schutzdiem went indoors.'

'Diemschutz. Yes. Or later even. I've been to examine that yard. There's plenty of places he could have lurked. He might have hid in one of the privies. Harry Lamb was the first constable to get there and he reckoned there was upwards of twenty people in the yard by the time he arrived, all milling about. And the gates were still open. It would have been easy enough for one man to slip away. But as I said, if he was to get to Mitre Square to kill Kate Eddowes at half past one he'd have had to look lively.'

I said, 'What I don't understand is how nobody saw anything. You know what Berner Street's like. There's always somebody about no matter what the hour. A man running, even a man walking in a hurry, somebody would have noticed him. Which way would he have gone?'

Ida was powdering her armpits.

'Round the corner to Fairclough Street.'

Tom said, 'Probably. Then Cherry Tree Passage, White Bear Court, there's plenty of shortcuts if you know the place.'

'He'd have had blood on his hands.'

'He would. Unless he ducked into a yard somewhere and rinsed them under a tap. But it's hard to think he did. If the killing fever was on him and he was determined to finish what he'd set out to do. Does a madman stop to wash his hands? I don't know, Dot. Perhaps he's a cooler character than we think. She was a foreigner, you know? Lizzie Stride. From Sweden. The pastor from the Swedish church knew her. Some of her acquaintances said she had teeth missing that caused her to have a funny way of talking, but perhaps that's how they speak in Sweden.'

'Did she have a husband?'

'They say she was a widow, but she had a friend, a Mr Kidney. He gave evidence today. A very diverting fellow. He had us in tucks. He said if Leman Street would only provide him with some men and a detective, he'd catch the murderer in no time. Wynne Baxter says to him, "My good man, I've received a hundred letters from persons who believe they can succeed where the police have so far failed. I daresay all those correspondents would like to have a detective at their disposal too." Raised quite a laugh. Of course Kidney wasn't amused.'

'And on Saturday night nobody saw anything?'

'Oh yes, there was plenty of accounts. Too many, if you ask me, because every one of them tells a different story. She was seen drinking in the Bricklayer's Arms before eleven, in the company of a man in a billycock hat. Supposedly. Now the Bricklayer's is on Settles Street, the other side of Commercial Road. Then there was a witness quite sure he'd seen her with a man on Berner Street, just before midnight. She was tall, you know? About your height, Dot. That's why he's convinced it was her. He said she was kissing and cuddling with a man in a black cutaway, smartly dressed, not young. Then another chap thought he saw her at about a quarter to one. He was on his way to the chandler's on the corner of Fairclough Street to get a pie for his dinner and he noticed a couple standing across the street, outside the Board School. And about the same time, a man called Schwarz saw a man throw a woman to the ground, on the street near Dutfield's Yard. He reckoned it was a young man, in a long coat and a wide-brimmed hat. Schwarz apparently ran away when he saw what was happening. I suppose he didn't care to get involved.'

'That was brave of him.'

'You can't blame him. It could just have been a husband chastising his missus. God knows you see plenty of that, and wives boxing their husband's ears as well. That's their own private business. And then, even if it's a prossie getting jostled, you still have to be careful. You might go to their aid and they'll as likely turn on you as thank you, particularly if they've been drinking. But here's another thing. When they took Lizzie Stride to the dead-house, she had a posy pinned to her coat, and yet none of those witnesses noticed it. So perhaps it wasn't her they saw at all.'

'And why is the inquest adjourned?'

'Because Wynne Baxter has engagements elsewhere. He's a busy man. There's still the doctor's evidence to be heard. It might even drag on till next week. I tell you what, why don't I come home with you, Dot? We can ride in together in the morning and I can make sure you get a seat at Golden Lane.'

I said, 'No, you go home tonight. I'm sure Mrs Bullen'll be glad to see you.'

'Ah, Dot,' he says. 'You're a tease. But anticipation makes the tastiest relish. How about Saturday?'

I told him it depended on Valentine. Whether he planned to be at home.

'How so? What's it to him if I stay? Don't tell me the lodger's dictating to the lady of the house.'

I said, 'It's your own fault, Tom. You make too much noise, crowing and carrying on. You embarrass him. He's only the other side of the wall, don't forget.'

Ida said, 'What scent do you wear, Dot? I can't remember the last time I made a man crow.'

Tom said, 'Me, embarrass an invert! That takes the cake! It was a bad day's work when you took him in.'

'You make him sound like a foundling. I didn't take him in. He pays me a fair rent, and he's cheerful company.'

Ida said, 'And he took her out for a slap-up today.'

'So that's who took you to the Great Eastern.'

'Yes. And when did you ever take me anywhere? Even Monty takes me to a chophouse once in a while, if I twist his arm.'

'It's not so easy. I'm a busy man.'

'You're a married man.'

'I've never pretended not to be. You know how it is.'

I said, 'I do. The only time I see you is when you're hoping for a bit of how's-your-father. Well not tonight. I'm going home to soak my feet.'

Off he went with a right old cob on him. He passed Clarence in the passageway, with his doll. I heard Percy's voice say, 'Cheer up, Tom. You'll be a long time dead.'

26

By the time the jury had been down to view Kate's body, half the morning was gone. The room was packed. I was grateful to Tom for getting me a seat. I shouldn't have liked to stand for so long. Mr Langham was the coroner.

'Sam Langham,' Tom called him. 'Known him for years.'

I'd never been in a courtroom before. That tells you what a spotless life I've led. Us Allboneses are a law-abiding bunch.

I said, 'How come they're all men?'

Tom said, 'What do you mean?'

'How come there's no women on the panel?'

He looked at me as if I'd gone soft in the head.

He said, 'Women can't sit on juries.'

I said, 'Why? Do they think murders are too upsetting for women to hear about? There's enough of us in the public gallery.'

'No, darling,' he says. 'It's not a question of upset, although Sam Langham has been known to clear the gallery if the evidence is liable to be too grisly. But an inquest is a serious matter. The jurymen have to apply their brains to a great deal of information. A woman's mind wouldn't be up to it.'

Well I wasn't letting that rest.

I said, 'Not up to it! There's a couple of those jurymen don't look all there to me. Look at that ginger one with his mouth hanging open.'

'Dot,' he says, exasperated, 'answer me this. Why are there no lady lawyers, no lady doctors, no lady professors? I'll tell you why. Because the feminine mind isn't suited to advanced cogitation.'

I said, 'I'll challenge you to tally up a column of figures faster than me. Any time you like.'

I thought that would shut him up but no, on he went.

'God gave you other qualities, and that's why us gents love you. And that ginger one, as you call him, is Chilcot, the tea merchant. He's made a packet of money and got a very nice house on Gracechurch Street, so there's nothing wrong with his mind. If his mouth is open, I daresay it's because he suffers from congestion of his passages. '

The first to be called to give evidence was Kate's sister, Eliza. Kate had told me she was known as Mrs Frost but the clerk called her Mrs Gold. I wouldn't have picked her out as Kate's sister. She was a dumpy little body, very stern-looking, but as soon as she was asked a question her face crumpled and she began to weep. First she said she hadn't seen Kate in several months but she believed her to have been living with a man called John Kelly. What did she know of her sister's way of life? Very little, she said. Only that she lived on Flower and Dean Street and was generally of sober habits. Sober habits! I can't think she really believed that. I suppose she said it for the sake of her own good name.

Mr Langham asked her if Kate lived on good terms with John Kelly.

'So far as I know,' she says. 'When I saw them three weeks ago they seemed to be.'

'But, Mrs Gold,' he says, 'you deposed that you hadn't seen the deceased for several months. Do you now say that you saw her more recently?'

She scratched her head.

'She knocked at my door. She'd heard I'd been in bed with a bad chest and she called on me, to see how I was going on.'

'Three weeks ago? Or three months?'

'Weeks,' she said. 'I was confused. It's because of the upset.'

'The court understands,' he said. 'Do you confirm that you saw your sister three weeks ago?'

'Yes. Thereabouts.'

'And do you confirm that you saw the deceased in the mortuary and identified her as your sister, Catherine Eddowes?'

'Yes.'

'Is the witness able to sign her deposition?'

The clerk said she was not. She'd had no schooling, I suppose, unlike Kate.

'Mrs Gold,' says the Coroner, 'put your mark on the document, then you may stand down.'

John Kelly was called next, the poor creature. He looked in pieces and his voice was so quiet they kept telling him to speak up. He said he and Kate had lived together for seven years. He portered at the markets, she had formerly done a bit of hawking but in recent times had worked as a char when she was well enough to work.

The last he'd seen of her was early on Saturday afternoon. He'd been on his way home from Leadenhall Market and bumped into her on Houndsditch. She'd told him she was going across to Surrey to see her daughter. Exactly what she'd shouted to me across the Whitechapel Road. 'I'm going to Bermondsey tomorrow to see my Annie.'

She'd told him she'd be back at Cooney's by four.

'But she did not come?'

'No.'

'Did you make enquiry after her?'

'Later. A woman told me she was in the Bishopsgate lock-up.'

'What woman?'

'I don't know her name. I asked about, had anybody seen Kate. A woman told me Kate had had a drop to drink and the police had taken her to Bishopsgate.'

'Did you go to the police station to enquire into the truth of that?'

'No. I knew they'd let her out when she was sober.'

'Was she a habitual drinker?'

'She liked a drop, when she had money. But she had no money on Saturday. I gave her none. That's why she was going to see her daughter. She hoped to get a few pence.'

'Was she at variance with anyone?'

'Sir?'

'Do you know of anyone likely to have injured her?'

'Not in the least. She was a good-natured person.'

'Did she ever stay away at night?'

'Only when she had work at the lying-in house. During the season.'

'What season?'

'The baby season.'

That caused laughter.

The Coroner said, 'Since when are humans a seasonal harvest? Surely they are born the year round?'

'Yes, sir,' said Kelly, 'but there's generally more come June and July. It's because the women go hop-picking and get themselves in the family way.'

'I see. Very interesting. But we've strayed from the point. Did you ever know the deceased to stay out at night for immoral purposes?'

'Never.'

'Did she stay with you every night at the lodging house?'

'No, sir. Sometimes I stayed at the Working Men's Home, or one of us might go to the Casual Ward. It depended what money we had.'

'What about last week?'

'We were mainly at Cooney's. Except for Friday. She went to the Mile End Casual on Friday night.'

'Why?'

'Because we hadn't enough to pay for two at Cooney's and as I had expectations of work on Saturday morning she said I should be the one to sleep there, to be handy for the market.'

'Why did she go to Mile End? Why not to the Thomas Street ward? Surely that was more convenient?'

'It was getting late. She thought she had a better chance of getting in at Mile End.'

'When did you next see her?'

'On Saturday morning.'

'At what hour?'

'Early. About eight o'clock.'

The jurymen started talking among themselves and Tom said, 'That can't be right. They won't let that pass.'

He was right. The Coroner said, 'How could she be out so early from a night shelter? Surely these people have to work before they're discharged, to pay for their bed and board?'

He appeared to be asking the whole court. One of the jurymen spoke up.

He said, 'They do, sir. They're given their skilly and then they must work. The men must do two hours at the stone-breaking, unless a doctor says they're not fit. The women must wash floors or pick oakum.'

'Thank you,' says Mr Langham. 'And at what hour are they released?'

'I'd say not before nine,' said the juryman. 'But I have no personal experience.'

More laughter. Kate would have enjoyed her inquest.

'I should think not,' says the Coroner. 'So, Mr Kelly, are you sure it was eight in the morning when you saw Catherine Eddowes?'

'Near as I can say.'

'We must perhaps hear from the attendant at Mile End. Is he in court?'

He wasn't.

'Very well, we'll consider whether he should be called. John Kelly, recount the events of Saturday morning.'

'We took my boots to the brokers. On Church Street.'

'To pawn them?'

'Yes.'

'You went to your work barefoot?'

'Yes.'

Suddenly up pops a man sitting at a table in front of the coroner's bench.

'Mr Langham,' he says. 'This seems at odds with the information given by the broker. The boots were pawned on Friday evening.'

Tom whispered in my ear. 'That's Crawford. Solicitor.'

'Why is he here?'

'Keeping an eye on proceedings. He's acting for the City Police.'

So then John Kelly was pushed to remember things more clearly. Was it Friday night or Saturday morning when they'd popped his boots? He said it might have been Friday. He was muddled. I couldn't see that it mattered.

'How much did the broker advance you for the boots?'

'Two shillings and sixpence.'

'And yet you hadn't enough for two people to stay at the lodging house?'

'I think we bought some tea. And sugar and bacon.'

'Did you spend money on drink?'

'Some. Very little.'

'But by Saturday afternoon you were destitute again.'

'Not quite.'

'Enough that the deceased needed to go to Bermondsey to seek assistance from her daughter.'

'She wanted to go there anyway. She was fond of her daughter.'

Mr Langham looked about.

He said, 'Is the daughter in court?'

'Not today,' the clerk said. 'But she will attend as required.'

'So,' says the Coroner, 'to summarise, you last saw the deceased on Saturday afternoon. You parted on good terms. And you understood her intention was to visit her daughter.'

'Yes, sir.'

'But when you heard she had been found drunk and arrested, you did not go to Bishopsgate to enquire about her.'

'No, sir.'

Sam Langham let out a great sigh. It was clear what he meant by it. The way these people live.

'You may step down, Mr Kelly,' he said. 'We have no further questions. We'll resume at two o'clock.'

Tom said, 'We'll go to the Hat and Feathers. They do a good pie.'

I wasn't hungry.

He said, 'Are you all right?'

I was perfectly all right. There had been nothing said so far to upset me. It was hearing about Kate's wounds that I was dreading. I just wished they'd get on with it.

I said, 'You know I don't generally eat at this time of day.'

'Oh yes,' he said. 'Unless some young mollyboy takes you to the Great Eastern. Well I have to eat so you might as well sit and watch me.'

What I really wanted was to speak to John Kelly. Tom thought it most likely he'd have fled the minute the Coroner had finished with him.

He said. 'Couldn't get his story straight, could he? He looked about ready to soil himself when Sam Langham pressured him.'

'Bad enough Kate's been murdered without him having to stand up and answer questions. That court would make anybody nervous.'

'It's meant to, Dot. So people think carefully about what they say.'

'But Kelly doesn't know who killed Kate. He's in a bad way and he shouldn't have been barked at. Nor Kate's sister. What wrong have they done?'

'No, well, that's just how it is. And they'll get over it. Actually there might be a few quid in this for Kelly. My life with Jack's victim. It'd make a nice little piece.'

'You're not going to hound a man for the sake of a story? He's just suffered a terrible loss.'

'No, no. Not now. What do you take me for? I'm talking about later on. You can ask him.'

I said, 'It's funny, isn't it, how he turned out to be called Jack?'

'Who?'

'The killer. When Annie Chapman was killed, you said the police were running around trying to catch Jack. Do you remember?'

'No. It's just a name.'

'That's what you said then. Still, funny you should get it right.'

'Jack Sprat, Jack-o-Dandy, Jack in the Pulpit. I'd say it's the first name anybody'd think of. Jack Frost. I hope you don't think it's me going round slashing these doxies.'

27

The afternoon session started. Wilkinson, the deputy from Cooney's, was the first to be heard. He spoke to me as we were going in.

'You're the lady off the halls,' he said. 'Mrs Kelly spoke very warmly of you. Terrible affair this. It's quite set Mrs Wilkinson back.'

He appeared very nervous on the stand. He said he'd known Kate and John Kelly for seven years and had found them to live on good terms.

'They were not given to quarrelling?' said Mr Langham, though what that was to do with anything I could not see. Everybody has their quarrels. Don't ever get yourself murdered. They'll pick over all your linen, clean and dirty, and it'll be in the papers the next morning.

'No,' said Wilkinson. 'No more than any married couple.'

That caused a roar. Even the solicitor smiled. After that Fred Wilkinson was less anxious. I knew what he was feeling. One good laugh from an audience and I know I have them where I want them.

Sam Langham said, 'You saw no violence between them?'

'No. They might have a tiff if Kate had had drink.'

'And Mr Kelly?'

'I never saw him the worse for drink. I'd say he's not in the habit.'

'But the deceased was?'

'Sometimes. Not regular. She liked a drink if she had the money. She was a good-natured person.'

Mr Wilkinson said the last time he'd seen Kate was on Saturday morning. He recalled she'd been in the kitchen at Cooney's, drinking tea with John Kelly. The Coroner asked him if he knew Kate was in the habit of walking the streets at night. I didn't care for that expression. Walking the streets is not the same as being a street walker. Just because she was out late on Saturday night, doesn't mean to say it was her custom. Some people seem determined to make her out a prosser. But Mr Wilkinson soon scotched that.

'Not at all,' he said. 'She was generally in by ten o'clock and I never saw her with any man but Mr Kelly. Some of them try to bring men into the house, but not her. And she'd never have had reason on my account to walk the streets at night. If she was short of her bed money I'd still have let her in. I'd known her long enough. Some people will take advantage but the Kellys always paid their debts, as soon as they were able.'

Tom whispered, 'I hope that doesn't get back to Johnny Cooney. I'm sure he wouldn't like Wilkinson hiring out his beds on the knock.'

The Coroner asked Mr Wilkinson if he remembered anything particular about Kate on that Saturday morning? How had she seemed?

What daft questions they do ask at these inquests. Did he think she expected to get murdered?

Wilkinson said, 'I think she was quite cheerful. Her usual self. And she was wearing her apron, so I supposed her to be going charring somewhere.'

'And John Kelly?'

'He went out. I cannot say what time. He was out all day and he was back in by ten on Saturday night.'

'Might he have gone out again, without your knowing?'

'No. At night we're very particular about comings and goings. He was in till Sunday morning.'

I said to Tom, 'It's as though the Coroner's trying to put her killing onto Kelly.'

'He has to be thorough,' he whispered. 'And it's a fair enough line of enquiry, Dot. When a woman gets killed, it's usually the husband did it.'

Such a waste of time. It was clear to anyone with a brain that John Kelly never harmed her.

'Mr Wilkinson,' said the Coroner, 'you say you're very particular about comings and goings at your establishment. Were there any arrivals or departures in the early hours of Sunday morning?'

'Two detectives came to the door. It was at about three o'clock.'

'From which force?'

'Beg pardon, sir?'

'Were they from the Metropolitan Police or the City Police?'

'I couldn't say. They asked if I had any women still out that I'd have expected to be in. They were going to all the lodging houses.'

'You told them Catherine Eddowes hadn't come in?'

'No. She hadn't asked me to keep a bed for her.'

Crawford, the solicitor, got to his feet. 'How many does your lodging house accommodate?'

'A hundred souls.'

'Were there a hundred in on Saturday night?'

'No.'

'How many were there?'

'I'd have to look at my register.'

'You have it with you?'

'No.'

'Go and fetch it.'

Another fine waste of time. I think that Crawford fellow just asked questions to prevent himself from falling asleep. While Fred Wilkinson went off to fetch his book, they called PC Watkin, the constable who discovered Kate's body. He explained his beat. Tom was drawing a little map in his notebook.

From the top end of Duke Street to Heneage Lane, right onto Creechurch Lane, left onto Leadenhall Street to where it meets Aldgate. Then left onto Mitre Street, into Mitre Square, round the square, back out onto Mitre Street, turning right towards King Street, through St James's Place and back to his starting point on Duke Street.

'It takes you how long?'

'Twelve minutes. Never more than fifteen.'

'At what hour did you commence your duties?'

'Ten o'clock.'

'Recount for the court the time immediately before you discovered the body.'

'I went through Mitre Square at half past one. The body wasn't there then.'

'You are quite certain.'

'Oh yes. I had my lantern and I always look into all the gateways.'

'What about the passageways?'

'I look into all of them but the one they call Church Passage. That's another man's beat.'

'Is that constable here today?'

'I couldn't say.'

Another sigh from the Coroner.

'Continue. You didn't look into Church Passage but there is another passage from the square, leading to St James's Place?'

'Yes. I look into that very carefully. It's a very dark place.'

'It is unmarked on the court's plan. What is its name?'

'It has no name.'

That caused me to shiver. A very dark place that has no name.

'Was anyone on Mitre Square when you went through it at one thirty?'

'No-one. I called at Kearley and Tonge's on my way past and left my tea can with Mr Morris, the night watchman. He obliges me with hot water.'

'Is this a regular arrangement?'

'Oh yes. I know Morris very well. He used to be on the force himself.'

'Continue.'

'I left my tea can with Morris, checked the passage to St James's Place, and then went back onto my beat, to Mitre Street. The next time I went into Mitre Square was at quarter to two. That's when I found the body.'

'Tell the court what you saw.'

'I saw a woman on the ground. Her feet were towards me and her clothes were thrown up towards her head. Her throat was cut and her stomach had been cut open.'

'You saw blood?'

'Yes, she lay in a pool of it.'

'Did you touch the body?'

'I did not. I ran across to Kearley and Tonge's and called to Mr Morris to come to my aid. He blew his whistle to summon help and I stood guard over the body.'

'The night watchman blew his whistle? Why not you?'

'I had no whistle.'

The Coroner turned to the solicitor.

He said, 'Mr Crawford, don't the City Police equip their constables with whistles?'

'Some have them, Mr Langham, but not all. Those without whistles signal with their lamps.'

'Much use a lamp would be in an enclosed place. Constable Watkin might have signalled till daybreak and no other officer would have been any the wiser.'

'Indeed, sir.'

'Constable, continue.'

'PCs Holland and Harvey were the first to arrive. Mr Morris found them on Aldgate and brought them to the square. They saw the body, then PC Holland went to Jewry Street to ask Doctor Sequeira to come and PC Harvey went to Bishopsgate to report the matter.

'Is PC Holland here, or Harvey? Is Doctor Sequeira here? Who do we have?'

The clerk said none of them were in court, but Inspector Collard from Bishopsgate Police Station was present, and Dr Brown, the police surgeon.

The Coroner took out his pocket watch.

Tom whispered, 'There'll be an adjournment.'

Mr Langham said, 'As they have taken the trouble to come here today, we shall hear from them.'

The police inspector was called first.

'Ted Collard,' said Tom. 'Know him well.'

Inspector Collard said he'd received notice that a woman had been murdered in Mitre Square just before two o'clock.

'Did you set off at once?'

'As soon as I'd telegraphed to Wood Street.'

'The gentlemen of the jury may not understand what you mean by "to Wood Street".'

'To the headquarters of the City Police. I also sent an officer to fetch Dr Brown.'

'Had he far to come?'

'Only from Finsbury Circus. I then proceeded to Mitre Square with my sergeant. By the time I arrived, Dr Sequeira was already there with two constables. He certified that life was extinct.'

'Had he touched the body?'

'I think not. He remained until Dr Brown arrived. The body was then loaded onto a litter and conveyed to Golden Lane.'

'The square was searched?'

'The square and the surrounding streets.'

'There was blood on the ground. Were there no footprints?'

'None.'

'Is there anything you wish to say about the deceased's clothing?'

'I imagine you're referring to her apron?'

'Yes. Tell us what you noticed.'

'The victim's apron had a sizeable piece cut from it. The missing piece was found later. A constable from the Metropolitan Police discovered it on Goulston Street on Sunday morning.'

'A body found in one jurisdiction and a piece of her apparel in another. An occasion for cooperation between the two police forces.'

'Yes, sir.'

Tom chuckled.

'That'll be the day,' he whispered. 'More like an occasion for them to lock horns.'

'Did the deceased have any money about her person?'

'None. There was very little of any note in her pockets except an old mustard tin containing two brokers' tickets. The mortuary can provide a detailed list of items. The pawn tickets both bore false names and addresses, but when news of them circulated they did lead to identification of the victim.'

Dr Brown came on next. He said a constable had rung his bell just after two on Sunday morning. He had gone with all haste to Mitre Square and arrived there at about half past two.

Tom said, 'Dot, are you sure you want to stay for this? He's bound to speak of her injuries.'

Well of course I was going to stay.

Dr Brown said Kate was on her back, her arms by her side. Her bonnet was still on her head, her skirts thrown up and her bodice torn open.

'Her injuries, Dr Brown, as you observed them at the scene?'

'The body was still quite warm. There was no rigor mortis. Her face was greatly disfigured and her throat cut.'

'In your opinion was the cut to the throat the cause of death?'

'Without doubt. It would have caused immediate death.'

'There was no sign of a struggle?'

'None.'

'But there were other wounds?'

'Yes, deep wounds, inflicted after the throat was cut. In my opinion.'

'And certain parts of the body had been removed?'

'Yes. Most of the uterus and the left kidney.'

'They have not been found?'

'No.'

'Would their removal require anatomical knowledge?'

'Yes, particularly the kidney. The position of the kidneys is not generally known by the man in the street.'

'But a butcher, for instance, would know?'

'A butcher would have some notion, yes.'

'And in this instance the deed seemed to have been done by someone who located those organs accurately?'

'I would say so. The cutting was precise and clean.'

'How long would it have taken?'

'With a sharp knife, five minutes if he knew exactly what he was about.'

'Would you expect the assassin to have been stained with blood?'

'His hands, yes. But if he knew what he was doing he could have stood so as to avoid being marked by any great issue of blood.'

'Can you suggest any reason for a person to remove organs in this way?'

'I cannot.'

'Can you suggest a reason for mutilation of the victim's face?'

'Diseases of the mind are not my field of expertise.'

Crawford, the solicitor, said something to the Coroner, very confidential, and the Coroner seemed to ponder for a minute.

Then he said, 'One final thing, Dr Brown. The deceased was wearing an apron, still tied to her body.'

'But with a piece cut from it.'

'I think you anticipate my question. Have you seen the piece of cloth found on Goulston Street?'

'I have. It fitted exactly the hole cut from Catherine Eddowes' apron.'

'Thank you,' said the Coroner. 'We shall no doubt have cause to return to the mysteries of Goulston Street before we're done.' He looked at his time-piece.

'That'll be it for today,' said Tom, and he was right. The inquest was adjourned until the following Thursday. I felt very flat. I don't know what I'd expected. Nothing anyone said or did was going to give Kate her life back. I had wondered if her boys would attend but there hadn't been any young men in the public seats. Perhaps they didn't know. Perhaps they didn't care.

It was good to get out into the fresh air. When we got onto the street I spotted Kate's sister.

Tom said, 'Go and have a word with her. I'll come with you. She might say something interesting.'

If you're a newspaper man I suppose you never stop.

There was a likeness to Kate, when I saw her close to. Not the features so much as her way of carrying herself, but Eliza Gold, Frost, whatever she goes as these days, didn't have Kate's spirit. I found her to be very cold, very watchful. I condoled with her, of course.

I said, 'I knew Kate. We grew up across the street from one another, in Wolverhampton.'

'Oh yes?' she said. 'Then you know she landed with her backside in the butter when they sent her there. Didn't turn it to good account though, did she?'

There was no denying it. Kate had been luckier than her brothers and sisters, raised by good people like the Eddoweses. She hadn't repaid them well.

She said, 'I suppose you're one of them that think I should have took her in these past years?'

I said, 'No. And I never heard Kate say so either. She seemed quite contented at Cooney's.'

'I couldn't have had her in my house. She had irregular habits.'

'I know she liked a drink.'

'All very well for people to say I should have looked out for her. They don't realise. They didn't know her.'

Tom urged me away.

'Nothing to be gained here, Dot,' he whispered.

It was true, for him and for me. It was like talking to a stone wall.

I said, 'You can understand it. Their mam died, then their dad. They were all farmed out. Kate got the kindly aunt and the good looks. Her sister got the orphanage.'

'And a face like a suet pudding. Are you going straight to Griffin's? I'll put you in a cab. I have to go back to the office but I'll come by after second house. See you home.'

'No need.'

'You sure you're all right?'

I could never have explained to him what had really undone me. All that business I'd listened to, about the blood and the kidney and her clothes disarranged, it hadn't troubled me. Do you know what weighed on me? Do you know what made me weep? The old mustard tin they found in her pocket, with her brokers' tickets and her precious twist of tea. Kate had had a happier life than some. She'd travelled about, seen more places than many do, and she seemed to have lived quite comfortably, till it went bad between her and Conway. Was she to blame for her own misfortunes? I can't say. Drink has never had a hold over me. All I know is that, in the end, that bloody mustard tin was about the only thing she had.

28

I received two pieces of correspondence on Saturday morning. The first lay on the mat when I came down, delivered by hand. Olive was giving her notice, or rather Olive's father was giving Olive's notice. *Could not allow her to work in such a house*, it said. It made no sense.

Valentine came downstairs just before twelve, suited and booted and on his way to have luncheon with his Dr Frank. I showed him the note.

I said, 'I don't understand this at all. What does he mean, "in such a house"? Olive's family's always known I'm in the theatre. They've never objected to it before.'

He said, 'I don't think it's about your theatrical associations. I think they mean about your friend getting murdered.'

'But how could they know? I've not seen Olive since Sunday. Nobody knew then who those women were. Anyway, I'm sure she never heard me speak of Kate. And if I had mentioned her, I wouldn't have said her name.'

'Ah,' he says. He chewed his lip. 'I think I may be to blame there.'

'You told her I knew Kate? How did that come about?'

'On Thursday. She brought my clean shirts in and she remarked it wasn't like you to be out so early in the afternoon. I told her you'd gone to the inquest. On account of being acquainted with Mrs Eddowes. She was wide-eyed, of course.'

'And then went home and told everybody.'

'Well, yes. You would, wouldn't you?'

'So now I have to find a new girl.'

'I'm sorry. I didn't dream it'd cause a problem. I just thought she'd be interested.'

'Olive didn't come here for interest, Valentine. She came to keep this house in good order. And something like this, you have to think before you speak. You never know how people are going to take things. They might be fascinated, they might be scandalised. People can be very narrow-minded.'

'They can.'

'Everybody's painting Kate to be a street walker. But John Kelly wouldn't have it and neither would Mr Wilkinson, who keeps Cooney's house, and they should know. "In by ten most nights," Wilkinson said. So I won't believe it either.'

'But she had been in the lock-up, drunk and disorderly. Olive's people will have read that in the papers. That might be bad enough for them. Olive'll be so upset though. I'm sure she liked working here.'

'She should have done. It's not every employer invites you to sit down and eat cake.'

'Well I'm sorry if I spoke out of turn. Is there anything I can do to make amends?'

I said, 'Yes, find us a new daily and be quick about it.'

The same morning another item came, by the penny post; a letter from my brother Albert. He'd read the news about Kate.

Dear Dotty, What a shock about Kate Eddowes. It must of knocked you back, you being acquainted with her. Everybody's talking about it. There's people saying they knew her that wasn't even born when she lived hereabouts. You have to laugh.

It was amusing. Olive's father might not have wanted his daughter even distantly connected with Kate, but the people of Bilston Street were apparently happy to claim her. Anything for a bit of excitement.

But I do worry about you out late at night without a man to watch over you, he wrote. I hope Monty still sees you home. He should do. You've earned him a few bob over the years. I'd thought he'd of made an honest woman of you by now. Ask me, he should pee in the pot or get off it.

Good old Albert. I couldn't ask for a better brother. I feel badly sometimes because I'm partly the reason he never married. He was very keen on one girl, Lilian, and when he came with me to London she said she'd wait for him. But she didn't. By the time he went back to Wolverhampton she'd married somebody else. He's never blamed me. 'It wasn't meant to be,' he says. Still, it would have been nice if he could have found somebody else.

It was my last night at Griffin's. I was engaged for the following week at the Hoxton Britannia, then two weeks at Gatti's, across the river. After that I had a resting week.

I said, 'I might go and visit my brother, first week of November. I should do. I haven't seen him in years.'

Valentine says, 'Oh do go, Miss Dot. That's a tip-top idea. It'll take you out of yourself after all this upset. I'll look after things here.'

It wasn't that I didn't trust him. He was a good boy, very clean, very careful. It was just the company he kept.

I said, 'I know you will. Only I don't want you entertaining certain people here. You know who I mean.'

'Yes,' he sighs. 'I do. But if it puts your mind at rest, you should know Frank's very rarely this side of town these days.'

'Then why does he keep lodgings on Batty Street?'

'He doesn't. He's given them up. It was only a temporary arrangement, while the usual tenant was away on business. Then the other gentleman came back and required his room. Frank did ask me about Mr Earp's old accommodations but I knew you wouldn't care to have him living next door so I told him they were already taken. See, I am mindful of you. And actually it suited Frank just as well to stay at the Charing Cross.'

Frank Townsend, Tumelty, whatever his name is, living the other side of my wall! I couldn't have borne it.

I said, 'I'd have thought he'd be packing his bags by now. Isn't it time he went home?'

'How you do go on about him. You'll miss him when he's gone.'

'Yes, like a stone in my shoe.'

'What if he takes me with him when he goes?'

'You wouldn't.'

'I might.'

'But to America? You don't know anybody there.'

'I didn't know anybody when I came to London. Neither did you, come to that. Anyway, Frank knows people everywhere. New York, Boston, St Louis. San Francisco. Theatre people too. He'd introduce me to his friends.'

'Are you in earnest?'

'Now you're worried.'

'I'd miss you.'

'You could come with me.'

'You, me and Frank Townsend? No thank you very much. I don't have a long enough spoon for supping with the devil.'

He laughed.

He said, 'You've got quite the wrong idea about him.'

I said, 'But I haven't. That's what troubles me. I haven't got *any* idea. All these months and I still don't know what he's doing here. I don't even know his name. Is he Townsend? Is he Tumelty?'

'Is Amazonia Amazonia or is she Blanche Smith? Is Celeste La Rue still Cissie Roundtree under that wig? Or could she even be Cyril Roundtree? There's no law against changing your name, Miss Dot.'

Lizzie Stride was to be buried that day, out at Plaistow. The Saturday papers were full of her inquest. At Friday's hearing there had been a great deal of discussion about the knife that had killed her. Would it have been long, or short, must it have had a pointed end? All the police-surgeon would say was that it must have been exceedingly sharp, to do her in so quickly that she never let go of the comfit packet she was holding in her hand.

They'd called witnesses too, who thought they might have seen her on the night in question. A Mr Marshall, a neighbour of Monty's on Berner Street, who'd seen a man and woman together near the George IV pub. It had been before midnight, perhaps a quarter to, and he was quite certain it was the woman he'd seen in the mortuary. He knew her by her dress, he said. Well that made no sense. In the mortuary they wear no clothes. As to the man he'd seen her with, it had been too dark to make out his face, but by his stoutness he guessed him to be of middle years and too well dressed to have been a labourer. He'd sported a dark cutaway and a hat. Mr Marshall had stood on his doorstep for a good half hour and had watched them go off together, very amicable seeming, and towards Ellen Street, quite the opposite way to Dutfield's Yard where Lizzie Stride was found.

A man from Fairclough Street believed he'd seen her too, but later, at a quarter to one he estimated. He'd gone out to buy his supper and seen a woman talking to a man outside the Board School. He could say nothing about the man's attire, not even if he'd worn a hat. Now if I was a juryman *that's* the kind of witness I'd trust. He was tired, he was hungry, and he was hurrying to the chandler's. Why would he study what some person across the street was wearing?

The inquest was adjourned for two weeks. How they do drag these things out.

Ida said Whitechapel was swarming with police. The word was that they'd brought in extra men, borrowed constables from other divisions.

'Saturday night,' she said. 'They're expecting another murder. But he'd be a chump if he goes out tonight. What he'll do is wait now, till it's all gone off the boil.'

'If he can, Ida,' says Dan Margolinski. 'If he can master his unnatural urges.'

Clarence said, 'Perhaps we shouldn't be talking about it like this, in front of Miss Allbones. She's had a personal bereavement, remember.'

Ida said, 'Hardly a bereavement. When your old mum dies, that's a bereavement, or your cat. Anyway, you don't mind do you, Dot?'

I didn't. Actually, I'd have been more grieved to think Kate was forgotten. Once they've caught him I suppose she will be, and the others he's killed. He'll be the one everybody remembers.

Dan said, 'You'd think they'd keep quiet about these bobbies they're bringing in from outside. You don't want your criminal types knowing that. All the police sent to Whitechapel, it'd be a good night to go burglarising in Stepney.'

'Finsbury more like,' says Ida. 'There's bugger all worth robbing in Stepney.'

'Nice language from an infant,' says Clarence.

Ida does look quite the part in her velveteen dress and her white stockings. From the back of the stalls. When the lights are down. And, of course, when she's doing her turn she pretendths to lithp.

She said, 'You going to your friend's funeral, Dot?'

'Of course.'

'You want company? I'll come with you if you like.'

I said, 'No thank you. Why would you do that? You didn't know her.'

'No,' she said, 'but while all them that did know her are weeping I could keep my eyes open for the one that killed her. It's a well-known fact that murderers like to go the funeral. They like to mingle with the crowd and hear what people are saying about them.'

I said, 'Well I doubt there'll be any crowd for him to mingle with on Monday. There won't be many to mourn Kate.'

But on that score it turned out I was mistaken.

29

I got to Golden Lane well before one o'clock and there was already a considerable throng and a great number of police. I found myself looking about, thinking of what Ida had said. What if the murderer was there? What if he was standing right behind me?'

Mr Wilkinson from Cooney's claimed me.

'I guessed you'd come,' he said. 'Sad day.'

I said, 'Why are the police here? Do they think he might be in the crowd?'

'If they do they'll need eyes in the back of their helmets to spot him. No, it's because of the size of the crowd. They don't want anybody getting trampled. They're going to escort her to the end of Old Street, then the Leman Street coppers'll take over. I hope she's watching from wherever she is. She'd be tickled pink to see this send-off. And just think, if she'd died peaceful in her bed there'd have been none of this. She'd be in the parish grave by now and never given another thought.'

The glass hearse stood empty. Two horses, with plumes, a nice piece of purple cloth for the casket to rest on, and two following carriages provided. Mr Hawkes had done her proud. On the stroke of one they brought her out. Four pallbearers and behind them John Kelly and three women. One was Mrs Gold or Mrs Frost, the sister. I knew neither of the others but I guessed by the age of the younger one that she was Kate's daughter, Annie.

Mr Wilkinson said, 'Come along then, Miss Allbones. I'll hand you up.'

I hadn't expected to ride in the cortège.

'Of course you must,' he said. 'You were her friend. Who else does she have to follow her? Come on, and I shall ride with you, on behalf of Cooney's.'

He pushed through the crowd.

'Passage, if you please,' he called. 'Kindly allow the bereaved to reach their conveyances.'

John Kelly looked like he hadn't slept. As soon as Kate's coffin was secured in the hearse, Mr Hawkes asked us to take our seats.

'Mr Kelly,' he said, 'you should ride in the first carriage.'

'No,' says John. 'I'll ride with Fred Wilkinson. I know who my friends are.'

'Yes,' says the younger woman. 'And I'll go with you.'

So Mrs Gold and the other person had the leading carriage to themselves.

Kelly said, 'They're welcome to it. I never met such a quarrelsome pair. Not sisterly at all.'

I said, 'I know Mrs Gold from the inquest. I didn't know Kate had another sister.'

'Oh yes. She had three. And three brothers. I can't speak for the rest of the family but that pair'd fight over the day of the week. I'd sooner sit with you and Fred Wilkinson. And this is Kate's daughter, Annie. Annie, this is Miss Allbones, an old acquaintance of your dear mother.'

Annie had Kate's colouring, but not her manner. She was altogether more refined.

She said, 'I wish there wasn't such a crowd. Why have they come? Ma can't have known all these people.'

I said, 'Some of them just like to go to funerals. But I think a lot of them came because they thought no-one else would. They mean it kindly. There was hardly any attended Lizzie Stride's burying.'

'I wouldn't know about that,' she said. 'Bad enough we have our own troubles. I can hardly believe I'm sitting here.'

I said, 'Did your mother come to call on you that Saturday?'

'No.'

'She told me she intended to.'

'I don't think she knew where to find me. We've moved since the last time she saw me. I wonder why she thought of coming?'

'Did she often visit you?'

'Hardly ever. My husband didn't encourage it, because of her habits, because of her drinking.'

'She missed you.'

'Oh yes? Is that what she said?'

'I'd given her two chemises, never been worn. I had the feeling she intended bringing them to you.'

'I'll bet she went to our old place and found we'd moved.'

Her eyes filled.

She said, 'If she'd known where to find me she might still be here. I should have let her know where we'd shifted to. If I know her she popped those chemises, when she couldn't find me, and spent the money on drink.'

John said, 'Don't blame yourself, Annie. When Kate wanted drink there was no stopping her.'

'But if she hadn't had money she couldn't have bought drink. If she hadn't bought drink she wouldn't have been put in the lock-up till she was sober. She wouldn't have been out on the street at that hour.'

I said, 'Annie, that's a lot of ifs.'

'Yes,' says Fred Wilkinson. 'As Mrs Wilkinson always says, if ifs and ands were pots and pans there'd be no work for tinkers.'

All the way to Manor Park there were little clusters of people waiting at the roadside, to see Kate's coffin go by. As we got towards Stratford, Annie seemed to grow anxious.

She said, 'John, do you think he'll be there?'

'He gave me his word,' he said.

I thought for one minute they meant Tom Conway, who had been Kate's husband. I had wondered whether he'd turn up. Annie read my mind. She shook her head.

'No,' she said. 'Not my father. I don't even know if he's heard of her death.'

John Kelly said, 'He must have, Annie. It's all over the papers. Unless he's in the grave himself.'

I said, 'You never hear from him?'

'No.'

'Nor your brothers?'

'No,' she said. 'And I wouldn't want Dad here anyway because I know what he'd say.'

'What would he say?'

'That Ma brought all this on herself. I don't need telling that.

She was still my ma. No, it's the cleric we were talking about. John here fixed it up for somebody to say the proper words over her.'

He said, 'They weren't going to. Mr Hawkes told me it wasn't the custom for women of Kate's type to be put into consecrated ground. I said, "Mr Hawkes, with due respect, my Kate was a woman who said her prayers every night." So then Mr Hawkes spoke to the chaplain at the cemetery and he agreed to do the honours. He's promised to meet us at the gates.'

And the chaplain was as good as his word. The Reverend Dunscombe. *Man that is born of woman hath but a short time to live and is full of misery*. Well that didn't sound right. Kate was forty-six, not bad for someone who lived on tea and rum, and I must say I never knew a more cheerful person in adversity.

John Kelly held up very well. Mrs Gold and the other sister, Mrs Fisher, provided the wailing. Annie never made a sound till they let the coffin down. I took her hand. I hope she didn't mind.

'What a waste,' she said.

I said, 'She spoke of you a lot, and your brothers.'

'Oh yes, I'm sure she did. I've heard it myself often enough. "Don't think I don't love you, Annie. Don't think I didn't want to be a good mother to you." But you see she loved the drink more. And I shall never understand it.'

Mrs Gold and Mrs Fisher left us at Mile End, to go into the White Hart for a preventative tot of brandy. Mrs Gold said cemeteries were famous places for catching deadly chills, which may be true as a general rule but we were having the hottest October I ever remember.

She said, 'You coming with us, Annie? Raise a glass to your mother's memory?'

'I will not,' says Annie. 'I have children waiting for me at home. And if you ask me, there's been too many glasses raised in this family.'

The rest of us parted at Banner Street, where Mr Hawkes has his establishment. John Kelly shook my hand. Annie thanked me for my trouble.

I said, 'I'll be at the inquest again, on Thursday. Will you be there?'

'I have to be,' she said. 'I'm to be questioned. Why are you going?'

I don't know why. I could as easily read about it in the papers the next day.

I said, 'Just trying to make some sense of it, I suppose.'

She smiled.

She said, 'Make sense of what? Why she was killed? That's easy. She went with the wrong man.'

I took her arm and turned her away from John Kelly. I didn't want him to hear what we were saying.

I said, 'Is that what you think? That she went with him willingly into that square, for money?'

'I don't reckon he dragged her there. Ma was a strong woman, for all her ailments. She went willingly, Miss Allbones. Perhaps she knew him. Perhaps he was one of those toffs who carries a saddle flask. One thing I know about my mother, when the mood was on her she'd do anything for a drink. When they catch him it'll all come out. How he lured her. How she could have been so foolish when all of London was talking about those murders.'

I said, 'I shall go to his trial. And when they hang him I shall go and stand outside Newgate. It seems the least I can do for Kate.'

I went home to rest for an hour. Valentine was in the kitchen making tea.

He'd been down to Christmas's laundry to pick up his shirt collars.

He said, 'I hear there was a big turnout.'

I said, 'Plenty of gawkers along the way, but only six of us at the graveside. It was nicely done though. Earth to earth, ashes to ashes, all that.'

'Dust to dust. Go and put your feet up and I'll bring the teapot through. I have good news for you. I've found us a daily.'

He said she'd come to the door and proposed herself for the position.

I said, 'But how did she even know there is a position?'

'Because she's Ethel Peck. She's Olive's cousin. I suppose the whole family knows Olive's given her notice. Ethel works for the Warlords, across the road. Remember Olive saying?'

'We can't steal servants from the neighbours.'

'No, we won't be stealing. Ethel only goes to the Warlords on Mondays, to help with their laundry. They have two live-ins for everything else. She said she has two gentlemen she does for in Haggerston but she can easily alter her hours to suit. So what do you think?'

'I should have to take a look at her. Does she have a testimonial?'

He said, 'I don't know. I spoke to her on the doorstep for five minutes. But I don't think Mr Warlord would employ her if she didn't have a good character, do you?'

Valentine was very keen, but of course his main concern was his shirts.

I said I'd think about it.

He said, 'Well think quick because I see her just coming out of the Warlords'. Shall I ask her to step across the road?'

Ethel might have been Olive's cousin, but she was a horse of a very different hue: much older, twenty-five at least. She had big red hands and a sharp eye. The first thing she said was, 'Your door brasses could do with a buffing.'

And the first thing I thought was, 'She'll expect higher wages than I paid Olive.'

I said, 'There's not a lot of work. Mr St John and I are tidy people and we go out to our work most evenings.'

She said, 'Your mantel shelf needs dusting. I'm very reliable. I have the reputation of giving satisfaction.'

'You know the circumstances of Olive leaving us?'

'Oh yes. Because of the murder.'

'Because I was acquainted with Mrs Eddowes.'

'That makes no difference to me.'

'Olive's father has no say over what you do?'

'No he don't! He's just my uncle. He's a one man Watch Committee, that one. Anyhow, no man has any say over what I do.'

Well then I began to warm to Ethel.

I said, 'I'd need you in the afternoons, to do a bit of cleaning and lay up my supper tray.'

'And take my shirts to the laundry,' says Valentine.

She said, 'This place needs a good bottoming first. I don't think

Olive was very thorough. I'll get it up to scratch for you. But I must tell you I don't work on Sundays.'

Valentine said, 'Church?'

'No,' she said. 'I go out on my safety bicycle. Me and my friends. We're a club.'

I'd been paying Olive one shilling and nine pence a week, not found, though heaven knows she'd enjoyed plenty of tea and toast and cake at my expense. I estimated Ethel would be looking for half a crown a week. We settled at two shillings and threepence, and no Sundays.

30

The Britannia in Hoxton is a big theatre though you wouldn't think it to look at it from the outside. From the street you might think it was still just a tavern but step inside and you'll find it very commodious, very well appointed. Mrs Lane runs it since her husband passed away and I'll say this for her. She's not afraid to spend money to keep it up to scratch. The only thing is, you only play one house, because she likes to put on one of her melodramas, halfway through the show. It's something a bit different, I suppose. Not to my taste, but there we are. Mrs Lane appears in them sometimes too. She must be sixty if she's a day, but she's spry.

There were some familiar faces – Betsy Ash, Dickie Dabney and his Crows, Stefan the Mentalist – and a couple of new ones – a skirt-dancer called Penny, and Il Gran' Orsone, Lyric Baritone. And then there were the actors for Mrs Lane's dramatics. They like to keep themselves apart. For some reason they consider themselves superior to people who can actually sing and dance and make people laugh. They were doing a piece called *The Brigand's Promise*.

Monty turned up.

I said, 'The face is familiar but the name escapes me.'

'Highly comical,' he says. 'I just wanted to let you know I'm back.'

'How was Herne Bay?'

'Refreshing.'

'And how's Mother?'

'Bearing up. You not got your face on yet?'

'Plenty of time for that. I'm not on till after the skit.'

'It's not a skit, Dot,' he says. 'It's a one-act play.'

'Well, whatever it is, it goes on twice as long as it should do and I don't start powdering my face until the brigand gets stabbed and commences his ten-minute death scene. Are you staying till the end of the show?'

'Yes.'

I said, 'Good. You can buy me supper.'

'Bullen deserted you, has he? Gone home to his wife?'

I said, 'No, my daily deserted me so there'll be no tray laid for me when I get home tonight. Anyway, it's been a while since you treated me.'

'I'll take you to dinner,' he says, 'but no hangers-on, no cadgers. Just you and me.'

I couldn't think what he meant.

I said, 'What cadgers? I don't have any hangers-on.'

'You know who I mean,' he says. 'The pair you had me take to Stott's that time. The dossers.'

Kate and John Kelly.

I said, 'You haven't heard?'

'Heard what?'

'Kate's dead. You won't have realised. She was the one who was murdered on Mitre Square.'

'No!' he says. 'Are you sure?'

That's what everybody said when they heard. 'Are you sure?'

I said, 'Of course I'm sure. I saw her in the mortuary. I never saw anybody so dead. You must have read what he did to her. Or don't they have papers in Herne Bay?'

He sat down.

'Oh don't say any more! That was her? Who went with us to Stott's?'

'I went to her burying this afternoon.'

The whole dressing room had fallen silent. Monty looked rather small and very pale all of a sudden.

'Oh my!' he kept saying. 'Oh my! What a shock.'

I offered him some of my Quieting Syrup but he wouldn't take it.

I said, 'I don't know why you're taking on so. You only saw her once in your life.'

'But I sat as near to her as I am to you.'

'Yes, and called her a dosser two minutes ago.'

'I ate a veal chop dinner with her. She was very personable. A lively conversationalist. Quite surprising really. It must have shaken you, Dot. It must have shaken you to the core.'

'It did and it still has. But you can still buy me a fish supper.'

He went to the pit to watch the rest of the show. As soon as he'd gone, they all started up. How did I know Kate Eddowes? Was it true there'd been an image of the killer on her dead eyes? Had he really sliced off her nose? Were her gizzards really draped around her throat like a necklace?

I said, 'I'm not talking about her wounds. You can read about them for yourselves. Kate lived across the street from me, thirty years ago. She was a fine-looking girl and she did pretty well for herself. Then she got the taste for drink and lost it all. That's as much as I'm saying. May she rest in peace.'

Betsy Ash said, 'Quite right. And for those of you who haven't worked with Miss Allbones before, when she ties that Indian shawl under her chin and starts powdering, woe to anybody who speaks to her.'

She tapped me on the shoulder.

'You all right, Dot?' she said. 'I thought Monty Hyams was going to faint when you told him about your friend. Did you see how pale he turned?'

'I did. Who'd have thought he was such a sensitive soul? You know he goes out on patrol, with this Vigilance Committee they've set up? I hope he's not the one to find the next body. It'd unhinge him.'

'Do you think there'll be another one?'

'Why not? Why would he stop?'

'My Reggie predicts the murderer will put an end to himself. They do that sometimes, when they wake up to what they've done, or if they think the game's nearly up. Or he might move on to a different place, with the police being all over Whitechapel. Reggie predicts he might start killing somewhere else.'

The Hon. Reggie Scrope-Lyttleton is one of Betsy's followers.

I said, 'Monty's going to be in a quandary now. He could dine out on this for years. "The Mitre Square murder? Knew the woman well. Had supper with her not long before she died." But of course people have Kate down for a prossie and he won't want them thinking he kept that kind of company. Particularly if it might get back to his mother. So what's he to do?'

'I see what you mean,' says Betsy. 'Poor Monty.'

Poor Monty took me to the refreshment salon after the end of the show. It was the first time I'd seen it since it was renovated. Pink walls, gold and white woodwork, new crystal lamps. Very elegant. They do a nice skate fried in butter.

He said, 'I've only been gone a week but a lot seems to have happened.'

I said, 'I'm not talking about Kate so don't ask me.'

'I appreciate that.'

'I've had enough of people picking over it.'

'Of course you have.'

'I'm thinking of going away for a few days. After I've played Gatti's. I've got a week off.'

'Good idea. Get a bit of sea air. Herne Bay is very pleasant.'

'I'm sure it is but I'm going to Wolverhampton, to see my Albert. How's the Authentic Warrior Maiden? She still indisposed?'

'Why do you ask?'

'Just curious. How many weeks has it been? You must be wondering whether to keep her on your books. You know? It's not like you to hang onto dead wood.'

'You never liked her.'

'Nobody liked her. Nothing about her to like. You got anyone else lined up?'

'I'm on the lookout. I think the interest in Strong Women acts might have peaked. Male impersonators are the coming thing. Girls in trousers.'

I said, 'I could do that. I have the build for it.'

'No, *girls*, Dot,' he says. 'Not ladies of your years. By the way, I should tell you I'm thinking of leaving Berner Street. Since all this to-do.'

'I heard Mr Simkin was attacked.'

'Mr Simkin. The woman killed in Dutfield's Yard. And then there's all those revolutionaries at the Socialist Club. I'm afraid it's not the neighbourhood it used to be.'

'Will you move your mother as well?'

'Of course. I won't sell. A murder is very deleterious to property values. I'll put tenants in for the time being. You might think of it, Dot. My house or Mother's. It'd be much handier for the theatres than where you are now. Think what you'd save on cabs.'

'No thank you. I'm happy where I am. So where will you go? Herne Bay?'

'No, Newington Green.'

'Sounds very countrified.'

'Not exactly, but it's nice. It's peaceful. No murders.'

'I'll bet there are. Only they'll be done behind lace curtains, not up dark back yards. But what about your high holidays? Won't it be a long way to come in to Duke Street?'

'I won't need to. There's a new synagogue on Poets' Road. Very handy.'

'I saw your church, when I went to see where Kate was killed. Valentine pointed it out to me.'

'I suppose she was engaged in a bit of business.'

'Hardly matters now, does it?'

'It's a dangerous trade, especially with this slasher on the loose. If these women will go out at night they know what they're risking.'

'They do. And I'm sure some of them must be thinking of changing their profession. Going into shopkeeping, or running an alehouse. Nice indoor work. Particularly if it's a wet night and you've got a hole in your boot.'

'I believe I detect a note of sarcasm.'

'I believe you do. But you know you called it "business", what Kate might have been doing that night, and when you think about it, it *is* a business. There's always men who need seeing to, lonely men who can't find a sweetheart, and there's always hungry women who'll do it for a consideration. It seems a fair exchange. Wouldn't you say?'

'How's your fish?' he says. 'The trouble with skate is you have to be very careful of the bones.'

31

I went back to Golden Lane on Thursday morning. Tom came along limping.

I said, 'What happened to you?'

'Tell you in a minute,' he says. 'Let's get inside first and grab a seat.'

Kate's inquest was due to resume at ten o'clock. Tom thought it was all likely to be over by four.

I said, 'Lizzie Stride's is still going on.'

Tom said, 'That's because there's more to be investigated. All those people who're convinced they saw her with a fellow. All those people trampling around Dutfield's Yard. And then, was it the same villain who did Kate Eddowes in? They still can't decide.'

'What, could there really have been two cut-throats about on the same night?'

'That's what some people think. Not that I agree with them, of course. It's clear to me it was one and the same fellow. He got interrupted, when Diemschutz's cart came rattling into the yard. Another five minutes and he'd have had Lizzie Stride's parts cut out. That might have satisfied him. He might have gone home after that and Kate Eddowes'd still be this side of the clay. But they have to consider all possibilities at an inquest, Dot. They have to be thorough. So, about my ankle. I injured it, in the line of duty you might say. Guess where I went yesterday.'

'Home? To give Mrs Bullen a surprise?'

'Now, now,' he says. 'My wife sees as much of me as she wishes to. No, I was in Epping Forest, getting hunted by sleuth hounds. There's a chap in Loughton breeds them, so I went out there to find out about them. I had to go ahead through the brushwood for about ten minutes, and then he let loose this hound, to see if she could find me.'

'Why?'

'Because there's talk of them bringing in bloodhounds, if there should be another murder. Warren's very interested, apparently. He's been given a demonstration of what they can do, in Hyde Park. So I thought I should look into it. It'd make a good piece for the dailies.'

'And did the dog find you?'

'She did. I leapt a brook, to see if that'd throw her off. That's when I turned my ankle.'

'But she found you anyway.'

'Yes. Very impressive. She did stop, when she got to the brook, but as soon as they loosed her she crossed the water and she was onto me in no time. Fine animal. Soft as butter. And I never heard her coming, she didn't make a sound till she'd found me. Then you should have heard her.'

'Like Fritz's Yodelling Dachshunds?'

'Something like.'

'So will they bring dogs in, if there's another murder?'

'That's the question. They say tracking a man along a pavement is a different matter altogether. But it seems to me there's nothing to be lost by trying it.'

I saw Kate's Annie come into the courtroom, and John Kelly. There were a lot of police in court too. Then Mr Langham, the coroner, came in and they started. The first to be called was Dr Sequeira. He had very little to say. Only that Kate would have died the instant her throat was cut, and that she wasn't long dead when he examined her just before two o'clock. Annie was next. She confirmed that Kate was her mother and that her father was Thomas Conway. She didn't know whether they had ever been married.

The Coroner asked her when she'd last seen her father. Eighteen months, she thought. He'd been living with her and her husband but they'd parted on bad terms and she had no idea where he was to be found. He hadn't lived with Kate for many years. He was a teetotaller and wouldn't stay with Kate because of her drinking.

Tom whispered, 'An Irish teetotaller. You don't get many of them to the pound.'

The Coroner asked her what work Tom Conway did.

'A hawker,' she said.

'Of what?'

'All sorts. Whatever he could get. And he had an army pension.'

'What was his regiment?'

'I think it was the 18th Royal Irish. But I did hear talk of the Connaught Rangers.'

Up popped Crawford, the solicitor. 'Mr Langham,' he said. 'The Connaught Rangers is the 88th. Perhaps the witness has confused the two?'

'I wouldn't know,' said Annie. 'It was before I was born.'

You could see she was losing patience with the questions. What was any of it to do with her mother's murder? Nobody with an ounce of sense thought Tom Conway had done it.

Mr Langham scratched his ear.

He said, 'Did your mother ever ask you for money?'

'Yes.'

'When did you last see her?'

'Two years ago and one month.'

'That's very precise.'

'I know it exactly because she looked after me during my confinement. I paid her for her help.'

'Did you ever receive letters from her?'

'No.'

'You have brothers and sisters?'

'Two brothers. They went with my father.'

'Do you know their whereabouts?'

'No.'

'Do you know John Kelly?'

'Yes. I know my mother lived with him as his wife.'

'So you lost all contact with your mother, your father and your brothers?'

'I know where my mother is now,' said Annie, quite sharp. I saw a flash of Kate in her then. Crawford scowled at her but the Coroner let it pass. There were no further questions. A constable from Bishopsgate was the next to give evidence.

On the night in question, on the Saturday evening, PC Robinson had been on his beat along Aldgate High Street and come upon a crowd that had gathered around a woman who was sitting on the pavement.

'You have identified her as the deceased?'

'Yes. I asked if anyone knew her name or where she lived but received no reply. I propped her up against the shutters of the furniture shop but she was unable to stay upright and fell to the side.'

'You assumed she was drunk?'

'She smelled of drink.'

I saw John Kelly hang his head.

'How did you proceed?'

'I signalled with my lamp and another constable came to my assistance.'

'Which constable?'

'PC Sturgeon. We took the woman to Bishopsgate police station. She refused to give her name to the custody sergeant. She was put into a cell.'

'Is the custody sergeant here?'

'Yes. Sergeant Byfield.'

'We'll hear from him. Step down.'

Sergeant Byfield said Kate had been brought into the station at a quarter to nine, so drunk she couldn't stand. He'd kept her in a cell until one o'clock.

'It was up to you when she would be released?'

'Yes. I don't keep people longer than I need to. She'd slept off the drink and was awake by half past midnight. She asked me when she should be released and I told her when she was fit to take care of herself. She said she was capable so we brought her up from the cells just before one o'clock.'

'At this point you ascertained her name?'

'She gave it as Mary Kelly, and her address as Fashion Street.'

'All false information.'

'Yes. She asked me the time. I told her it was too late for her to buy more drink. She laughed and said she'd be in trouble when she got home.'

'Did you see what direction she took when she left the police station?'

'Towards Houndsditch.'

'In the opposite direction to the address she had supplied.'

'I suppose it was.'

'There is no supposing about it.'

'I thought nothing of it at the time.'

'And did the deceased say anything more to you?'

'She said, "Good night, my old cocker. Tararabit."'

That caused a laugh. It took a minute or two for the court to settle down. The night watchman from Kearley and Tonge's warehouse gave evidence next. He said he'd had the street door onto Mitre Square ajar for several hours, it being a mild evening. He'd been sweeping near the open door and expecting PC Watkins to call in for his tea can, but he'd heard nothing until Watkins raised the alarm.

'What did PC Watkins say to you?'

'He called out, "For Gawd's sake help me, mate. There's another woman been cut to pieces."'

'What did you do?'

'I went with him across the square and saw the body. Then I ran up Mitre Street towards Aldgate, blowing my whistle.'

'You had a whistle but PC Watkins did not?'

'I have mine from when I served with the Metropolitan Police. A whistle is a very useful thing.'

'Indeed. Perhaps we should all carry them. Did you see any suspicious persons about?'

'None, except two constables. Not that they were suspicious, of course. I mean to say they were the only persons I saw.'

'And you informed them a body had been found?'

'Yes. I brought them to the place where the body lay. Then I went back to my post.'

Tom whispered, 'Now, Langham, it's time for a recess. I have to answer a call of nature.'

And as if he'd read Tom's mind, the Coroner took out his watch.

'What else have we?' he said.

'Two possible witnesses,' says the clerk, 'and then the matter of the writing.'

'Ah yes,' says Mr Langham, 'the writing. We'll resume at two o'clock.'

By the time Tom had done what he had to do and hobbled as far as the Hat and Feathers, it was nearly time for him to hobble back.

I said, 'What's this about writing?'

'Found on a wall in Goulston Street on the Sunday morning.'

'What did it say?'

'Something about Jews.'

'Will the jury have to go out to see it?'

'Nothing for them to see. It was wiped clean. Langham'll have something to say about that, I'll wager.'

★

The witnesses were called first. A cigarette salesman called Lavender and a Mr Levy, a butcher, friends who'd been out together that Saturday night. Mr Lavender gave his account first. He was a Pole but his English was very clear. He said he and Mr Levy and another friend had been at the Imperial Club until half past one.

'The Imperial Club is where?'

'On Duke Street, sir.'

'What is its nature?'

'It's a social club.'

'A Jewish club?'

'Yes.'

'Continue.'

'As we left the club I noticed a man and woman talking at the corner of Church Passage, where it leads into Mitre Square.'

'Did you recognise the deceased as that woman?'

'I can't swear to it. She had her back turned to me. But I was shown her clothes and I think they're the same.'

'And the man? You have described him to the police?'

'To the best of my ability. He was taller than the woman. Not well dressed. And he wore a hat. A cloth cap, I think.'

'Would you recognise him again?'

'I doubt it.'

'Did you hear anything they said?'

'Nothing.'

'Did there seem to be any quarrel between them?'

'No.'

'And you didn't observe them to see where they went?'

'I had no reason to.'

*

Mr Levy had nothing more to add to Mr Lavender's account. He said he hadn't looked closely at the couple because he guessed what they were up to. That caused some sniggering.

The Coroner said, 'You were more concerned for your own safety, perhaps?'

'Not exactly,' says Mr Levy. A fair enough answer. What sensible person goes around examining everybody they see on street corners? At half past one in the morning he wants to get to his own bed.

And so they came to the business about some writing on a wall and a piece of cloth.

I said to Tom, 'Is this anything to do with Kate?'

'The cloth is,' he said. 'The writing? I'm not so sure.'

A constable from the Metropolitan Police was called on. PC Long. Tom didn't know him. First time for everything.

He said, 'There's a lot of new faces been brought in, since Annie Chapman's murder. This one's from A Division, apparently. Whitehall.'

PC Long had been on his beat along Goulston Street at three o'clock on the Sunday morning and found a rag with blood on it. It fitted the piece cut from Kate's apron and had been brought to the inquest, to be shown to the jury.

The Coroner began his questioning.

'You found the piece of cloth on the pavement?'

'No, it was by the foot of the tenement stairs, and the writing was on the wall in the passage to the building.'

'We'll come to the writing in due course. So the piece of cloth was not in clear view of anyone walking along the street?'

'No, not really.'

'You had passed that way before on your beat. How much time had passed?'

'Half an hour. Perhaps a bit longer.'

'It's possible the piece of apron was already there but you failed to notice it?'

'I'm sure it wasn't.'

'What did you do next? After you noticed there was blood on the cloth?'

'I shone my lantern around the staircases, to see if anyone was injured.'

'How many staircases are there?'

'Six, I think. I searched them all from bottom to top. Then I took the piece of cloth to Commercial Street police station.'

'You were aware that two women had been murdered?'

'I'd heard there was a body found at Mitre Square. There was talk there had been another killing but it wasn't confirmed.'

'Now about the writing. When did you discover it?'

'After I found the cloth. When I was casting about with my lamp.'

'What did the writing say?'

'The Jews are the men who will not be blamed for nothing.'

'You are certain?'

'I wrote it in my pocket-book.'

'You have the pocket-book here?'

'No. It's at King Street.'

'Why?'

'Because I'm generally with A Division, sir.'

The Coroner was growing impatient.

'Have it fetched. In the meanwhile, Constable Long, tell us about the style of the writing. Was it done in a clear hand?'

'Quite clear, sir. In chalk.'

'Did it appear to be freshly done?'

'I could not form an opinion.'

The Jews are the men who will not be blamed for nothing.

What did it mean? It didn't make any sense to me.

'When you took the cloth to Commercial Street, did you leave the place on Goulston Street unattended?'

'No, I left it guarded by the constable who came onto the beat to relieve me.'

'Guarded from the front? What about the rear?'

'I didn't know there was a rear. It was my first time on that beat.'

A detective from the City of London Police was called. Dan Halse.

Tom whispered, 'Hold on to your hat. Now there'll be ructions.'

Detective Halse said he had been on duty with several plain-clothes officers in the early hours of Sunday morning. When they heard that a body had been found in Mitre Square, they had dispersed to search the surrounding streets. He himself had gone up Middlesex Street and then back along Goulston Street.

Tom whispered, 'Off his patch. That's the Met's territory.'

'From Goulston Street I came to the mortuary. I then accompanied Major Smith to Mitre Square to view the site of the murder.'

'Perhaps you had better identify Major Smith to the jury?'

'Major Smith is our Acting Police Commissioner. When we got to Mitre Square, someone told us that a piece of apron had been found on Goulston Street, stained with blood. I went there directly and saw the writing. I asked for it to be photographed but I was over-ruled by the Metropolitan Police. They said the writing must be removed at once before people were on the street. I think they feared a riot against the Jewish people. There's a Jewish market on Middlesex Street and Goulston Street on Sunday mornings.'

'You made a note of what was written?'

'I did. The Juwes – the word was misspelt – the Juwes are not the men who will be blamed for nothing.'

'Your version differs from Constable Long's.'

'I have my pocket-book here.'

'Did you protest at the removal of the writing?'

'Very strongly. I felt it should be photographed first.'

'When was it removed?'

'At about half past five. It was starting to get light. People were bringing out their market barrows.'

One of the jurymen asked why enquiries hadn't been made, door to door, around the Goulston Street dwelling house.

Detective Halse said, 'They were, by City detectives, but by then two hours had passed since the Met constable had found the blood-stained cloth.'

The Coroner said, 'Well as the writing was so zealously removed, we cannot verify either Detective Halse's note of it or Constable Long's. I see no need of any further adjournment. Members of the jury, I will be happy to refresh your memories on any salient points. Otherwise I presume you will return a verdict of wilful murder by a person or persons unknown.'

The jury foreman said they were agreed on that. They were all eager to collect their fee and be off. Tom seemed dejected.

He said, 'I thought Sam Langham would have had more to say about the writing being scrubbed off. It was done too hastily.'

'Do you think it matters? Do you think the murderer wrote it?'

'We'll never know now, will we? Long said it looked fresh, but he wasn't familiar with Goulston Street. A local bobby might have been able to say if it was new. The thing about Goulston Street is there's things written everywhere. *Forward to the Revolution. Ireland for the Irish. Sarah Jane'll play your bagpipes for a penny.* The whole bloody street needs scrubbing. But the point is that writing shouldn't have been taken down before it had been photographed. Now they can't even agree what it actually said.'

'Who ordered it to be done?'

'Abberline probably. Somebody at Leman Street. But it might have come from higher up. Could have been Warren himself.'

'Why?'

'To remind the City bobbies whose parish they were on. To remind them who was in charge. And that's the trouble, Dot. They should be working together to catch this villain, not quarrelling over whose yard they're playing in.'

I said, 'They should bring in some women. They'd get the job done.'

He laughed. 'Women bobbies!' he said. 'I suppose you think we should have them in Parliament too? God help us. They'd spend all their time comparing bonnets. Nothing would ever get done.'

The Coroner wound things up. Catherine Eddowes, wilfully murdered by a person or persons unknown.

*

On Saturday night, Tom and Monty's paths happened to cross. Tom had come by hoping to avail himself of my hospitality after the show. Monty had come to collect my box money from Mrs Lane. He had a look about him: *I know something you don't know*.

He said, 'So, Bullen, it seems like this villain might be on the move again.'

Tom grunted.

Monty said, 'Unless he's kidding us. He could be. Or even it could be somebody else. It could be an imposter. Some people have strange ideas of fun and games. '

Another grunt from Tom.

I said, 'What's this then, Monty? You sitting on a story?'

'Just the new postcard,' he said. 'The one that George Lusk got yesterday.'

'Who's George Lusk?'

Tom jumped in. 'The fellow who dreamed up the Whitechapel Vigilantes. Shopkeepers playing at coppers.'

Betsy Ash was changing her stockings, listening in.

She said, 'I didn't see anything in tonight's paper about a postcard. Have you missed a trick there, Tom?'

'No,' he said. I could tell he was rattled. 'I haven't missed anything. But sometimes there's good reason to hold back news. The papers don't always publish everything they know as soon as they know it. They wait till they're in possession of the facts.'

Monty said, 'Except most of the time they go ahead and publish whether they're in possession of the facts or not.'

Tom refused to say if he'd seen the postcard sent to George Lusk.

He said, 'I'm afraid I'm not at liberty to comment.'

Monty said, 'Really? Well I've seen the card and nobody's told me I can't speak about it. It said he knows he's got us worried and he'll give us good reason when he's not so busy. Something like that. A threat. So you be careful, Betsy, and you, Dot. I reckon he's getting ready for another spree.'

I've never known Tom Bullen so quiet as that night. He stayed in my bed but there were no melting moments. He was like an empty gas bag.

I said, 'You all right? What's ailing you tonight?'

'I'm very tired, Dot,' he said. 'It's been a busy week.'

Of course I knew what it was. Monty had seen something he hadn't even known about. And him supposed to be the newshound! I'm afraid I needled him over it.

I said, 'Funny that man Lusk getting a postcard. Do you know him?'

'Oh yes,' he said. 'We all know Lusk. He's a builder. Very full of himself. Well you'd have to be, wouldn't you? Going round setting up committees. Sending mother's boys like Monty Hyams out on patrol. What a joke. But George Lusk thinks he's the dog's diddles. I daresay he's enjoying these murders. I daresay he's hoping to make a name for himself. He probably wrote that postcard himself.'

'Why would he do that?'

'To make himself seem more important than he is. So people won't forget his committee. So they'll think his vigilantes are worth a candle. Wake me early, sweetheart. I'll be a different man in the morning.'

32

Ethel commenced working for us the following Tuesday. I wasn't in the best of moods. I'd hurt my back on the Sunday being obliged to empty my own bath tub.

I said, 'Are you sure you can't give me two hours on a Sunday afternoon?'

'Oh no,' she said. 'I must have my Sundays off. Now this week I'll do all your picture rails and I'll black the grates and the kitchen range. It looks to me as though Olive had been letting things go.'

Valentine pulled a face. He whispered, 'I don't think we'll be having any tea parties with this one.'

He was appearing at the Old Mo on Drury Lane, engaged for two weeks.

I said, 'Very nice. If you keep getting engagements like that I'll have to consider putting your rent up. Or are you still threatening to go to America?'

'Yes,' he said. 'Well no, not really. I mean it is tempting, but it'd be very hard to leave all my friends. Starting afresh, not knowing anybody.'

'What about Dr Moneybags?'

'Frank's a busy man, Miss Dot. I couldn't expect him to look after me.'

'You don't seem to see him so much these days.'

'We see each other when it's convenient,' he says. 'And I'd have thought you'd be glad. You've never had a fair word to say about him.'

I guessed then that the shine had gone off the friendship but I didn't say anything more.

I was at Gatti's, Charing Cross, for the week. I was out of the habit of working so far west. It can take an age to get home. But I did have a small affection for Gatti's because it was one of the first proper engagements Albert got for me when we came to London.

Gatti's have two establishments, the small one at Villiers Street and a bigger one in Southwark. I remember Albert making enquiries, telling them my history and which theatres had engaged me up in Brum. They said they'd take a look at me and it was so cold I went on in my coat and muffler. I did two verses of 'What's the Use?' and the chairman said, 'Yes, quite nice. You can start on Monday week. We'll try you out on the dog.'

By which he meant the Villiers Street establishment.

That was when? 1870, 1871? A long, long time ago. And now I'm back there.

I said to Monty, 'Valentine's working on Drury Lane and I'm back in a fleapit. This isn't progress.'

He said, 'Gatti's is not a fleapit. And Valentine St John is a different class of artiste. Operatic almost. You're better suited to somewhere like Gatti's. It's a nice, intimate space. It doesn't put such a strain on your voice.'

My voice is as strong as it ever was.

He says, 'You have to appreciate, Dot, we're none of us getting any younger.'

He said he'd come down on Tuesday evening, to see second house.

'I'll buy you a chocolate ice afterwards,' he said, as though that was recompense. In the event, he didn't turn up anyway and neither did Tom. I shared a hansom with Mr Sylvester, the Canadian tenor, a perfect gentleman. He insisted on seeing me right to my door although it was quite out of his way. He said he prayed the Whitechapel fiend would be apprehended before the winter set in because the murders had made his wife so fearful she wouldn't step outside after dark, even in Camden Town.

The gas mantle was burning in the front hall, my supper tray was nicely laid out and covered with a tea cloth, and the parlour grate was gleaming. Ethel had come up to expectations. The only thing was she tidied up so thoroughly I couldn't find the evening paper. Since the murders, Valentine generally brings in the *Evening News* before he goes to the theatre and leaves it for me at the foot of the stairs. It was only when I went to make myself a cup of cocoa that I thought to look in the sack tied up ready for the vestry van.

It was as well I found it. It contained several stories I shouldn't have liked to miss and the first that caught my eye was that Tom Conway had been found. He'd turned up at the police station in Old Jewry with his two boys. Said he'd only just learned that it was Kate who'd been killed in Mitre Square. He'd told the police that he and Kate had lived apart for eight years, on account of her intemperate habits. He had seen her once or twice when they first parted, but then he'd shifted Pimlico way, so as not to encounter her. The police had judged Conway to be a man of exemplary character and sent him on his way.

There was a piece about bloodhounds too. It said that a great deal of nonsense was talked about scent hounds by people who are wholly ignorant of the matter. There was no by-line but I saw Tom's hand in that. An hour getting chased through Epping Forest and he fancies himself quite the expert. The article said a hound must be trained up from a puppy to whatever kind of work will be required of it. If a hound is to work on city streets it must be trained on city streets.

Then there was a story I nearly missed. It was at the bottom of a page. A lodging house was believed to be under observation, in connection with the Whitechapel murders, after information had been received from a German landlady. On the Sunday morning Kate and Lizzie Stride were found, one of the landlady's gentlemen lodgers had come in in the early hours and disturbed her sleep, moving about in his room and packing his valise. She had risen, to see what all the noise was about, and the lodger had told her he was going away, which he was in the habit of doing from time to time in the course of his business. He had left his laundry for her to have ready for him when he came back. When she undid the laundry bundle, she'd found a shirt, stained with blood on its cuffs. Her neighbours had persuaded her to report the matter to the police, which she had eventually done when it began to seem that the lodger might not return. The house was now being watched by plain-clothes detectives.

I kept the page out to show Valentine the next morning. He didn't appear to be very interested.

I said, 'Didn't Frank Townsend lodge with a German lady?'

'He did,' he says. 'For a while. They don't say what street though, do they? There's an awful lot of German landladies around. So is that what the police call an undercover operation? They tell the press what they're up to so the press can put it in the papers? How cock-eyed is that? Now the lodger'll have read it and if he has anything to hide he'll never go back – not even for his laundry.'

'Perhaps it wasn't the police who told the press. Perhaps it was the landlady.'

'I daresay your friend would know the answer to that.'

I said, 'I don't know. Tom doesn't always have his finger on the pulse, not like he used to.'

I left a note for Ethel, not to throw out the evening paper in future. She left me a reply. She'd crossed out my words and written, *WEREN'T ME. E. PECK*

I didn't see Monty until Thursday evening.

I said, 'You're two days late.'

'Sorry about that,' he said. 'A few things cropped up. But I've got some very good news, Dot. The Paragon.'

Well!

'A definite engagement?'

'Third week of November.'

'Did somebody die?'

'What if they did? Are you happy?'

I did no more than put my powder puff down and give him a big kiss.

'Steady on,' he said. 'You'll have people talking. So, have you seen Tom Bullen since Tuesday?'

'Why?'

'I thought he might have said something to you, about what's happened.'

'No. What has happened?'

'I'm not sure how much I should tell you.'

I said, 'It's entirely up to you, Monty. If you can't speak about whatever it is, I certainly won't press you to tell me.'

'Still, I know you're not one to tittle-tattle, Dot.'

'I'm not. And I think whatever it is you'd better spit it out before you choke on it.'

'Well,' he says. 'George Lusk received a parcel. And you'll never guess what was in it.'

'Go on then.'

'A body part.'

One of the Daring Damzelles let out a scream. Well, more of a squeak.

'Mr Hyams,' she says, 'did you say what I thought you said?'

'Not to be repeated, Sadie,' he says. 'You shouldn't even have been listening. Now you must promise it'll go no further than these four walls.'

'It won't,' she said, 'but I'm not Sadie, Mr Hyams. I'm Phyllis. Was it a woman's part?'

He went from pink to scarlet in short order.

I said, 'Well? Was it?'

'No. According to the letter that came with it, it was a kidney. Half a kidney. The sender said he took it from, you know, your friend . . .'

Monty dropped his voice. 'He says he ate the other half.'

'Oh my good God,' says Phyllis. 'Now I'm going to cat.'

I said, 'Then go outside to do it, away from my gowns and private conversations.'

George Lusk had received a package, through the post, with a letter and half a kidney.

I said, 'Did it look like a kidney?'

'It was hard to say. It smelled pretty rank.'

'What did the letter say?'

'Just what I've told you. Where he got the kidney and all that. And that he might send Lusk another package, with the knife.'

'Was it signed "Jack" like the other letter?'

'No, it was signed "Catch Me When You Can".'

'Lusk took it to the police, of course.'

'Not yet. He took it to his doctor first, to Dr Wiles on Mile End Road, to see if it was a genuine kidney, and Dr Wiles said it was but it could have come from any butcher's slab, so now he's taken it, Dr Wiles that is, to the London Hospital, to a Dr Openshaw. He's a great expert in such things, apparently.'

'I've heard Tom speak of him.'

'Dr Wiles said Openshaw'll be able to say if it's human or from some other creature.'

'What a horrible thing to find when you open your post. Is there a Mrs Lusk?'

'Oh yes, and a number of children too. But Lusk kept it from them, of course. Just some of us from the committee saw it. We meet at the Crown, in the back room. That was why I didn't get to see you on Tuesday.'

'Was it bloody?'

'Not at all. It looked quite dried up. I didn't touch it though. As Joe Aarons rightly said, we have to assume it wasn't kosher.'

'Kosher? You don't usually bother about all that.'

'I do. A bit.'

'What about the veal chops you like when we go to Stott's?'

He had no answer to that.

'Anyway,' he says, 'I never touched it. And I'll tell you something, if this fellow really ate half of it as he says he did then he's no Jew.'

We shared a cab. The driver said Commercial Street was closed because of a fire and, sure enough, as we came up Aldgate, we could see the glow of it. We dropped Monty at the top of Berner Street then cut up through New Road to Whitechapel Road. Valentine was home before me.

'Did you see the fire?' he says. 'I caught a tram as far as Liverpool Street, thought I'd pick up a growler at the station but when I saw the flames I walked round to take a look. It's a warehouse burning, opposite St Jude's. Furs. You might be able to get yourself a new fox tippet, nice and cheap. Slightly water-damaged.'

'How did it start?'

'No idea. There were people inside but I think they got them all out. The flames were right up to the roof though. The whole street was blocked with steamers but half of them weren't pumping. They weren't properly fired up. Nothing works these days. The police can't catch murderers. Fire brigade can't pump water. But I do have a cold bottle of Bolly ready for you.'

I said, 'You're very gay this evening.'

'Am I?' he says. 'Yes, I suppose I am. I've had interest from the Savoy.'

'Just interest?'

'Keen interest, I'd say. I think they definitely want me. I'm going to see Mr Edwardes next week.'

'Is the money good?'

'I'm sure it would be. I mean, the *Savoy*. It's a top venue. They have the incandescent lamps, you know.'

Electric lighting. I have heard about it. Don't ask me how it works. I don't understand it at all, but they say it's the coming thing.

Ethel had left us cold chicken and a jar of her own piccalilli. And she'd done the front step. You could have eaten your dinner off it. It seemed she was going to suit us very nicely.

I said, 'I've got a bit of news myself. The Paragon. Middle of November. Dead men's shoes but do I care?'

Valentine opened the bubbly.

He said, 'That story you were asking about? The German landlady and the bloody shirt? Turns out it was the place where Frank used to stay. Mrs Kuhr's.'

It was in the evening paper. Actually the story appeared twice. The first piece said the lodger had returned and been questioned by the police. He had given a satisfactory account of himself and been released. Then on the back page the story had changed. He wasn't a lodger at all. He was a bachelor gentleman who left his shirts with this Mrs Kuhr regularly, for laundering.

I said, 'She's changed her tune. What about him coming in late and waking her? And who drops off their laundry at three in the morning?'

He said, 'Miss Dot, I wouldn't believe anything I'm told nor anything I read. Like last night in the dressing room, they were all saying a woman had been found with her throat cut in Bermondsey. Everyone was talking about it. Turns out she'd fallen down drunk and cut her chin open. See what I mean? You can't trust anything you hear. Least of all the papers. All they care about is getting you to buy the next edition.'

I told him about Monty and the kidney. He put his knife and fork down.

'Don't say another word. You'll put me off my supper.'

But as soon as he'd finished eating, he came back to the topic.

'Was it really a kidney, do you think?'

'Monty said he saw it with his own eyes. And the doctor they took it to seemed convinced it was.'

'Jiminy Christmas, how do you send a thing like that through the post?'

'Wrapped in plenty of brown paper I suppose.'

'I'll bet it was a pig's kidney. Somebody playing a nasty prank.'

I said, 'Well if it was Kate's kidney, I hope it was her bad one he took. And if he did eat it I hope it gave him a belly ache.'

I didn't have long to wait for further information. It was all over Friday's papers.

> Half Victim's Missing Kidney Restored. Other Half Eaten By Cannibal Assassin.

Dr Openshaw had given his opinion. The item received by Mr Lusk was indeed a human kidney, a left kidney, which was what had been taken from Kate's body. It showed signs of being diseased and of having been kept *post mortem* in spirits of wine. Upon receiving this information, members of the Vigilance Committee had taken the remains of the organ, the postcard and the letter to Leman Street police station. In the light of what was known of the Mitre Square victim – that she suffered from a kidney complaint, and that one of her kidneys had been missing when her body was found – Inspector Abberline had later ordered everything to be handed to the City of London Police.

Friday's paper was all the fire and the kidney. The top three floors of Konigsberg's warehouse had been gutted, but the only person injured was a worker who'd panicked and jumped from a window rather than wait for the escape ladder to be raised. He'd smashed his ankles. Everyone else had preserved their health but lost their jobs.

The report about the kidney told me little I hadn't already learned from Monty. The wording from the postcard and the letter were given in full, a rambling scribble from someone who'd had little schooling. Couldn't spell knife, couldn't spell kidney. Dr Openshaw was quoted too. He said it was the left kidney of a female who was in the habit of drinking. To think, give a man enough of a medical education he'll be able to look at a lump of your flesh and tell you the story of your life. I don't care for the idea of it. Some stranger peering at your parts after you're dead and gone.

I said to Valentine, 'When I go, make sure they put me straight into my shroud and into the ground without delay.'

'I'll make a note of your wishes,' he says. 'Only take care not to get murdered. If you're found murdered, I think they're obliged to anatomise you. How cheerful we are today.'

Directly beneath the story of the kidney was a report of an arrest in Bermondsey. A man 'whose conduct, demeanour and appearance had given rise to great suspicion'. He was said to be an American.

I said, 'What's this, then? Has your Dr Frank been up to some mischief?'

'Miss Dot,' he says, 'do you have any idea how many Americans there are walking about the streets of London?'

'I only know of one.'

'There are many, trust me. Same as there are many German landladies and many men who wear leather aprons. This is one of the daftest stories I've ever read and, heaven knows, there have been plenty of them just lately.'

A man had been seen first outside the Grave Maurice pub on Whitechapel Road, apparently looking for commerce with a doxy. Nothing remarkable about that but two drinkers had decided to follow him on the grounds that he was funny-looking and they thought he might be the murderer.

Valentine said, 'I wonder how much ale that pair had taken? Funny-looking? What does that mean? "There's a man with jug ears. He must be up to no good. We'd better observe him."'

They'd pursued the funny-looking man to Aldgate and thought he seemed aware he was being followed because he kept stopping and pretending to look in shop windows and then had doubled back and gone down Leman Street. At some point he'd gone into a house on King Street and his followers had waited outside and seen him come out differently attired. Instead of the short frock-coat he'd been wearing, he had on a long, dark overcoat and was sporting a large moustache, such as might be stuck on with spirit gum and worn for theatricals. They described him as tall, of middle years, and American-looking.'

Valentine said, 'And American-looking? What does that mean? Did he look like Buffalo Bill?'

The man in the false moustache had then headed back towards Whitechapel Road but his followers had lost him in the fog and smoke from the fire on Commercial Street.

Valentine said, 'I reckon the fog and smoke was between their ears. And it gets worse. If you read on, it says he went across London Bridge, not to Whitechapel at all. And then he was arrested in Bermondsey. For what? Wearing a false moustache? And then it goes on to say he wasn't actually arrested. He was questioned. A different thing altogether. Nobody was arrested in Bermondsey on Thursday night. That's hard to believe. I'll tell you what, Miss Dot, let's stop wasting our eyesight on the dailies. They're full of nonsense. Let's get *Tit-Bits* instead. That's always good for a chuckle.'

But we did continue to read the dailies because Lizzie Stride's inquest was resumed, which perked up people's interest again and had us all wondering how long before there was another murder. On my way home at night I'd look out at women going along the street and feel my skin crawl. I started hurrying again, just those few steps between the cab and my front door.

Tom said the only reason for another hearing at Lizzie Stride's inquest was that there had been such confusion at first over who the woman found in Dutfield's Yard really was.

He said, 'You may recall there was a woman who claimed Lizzie Stride's body and swore it was her sister. Said she'd been a drunkard and God knows what else. Then the supposed sister turned up alive and well. A Mrs Watts. So she wanted her five minutes, to clear her character, and Wynne Baxter allowed her to say her piece and she seemed satisfied. But Baxter had a bit of fun with his summing up. "Like The Comedy of Errors," he says. "The deceased and Mrs

Watts both had the name Elizabeth. They were the same age. Both had lived in Poplar, both had lost their front teeth and had misplaced various husbands, both were reputed to suffer from epileptic seizures though there seems to be some doubt as to the veracity of that. In spite of these and many other marvellous similarities, we can now be quite satisfied that the woman killed in Dutfield's Yard was Elizabeth Stride." So that was that. Wilful murder by person or persons unknown.'

'What do you think about the kidney?'

'It seems to be the genuine article. I'd trust Openshaw's opinion.'

'Can't they find where it was posted and get a description of the man who sent it?'

'The postmark was smudged. It couldn't be properly made out.'

'So the police are no nearer to catching him.'

'It's hard to say. They might have their eye on somebody. But one thing I will say, he's getting cheekier. Killing two in one night, and then sending that kidney to Lusk. He's daring them to catch him at it, and maybe they will, next time. One of these nights he'll get too cocky and they'll nab him.'

I told him I was going away for a few days. His face fell.

'Away?' he says, like I'd told him I was going to Zulu Land.

I said, 'Just to Wolverhampton, to see my brother.'

'Why?'

'Why not?'

'I know I haven't been attentive to you lately.'

I said, 'That's not true. But you can be attentive to Mrs Bullen while I'm gone.'

'When are you going?'

'Monday.'

'Then you shall have my undivided attention on Sunday night, barring any more murders. Body and soul, I'll be yours. And see if you can't get that molly who lodges with you to stay with his American friend. So we can have the house to ourselves.'

'Valentine doesn't see so much of Townsend as he used to.'

'Tumelty.'

'Whoever. I always think of him as Townsend. You know he used to have rooms at that house where the blood-stained shirt was left?'

'I knew he lodged on Batty Street. You're sure it was that very house?'

'That's what Valentine told me and he should know.'

'Of course that was a story that changed every time you heard it. I put no great store by it myself, and neither did the police.'

'I thought they were watching the place?'

'That woman couldn't be relied on. If a witness can't get their story straight they're no use to anyone. What time are you going on Monday?'

'Nine o'clock.'

'Then I'll take you to Euston station in a cab and help you with your portmanteau.'

And so he did, though there was really no need. A porter is easy enough to find. But Tom fussed over me. First he insisted he should go to the booking office to purchase my ticket.

He said, 'You have to deal firmly with these people, Dot. Make sure they know who you are, then you won't be fobbed off or overcharged.'

He told the clerk the ticket was for Miss Dot Allbones.

'Oh yes?' says the clerk. He was so impressed he could hardly keep from yawning.

I had half an hour before the train left. I told Tom to get off to his work, but he wouldn't hear of it. I must have a bag of oranges. He must fetch me a gristle pie from the refreshment room. I must choose a novelette or two from the yellow-backs on WH Smith's bookstall. I tried *Murder or Manslaughter* as far as Wolverton, but I couldn't get on with it. To tell the truth, I'm not much of a reader. I'd as soon pretend to sleep and eavesdrop on people's conversations. If I ride on a horse tram or in a crowded growler, there's generally something I overhear that I can use in my skits.

Two ladies got in at Rugby and as they sat down one of them said, 'I wouldn't have minded so much, Bessie, but he didn't even wash it first.'

33

It was dusk by the time the train pulled into Wolverhampton. It was no great distance to Bilston Street, but blow me if I didn't get lost and have to ask the way. The old lock factory had been pulled down and there were new buildings going up. For a minute I couldn't place where I was.

The house was in darkness. I rapped on the door good and loud, twice, three times. Then I heard him coming. Albert's a terrible shuffler. He has fallen arches. He peered out at me.

I said, 'What kind of a welcome is this? I thought you'd have the flags out.'

'Dotty?' he says. 'I thought you was coming on Monday.'

I said, 'It is Monday.'

'Is it?' he says. 'Are you sure?'

He'd been sitting in the kitchen. He said he never used the front parlour.

'It's not worth warming it for one,' he said.

'How about for two?'

'Can do. Whatever you want, Dotty.'

I looked in. It smelled of damp.

He said, 'I wipe a paraffin rag over it every spring, to keep the moths out. I keep it ship-shape in case of funerals. Mine'll be the next I suppose.'

I said, 'You're a cheery soul. Well tomorrow let's bring in a bag of coal and make it cosy for the evening.'

'Anything you like, Dotty. We can get some ale in too if you like.'

'Where am I sleeping?'

'Front bedroom of course, with the new linoleum.'

'I'd have thought you'd have taken that room. It's the best room in the house.'

'I'm all right where I am. What would I want with a great big bed like that?'

'You might find a sweetheart.'

'I'm not looking for one.'

'I'll bet there's a few widows around here who'd jump at the chance.'

'And have some old besom niggling at me day and night? Not so likely. I'm all right on my tod. Same as you. I can please myself.'

'I've got a lodger now, you know. He's in the business, male soprano, so we keep the same hours. It's company sometimes, and a bit of extra money coming in.'

'That's nice,' he said. 'Dotty, are you sure it's Monday?'

He ran out for pie and mash and a jug of ale from the Crown and Cushion. I put a hot water jar in my bed. Those sheets were so damp I swear they began to steam.

We talked all evening. He told me all the changes he could think of. Biddle the grocer was gone and Daniels' the butcher, the Boot and Star had changed its name to the Gaiety and proceeded to go downhill fast.

He said, 'But I'll tell you a place that's on the up and up. The Old Prince of Wales. They go under a different name now, I'll think of it presently, and they've got new premises. They're doing all sorts, pantomimes, melodramas. If ever you thought of coming home, Dotty, I'm sure they'd engage you.'

Coming home. As if I could ever leave London. It shocked me though to see Albert, his hair white, what was left of it, and his teeth gone. He's a good age. Sixty-two or three. But I still thought of him as a young tyke. I still pictured him when he first started at Bilston Steel, handing his wages to Mam, kicking a football up and down the street on a Sunday. I was glad to see him. Everybody should have a brother like Albert.

I said, 'You never come to see me.'

'No, well, it's been a long time since I was in London. I don't think I should like it nowadays. I shouldn't know how to go about things.'

'You wouldn't need to. I'd look after you.'

'I know you would, Dotty. But I wouldn't want to be any bother.'

About eight o'clock, somebody tapped on the scullery window.

Albert said, 'You sit tight. Don't make a sound.'

He went to the back door and I heard him say, 'Yes. But she's very tired, been travelling all day. She's just gone up to bed.'

He came back in. 'Mrs Turner,' he says. 'Gagging to quiz you about Kate Eddowes.'

Mrs Turner was just the first. Albert was up and down all evening, turning neighbours away. My arrival had been noted.

He said, 'You'll have to face it tomorrow, Dotty. There'll be no avoiding it. The whole street's been a-bubble since they heard you was coming. Since they heard you knew Kate Eddowes of late.'

'But who told them?'

'Well, I was in Sutton's getting a bottle of Camp. I thought you might have got the taste for coffee drinking. Mrs Sutton asks was I expecting company so I told her you was coming up from London. "Oh that terrible place," she says. "I wouldn't go there for a sack of gold. Look what happened to the Eddowes girl. Had her heart ripped from her chest." Then, of course, I corrected her as to the particulars, because it wasn't her heart that was took at all, was it?'

'No, and Kate was no girl.'

'True, but of course there's still a few round here that remember her as a girl. Mrs Sutton says, "You seem to know a lot about it, Mr Allbones. You been studying up on it?" Which got a laugh out of everybody that was in the shop. So then I'm afraid I let slip how you'd been reacquainted with Kate Eddowes and gone to the inquest and everything. And once Mrs Sutton has any information, you might as well place an advertisement in the *Chronicle*. I'm sorry about that. I should have been more cautious. So now you know. Everybody'll want to see you.'

Of course I'd expected to be gazed at and whispered about. It's not every week a star of the London stage visits Bilston Street. But Kate was all they were interested in. Well, poor soul, I could hardly begrudge her the limelight. The least I could do was put on a good show for her. I decided they'd get no watered-down version from me. I know how to tell a story.

The only person Albert allowed into the house that first evening was his friend Ezra Dick, and he didn't ask a single thing about Kate. He just stood clutching his cap and the principal thing he wished to know was how long would I be staying. It's a difficult thing to converse with a person who has a wall-eye. He may appear to be looking at you, but you can't be sure.

I said, 'I'll probably stay till Saturday.'

'Ah,' he says, 'Saturday,' and I guessed from the way he squeezed his cap that that wasn't what he'd hoped to hear.

I said, 'Albert, do you have prior commitments?'

'No, no,' he says, 'nothing special.' But I noticed he shot a look at Mr Dick.

I said, 'But you know I might go on Friday. The trains won't be so crowded.'

'You're right,' says Mr Dick. 'They won't. They say the Saturday trains are packed like herring in a barrel.'

He seemed a happier man as soon as it was decided I'd leave on Friday, but he still wouldn't stay and take a glass of ale.

'He's a bostin chap, Ezra,' Albert said, after he'd gone. 'Always there if you need a hand but he never outstays his welcome. And he won't say a word about you still being up and about when I'd told people you were sleeping. You can depend on Ezra.'

I said, 'And what was all that about Saturday? Is that the night you two get soused?'

'Never!' says Albert. 'Ezra's Band of Hope. Total abstainer. No, it's just that the Wanderers are at home on Saturday. They're playing Derby County. I reckon he was worried I might not be able to go to the match. But you don't have to leave on account of that. I'm glad to have you here, Dotty. You're always welcome, you know that.'

'I do know. But I will go on Friday. You'll have had enough of me by then.'

He laughed.

'I'll let you know,' he said. 'Remind me again, what day is it today?'

The following morning I put on my health bustle and my peacock-blue gown and frizzed my front hair.

Albert said, 'You'll turn heads looking like that.'

I said, 'Wait till they see my hat. It's got a feather a foot high. If they're all so keen to see me I might as well give them their money's worth.'

As soon as we stepped out into the street every door seemed to open, every neighbour suddenly had a step to scrub or a duster to shake.

'Here we go,' said Albert.

The woman from number 27 was the first.

'Albert,' she said. 'I see you have a visitor.'

'My sister, Dotty,' he said. 'Come all the way from London to see how I'm going on.'

Two more women sidled up.

'This your famous visitor, Albert?'

'From London, I hear. Terrible place. All them murders.'

I said, 'Don't people get murdered in Wolverhampton? I think they do. I remember when Baggot the pawnbroker had his head staved in, and that was in his own parlour.'

'Of course the Eddowes girl was asking for trouble.'

I said, 'Do you think so?'

'Oh yes. And always did.'

'Knew her well, did you?'

'I didn't need to. I heard enough about her. Giving men the eye. Putting temptation in their way. Broke her aunt's heart.'

I said, 'Well, the years took their toll of her as they do with all of us. I doubt many men were tempted by her lately.'

I had five of them gathered.

'Acquainted with her, was you?'

'I was. I saw her just two days before she died.'

That opened wide the sluice. Had I seen her in the mortuary? What were the last words she said to me? How had she fallen so low?

I said, 'It was drink that undid her, nothing else. It cost her her husband, and her children. It'll be hard for you to comprehend. I'm sure you're all abstainers. But strong drink can pull a person down. She was a sick woman, and if that murderer hadn't put her in her grave she'd have been there soon enough anyway.'

Somebody said, 'She got above herself. She should have stayed here. Settled down.'

I told them about Mitre Square. I told them how one false turn had cost Kate her life. I even told them about Mr Lusk and the kidney.

'It just goes to show,' said one of them.

'Yes,' said another. 'The way I look at it, if she'd been in her bed like regular, decent people it wouldn't have happened to her. She should have had more sense.'

'True. If you're not there it can't happen to you. You wouldn't catch me outside at night. If I get a call of nature, I go in a pail. You never know what's lurking, even in your own back yard.'

Someone said, 'Only one thing likely to be lurking in your yard, Lil. Your old man having a crafty smoke of his pipe.'

We moved on.

Albert said, 'You realise who that was? The one who won't go out to the privy at night?'

'The one they called "Lil"?'

'That's Lilian. Remember Lilian?'

'Who jilted you?'

'She didn't jilt me. She just didn't wait for me. Luckiest escape I ever had.'

Me and Albert had some good laughs that week and I told Kate's story up and down the street. People never seemed to tire of hearing it. I think she'd have been well satisfied. Albert thought I cast her in a kinder light than she deserved.

He said, 'I know you shouldn't speak ill of the dead, Dotty, but she was a bit of a trollop. Well she was when she lived around here. You were still a nipper, you wouldn't have understood.'

'She didn't walk the streets.'

'She didn't need to in them days. She was with her Irishman, hawking his ditties. But before she met him, she did lead men on. She was a good looker, you know? Pretty hair, nice little ankles.'

'As I recall, it wasn't her ankles you lads were interested in. I wasn't that much of a nipper.'

'All I'm saying is, you can't blame people for thinking the worst of her now. She wasn't well liked round here. Mam didn't like her.'

'Mam didn't like a lot of people. Anyway, Kate went away so she didn't trouble anybody here for long. But people don't like that either, do they? They want you to stay put and be the same as them. How many times have I heard that this week? "She should have stayed here and settled down." And if you don't, if you have the gumption to go off into the world, heaven help you if you ever come back. They'll look at you like you've grown horns.'

Albert said he hadn't found that to be the case when he came back and what did I expect if I paraded along Bilston Street with a two-foot feather in my bonnet. That feather was nowhere near two foot.

On the Thursday, Ezra Dick came to tea. Albert fetched in some sliced ham from Sutton's and a jar of pickled beetroot. I preferred not to go into that gossip shop, so I took a walk up to High Green to buy a packet of squashed fly biscuits and some new cups and saucers. I don't think Albert sees as well as he used to and I abhor a chipped cup.

Ezra actually hung his cap on the peg and sat down, just when I'd begun to think he must have some bodily peculiarity that prevented him from bending in the middle. I must tell you another thing about Ezra Dick. He had the biggest ears I'd seen since Batty's Circus brought the elephants to town. He didn't have a great deal to say until Albert went out to water the horses but as soon as he heard the scullery door close, he seized a chance he seemed to have been waiting for.

'Miss Allbones,' he says, 'how have you found your Albert?'

'Not much different.'

'You surprise me.'

'He's a bit forgetful.'

'He's very forgetful and it troubles me. What's to become of him, all on his own here?'

'He's getting up in years. Everybody forgets things.'

'I don't.'

'Well what am I supposed to do about Albert?'

'You must think of coming home, to care for him.'

I hardly knew what to say. Me, back in Bilston Street! And just when Monty got me an engagement at the Paragon. I couldn't countenance it.

He said, 'I do what I can. I look in on him every day. We go to the match, when Wolves are playing at home. Summertime we do a bit of fishing in the cut. But he needs regularity, Miss Allbones. He needs a woman in the house.'

I said, 'I'm in the theatre. There's nothing regular about my life. Perhaps he should go to our May's to live.'

He put down his cup.

He said, 'Do you mean to your sister?'

'She'd have room for him.'

'But, Miss Allbones,' he says, 'your sister passed away. February, or it might have been March. Before Easter, any road. Surely Albert let you know?'

'No. When he wrote to me last month he said the last he'd heard May wasn't well but no worse than she'd been for years.'

He shook his head. Then the scullery door squeaked open and Albert returned.

Ezra said, 'You need a bit of grease on them hinges, chap. I shall bring my oil can round tomorrow.'

I put it off. I packed my valise before I tackled Albert.

I said, 'I was thinking I might call on our May, seeing as I'll be going through Birmingham tomorrow. Have you had any word from her?'

'Don't think so,' he says. 'She never was much of a correspondent.'

'Only your friend Ezra seemed to think she'd passed away. He must have been thinking of somebody else.'

'Ah yes,' he says. 'May. That's right. May passed over. But you knew that, Dotty. I wrote you about that.'

'Are you sure? Did you go to the funeral?'

'I think so. It's a long time ago now.'

'Is it? Wasn't it this year?'

'It might have been. Get to my age you go to a lot of buryings.'

'Well I don't think you ever wrote to tell me.'

'Dotty,' he says, 'I hope you won't mind my saying, but you're getting quite forgetful.'

I hardly slept. I lay there going over it, back and forth. Ezra Dick was just a worry-wart, making much of little. No he wasn't. He was just being a true friend to Albert. He just didn't understand my circumstances. He didn't understand that I couldn't be expected to give up my life and come back to Bilston Street. Somebody else would have to do it. Who? Our May's gone, apparently. Typical. She was never any help when Dad went peculiar. But then neither was I. Albert's always been the one. He had no business getting forgetful. He was supposed to stay hale and hearty. Until what? Until it was more convenient to me to look after him. And when exactly would that be? And then, who'll look after me?

34

Valentine was appearing at the Marylebone. I was resting, as we say in the business. Wednesday morning he came tapping at my bedroom door quite early. I wasn't asleep, but I wasn't exactly awake either. Could he have a word?

He came in and sat on the edge of the bed.

He said, 'There's something I have to tell you.'

I said, 'You're leaving.'

'No. Something happened yesterday. I expect Tom Bullen will know all about it, but I wanted you to hear it from me first. Frank got arrested. But it was all a silly mistake so you shouldn't believe what the papers say.'

'What do the papers say?'

'Nothing yet.'

'What's he supposed to have done?'

'Gone with boys. In Hyde Park.'

I said, 'But, Valentine, he probably did. He's not exactly a ladies' man, is he?'

'He's a respectable person. He doesn't wander around parks looking for company.'

'Was he in Hyde Park?'

'Yes.'

'What was he doing there?'

'Just conversing.'

'If you say so. Is he locked up?'

'No. But he has to go to court this morning. Marlborough Street. So it'll probably be in the papers tomorrow.'

'Don't look so worried. It's him that's in trouble, not you. Let it stay that way. What you need is a sweetheart. Luncheons and suppers with an old man like him, it's not natural. All those pierrettes you work with. Isn't there one of them that's tickled your fancy?'

'Seeing as how I've disturbed your sleep,' he says, 'I'll make you a pot of tea.'

Tom was on my doorstep that afternoon, full of it, of course.

'Four counts of gross indecency!'

'Have they locked him up?'

'No, he's bailed till next week. Five hundred pounds, thank you very much! Put up without a blink. I hope young Valentine's learned a lesson from this.'

'I think he has. It's shaken him. Will it be in the papers?'

'Oh yes. One line probably. Depends if there's any tastier news.'

'Will he go to prison?'

'He could get two years. How the mighty have fallen, Dot.'

But there was nothing about any Tumelty or Townsend in Thursday's paper and by Friday evening there was a much bigger story to fill the pages. Another woman had been murdered, not on the street like Kate and the others, but indoors, in her bed. Still, word spread like the pox. She'd been so cut to pieces it had to be Saucy Jack at work again.

The woman's name was Mary Jane Kelly and she had a room in one of the courts off Dorset Street. The rent collector had gone to collect money she owed and got no reply when he knocked at her door. He thought she must be at home so he'd gone to look through her window and found a pane broken and a smear of blood on the glass. When he looked closer he'd seen something inside he didn't like the look of. He'd gone directly to tell the landlord, a Mr McCarthy who kept the chandlery just around the corner. It was the landlord who'd looked properly through the broken window and seen the body on the bed. *Without clothing and terribly mutilated,* it said. *A most horrifying spectacle.*

The police had been sent for and had broken down the locked door. Ethel Peck was usually a woman of few words. She'd come in, tie on her apron and go straight to her scrubbing, but even she found something to say about Mary Kelly's murder.

'How can that be?' she said. 'If the door was locked from the inside, however did the murderer get out?'

I said, 'I suppose he took the key out of the spring-lock and pulled the door shut behind him.'

'I don't know,' she said. 'If you ask me, he's not of this world. Nobody ever sees him, nobody ever hears him. And now he passes through brick walls, so we're not even safe in our own beds.'

She said she intended sleeping with a Bible and a poker beside her pillow.

She said, 'If it's the Devil he won't come near the Word of God and if he's human I shall anoint him with my poker and he'll be caught by the bruises on his head.'

We had a laugh about Ethel's precautions, but I decided I'd put a chair against my bedroom door until further notice.

Mary Jane Kelly was only twenty-four. *Of fresh complexion and attractive appearance*, the papers said. She evidently hadn't been living long enough on Dorset Street to have the bloom taken off her. She'd last been seen on Thursday night, though one of her neighbours in McCarthy's Rents swore to have heard her singing well after midnight. When she was found, her nose and ears had been cut off and certain other parts, not named by the papers, had been cut out and left on the table beside her. The courtyard where she'd lived had been closed off most of the day so no-one could leave or enter and there was talk of bringing in bloodhounds.

Tom came round late that night, tapping on my parlour window with a florin and nearly causing my heart to stop.

'I guessed you'd still be up,' he says. 'What a day. I haven't stopped since two this morning. Boil me an egg, there's a darling, and I'll take a drop of your brandy.'

He hadn't actually seen Mary Kelly's body. As she'd been found in her own lodging and there was no doubt as to the name of the poor dear, she'd been carried directly to the Shoreditch dead-house. No press were to be admitted till Monday when the inquest opened, but Tom had seen the photographs taken by the police.

'Like a slaughter yard,' he said. 'I pity the woman who has to clean up that mess. And, once again, nobody heard a dicky-bird, Dot. Not the woman across the yard, not even the neighbours upstairs, and you know what the walls are like in those houses. Just a bit of thin matchwood and scrim. You could hear a bedbug fall the other side of one of those partitions. Of course, they're all drinkers. I suppose they were all spark out.'

Tom told me as much as he knew. Mary Jane was Irish or possibly Welsh, she lived with a Billingsgate porter called Barnett, except when they quarrelled, and she was known to the police as a doxy and a drunkard. She'd been seen up and down Commercial Street on Thursday night, drinking in the Britannia and the Ten Bells, and then later, outside her house with a jug of ale, entertaining a gentleman, heavy-set with a ginger moustache.

I said, 'Don't we know a heavy-set gentleman with a ginger moustache? Oh no, he goes with boys in Hyde Park, not girls on Dorset Street.'

'Tumelty?' he said. 'No. Dorset Street wouldn't be his style at all. There's men in and out of that rookery all night. It's hardly a secluded spot.'

I said, 'I suppose that's why he went indoors to kill her. He's being more careful now.'

'If it's him.'

'Do you doubt it?'

'I don't know. Villains don't usually change their ways. They're not bright enough to think of it. That's how they get caught.'

'But if her parts were taken? Surely that signifies it's the same man who killed Kate?'

'Dot,' he says, 'it's common knowledge now what Jack does to them after he's cut their throats. Any madman could have taken it into his head to copy him. There's lunatics a-plenty in the world.'

'And what about the bloodhounds they talked of bringing in?'

'Bloodhounds! Another fine mess. It was left too late. Commercial Street thought Leman Street had sent for them.

Leman Street said it was Commercial Street's duty seeing they were the station that was first to the scene. The net of it was, no hounds were sent for and by the time it was realised, half the boots in H Division had trampled over the scene. That's the trouble with the police these days. There's too much brass and not enough common sense.'

Tom attended the inquest. It was all concluded in one day in spite of a delay at the start. Two of the jurymen had objected to being summoned because the murder had happened in Spitalfields and they lived in Shoreditch and they didn't see why they should lose a day's work over something that was none of their business.

Tom said, 'They picked the wrong coroner to argue with there, I can tell you. Dr Macdonald. He says, "I will not have my time wasted by men presuming to teach me my business. Jurisdiction lies where the body now lies, not where it was found. The body lies here in Shoreditch and I am the appointed coroner for this mortuary. If anyone persists in objecting, let him speak up at once. I shall know how to deal with him. He'll find he loses more than today's work." That shut them up.'

Mrs Kelly's friend, Mr Barnett, had been called first. He said her correct name was Marie Jeanette, not Mary Jane, and he'd only ceased living with her because she was in the habit of allowing her friends to bring men to their room for immoral purposes and he disapproved of it. He'd seen her on the Thursday evening and they'd parted on friendly enough terms. He said he was very fond of her and the only trouble there had ever been between them was because of the low company she kept.

Then the rent collector had told how he'd gone to collect arrears that were owed, nearly two pounds, and when no-one came to the door he'd put his hand through the broken window and moved the curtain to see if she was hiding and pretending not to be at home. That was when he'd seen something unnatural on the table next to the bed.

'What was it?'

'He said it looked like some kind of meat. Then he ran to fetch the landlord. McCarthy.'

Mr McCarthy had explained the broken window. It had been like it for some time after Mrs Kelly had had a fight with Mr Barnett.

Tom said, 'Four shillings and sixpence a week and you don't even get a broken window mended.'

Various neighbours had given evidence. A Mrs Cox, who'd seen Mrs Kelly in the courtyard with a man. She gave his description as stout, with a carroty moustache, very full, but no beard. He'd been wearing a long coat and a billycock hat. She'd seen them go indoors, quite drunk and with a pot of ale. Mrs Cox said she hadn't slept a wink that night. She'd been in and out, looking for trade, but she'd seen nothing and heard nothing from Mary Jane Kelly except her singing which had gone on to an inconsiderate hour.

A Mrs Prater who lived directly above Mrs Kelly said she'd come in at one o'clock and heard no singing. The only thing she recalled was a faint cry of 'Murder!' some time between three and four but she'd paid no attention to it because there were often cries of 'Murder!' along Dorset Street.

Then there had been a bit of an upset to the proceedings. A

Mrs Maxwell, who lived across from the entrance to McCarthy's Rents, swore she'd seen Mary Kelly alive at eight o'clock on Friday morning on Dorset Street, not once but twice, and had spoken to her. Mrs Kelly had told her she wasn't feeling well. She'd said that she'd had a glass of beer and it had turned her stomach sour. Mrs Maxwell had wished her well and then walked on, to fetch her husband's breakfast. When she came back from the chandler's, she'd noticed Mrs Kelly was back outside Ma Ringer's beer shop, in conversation with a man. She could not describe him well. She thought he was stout, in a plaid coat and a hat. More than that she couldn't say, but she was quite certain it was Mary Kelly she'd seen.

Another witness had called on a friend who lodged down the courtyard. She'd arrived at half past two on Friday morning and seen a man nearby, stout and wearing a black wide-awake.

I said, 'Paying calls at half past two? Don't these people ever sleep?'

'Not much,' he said. 'They're all toms, the women round there. They go out, do a bit of business, come home if it turns to rain, go out again if they've a mind to earn a bit more. That one said she'd dozed in her friend's chair for a while. She'd heard a cry of "Murder" too but she paid it no attention. She was probably half-puddled. Give me another tot of brandy, Dot. The thing is, there's not one reliable account. Some heard cries around three or four o'clock, but then that Mrs Maxwell, and I'd credit her with a clearer mind than the rest of them, she was convinced she saw Kelly puking up beer at eight o'clock in the morning. So what do you make of that?'

*

Fred Abberline had been the last to speak, regarding the mix-up over sending for bloodhounds and the breaking down of Mrs Kelly's locked door. He had some new information to add. There had been a fire burning in the grate, so hot it had melted the spout and the handle of the tea kettle, and from examination of the ashes it was believed clothes had been burned there, and a bonnet.

Tom said, 'Kelly was wearing nothing but a chemise, what was left of her, but her usual clothes were folded on a chair at the foot of the bed. So the fire is a bit of a mystery. What was burned? And those who knew her say she never wore a bonnet. She liked to show off her hair. Abberline thinks Jack must have built up the fire to give him light to work by, to carve her up. There was only a nub of candle in the place. Still, I don't know that I agree with his reasoning. Hanging about, taking time to build up such a fire? What if one of her doxy friends had come to the room, or a neighbour?'

'The parts he took? Was it the same as Kate?'

'Much worse, Dot. I hardly like to tell you.'

But he did, after another brandy.

'Her belly was empty. Everything had been ripped out.'

That word 'ripped' made me tremble every time I heard it.

'Liver, gizzards, kidneys, female parts. I think he left the lights in her chest, but her bosoms were sliced off, and her face. Even the flesh off her legs, which was what the rent man saw on the table when he peered through the window. Like mutton hams. So he's really gone to town this time. And it was all laid out around her, like you might put dishes out on a table.'

'So he's quite insane.'

'When his blood's up. But the rest of the time he must go about like any normal person. He could be some mild little counting-house clerk.'

'Don't say so. That makes it worse. Who can a woman trust these days?'

He took me in his arms and held me tight. I was glad of the comfort of it.

'You can trust me,' he whispered. 'How's that for a start? And you can trust that powder puff you live with. And I daresay you can even trust Monty Hyams.'

'Was everything accounted for? The Kelly woman's parts? Did he take anything away?'

Tom hesitated.

'He took her heart. But it's not generally known, so don't go talking about it. The jury never heard the details. Dr Macdonald said there was no reason for them to know all the terrible particulars. She was murdered, that's clear enough. It wasn't a mishap and she didn't do it herself.'

He fell quiet. I said, 'Are you staying the night? Valentine's already in and gone to bed.'

We went up but we both lay awake. I always know when Tom's fallen asleep. He soon commences a whistling noise in his nose.

'Dot,' he says, eventually. 'Listen to this. What if that wasn't Mary Kelly he slaughtered? What if it was one of her friends that Barnett spoke of, that used her room for business? Her face was so cut up, how would you know who she was?'

'By her hair. By the shape of her. If you know a person you'd be able to tell at once.'

'But I'll bet Barnett only took a quick look. You wouldn't want to dwell on a sight like that.'

'Then if it wasn't Mary Kelly, who was it? And if she wasn't murdered, where is she now?'

'That Mrs Maxwell was quite sure she'd seen her on Friday morning, and she's not the only one. There's others saying the same thing, only they weren't called to the inquest.'

I couldn't see what he was getting at. So he went over it again, slowly. I felt him counting off the points on the counterpane.

'One: Mary Kelly allowed other doxies to use her bed. That's why Barnett left her. Two: She owed McCarthy a great deal of money. Three: Say she's out all night, down the docks, doing business, comes home in the morning and finds one of her friends murdered. Four: Well, she thinks, here's my chance to flit and let them all think I'm dead. That'll stop McCarthy dunning me for the rent. Do you see what I'm saying?'

I said, 'I do and I don't. If I came home and found my house all blood and body parts, I'd scream so loud they'd hear me at Leman Street lock-up.'

'But you're no Mary Kelly. Those prossers, they're quick and cunning and hard as flint. They have to be. And why was she spewing up beer at eight o'clock in the morning? Because of what she'd seen? That'd turn anybody's stomach sour. And here's another thing. When the Maxwell woman was telling her version, the Coroner grew quite testy with her and told her to be very careful to say only what she could swear to because her story was at odds with everyone else's. He wanted that inquest finished, no adjournments, and that's exactly how it turned out.'

I said, 'But, Tom, where's the point to any of it except to Mary Kelly? If she's run away, she'll have had to go somewhere she's not known. And if the police aren't sure it was her that was killed, why don't they say so?'

'Because, Dot, they look bad enough already. How many is it he's killed now? Five, six? And anyway, one trollop's much the same as another. Whoever she was, there's plenty more where she came from. You ask Saucy Jack when he's caught.'

'That's a terrible attitude.'

'And these are terrible times.'

35

Whether it was truly Mary Kelly or not, that's how she was buried. That's the name they put on her box. She was taken out to the Catholic cemetery at Leytonstone and as she had no family and her friend Barnett was out of work and without funds, the sexton from St Leonard's kindly paid for her funeral. These may be terrible times, but there are still some generous Christian souls. She had a fair crowd to follow her, some who knew her, some who just enjoy a good Irish funeral. They say the Crown and Shuttle did brisk business that morning.

If Tom was right, if it was some other woman in that casket, I wonder if Mrs Kelly was in the crowd that followed it to the cemetery? What would that be like, to attend your own funeral?

I saw nothing of the procession myself. I was opening at the Paragon that night, so my guts were all of a flutter. I rested at home till it was time to go in. Valentine wasn't working that week. He had two weeks off before he opened at the Savoy and he was like a dog with two tails. The Savoy was a considerable step up in the world for him. Frank Townsend gave him dinner at the Café Royal to celebrate.

I said, 'I wouldn't have thought a man waiting to be tried at the Old Bailey would be in the mood to celebrate anything.'

'Oh that's all going to be taken care of,' says Valentine. 'Frank has friends, you know, people of influence. The police are likely to drop the charges, which anyway should never have been brought. The last I heard, this is a free country. A man can walk through Hyde Park and strike up a conversation without getting hauled before a magistrate.'

That was on the Monday.

Monty came to the theatre before first house.

He said, 'I hope you're in good voice, Dot. This could be the start of bigger things.'

I said, 'I'm always in good voice.'

'Nobody's *always* in good voice,' he says. 'What are you doing for your finale?'

'"The Boy I Love".'

'That's Nelly Powers' song.'

'And Nelly Powers is six feet under in Abney Park. She won't be singing it again.'

'Even so, Dot. Are you sure it's the right number for you? It's not your usual style.'

'They'll be glad of it after all that juggling and skating and Red Indian drumming. A nice sweet song everybody knows. I've tinkered with the verses a bit, to play it for a laugh or two, but it's the chorus they like, Monty. And I've got a bit of a head cold so I can give it just a touch of huskiness.'

'So you're not in good voice at all. Well isn't that just my luck. I get you an engagement at the Paragon and you let me down.'

I said, 'I never let my audience down. Stop fretting. They'll love me.'

He was fiddling with my make-up box, taking out my

brushes and my grease sticks and putting them back in the wrong place.

I said, 'Anybody'd think it was you debuting at the Paragon. I don't know why you're so jittery.'

'I'm not,' he says.

But he still seemed to be lingering.

'You all right?'

'Yes.'

'You still set on shifting to the country?'

'Yes,' he says. 'Mother's there already. She's got rooms with a Dutch lady. Very pleasant.'

'That's nice.'

'We'll have a garden.'

'I didn't know you liked gardens.'

'No, but a garden can be a good thing.'

'If you have a gardener.'

'Or a family.'

I looked at him in the mirror. His ears had turned red.

I said, 'A family? What are you telling me, Monty?'

'Blanche,' he says. 'Me and Blanche.'

I got the ten-minute call.

He said, 'I thought you'd already guessed.'

I told him I had. I couldn't have him thinking anything escapes me. I mean, I'd suspected the reason for Blanche's indisposition. It happens all the time. But with Monty! What a shocker. It quite threw me. But the ten-minute call is holy writ to me, so I tied on my shawl and started powdering and that saved me having to make pleasant enquiries about Blanche's health.

★

It was a top-notch show, very lively, very fast. Mr Cinquevalli, King of the Jugglers, The Splendido Sisters, who skate on a kettle drum, Soaring Eagle the Pawnee Indian. He actually rides his pony through the stalls and up onto the stage. The only familiar face in the line-up was Lionel Neve, the blind pianist.

He said, 'I've worked with all sorts, Dot. Crows, dogs, snakes, even the Norbury fucking Nightingale. But horse shit in the wings beats all. Mind where you step.'

Peggy Splendido said, 'He's a bonny-looking lad, that Soaring Eagle. Have you seen the thighs on him? He can play cowboys and Indians with me any time he likes.'

Lionel said, 'I hate to be the bearer of disappointing tidings, Peggy, but I heard Soaring Eagle is actually Yudel Snapperman from Clarksburg, West Virginia.'

I had no idea where Lionel got his information. Hebrews aren't generally known for taking their shirts off and riding bareback horses. But if Monty Hyams was getting a garden in Newington Green and a baby with Ammonia, anything was possible. The world was going mad.

I'd hardly seen Valentine all week. The hall lamp was burning when I came home every night but I was never sure if he'd lit it and gone to bed or lit it and gone out again. I slept soundly anyway. The Paragon is a big theatre and the bigger the audience, the harder you have to work.

Sunday morning, I knocked on his door. I heard him say something, I couldn't tell what.

I said, 'It's gone eleven. Will you be going to Friedman's?'

Not that I cared about cake. I was actually hoping he'd give me a hand filling my bath tub. I did miss Olive on a Sunday.

'Not today,' he said. He sounded very groggy. 'I'm not feeling so well.'

So I went in to him.

What a sight. Valentine's a fine-looking young man, but not when he hasn't shaved, not when his eyes are rimmed with red.

I said, 'What's ailing you? Have you caught my cold?'

'No,' he says. 'I've had a bit of a setback.'

'At the Savoy?'

'No. It's Frank. He's gone.'

'Back to America?'

'I don't know.'

'Is he still on bail?'

'Yes. I think he's run.'

I opened the curtains.

I said, 'Well that's no reason for you to lie a-bed moping. You knew he'd be going sooner or later. And he's the one who's in trouble. You didn't put up money for his bail?'

'No. But he said everything was going to be sorted out.'

'Perhaps it was. Useful people in high places and all that. Perhaps he was told he was free to go.'

'But he didn't settle his bill, at the hotel. They said he'd taken his things and done a bunk.'

'Then good riddance. You don't need a friend like that. Think of your own good name. Now get up and pull a brush through your hair. How about a few rashers and an egg?'

'Miss Dot,' he says, 'there's something else.'

'What?'

'You won't like it. Frank left a few things with me.'

'When?'

'A week ago. He said you couldn't always trust hotels.'

'Though as it turns out it was hotels that couldn't trust him. What did he leave?'

'I'm not sure.'

And as he said it, I suddenly had a horrible thought. Dynamite.

'Is it in this room?'

'Yes. There's a few things. Some books and some herbal remedies. It's the other thing. I don't know what to make of it.'

'Could it be dynamite?'

'Dynamite!' he says. 'Why would Frank have dynamite?'

'To blow the government to kingdom come. Where is it?'

He started to get out of bed. Valentine has surprisingly hairy legs for a soprano.

I said, 'You mustn't touch it.'

He said, 'It's not dynamite.'

'Do you know what dynamite looks like?'

'No,' he says. 'Do you?'

He went to his tallboy and brought out a bag, a small portmanteau. There were a few medicine bottles, not labelled. I had a sniff. Nothing but water and floor sweepings if you ask me. The books were just pictures, no words. Boys wrestling, in their birthday suits.

I said, 'These need fire-backing. What else?'

There was a parcel wrapped in butcher's paper, no bigger than my hand. He held it out.

I said, 'We should have a pail of water ready to drop it in.'

He said, 'I'm fairly sure it's a medical thing, Miss Dot, not dynamite. You'll see.'

'Open it then.'

'I'd sooner you did,' he says.

It smelled faintly of chlorodyne. Does dynamite smell? A person should know these things, for their own good. My chest was pounding. I thought, 'Any minute now I'm going to wake up and find myself outside the pearly gates.' But when I looked it was just a leather pouch.

I said, 'It probably holds his collar studs. Have you looked inside?'

'No.'

'What's wrong with you?'

'I don't think it opens. I didn't like the feel of it. You touch it, see what you think.'

I took it out of the paper. It was quite soft, like pigskin. The moment I held it in my hand and turned it over I guessed what it was.

36

We were halfway to Mare Street looking for a cab when Tom Bullen came striding along.

Valentine said, 'Don't tell him where we're going. I don't want my name in the papers.'

I said, 'There's no reason you should. You've done nothing wrong, except ignore my advice and chum around with undesirables. But we shall have to tell Tom where we're going. He's not shaken off that easily and, anyway, he might be able to help us.'

Tom said, 'You two look like the hounds of hell are after you.'

I said, 'They are. We're going to Leman Street. I have to see Fred Abberline.'

'What's happened? Have you witnessed a crime?'

'We have information. If you'll come with us and help us to see Abberline I'll tell you what it's about. Otherwise, bugger off home to Mrs Bullen.'

My nerves were stretched tight as a fiddle string.

He said, 'Of course I'll come with you. Anything for you, Dot. But I doubt Abberline will be in on a Sunday. I know where he resides though, if that's of any interest to you.'

I had no intention of traipsing across the river, going to Abberline's place of residence.

I said, 'When he hears what we've got he'll soon pull his boots on.'

There are two things that are guaranteed to make Tom Bullen's eyes shine: one is the tickle of a news story and the other is, well, nobody's business but his and mine.

'Go on then,' he says. 'What have you got?'

'A heart.'

He squinted at me.

'You mean an actual heart? Like you'd get from a butcher?'

'A heart's a heart. It could be Mary Jane Kelly's.'

'You're codding me. Show me.'

'In the street? I will not.'

'Where did you get it?'

'Frank Townsend Tumelty left it with Valentine. It's been in my house this past week, wrapped in paper. First I heard of it was this morning. And, he appears to have left town. Done a moonlight and never paid his hotel bill.'

'So he's jumped bail? But are you sure it's a heart, Dot? You'd need a doctor to verify that.'

'I don't need a doctor to tell me it's a piece of flesh. You can see the pipes, where it was cut out.'

'Oh my good God,' he says. 'Then give it to me and I'll take it to Abberline.'

'No. *I'll* give it to him.'

'Then I tell you what, you go home and I'll bring him to you. If you take it to Leman Street on a Sunday, there's no saying who you'll have to deal with.'

★

So Valentine and I turned for home and Tom went bustling off to fetch Fred Abberline.

Valentine said, 'I wish now I hadn't showed it to you. I should just have thrown it away.'

'And let Frank Townsend get away with murder? He must be brought back.'

'We don't know that Frank murdered anybody. He's a doctor. They carry all sorts in their bags.'

'Not hearts, they don't, and you know it. You did right showing it to me and now we're doing right telling the police.'

'I shall be in trouble.'

'For what?'

'Harbouring it. I bet I'll forfeit my engagement at the Savoy when this gets out.'

'Nonsense. When they capture him it'll be thanks to you. Now buck up. And when Abberline comes, you get a grip on yourself. Just tell him the truth. Your friend asked you to look after a bag for him. You only opened it after you heard he'd scarpered, and you weren't sure what this was until you showed it to me. You don't need to go into a long rigmarole about it and you can leave most of the talking to me. I'm not afraid of Fred Abberline. We go back a long, long way. He used to bring his wife to my shows when he was courting her.'

The afternoon seemed endless. Valentine kept going to the window but there was nothing to see. Victoria Park's not like Bilston Street. Nobody stands on a doorstep, nobody brings a chair out to catch a bit of sunshine. If they're watching your comings and goings, they're doing it from behind their curtain lace.

It was getting dusk when a hansom came rumbling along and Tom and Abberline stepped down from it. Valentine was trembling.

He said, 'Don't let him arrest me, Miss Dot. I couldn't endure it.'

I said, 'He'll thank you, you barmpot, not arrest you. Now leave this to me.'

Fred Abberline had put on a bit of weight since I'd last seen him, but he still wore his whiskers mutton-chop style.

'Dot Allbones,' he says. 'Here's a turn up. How are you, my dear?'

I said, 'Older but no richer. You should bring Mrs Abberline to the show one of these nights.'

'Nothing I'd like better. When this terrible business is cleared up.'

I told him Valentine was very shaken by our discovery.

'No need to be anxious, Mr St John,' he says. 'Just show me the item you were given and tell me what you know.'

The package lay on my occasional table. Fred opened it very delicately. He looked at it for a good while before he touched it. Then he turned it over. Tom was peering over his shoulder. He made a little sound when he saw where the pipes had been cut, but not Fred Abberline. He just nodded and closed up the paper.

'Certainly a heart,' he said. 'But we'd need a surgeon to say whether it's human.'

'You'll give it to Openshaw, I suppose.' says Tom.

Fred said, 'I don't think we need trouble Dr Openshaw on a Sunday. Any surgeon worth his salt will be able to tell us, and probably any Aldgate butcher too. Now, young man, tell me how you came by this.'

He brought out his notebook and pencil.

Whatever goes on in Fred Abberline's mind, you can never guess it from studying his face. He listened to Valentine, wrote things down, never moved, hardly blinked.

'So, to summarise, your friend is known to you as Frank Townsend but you were aware that he also uses the name Tumelty?'

'Yes.'

'Did you ever know him to use any other name?'

'No. Well, some people say Tumblety.'

'But no other name?'

'No.'

'When exactly did he give you the package?'

'Last Thursday week.'

'Did he say why?'

'He was having a bit of trouble. He'd been wrongfully arrested and he had to go to court again on the Friday. He said he was worried he might not get bail and he didn't like to leave things unattended in his hotel room.'

'But he did get bail.'

'Yes.'

'Did you see him, after that?'

'Last Saturday. He said he was thinking of moving to a different hotel.'

'And since then?'

'I haven't seen him. He's left the Charing Cross and I don't know where he is.'

Fred put his notebook away, cracked his face into a smile and jumped up.

'Not to worry, Mr St John,' he says. 'You may not know where he is, but I can assure you the Metropolitan Police are hot on his heels. He'll be brought back. I'll take the other items he left with you, if you'd be kind enough to fetch them.'

Tom waited till Valentine had left the room.

He said, 'I've been telling Dot for months that Tumelty was bad company for a young fellow.'

I said, 'Valentine's my lodger, Tom, not my child. He got plenty of advice from me but he chose not to listen. Well, now he's learned the hard way.'

Valentine came back with the bag. Fred opened it and sniffed.

'Herbal remedies indeed!' he says. 'Some people have more money than sense.'

He wound his muffler round his throat.

He said, 'I'm told you have a very fine voice, Mr St John.'

'I'm opening at the Savoy this coming week. *Yeomen of the Guard*. I'm playing Elsie Maynard.'

'I shall mention it to Mrs Abberline. She's fond of operetta. Bullen, share a cab with me?'

I could see Tom was torn. To stay behind and chew over what had happened or to go with Fred Abberline and fish for a few words that could be published? He went with Abberline. Valentine watched from the window till they were out of sight.

'Curtain twitching over at the Warlords',' he said. 'I'll bet Mr Warlord recognised Inspector Abberline.'

I said, 'Well? Do you feel better now? It wasn't as bad as you thought, was it?'

Then he turned to me.

'What did you do with them, Miss Dot?'

'What did I do with what?'

'The picture books.'

I said, 'I don't know what you're talking about.'

'Did you burn them?'

They'd made a fine blaze in the kitchen range. Better than that last load of coal we had delivered.

I said, 'I don't recall any picture books. But then, my brother Albert told me I'm getting very forgetful. You haven't done your vocalisations today.'

'I'm not in the mood.'

I said, 'You don't have to be in the mood. You're opening at the Savoy tomorrow. Go up and do them.'

Tom came back about eight o'clock.

'Well, well, well,' he says. 'So who's a clever boy, then?'

I said, 'Valentine's not been clever. He's been a fool. And it was me insisted he went to the police.'

'Not Valentine, you cuckoo. Me. Didn't I tell you there was more to Tumelty than met the eye?'

'You said he was a Fenian. What about the American who'd been trying to buy wombs? What about the man with the ginger moustache seen with Mary Kelly? I was the one who remarked on that. Oh no, says you, Dorset Street's not his style.'

'I think you're misremembering, Dot. Anyway, now they've gone and lost him.'

'But Fred Abberline said they knew where he was.'

'He did. Well he would say that. He wanted to put your mind at rest. In the cab with me he changed his tune. He said they had a good idea where he was, which is not the same thing at all as being hot on his heels. If you ask me they've accidentally on purpose lost him.'

'How?'

'He caught a packet to France. They do know that much. They had a detective following him, supposedly. A detective following a shirt-lifter? Because he jumped bail? Never. They'd be glad to be rid of him. Save the courts time and money. Same thing if he's been in their pay, if he's been passing them information about Fenian dynamiters. They don't want that to come out. They won't want him questioned.'

'But none of that matters now. The murders are what matter.'

'Do you think so? I predict he's sailed. He'll be safely on his way to America by now. And you know what? They'll never bring him back. You heard it here.'

'But why not? If he murdered Kate and all those others?'

'Because those doxies are the least of it. He was a nasty piece of work but he's gone, so there'll be no more rippings. This time next year nobody'll even think about it. I put it to Abberline. I said, "Of course Tumelty had Fenian written all over him. He was probably working for your lot as well. Turned informer. He always had plenty of money to throw around."'

'What did Fred say?'

'Nothing. He just smiled.'

'I told him, if I was Home Secretary I'd sit on my hands, let our friends across the water deal with Tumelty. If the American-Irish get wind he's been taking the Queen's shilling as well as their dollars, they'll soon bring him to account. He'll be going for a dip with rocks in his pockets. Save the Met the trouble of finding him and bringing him back here.'

'And what about the women he killed? What about Kate?'

'A trial won't bring them back, will it, nor a hanging? And Tumelty's a clever fellow, and slippery. He might get acquitted. Then how would you feel? No, let him sail to New York. This time of year, sooner him than me. Who knows, perhaps his ship will founder. Now, Dotty, my sweet, if I'm not mistaken, with all this excitement you've not had your bath today. Allow me to give you a hand. I'll bring the tub in. You slip into your nothings.'

37

Tom was right about one thing. Frank Townsend Tumelty never was brought back, though he was followed to New York and his whereabouts were known. He wasn't the kind of man to stay in the shadows for long. It grieved me to think of him still living while Kate lay at Manor Park, unavenged, but one good thing came of it. After Dr Frank left town there were no more rippings. I won't say there were no more murders. London's London after all. But as the Infant Prodigy said, 'We've gone back to regular murders now. Husband lamps his wife too hard. Wife puts too much rat poison in her old man's soup. Nothing to keep us awake at night.'

But Ida didn't know what I knew. Every time I looked at my mantel shelf I remembered how he'd leaned upon it and held forth that Sunday afternoon. 'As I once remarked to Mr Lincoln . . .' Valentine and I never spoke of him, but if he haunted me I'm sure he gave Valentine some sleepless nights. One thing I do know. I never saw him wear that pocket watch again.

*

One evening, Tom brought in an American newspaper, the *New York World*.

'Here,' he said. 'Show this to your lodger. In case he's still in any doubt.'

TUMBLETY'S PROTÉGÉ TALKS, was the headline. *Lived with the doctor and was his constant companion.*

Another paper, the *New York Tribune*, had reported that Dr Frank was suspected of involvement in the recent murders in Whitechapel, London. So a certain Mr McGarry had given an interview to the *New York World*, to speak in his defence.

> 'I was engaged in his service in 1882 and travelled with him widely. He is a surgeon, not an herb doctor as has been erroneously stated. He studied in Dublin and in New York and served with distinction as an army surgeon during the Civil War. He is a cultured man, very fond of the theatre, and a generous man. He assisted me financially in setting up my speaking-tube enterprise and I owe my success in business entirely to him.' When asked about Dr Tumblety's alleged aversion to women, Mr McGarry replied, 'It is true he had no place for them in his life. He thought them deceitful and untrustworthy. He often said all the troubles of the world were caused by women.'

I didn't show it to Valentine. He'd mentioned a new friend a couple of times. Edgar. There's talk of them taking a house together. Anyway, no sense opening old wounds.

I played the Canterbury just before Christmas and the Abberlines came to see me. They came round after the show.

I said, 'What happened, Fred? I thought you had a detective following that devil Tumelty? Did you send a boy to do a man's job?'

'It was complicated,' he said. 'Very complicated. Top show though, Dot. I will say, you haven't lost your touch. Where's your next engagement?'

'Theatre Royal.'

'Blimey,' he says. 'You're going up in the world.'

I said, 'Not Drury Lane, more's the pity. The Theatre Royal in Birmingham.'

'Monty Hyams still managing you?'

'No, I'm managing myself. Monty's got other fish to fry. He got married, you know? To Amazonia, the authentic warrior maiden. Blanche Smith. There's a baby on the way which I can promise you won't be winning any beauty contests.'

'Monty'll miss you. You've been one his stars.'

'He won't miss me. He's branching out. When I told him I was leaving, do you know what he said? "I've seen the future and I've got just one word to say to you, Dot. Seaside piers."'

We laughed.

Fred said, 'Nothing wrong with Birmingham though. Going back to where you started. You got family up there?'

'Yes,' I said. 'I have. I've got somebody.'

AUTHOR'S NOTE

The Whitechapel Murders present a tempting minefield to a novelist. So much is already known and yet so much is uncertain and unverifiable, in spite of the tireless research of Ripperologists. We do well to remember that forensic science, now a rather popular subject for university degrees and TV shows, was non-existent in 1888. It would be another thirteen years before Scotland Yard established a fingerprint bureau, and such crime scene reports as exist regarding the Ripper murders are blurred by erratic detective work and overlaid by the heavy tread of constables' boots. So, how to tell this oft-repeated story?

My chosen mouthpiece, Dot Allbones, is a fictional character, as are Valentine St John, Monty Hyams, and the long playbill of acts and artistes with whom they work. Marie Lloyd is the only real performer identified in the book and in 1888 she wasn't yet a household name. Music hall was very popular but it hadn't reached its zenith.

Kate Eddowes was, of course, an actual victim of the Ripper – his fourth or his fifth, or perhaps only his third, depending on which school of thought you subscribe to. We know quite a lot about Kate – you can find her in the 1851 census, aged ten and living in Bermondsey, one of seven children. You can find her in the 1861 census, on Bilston Street in Wolverhampton, lodging with her aunt and uncle. We even know what she looked like, in death at least. The photographs of her in the Golden Lane mortuary have become one of the most famous images of the Whitechapel Murders. Her name, anyway, will be familiar to readers.

The same is true of Inspector Fred Abberline, the Scotland Yard detective sent back to his old Whitechapel patch to oversee the hunt for the Ripper. Inspector Abberline, played somewhat improbably by Johnny Depp in *From Hell*, was a middle-aged career policeman and I have portrayed him as such. The other police officers I've named, the coroners and the politicians, are all taken from the press records of the time.

Between these real people and my entirely fictional creations, there is a grey area occupied by two important characters: Francis Tumelty and Tom Bullen. The American Dr Tumelty, also known as Twomelty, Tumblety, Townsend and various other handles, will be a familiar name to students of the Whitechapel Murders. His colourful and bizarre life before, during and after 1888 is well documented and as a suspect he has his detractors and his advocates. I have played my hand.

And then there is Tom Bullen, or Bulling: the matter of people's names was still quite free and easy in the late nineteenth century as was clear when it came to identifying some of the Ripper's victims. Mr Bullen certainly existed. He was employed by the Central News Agency, was known to be fond of a drink, and has been suggested as the possible author of the Ripper letters published in the newspapers of the day and therefore the person who first gave the supposed murderer the name Jack. Did he or didn't he? For readers interested in forming their own opinion about Francis Tumelty and Tom Bullen, I recommend the exhaustively thorough website www.casebook.org, where you will find theories of every stripe.